MW01698605

The author, Paul Fox, was born and raised in the UK and immigrated to Canada in 1993. He worked in sales for a major Canadian energy company for over twenty years. He's an avid collector of all types of detective fiction and mysteries. *The Connie* is Paul's first foray into this genre. He is currently working on the second Rick Marshall Mystery. Paul has previously published a comic crime caper set on a Caribbean cruise ship called *Going Overboard.*

For Dad

Paul Fox

The Connie

The Rick Marshall Files

Austin Macauley Publishers™
London • Cambridge • New York • Sharjah

Copyright © Paul Fox (2021)

All rights reserved. No part of this publication may be reproduced, distributed, or transmitted in any form or by any means, including photocopying, recording, or other electronic or mechanical methods, without the prior written permission of the publisher, except in the case of brief quotations embodied in critical reviews and certain other non-commercial uses permitted by copyright law. For permission requests, write to the publisher.

Any person who commits any unauthorized act in relation to this publication may be liable to criminal prosecution and civil claims for damages.

This is a work of fiction. Names, characters, businesses, places, events, locales, and incidents are either the products of the author's imagination or used in a fictitious manner. Any resemblance to actual persons, living or dead, or actual events is purely coincidental.

Ordering Information
Quantity sales: Special discounts are available on quantity purchases by corporations, associations, and others. For details, contact the publisher at the address below.

Publisher's Cataloging-in-Publication data
Fox, Paul
The Connie

ISBN 9781645758884 (Paperback)
ISBN 9781645758877 (Hardback)
ISBN 9781645758891 (ePub e-book)

Library of Congress Control Number: 2020909839

www.austinmacauley.com/us

First Published (2021)
Austin Macauley Publishers LLC
40 Wall Street, 33rd Floor, Suite 3302
New York, NY 10005
USA

mail-usa@austinmacauley.com
+1 (646) 5125767

Author's Note

This story is set in 1952. The language and attitudes of the narrator and characters regarding race, culture, and gender are contemporary to that time and may be disturbing to some.

Chapter One

I didn't see the explosion but just like everyone else in San Francisco on Friday the 4th of July, I heard it. Unlike most everyone else in San Francisco on that day, I knew what it was. I'd heard a large aircraft blow apart before, only from much closer than this one. On the 4th of July 1952, the plane that blew up over the Golden Gate Bridge was a Lockheed Constellation with forty-nine passengers and nine crew on board. There were no survivors. The plane that blew up just off my port wingtip in 1943 was a B17 called 'Suzie Q.'

One minute it was right there alongside us over Bremen and the next minute large chunks of it were tumbling to the earth eleven thousand feet below us. The explosion took out my port outer engine and a large chunk of the wing. On the homeward leg over the North Sea, my port inner caught fire. I managed to put my B17 down in a Lincolnshire potato field but not before the fire had given me second-degree burns on the left side of my head and my left hand. We were lucky I guess; you know what they say: any landing you can walk away from is a good landing. I didn't think so at the time.

The passengers and crew of the TWA Connie weren't so lucky. I didn't know any of them personally although a lot of long-haul TWA pilots were ex B17 guys like me. I was soon to become very familiar with some of the victims of that explosion, but I didn't know it at the time.

Since the war I'd had a number of jobs, most of them involved selling household gadgets door to door or driving trucks full of gadgets warehouse to warehouse. I did okay at sales, I wasn't too proud to play the 'wounded vet' card but there were a lot of us out there doing the same thing. You couldn't make a decent living at it. I couldn't get a job flying for anyone. I was partially deaf, and the fire had done quite a bit of damage to my inner ear. All the medical examiners I spoke to (I spoke to a lot) said they couldn't clear me to fly because they were afraid damage to my left ear would affect my spatial awareness when flying on instruments or at night; so, no more night flying for me.

I answered a 'help wanted' ad and joined The Homer Georgeopolous Detective Agency and I know Detective Agency sounds very Sam Spade but in truth I got a job helping one old Greek guy chase down younger American guys who owed clients' money or cheated on their spouses. There is a surprising amount of both going on in San Francisco, who knew? Three months into the job and the old guy croaks following some broad up the steps on Lombard Street. His second heart attack I was told. His widow, Mrs. Georgeopolous didn't want anything to do with the business (who can blame her?) So I sort of took over the client list and carried on. I pay the rent on Homer's old office and I slip his widow a few dollars every now and then to help her out.

What can I say? I'm a soft touch! I don't have a cute dame as my receptionist; I don't have any kind of dame as a receptionist. I do all my own filing, accounts, and typing and I do all the legwork. I did get in contact with an answering service that took my calls and saved my messages. This was a God-send and it means that I don't have to keep calling in at the office to pick up messages.

I sometimes sleep on an army surplus cot behind the desk when work keeps me out late and I don't feel like driving all the way back to Oakland. I can`t afford to have the name changed on the door and I can`t afford new letterhead or business cards so I`m now known in some circles as Rick the Greek. This is not like in the movies, well not like any movie I've seen.

I learned the tricks of the trade as I went along, they don't do night school classes on chasing down cheating husbands. That's not a bad idea though, is it? They would always be busy because, let's face it, most married guys I know would cheat on their wives if they thought they could get away with it, and most of the guys I follow think they are doing just that; getting away with it; the women too. That's until the 8 x 10 glossies drop on the doormat.

I was just coming out of the Buena Vista Cafe on Hyde Street when the Connie went down. It's a classy joint; friendly staff that don't chase you out of the door when you're watching someone on the street. I was following a guy who was allegedly seeing his sixteen-year-old niece. I say allegedly because I hadn't caught him with his pants down yet. It was only a matter of time, she was a honey, looked a lot like Lauren Bacall when she first got into movies only with more going on up-front if you catch my drift. So, I'm a few yards behind the two of them heading west, he's got his arm around her waist in a very friendly manner. He's got no idea he's being followed. His mind is on other things and they are wrapped up tight in the fluffy white sweater the blonde is wearing.

When the explosion came, most of us in the street froze; some actually ducked. It was like an atom bomb went off over Alcatraz. It felt as if the loudest crack of thunder ever heard was echoing around the bay. I forgot all about

Mario Vitali and his sixteen-year-old niece and hurried down the hill toward Hyde Street Pier.

When I got to the pier, there wasn't much to see, just the backs of hundreds of people all looking west toward the Golden Gate Bridge. I asked around. No-one had actually seen the explosion; everyone had heard it sure enough, but I couldn't find an eyewitness if my life depended on it. After maybe twenty minutes the crowd began to thin a little. That was when the police turned up. Three black and whites skidded to a halt by the entrance to the pier all squealing tires and wailing sirens. A Whole schlock of uniforms tumbled out of the cars and hurried through the crowd to the end of the pier.

They came back to the cars a short while later escorting maybe three or four people all of them carrying cameras. I knew one of them; Sammy Kirk was ex-navy, lost his left leg at Pearl. He made his living now taking pictures of couples walking on Hyde Street Pier. You know the kind of thing, happy holiday snaps for a buck, developed overnight, present your ticket at this display stand.

I caught his eye as the police led him toward the black and whites. He was deathly pale; his eyes were rimmed with red. He looked as though he was back on the U.S.S. Virginia that Sunday morning. He looked like hell.

I would have followed Sammy to the police station, but I had another appointment at a real station. I had to be at Southern Pacific's Third and Townsend Depot to meet the Coast Daylight express from Los Angeles. My wife Josephine was returning from a three-day business trip with her boss, Jacobus den Hamer. Ko den Hamer (as he liked to be called) was a property developer who was looking to get into real estate in some place just to the north of the Bay area called the Napa Valley. Apparently, he planned to switch a bunch of orchards from producing apples to growing grapes. It seemed like a crazy stunt to me, but Ko den Hamer Developments was investing millions of other people's money in this hair-brained scheme. Some of the people he was talking about were big-shot Hollywood producers and actors, hence the trip to Los Angeles.

Jacobus den Hamer was at least ten years older than me, maybe even late forties; he was originally from Holland where his family were potato farmers and distributors. Josephine had worked for him all through the war and I guess she enjoyed her role as 'Executive Assistant.' We were glad of the money she earned when I was de-mobbed and couldn't find a job.

Ko was tall, like every Dutch guy I've ever met (I haven't met a lot) he wore his thick blonde hair swept back from a high, tanned forehead. He always dressed in the latest fashion, favoring double-breasted pin-striped suits. He never wore a hat, that normally would set alarm bells ringing with me, but

Josephine said he was the perfect gentleman in the office and when they travelled to see potential investors. I wasn't worried about this guy turning Josephine's head even if he looked like Johnny Weissmuller's better-looking brother; she was a great gal who'd stuck by me when things were at their worst. Why would she even think about fooling around on me now, just when things were going so well for us?

Josephine could have had any guy she wanted. She looked like a film star even when she wasn't trying. She had the kind of beautiful face that men just stared at. She had a fabulous figure and the darkest long wavy hair that she nearly always wore down. There have been lots of times when we've been stopped in the street by folks who think she's Rita Hayworth or (what's the other one called?) Hedy Lamarr. Why she stuck by a burned up battle-scarred wreck like me I will never know. I'm just glad she did.

The train was a few minutes late, so I had time to grab a coffee before heading down onto the platform. I got down there just in time to see the Daylight pull in. It was a hell of a sight to see, a massive streamlined orange-red and black locomotive with a blinding light on the front in the center of a silver shield. It was pulling a line of matching coaches, all with the same striking paint job. I dropped my coffee cup in a garbage can and hurried down the platform.

Josephine and her boss were just getting off the train. She was carrying a fancy package in a large paper carrier bag with French writing on the sides, he had both their cases. When Josephine saw me striding toward her, she dropped the package. She scooped it up again real quick and they both stepped away from the coach as a steady stream of well-heeled passengers came down the steps. A porter hurried forward to offer assistance. Ko waved him away.

Jo and I hugged awkwardly for a second then we all set off down the platform as steam billowed from the locomotive. Den Hamer insisted on carrying Jo's case. Back out on the street, I offered to give Ko a ride. He wouldn't hear of it. He commented:

"You're heading in completely the opposite direction to me." He shook both our hands before turning to Jo:

"Thanks for all your help in Hollywood, Jo, you were a great asset. Why don't you take tomorrow off? You deserve a rest after all you've done for the company in the past few days."

Jo smiled as if she'd just been handed her very own Oscar.

"If you're sure you can manage," she said. He shook my hand again, squeezing just a little harder than was strictly necessary; then we headed off to collect the car. Did I tell you we live in Oakland? I thought I might have mentioned it. We're not too far from Berkeley at Telegraph and Derby. The place cost us everything we had and continues to take everything we both earn. It's an old house, it needs a lot of work.

Have you seen that movie: Mister Blandings builds his Dream House? Came out a few years ago? Well, I'm Cary Grant, without the accent and the good looks. The house is just like his, only way smaller. I could maybe do odd jobs on it at the weekends, but I work a lot at weekends.

As we headed home over the Bay Bridge, Josephine stared straight ahead, not saying a word. She held the mysterious package with her legs, occasionally messing with the pink wrapping paper sticking out of the top of the paper carrier bag. She played with her pearls all the way home. This was a habit she had when she was bored. I'd bought her the pearls on our second anniversary. I think I've almost paid off the loan I got to buy them. When we got home, she stuffed the package at the bottom of her wardrobe and went straight to bed. It was barely eight.

"Try not to wake me when you come up," she said. Message received and understood. I put on a Louis Jordan record, kept it turned way down, fell asleep in the chair listening to: 'Let the Good Times Roll.'

The next day The Chronicle confirmed what I knew in my gut. A passenger aircraft had exploded mid-air somewhere between the Point Bonita Lighthouse and The Golden Gate. Turns out it was a TWA Constellation which had taken off some twelve minutes earlier bound for Seattle and eventually Vancouver, Canada. The Chronicle was quoting un-confirmed rumors that Howard Hughes, the reclusive billionaire, and owner of T.W.A. was amongst the passengers.

I digested the grim news along with my usual breakfast: two black coffees, and a Danish. I had my usual table in the window of the Cozy Cove coffee shop; half a block from my 'palatial' offices on Clement Street, Inner Richmond. I was just a few blocks south of The Presidio which led onto The Golden Gate, so I was much closer to the scene of yesterday's tragedy.

I decided not to join the steady stream of Lookie Loo's heading toward the bridge. A recovery operation was planned for later in the day, but I wasn't too keen to see it. Call me squeamish, call me over-sensitive; call me anything you like but I did not want to see bits of aircraft with bits of people attached being fished out of the harbor. Let's just say it's not my thing. Instead, I took the car and drove across town to see if I could get hold of Sammy Kirk. I wanted to know what the police had asked him about. I wanted to know what he had seen.

Along with the business and the lease for the office I had 'inherited' a light blue '47 Plymouth Convertible from the saintly Mrs. Georgeopolous. All I had to do was pick up her groceries every now and then and once a month run her over to see her sister Gladys who lived in Emeryville. The car was a peach and ran great, even though it had never seen the inside of a garage since I'd got hold of it. It wasn't fast compared to some of the newer cars out there, but it started first time every time and the price was right.

I got to the pier just after ten. The early morning fog was burning off nicely as I parked in a bay about a block from where I'd seen Sammy yesterday. I picked up my hat from the back seat and put on a pair of sunglasses. I didn't go anywhere without the glasses and the grey fedora. They hid the scarring and my half-melted left ear pretty well, which meant fewer folks stared at me. This was a good thing for a private detective.

I found Sammy at the end of the pier loading a roll of film into his Canon IIB. He looked up as he closed the case.

"Oh, hi Rick, I thought I saw you yesterday when the cops took me away," he said.

"They didn't keep you in overnight, did they?" I asked.

"Nothing like that, they took my roll of film is all."

"You got pictures?" I asked incredulously.

"Well, I'm not sure what I got; they haven't released any prints yet. I didn't get the explosion but I'm sure I got some of what happened next."

"And what did happen next?" I asked.

Sammy looked out west, over the bay. Out toward Alcatraz and the bridge. His eyes filled with tears and his words seemed to catch in his throat.

"Bits of the plane fell into the bay, just past the bridge. Big bits. It broke into two main parts."

"You know you should get those pictures back; you would make a mint if you sold them to the papers."

"I don't think the papers could use them, they might be a bit too, you know, graphic. I'm sure I saw bodies falling, or parts of."

I had to get a look at those pictures somehow. What Sammy was describing sounded like the plane had been hit by anti-aircraft fire. But that couldn't have happened. So, there was only one explanation for what he'd witnessed and may be captured on film.

"I know a couple of decent lawyers Sammy; they can maybe help you get your film back."

Sammy took a hip-flask from his camera case, popped the lid, and took a slow swig.

"I don't want any trouble." He said.

"Won't be any trouble, Sammy," I said, as cheerfully as I could. "I'll make a few calls. Where can I get hold of you?"

Sammy gave me the number of his rooming house. Out in the bay, two giant cranes on barges were being towed slowly westward by four ocean-going tugs. We both stared out as the spectacle unfolded for what seemed like an hour.

"They'll be from the Kaiser Shipyards I guess," said Sammy, taking another belt from the hip-flask. He offered me a shot.

"Bit early for me, besides you look like you need it more than me."

"You may be right," said Sammy. "Do you think Howard Hughes was on board like the papers say?"

"I'm not too sure. No-one's seen him since that crash he had in Beverley Hills, that was just about a year ago. It would be a bitch to survive a crash like that only to die in another just a year later."

"You know what they say. When your number's up," said Sammy.

I shook his hand.

"I'll give you a call this evening; maybe give you a lawyer's name and number."

"If you think it will do any good."

"Sure, it will Sammy, sure, it will."

When I got back to the Plymouth the steering wheel and seat were already red-hot. I guess that's the price you pay for traveling in style in California. I pulled out a handkerchief, wrapped it around one hand so I could grip the wheel, thought for a moment about buying a beach towel to put along the front seat then I headed back to the office to make a few calls.

I knew at least three lawyers I had done work for recently. All divorce work obviously. I started calling around. The second guy I spoke to was an old Jew called Melvin Hammerstein. He'd lost nearly all of his European relatives in the camps and he'd been in the papers when he helped prosecute some Nazi sympathizers living in Carmel just after the war. Most recently I'd seen him in the papers again working on what he called 'civil liberties' cases. I had no idea what they were, but he seemed to be on the side of the little guy, and he was none too popular with the local Police Captain. He was happy to help out.

Then I got back to work following Uncle Mario and his teenage niece. Remember them? I knew Mario worked at an Italian Bakery at Folsom and Spear, down near Embarcadero. Working as a baker was a real break if you were looking to schtup your young niece after school. In fact, working as a baker worked real great if you wanted to meet and or schtup anyone when most other citizens were still slaving away in the afternoon heat. You see, bakers start work early but they also finish work early, around lunch-time. So, at around twelve I drove down to Folsom and Spear and parked up across the street from the San Marino Bakery. The place smelled great and I was beginning to think about heading inside to buy a sandwich. I was just opening the car door when Mario Vitali comes out of the front door of the bakery. He's wearing a sport coat and he's tried his best to knock the flour off his work pants. His thick wavy hair is wet where he's run a damp comb through it. He's in a hurry. I shut the car door and set off following him on foot.

Mario was maybe my age, he was thick-set, and his middle was the thickest bit about him. I got the feeling that he's been a bit of a Don Juan in his youth. He was a good-looking guy in a swarthy, hairy Italian way. It looked as if he knew a lot of people in the neighborhood. He was continually shouting greetings to people he passed in the street. This guy had balls; I'll give him that. If I was off to meet my niece for some seriously illegal incest, I'd most likely keep my head down. But not this guy, he was full of the joys of spring and he didn't give a shit who knew it.

I began to think we weren't on our way to a lover's rendezvous when Mario turned a corner and there was the niece, standing in front of the Folger's Building on the corner of Howard and Spear. If she'd been to school that morning, she must have skipped out early and found somewhere to change. She was carrying a small round case like a hat-box. Her school clothes would be inside I guessed. No-one would have thought she was still at school. She had on the same tight white sweater she'd worn a couple of days ago. She wore it with a slit pencil skirt that hugged her legs down to her calves. She had on high heels and nylons. She could have passed for twenty-five.

From what I could tell they didn't say anything to each other. They just started walking side by side down Howard toward the water. After a block and a half, they came to the Daniels Hotel. They went straight inside. I hurried across the street and entered the lobby just in time to see the niece's legs walking up the stairs. I assumed the niece was still attached to her legs, so I followed them up the stairs, keeping a safe distance. Luckily the old guy on the desk was tied up with another client so I wasn't noticed. I saw Mario and the girl enter room number nine which was at the rear of the building. They wouldn't have a view of the bay, but I figured that wouldn't worry Mario too much. He was thinking about getting a look at something else.

I left them to it; headed back downstairs and round the back of the hotel. I was in luck. The fire escape wasn't locked and by my calculations that open window just to the left of the fire escape on the second floor would be room number nine. I got my trusty CMC Miniature camera ready and started quietly up the metal steps. When I got to the second floor, I could hear a radio playing a Les Paul tune. I leaned over and sneaked a look through the net curtains. It was your usual low rent hotel room: metal bed frame, sagging mattress, peeling wallpaper, a bed-side table with a Mickey, and two glasses on it.

The blonde niece didn't look twenty-five anymore. Without the high heels and the fancy clothes, she looked just like a sixteen-year-old school kid being raped by a hairy fat guy. She was naked, her clothes strewn around the room. Her hat-box was open on the floor next to the bouncing bed. The niece was pale-skinned, painfully thin, and flat-chested, evidenced by the mounds on toilet paper spilling from her over-stuffed bra as it fell from the violently shaking bed. He had his hand over her mouth stifling her sobs and he was just about to put his Ciabatta to use. She was kicking feebly with those long legs of hers, but she wasn't strong enough to hold Uncle Mario off for much longer. I put the camera back in my pants pocket. I leaned over as far as I dare and grabbed hold of the window frame. Then I swung one leg onto the frame and kind of rolled my body into the room. I landed on the floor with a clunk. I jumped to my feet as quickly as possible shouting:

"Truant Officer! This young lady is missing Bible studies and I want to know why." It was the best I could come up with at such short notice. I thought it wasn't bad. Uncle Mario had a different opinion. He clambered off the bed and came at me like an angry bear. Unfortunately for Mario, he was an angry bear with a hard-on and his pants around his ankles. He stumbled forward closing the gap between us. Uncle Mario stumbled forward head-first…head-first onto my shoe (which was swinging upward to meet his jaw). There was a very satisfying cracking sound as leather met bone and Uncle Mario bit the dust.

The schoolgirl on the bed clawed at a sheet, desperately trying to cover her bee-sting breasts.

"You're not the truant officer," she said.

"No shit," I said. "Get dressed, I'm taking you home." She started scrambling around for her underwear and clothes.

"Could you take me back to school instead? I don't want anyone to find out about this."

"Too late princess, somebody already has." I got the girl downstairs past a very nervous desk clerk and out into a cab. She cried all the way back to school. I decided not to tell Mrs. Vitali who her husband had been seeing. It wouldn't help anyone in that family, least of all the girl, who it turns out was called Jessica. She was fifteen.

Two days later Sammy gave me a call with the good news, he'd got nearly all of his pictures back. We arranged to go to Melvin's office on Turk Street in the Tenderloin so we could go through them. Nine fifteen, the next day I picked Sammy up outside his rooming house and drove him over to Turk Street. Sammy had the photographs in a manila envelope, but he wouldn't let me get a look at them until we were with Melvin the lawyer. Sammy sat straight-backed on the edge of the seat clutching that envelope like it held a jar of nitro.

He was sweating although that morning was way cooler than when we last met. I drove around the block a couple of times looking for a place to park.

"What's wrong? You don't look so good."

"Maybe this isn't such a good idea," said Sammy.

"Hey, we've done the hard part, my friend. We got the film back. All we have to do now is make a deal with the papers, Melvin can handle that."

"I…I'm not so sure I want to go through with this."

I pulled into a recently vacated parking space. Sammy sat perfectly still, staring out through the windscreen, both hands clutching the envelope on his lap. I jumped out, walked round to the sidewalk, and opened the passenger's door.

"Let's see what Melvin has to say."

After another couple of minutes, Sammy got out of the car. I practically had to lead him by the hand. He moved like a man sleep-walking. I'd never seen anything like it. We took the elevator to the third floor. As I closed the gate and pressed the button, I asked Sammy if someone had been threatening him. He answered:

"It's nothing like that Rick; no-one ever calls me. It's just…I've seen the photographs now and I'm not sure I want to go public with them. No-one needs to see what's in here."

He patted the envelope as the elevator clattered to a halt on third. I yanked the gate open. I must admit I was getting a little pissed with Sammy. What could be on the pictures to make act so ape-shit?

We went through an empty reception area complete with a typewriter and phone on what looked like an old school desk. Then I knocked on the glass-paneled door. A familiar voice called out:

"That you Rick? Come in, come in my boy."

In one way Melvin Hammerstein's office was a lot like mine. They were both roughly the same size, tiny. Apart from that they could not have been more different. I thought my place was crammed, what with the big old desk and chair and the cot I slept on sometimes. This place was like walking into the world's smallest library. Every wall was covered in bookshelves which in turn were filled to overflowing with books the size of family albums. There were stacks of books waist-high in every corner.

Melvin's desk must have been close to collapsing under the weight of all the (you guessed it) books. There were piles and piles of books on the floor, some leaning precariously awaiting the slightest touch which would send the whole tower tumbling. The place smelt like an old schoolroom that had been left out in the rain. Sunlight slanted through a large arched window behind Mister Hammerstein's desk and chair, dust motes danced a lazy tango.

As we entered the office Melvin hurried around from behind his desk, miraculously avoiding the book towers, he cleared two battered brown leather chairs for Sammy and me adding to one book structure on his desk.

We tipped-toed along the narrow winding pathways like infantry walking through a minefield, then carefully sat down. Melvin hurried back behind his desk shouting out:

"No calls please Mrs. Finkelbaum!"

I leaned forward in my chair and whispered:

"Melvin, there's no-one out in reception."

"There isn't?"

I shook my head. Melvin Hammerstein looked confused for a moment. We waited.

"Oh, that's right, Moira Finkelbaum died last year."

Sammy glanced across at me with a very worried look in his eyes.

"So, who's been making my coffee and typing my letters for the last nine months?"

Sammy stood up, about to leave. The look on his face was priceless. I reached over.

"Sit down Sam, Mel's just messin' with you."

Mel Hammerstein was laughing out loud, almost falling out of his chair, tears in his eyes.

"It's been years since I've done that one, worked like a charm!"

I turned to Sammy.

"Melvin's wife is his receptionist, but Sylvia doesn't start as early as Mel, she likes to start the day slowly, isn't that right Mel?"

"None of us are getting any younger Rick, even Sylvia. She likes a lie-in every now and then. She'll be along shortly. How's the hand?"

"Still burned to hell." I quipped as I took off my hat.

"The ear's looking a lot better though," said Mel.

I said: "I have to keep it out of the sun, which isn't too hard in this town."

Melvin turned to Sammy.

"So, what do you have there, Mister Kirk?"

Sammy's grip on the envelope tightened. I said:

"Come on Sammy, let's see them."

Sammy reached between two book towers and handed the envelope over to Melvin Hammerstein. Mel pulled a pair of small horn-rimmed glasses from his breast pocket, wiped them on a paisley handkerchief from the same pocket. Then he opened the envelope. One by one he looked carefully at the 8 x 10's before handing them back over the desk to me.

Sammy stood up and squeezed his way to the window behind Mel's desk. He stared down at the street below. He didn't want to see the photographs again, I guess.

Mel passed the first two photographs over to me dismissively; they were hard to make out, just a brown blur really. Sammy apologized:

"The first couple are my feet and the boardwalk; I must have pressed the shutter as I ran to the railing."

Mel held onto the next one. Sammy spoke very quietly:

"The cops did blow-ups of the next four or five, they pushed the enlarger to the limits, I guess. Did the best they could." Sammy's voice kind of trailed away.

"Oh my," said Melvin. "Oh my."

His hand was trembling as he handed over the 8 x 10. It was out of focus a little and the subject matter was way too far out to get any detail, but it was all too clear what we were looking at. It looked to be almost directly above the Golden Gate Bridge which formed a kind of frame for the main subject. The Connie was in two very large pieces that were falling vertically about fifty yards apart. You could clearly make out the nose section including the cockpit followed by the rest of the aircraft which looked like a giant black cross falling from the sky. The Connie had been blown apart somewhere behind the cockpit but before the wing roots. It looked as if the engines were still running as it tumbled into the sea. You could clearly make out the distinctive triple tail section.

I felt the bile rise in my throat as I turned over the photograph and handed it back to Mel Hammerstein. Sammy would not turn from the window. Mel was looking at the next two photographs. He was reluctant to hand them over to me.

"Dear God!" Mel exclaimed. "You got the tail hitting the water."

Very quietly Sammy said:

"I know what I got."

Chapter Two

Sammy said he wasn't sure if he wanted to sell his pictures to the newspapers so we agreed that Melvin would keep them in his safe for now, along with the negatives. I told him if the pictures were sold to Life magazine or a syndicated newspaper group, he'd make a mint. Sammy said he wasn't interested in making money off of people dying in his pictures. I kind of understood that. We'd both witnessed death at close quarters. Maybe Sammy would re-consider when next month's rent came due…I wasn't sure. After thanking Melvin for his advice and assistance I drove Sammy back to Hyde Street Pier so he could get to work. He seemed relieved not to have the prints on him anymore.

I drove to Clement Street, parked up in the alley, and got to my office just before eleven. I was somewhat surprised to find the door un-locked. I was more surprised when I went in. A tall, very thin guy with spiky, short, very blonde hair was standing behind my desk in just the same way that Sammy had stood by the window of Melvin Hammerstein's office less than an hour ago. The tall blonde guy wore a very expensive looking black suit.

"Do you mind telling me what the hell you are doing in my office?" I asked, which was (I thought) a reasonable question in the circumstances.

"The door was locked; how did you get in bub?"

Without turning or saying a word the tall guy held up a set of skeleton keys in his left hand. The guy had very small hands with long fingers. He appeared to be wearing nail polish, although I couldn't be sure. This struck me as kinda weird.

"Why don't you sit down and start talking?" says I. The tall figure turned from the window and appeared to be holding a Beretta in his right hand. He also appeared to be female. This was really weird. She was wearing a suit all right but there were bumps where there shouldn't have been bumps, really quite impressive bumps. Also, the scarlet lip-stick was a dead giveaway. She had the palest blue-grey eyes and her hair was cut like she was going to play Peter Pan on stage somewhere. She had a short up-turned nose and an over-plump bottom lip. Not that I was paying attention.

"What's your name toots?" I asked, by way of being friendly.

"Not toots," she answered, by way of being business-like.

"Look if you're not going to use that pea-shooter how's about you put it away in that snazzy shoulder holster you're packing, and I'll forget all about punching that lip-stick off your face?"

Blondie put the gun and keys away and sat down. With her left hand, she extracted a business card from a jacket pocket. She tossed it across the desk. I caught it.

"I'm Inga," she said.

"I'm not the slightest bit surprised," I said…I can be snippy when strange people break into my office even if they look like the tall blonde. I looked at the business card. It didn't say: 'Inga' on it. It said this:

Douglas P. Brady Import And Export

Obviously, I wasn't at my sharpest that morning because it took me a full thirty seconds or more to work out who Douglas P. Brady was. Then the penny dropped. It made a hollow metallic clunking sound, kind of like you might imagine a guillotine would make.

I'd never heard anyone call him Douglas before. That's why I was a little slow making the connection. Everyone just called him Patrick Brady or more commonly 'Big Paddy Brady.' He was the most notorious ex-bootlegger on the West Coast, an Irish/Canadian old-style gangster, born in Ireland but brought up in Toronto, Ontario. Supposedly he'd now gone legit, moved into hotels, trucking and bars. He's come up in the world it's true, but he was still as tough as nails and anyone stupid enough to cross him wound up floating in the bay with several body parts missing. I'd met him a couple of times over the years; I did not enjoy the experience.

"What does Big Paddy want with little ol' me?" I asked.

"Mister Brady wants to talk to you."

"I guessed as much. Why didn't he come down here to see me? We could have skipped all the unpleasantness and got straight down to business. I'm a straight-talking guy. Tell him to give me a call if he…"

The Beretta was back on display.

"Mister Brady wants to see you now."

"Why didn't you say so Toots? Let's not keep him waiting. That would be rude."

I made a point of locking my office as we left then I followed blondie down to the street. A new dark green Cadillac Fleetwood sat outside my building. It also sat outside several neighbor's buildings. This thing was as long as a city block! Blondie opened the back door for me.

"Get in."

"No please?"

"Get in or I will shoot you in the gut. Then I'll make you clean up the blood from the back of the car."

"Don't you wish you had a dick to go with the suit and all the tough talk?" I asked. This did not go down too well. Blondie chopped me on the back of the neck as I bent over to get in the car. I fell face-first onto the back seat, and everything started to look black for me.

I came round as we were passing the Army base at Cavallo Point. The back of my neck hurt like hell. I owed Inga some form of retribution, but I couldn't hit a girl, now could I? I would have to plan something else. I rubbed my neck for a while as we headed toward Sausalito. I knew that Brady now owned the Sausalito Hotel, so I thought we'd be going there. Instead, we turned right shortly after the base and headed down toward the water.

We turned right again on Sommerville Road and seconds after that we pulled up at the Presidio Yacht Club. This place wasn't as fancy as the name suggested, just one average white barn of a building facing out onto the marina. Some of the yachts tied up at the marina were probably worth more than the whole set up on-shore. I was led down a jetty toward the biggest, swankiest motor-boat I had ever seen.

It was sleek, it shone brilliant white in the afternoon sun; it was as big as a destroyer. We went aboard, climbing the steep gang-plank. The decking looked like polished mahogany. The boat was called The Kilkenny. It had a brass name-plate the length of a surfboard. Blondie dug the gun in my ribs again and ushered me toward the stern. Under an awning that could cover a cow field was a lounge area complete with about a dozen wicker deck chairs and a very well-stocked bar. I was told to sit down. I sat down. I heard a radio somewhere on the boat playing a recent top 50 hit. I think it was 'Tenderly' by Rosemary Clooney. I like Rosemary Clooney.

After about ten minutes Patrick 'Big Paddy' Brady appeared. He was dressed like Mussolini's flamboyant uncle. He wore whites, some kind of Captain's uniform complete with enough gold braid to make an admiral jealous. Normally I would have found this kind of get up immensely funny, not today. One look at Patrick Brady's face told me that merriment would not be a good idea at this time.

As you might expect 'Big Paddy' was a large man, with big hands, broad shoulders, and a broader belly, straining his Captain's jacket to bursting. He was taller than me, red-faced with black wavy hair, bushy black eyebrows, and an astonishing amount of black nasal hair. The backs of his hands and fingers were like small forests. Under the bushy eyebrows, he had pale green eyes that seemed to read your thoughts as he talked to you.

"Drink?" he asked.

"Only if you're having one."

"Whisky?"

"Sure."

Brady squeezed himself behind the bar and came up with a bottle of Kilbeggan, an Irish Whiskey I'd never heard of before. He half-filled two tumblers, handed one to me. He stayed behind the bar. I got the impression he felt at home there.

"Slainte!" he said. I'd heard this greeting before when I was stationed in Norfolk, England.

"Cheers!" I said; then I took a good slug of the peaty amber nectar. Trust me; it was good, very good. I held the glass up to the light for a moment, savoring the flavors still in my mouth.

"Wow," I said. Brady had finished his tumbler already.

"Irish Whiskey," he said proudly.

"Mister Brady," I said, trying to appear relaxed and confident. "Why all the cloak and dagger stuff? My name's in the phone book, if you wanted to see me you only had to call."

"Another?"

"No thanks Mister Brady, I've only just got going on this one."

"You heard about the plane blowing up?"

"Who hasn't? You would have got a great view of it if you were out on this floating palace. I figure they'll be lifting the bits and the bodies out of the bay in the next few days."

"My wife Constance was on that plane."

Suddenly the whiskey didn't taste so good. I just stood there dumbfounded. I don't know how long we stood looking at each other over the top of that bar. Eventually, I managed some kind of response:

"I…I…errr."

"I want you to find out what the fuck happened," said Brady.

"I…I…"

"I'll pay you five thousand dollars now. You'll get a bonus if you find out who killed my Connie."

"Your Connie?"

"My wife Constance; Constance Louise Brady. Connie."

"Your Connie, right."

"Whose Connie did you think I meant?"

“It’s not that Mister Brady, it’s just that most pilots call the Lockheed Constellation a Connie. It’s a bit of a coincidence that’s all.”

Brady looked me in the eye. He had gone very pale.

“Do I look like I give a fuck about the name of the fucking plane?”

He did not. I had the sense to shut my big yap. Brady reached under the bar and handed me a package that felt a lot like five thousand dollars. I did not think it wise to count it.

“Your wife was flying to Seattle?”

“Vancouver. She was Canadian. She was heading north to see her Mother. She lives in Calgary.”

“Funny time to travel, with the holiday and everything.”

“Her mother’s not well, she’s in hospital.”

“I see. When did your wife decide to fly to Canada?”

“Is this relevant? It won’t tell us why the plane blew up.”

“You’re probably right. I just wanted to get some background.”

“Fuck background!” shouted Big Paddy Brady.

“Got it,” says me. “Background fucked. One last question Mr. Brady. Why me?”

“Why you?”

“There are lots of agencies in town, all of them bigger, most of them with more experienced detectives.”

‘Homer Georgeopolous did some work for me once or twice. He mentioned taking you on. At his funeral, his widow mentioned you were a pilot, some kind of war hero. I figured you’d know one end of a plane from another and you might have the right connections.’

So, I had the widow Georgeopolous to thank for this poisoned chalice of a job. I would have to make sure I thanked her, if I lived long enough.

“You can start right away; Inga will be your driver.”

“I don’t need a…”

“Inga will be your driver and assistant.”

“I don’t usually work with…”

“She’ll make sure you get access to anywhere you want to go. You’ll be able to speak to anyone you feel can help us. And she’ll act as security for you. And don’t say you don’t need security! She’s going to be your shadow until you find out what the fuck happened to my Connie.”

“Can you guarantee she won’t club me with her gun again?”

“No.”

Brady reached under the bar and somewhere else on The Kilkenny a buzzer must have sounded. Inga appeared seconds later.

"Inga, take Mister Marshall back to his office. Make arrangements to meet him first thing tomorrow morning."

Inga didn't look too pleased by the whole 'driver and assistant' scenario. Without a word, she headed outside. I turned to follow.

"Don't fuck this up, Rick," said Brady. This was the only time I ever heard him use my Christian name.

As we cruised back over the Golden Gate Inga sat up-front with the driver, she did not turn around. Back at the office, I didn't bother popping upstairs, there was no point. Before the Cadillac pulled away, I leaned into the car and told Inga that I would pick her up.

"I don't want to be driving around town in this hearse. We'll use my car. Your boss said you have to be with me but let's get one thing clear. I'm doing the investigating, you are doing the driving, maybe. When I speak to someone, you keep your pretty mouth shut."

Inga, opened that pretty mouth to comment. I held up my hand.

"And I don't want to know why you feel you have to dress like a matinee idol but please don't dress like this tomorrow. This outfit might give your girlfriend hot pants, but it won't help us. The name of the game is blending in, being inconspicuous. Do you get that?"

She nodded. I could see the hate in her eyes.

"And keep the pea-shooter under wraps, for now, okay?"

The Cadillac pulled away with a squeak of protest from its whitewall tires. I checked for messages with my service then decided to head home early for once. I didn't want to keep the five big ones in the office overnight and I wouldn't be working on any other cases for a while. Besides, the Vitali assignment had come to a satisfactory end with the skinny princess still virgo-intacta and I only had one or two more cheating husbands on the books at the moment.

Getting home early isn't always what it's cracked up to be. As I came in the front door, I heard the unmistakably awful sound of Vaughan Monroe singing 'You are the One.' He was a crooner my wife adored. I did not share her enthusiasm for crooners apart from the aforementioned Miss. Clooney. I was more of a Louis Jordan fan, maybe Cab Calloway. She loved big bands and crooners, people like Guy Lombardo. This was most likely because she'd worked with a lot of them in the early forties.

I liked the smaller combo's, I associated big band swing with the war years, and that was a long time ago. Swing music reminded me of time spent in village dance halls chasing English girls with my buddies. A lot of my buddies were still over in England. They wouldn't be coming back any time soon and they wouldn't be chasing English girls anymore either.

I went into the small square space we laughably called the lounge, walked over to the phonograph. Took Vaughan Moore off the turntable and turned it off. I called out Josephine's name but there was no reply. I grabbed myself a cold one from the fridge and wandered around downstairs. She wasn't there. Maybe she'd gone shopping and forgotten to turn the music off? I decided to get out of my suit, so I went upstairs to get changed.

As I opened the door to our bedroom I was greeted by a very uplifting sight. Jo was admiring herself in the full-length mirror and let me tell you, there was lots to admire. She had just applied deep red; glossy lipstick and she was wearing the sexiest underwear I have ever seen. A cream and black silk outfit complete with black stockings and a garter belt. She looked better than any film star I could think of. I nearly dropped my beer! She looked jaw-droppingly hot.

"Wow!" I gasped. Jo turned; surprised, she put down her lipstick and reached for a robe.

"Don't feel you have to get all dressed up on my account," I said. "I like what you have on just fine."

She forced a smile and picked up the robe anyway; it was on the bed next to the fancy box the lingerie had come in; all the way from Frederick's of Hollywood if the label was to be believed.

"You look like a million dollars." I panted. "Whatever this lot cost it was worth it."

Jo was obviously well aware of the perpetual lack of spare cash in the Marshall household. She wrapped the robe around her and started to say:

"I didn't…" then she stopped herself. I took a long drink of beer.

"You didn't what?" Jo played nervously with her pearls.

"Nothing, nothing." She said. "You're home early, is everything okay?"

I was feeling a little full of myself, so I threw the five thousand dollars on the bed. The notes kind of fanned out across the covers. For a second, I thought about taking the money to the bank.

"I got a new client today, insisted on paying up-front."

Jo stared at the money on the bedspread.

"How much did they pay you?"

"There's five thousand dollars there. I get a bonus if I get a result."

Jo started picking up the bank-notes.

"Five thousand dollars! What have you got to do, kill somebody?"

"I wish it was that easy. Do you know the Connie that blew up over the bay? I have to find out what happened."

"Why? Who's paying you five thousand dollars for that?"

"Turns out the wife of one Douglas Patrick Brady, famous ex-bootlegger of this parish was on the plane. He wants answers."

Jo sat down heavily on the edge of the bed, took my beer from me and took a long drink.

"Holy Christ!" she said, then drank some more. She finished the bottle.

"Do you think you can do it?"

"I don't see why not," I said.

"And this is really what five thousand dollars looks like?"

I leaned down, kissed her on the top of her head.

"It sure is," I said. "I'm going to get another beer. Do you want one?"

"Couldn't we hang around and roll about on top of five thousand dollars for a while?" She said, untying the belt of her robe.

"Now that is an offer I can't refuse," I said. Jo slipped off the robe, kicked off her shoes, and lay back on the bed.

"Come here," She said.

I pushed the fancy box onto the floor and joined my luscious wife on the bed of greenbacks. We made out like it the first time; crazy, reckless, laughing out loud. I worked around fancy underwear for maybe ten minutes just so I could keep looking at Jo wearing it. Then I eased the silk panties down her legs, and we continued with Jo wearing only the bra and stockings.

Finally, they too were tossed onto the floor as ten-dollar bills were scattered all over the room. Jo had the smoothest, palest skin. I ran my hands slowly along her stomach as she kissed the scarring over my eye. She nibbled on my mangled ear which hurt like hell. I decided to put up with this minor inconvenience for a while. I traced a line south from between her breasts with my tongue. She tasted salty.

Eventually, we fell asleep on top of the bed. We slept in each other's arms until it was dark. Then we got dressed and went out in search of a meal. We frequented a diner a few blocks down the hill so that was where we headed; still laughing like school kids on a spree.

The place was quiet, it was getting late. So, we both ordered the meat-loaf special and a couple more beers. We sat and talked about nothing much for a couple of hours. She told me about her trip to Hollywood, about meeting Errol Flynn and Frank Capra. I told her all about Sammy's pictures and my meeting with Big Paddy. What a night.

Chapter Three

When we got back to the house, there were two cars parked outside. One was an unmarked police car. I knew it was an unmarked police car because there was an unmarked police officer in the driving seat. The second car was a little more up-market. In its back seat was the Assistant District Attorney, Elton P. Dwight. He was a rising star in San Francisco law enforcement. A well dressed and very well-groomed small man in his early thirties; he dressed like someone much older and always wore a bow-tie. There was really only one word to describe Elton P. Dwight. He was dapper. This evening (from what I could make out) the dapper Mr. Dwight wore a cream linen suit, crisp white shirt, and a paisley tie. He looked like a Louisiana Plantation owner, a very dapper plantation owner.

Elton P. Dwight was tipped to make D.A. by the time he reached forty. So why was such a luminary waiting in a Black 51' Packard outside my humble abode at close to midnight? Josephine didn't care to find out. She took the house-keys from my hand, walked by the car, up the steps, and into the house. I was thinking maybe I should join her when Dwight wound down the window and beckoned me closer. I could almost taste the flowery cologne Dwight was wearing. He certainly had enough on. Maybe he was on his way to a hot date?

The driver hurried around and opened the door for me. I took this as a request to step inside, so I did. Dwight smiled like a shark eating sardines and said:

"Mister Marshall, good of you to join me. Mind if we have a quick word?"

"Not at all, Mister Dwight, what's up?"

"If you don't mind, I'll get straight to the point Mister Marshall, as it's late and we all have homes to go to."

"I certainly do, mine's right here but you already knew that."

"Indeed, I do. I'm reliably informed that you met with Patrick Brady this afternoon out in Sausalito."

"Correct."

"Would you mind telling me what the meeting was about?"

"He hired me to do a job."

"What kind of job?"

"I'm sure you know what I do for a living Mister Dwight; I'm a detective."

"License Number 61781, yes I know quite a lot about you."

"He hired me to get some answers for him. It's what I do. I get answers."

"And what kind of questions does Mister Brady need an answer to?"

"He wants to know who killed his wife."

"His wife is dead?"

"You see, you don't know everything that goes on in this town Mister Dwight."

"Enlighten me."

"Mister Brady's wife Constance was one of the passengers on the TWA Constellation that blew up over the bay four days ago."

Dwight leaned back in the seat.

"That is a very interesting development. I will have to send my condolences," I reached for the door handle.

"Why don't you do that? Me, I'm going to bed. Goodnight Mister Dwight."

I made to get out of the car. The driver made to stop me. Dwight put his hand on my arm. I wasn't sure I liked that.

"If you could spare me just a few more moments of your time, I'm sure Josephine won't mind waiting. You are a very lucky man, Mister Marshall; your wife is particularly attractive, in a somewhat obvious way."

I was going off this guy real fast. I didn't like the way he smiled, I didn't like the way he smelled, and I didn't like the way he kept letting me know he knew all about my business. When he mentioned Josephine, he spoke as if he'd just been rummaging through her underwear drawer.

"What is it you want Mister Dwight?"

"I'd like you to keep me informed of any developments in your forthcoming investigation, not every day you understand, but on a regular basis, regular up-dates. I do like to be kept abreast of certain matters. Particularly matters pertaining to individuals like Douglas Patrick Brady."

"All I know about Mister Brady is he's a very successful businessman who's recently suffered a tragic loss."

For the first time, Dwight's face began to show his impatience. His voice was growing harsher too.

"Let's not be naive Mister Marshall you know as well as I do. Brady is an old school gangster and he's currently involved in more forms of criminal activity in this city than…"

"So, arrest him, Mister Dwight."

"All in good time; all in good time."

I leaned against the door again and said:

"I gotta go."

The cop let me out this time. Dwight leaned out of the window.

"You will keep me informed of any progress?"

I turned and looked the Assistant D.A. in the eye.

"What's in it for me?"

A smile slowly spread across his boyish face.

"Let's just say I can arrange a little help during this and future investigations. Maybe open a few doors that might otherwise have remained closed to you. Oh, and I can speak to the newspapers and tell them it's okay to publish your friend Sammy Kirk's pictures. That's if he ever decides to sell them."

"How did you know about the pictures?" I asked.

"I told you earlier, I do have my sources, Mister Marshall."

The Assistant D.A. handed me his business card.

"If you run into any push back or resistance call this number. We'll do everything we can to smooth things along. Provided you keep in touch."

I was just about to say: 'I'll think about it.' Too late, the unmarked police car was already pulling away. Elton Dwight's Packard followed.

I was at the office early the following day but not early enough to beat my new assistant. Inga had let herself in just like before. She was sitting at my desk wearing a long black skirt with a matching jacket, and a pin-striped white blouse. She was also wearing the sourest expression I'd seen for a long time. I decided to have a little fun at Inga's expense.

"Inga, you look marvelous! Stand up, come out front of the desk; let me get a good look at you."

She did not move.

"You know with a fashionable outfit like that you'll have all the guys chasing after you. You'll have to beat them off with a stick!"

"Super funny, asshole," she said as she toyed with the Beretta. "Say something else funny, see where it gets you."

"You wouldn't want to kill me toots, your boss wouldn't like it."

"And he can go fuck himself too."

"Do you kiss your girlfriend with that mouth?"

Inga levelled the pistol at my groin. I knew she was bluffing. At least I thought she was. I soldiered on.

"I hope you brought your driving gloves; we're going on a trip."

Inga did have her driving gloves, so I put her to work behind the wheel of the Plymouth. We headed south out of town on the 101. The usual early morning fog had long since faded by the time we got to San Bruno and the turn off for the airport. We parked out front of a long white Mexican looking building with the control tower at its center.

We entered the terminal building and went to find the T.W.A. desk. I needed clearance to speak to maintenance crews and any staff on duty during the pre-flight preparations of flight 402 to Vancouver, British Columbia. Before we spoke to the T.W.A. I found a payphone and called the number on Elton Dwight's business card. I told whoever was on the other end of the line where I was and what I planned to do.

"Give us ten minutes, we'll make a call," said the D.A.s office. I checked my watch and strode over to look out on the apron. The familiar smell of aviation fuel brought back all sorts of memories; some good, some not so good. Two DC3s were shuffling back from the ramp, a long line of passengers snaked up the steps of a Pan Am Stratocruiser. It was business as usual. You would not be able to tell that an aircraft had left here just a few days earlier and ended up in San Francisco Bay. Inga stood silently by my side, looking at the panorama dispassionately. She must have put her pistol in her purse. There was nowhere else for her to hide it.

"Just let me do the talking in there. I know these civil aviation types; I was planning on being one. You know you really do look good in that outfit. I wasn't joking."

Inga looked at me with icy blue-grey eyes. She did not smile. I held up my hands.

"Okay, okay. I won't say another word about how you look. Where are you from originally?"

"Iceland."

"I don't think I've ever met anyone from Iceland before."

"It's not a large country," she said. Was she trying to be funny? I couldn't tell from her face which was still a frigid mask. We walked over to the T.W.A. desk. There was a buxom boxy young woman behind the counter; she was about as wide as she was tall, her mid-blue uniform emphasizing her broad hips and shoulders. Her red hair was a lion's mane of curls tied at the back with a blue bow and her nose was sprinkled with freckles. Even as we walked toward her, she was looking around nervously. I said:

"Hi, my name's Rick Marshall, the District Attorney's office should have called ahead. I'm a Private Investigator working for a very important local businessman."

She reached for the phone.

"Ah, Mister Marshall; if you could show me some identification."

I dug in my wallet for my driver's license. Boxy red-head held up a finger to me and whispered into the phone.

"Mister Wallace? He's here. Yes here, now, at the main terminal."

She put down the phone; all of a sudden, she seemed close to tears. I had no idea why.

"If you wouldn't mind waiting just a few minutes, Mr. Wallace is coming down to see you."

"And Mister Wallace is?"

"West Coast Operations Director; he won't be a moment," she said, she ducked behind the counter and came up with a purse. She dug around in it for a while till she produced a handkerchief. She put the handkerchief to good use, wiping at her nose constantly.

Mister Wallace rushed across the concourse like the white rabbit from Alice in Wonderland. He even had a fob watch tucked into the waistcoat of his three-piece Sear's suit. He was a little shorter than me, about 5'9", about forty. He looked like a guy who ate too much home cooking. He was pear-shaped and decidedly soft boiled. He had a soft-boiled handshake to go with the look. He nervously looked us up and down.

"Mister Marshall? From the D.A.'s office?"

"Not exact..."

"That's right," said Inga. "Mr. Marshall would like to talk with your maintenance chief, and we'd like a list of all the passengers and crew on flight 402."

I looked around at Inga. She was once again the Ice Maiden, playing the part of an efficient secretary/assistant perfectly. Wallace was a little taken aback by Inga. He was obviously used to bossing submissive female underlings around. The spurious connections to the D.A.'s office won him over though.

"If you'll wait here a second, I'll get Miss Harper to type up those lists for you. You can collect them when you leave. Then I'll drive you over to the hangar. It's quite a way and there's lots of construction going on at the moment, they are building a new terminal. There are trucks and planes everywhere. The airport can be quite a dangerous place. I'll meet you out front in a few minutes; I've got a company car."

He said, 'I've got a company car' like he was saying: 'I'm having an affair with Marilyn Monroe' or: 'I've got a foot-long schlong.'

We stepped back out into the sunshine and waited for Wallace to collect his company car.

"Nice work back there, Miss.?"

"I don't think we should bother with that," said Inga.

"No really, I'd like to know. I can't introduce you as Miss Inga or Inga, it doesn't sound right. What is your full name?"

"Do you have a pen? Because you are going to have to write this down."

"Come on, it can't be that hard."

At last, Inga smiled.

"Ready?" she asked. I nodded.

"Inga Bjarkardóttir."

"I'm sorry?" I said.

"Inga Bjarkardóttir."

"Maybe we'll stick to Inga," I said.

"Maybe we will," said Inga.

A 49' Ford Woody wagon with a T.W.A. emblem on the door pulled up. We got in. I let Inga take the front street as I figured the more we could distract our new best friend, the better. Wallace drove us away from the terminal building, a few hundred yards around the perimeter, and we came to a security barrier.

"These people are from the D.A.'s office, they are with me," said Wallace. I nodded a greeting to the guy on the gate. He made a note on his clipboard and the barrier was lifted to let us through onto the apron. We dodged taxi-ing aircraft and tractors pulling trains of luggage and eventually got to a quieter part of the airport, away from all the noise and dust of the construction site. We pulled up in front of one of the biggest hangars I've ever seen. Lined up out front were three Lockheed Constellations. Mr. Wallace turned to me:

"We've grounded the whole fleet of Connies, don't know for how long. We're pulling them into the hangar one after the other for a complete going over. We're concentrating on the fuel system to start with as it looks like the likeliest cause of the crash."

I knew it wasn't the fuel system. If the fuel had stopped flowing to the engines, I would have heard miss-fires. I heard an explosion. We got out of the car. Wallace hurried round to open the door for Inga. She made sure her skirt rode up a few inches as she stepped out. Then she took his hand; held it for a few seconds longer than strictly necessary. I could practically hear his heart rate climbing, poor sap. She was absolutely brilliant. I brought Wallace back down to earth with a bump.

"Mister Wallace, I don't think there was a fuel management problem. I heard an explosion. And I've seen photographs of the wreckage falling out of the sky..."

"Which photographs? Where?"

"...And I can tell you all four engines were still under power when the aircraft hit the water."

"Scared the bejesus out of me," quipped Inga. "I was really close."

"Oh my, where were you?"

Just for a second, I thought Inga was going to say she was on Mr. Brady's yacht off Sausalito. I needn't have worried; she was way too smart for that.

"I'd just gone over the bridge; I was heading out to Marin City, to see my aunt." Inga smiled sweetly at Wallace; virginal innocence personified.

We walked through the main doors of the hangar, past one Connie with two of its engines removed and up a flight of stairs to the office. We were met by the crew chief. He was just the kind of guy I expected him to be. Except his company overalls were surprisingly free of oil stains.

The chief was maybe late fifties, the stubble on his chin looked like it could scrape paint off a house side. He was about my height, 5' 11' and he had broad shoulders and arms like tree-trunks.

His hands were the size of dinner plates and his nails were encrusted with black gunk. I knew this guy; I'd known lot's like him.

Of course, he didn't know me, and he didn't look like he was too interested in talking to a complete stranger about the biggest disaster he'd ever been close to. He wiped his hands on a rag then shook mine as we were introduced.

"Mike Halloran," he said. "I hope this won't take too long, Mister Wallace. We're under the gun here."

Behind Mike's large head I noticed a crest from the 390 Bomber Group; who were stationed at Framlingham.

"I see you worked on B17's in Europe."

Mike turned to look at the crest, when he turned back, he looked at me in a whole new way.

"You were over there?" he asked.

I took my hat off, rubbed what was left of my left ear. Just for show, you understand, every little bit of leverage helps.

"I was with the 482nd at Alconbury just the other side of Cambridge from you until spring '43. After this, I was shipped back Stateside."

"Can I get you a coffee sir, miss?" he asked. We had him now.

"Tell you what Mike, why don't we have a look around the Connie downstairs, you can talk me through the maintenance logs, how you usually handle pre-flights and let me know what you think might have happened with flight 402," Mike Halloran was heading for the door in a flash.

"I'll make the coffee," volunteered Inga. "If Mister Wallace will show me where everything is."

Halloran was already heading down the steps.

"I knew you wouldn't be able to resist a look around the flight deck of the Connie, she's one hell of an aircraft. Cruises at 340, that's faster than some fighters in the war. She's got a range of over five thousand miles...follow me, sir."

I left Inga to talk some more with Wallace and followed Halloran down onto the hanger floor.

We climbed aboard the Lockheed Constellation using a metal ladder up to the rear door; Mike Halloran led the way forward to the cockpit before thoughtfully stepping aside to let me squeeze into the left-hand seat.

"I knew this would be your seat," he said. He took the flight engineer's seat behind and to the right.

"It's been a while. There's a lot more to this cockpit than a B17's… You know I applied to T.W.A. in 1946. Did the interviews, even flew a few shake-downs in a DC3, then I did the medical."

"What happened?"

"They said I may have damage to my inner ear. They couldn't clear me for night flying etc. etc. etc. and that was all she wrote."

"Sorry to hear that sir."

"Call me Rick," I said. "I got the same story when I tried to enlist for Korea. I could have flown supply flights; that kind of thing, maybe not combat anymore, I'm a little too old for that…but, no dice."

I took my time gazing over the instruments in the Connie's cockpit; I began to find my way around. Everything felt the same, smelt the same as the B17. I realized just how much I missed flying.

"There was nothing wrong with 402 when she left here that morning. I signed off on her myself. I can show you the maintenance logs if you like but there's nothing to see. And the flight engineer was one of our most experienced men. The crew could have handled almost any emergency apart from an explosion on board at less than a thousand feet."

"I believe you, Mike. I've seen photographs taken just after that explosion."

"How in the world did you get those?"

"Just someone with a camera in the right place at the right time."

"How come we haven't seen those pictures yet? They could be important to the investigation."

"The guy that took them isn't sure if he wants them in the newspapers. It's not something you want to look at over breakfast. I'll get in touch and see if we can send you copies if you think it'll help."

"Thanks, Rick; that would be helpful."

"What I can tell you is flight 402 broke in two after the explosion somewhere right about where you are sitting. You can clearly see two large pieces of fuselage."

"Jesus! Poor guys."

"You know it looked kind of like she'd been hit by a burst of cannon shells. Now we know that didn't happen so the only other thing it could be is…"

"…A bomb."

I said: "It seems unbelievable."

"No, you're right; it's the only logical explanation so far. I mean its only guesswork until they recover the Connie."

"How long will that take?" I asked.

"Your guess is as good as mine on that one captain."

Mike took a last look around the instruments on the flight engineer's panel.

"Well, if it was a bomb and it went off near here Stu wouldn't have known much about it."

"Stu was the flight engineer?"

"Yeah, Stu Brown, great guy; been with us since '46. He was a bit of a ladies-man. Half the women at this airport are in mourning right now; over the years Stu Brown has had his wicked way with practically every passable female in this company. His wife lives on the family farm some ways north of the bay area, hardly ever comes into town. So, Stu used to stay in a boarding house through the week when he was flying and drive up at weekends. That was a very busy boarding house if you catch my drift… He told me once his wife is a bit of a loner, doesn't do well in crowds. He said she worked in a munitions factory during the war; they met at one of those big dances over on Alameda…never met her myself."

I clambered out of the captain's seat and we headed back through the luxurious passenger compartment then back out of the rear door. I asked Mike what he thought of the new jet airliner coming into service in England, The Comet. He was impressed that I was so well up on the industry. I told him I had a couple of buddies who had stayed on in England after the war and got jobs at the Hatfield factory where the Comet was being developed.

"They have a couple being tested by B.O.A.C. right now," I said. Mike asked:

"Don't those four big jet engines get through a ton of fuel?" I wasn't sure. But I decided to keep quiet about the new jetliner. Mike thought so much of the Connies in his charge that it was kind of cruel to even suggest they might be obsolete in just a couple of years. Back in Mike's office I took note of his address and said I'd try to get copies of the pictures to him as quickly as possible. We shook hands at the top of the stairs.

"The Constellation is one hell of an aircraft Mike. I'm sorry I didn't get the chance to fly them."

"You know Howard Hughes himself had a hand in the design…"

"Really, I did not know that…"

"Like I say, she flies like a fighter. We had some engine problems on some of the early models, but we got that licked a while ago."

I'd read about the engine fires on a number of Constellations. There was a well-worn joke that the Lockheed Constellation was the best tri-motor money could buy. I did not share that joke with Mike Halloran. I did not think he'd appreciate it.

I followed Wallace and Inga down the stairs and back out to the station wagon.

Chapter Four

When we got back to the T.W.A. counter, Miss Harper was M.I.A. The passenger and crew details were on the counter, neatly typed, awaiting our scrutiny. Miss Harper had obviously been crying as she typed; tears had smudged a number of names on the list. 49 passenger's names listed alphabetically then a separate sheet for the crew. I thanked Mr. Wallace for his attention and promised to keep him in the loop if there was any progress in the investigation. He gave me a business card.

"Call me anytime, anytime you get some news," he said.

"What do you think of the rumors that Howard Hughes was on the Connie, that's why it was blown up?"

Wallace looked decidedly uneasy. He took a deep breath before answering.

"We don't know what happened to flight 402 Mister Marshall and I would be grateful if you would not use phrases like 'blown up' when referring to this 'incident.' Not until we have proof, one way or the other. What I can tell you for certain is that Mister Hughes was not on flight 402."

"And how's that?" I asked.

"Because I spoke with Mister Hughes this morning personally. He was very concerned about the incident and requested daily reports of any progress."

"Where is Mister Hughes?"

"I'm not at liberty to say."

"So, you don't know?"

"I didn't say that; now if you will excuse me, I'll say good-day."

After the most cursory of handshakes, he moved over to say goodbye to Inga. He looked her up and down one last time, like a county auctioneer looking over a brood-mare. I thought for a second that he was going to kiss her hand and I wondered how she might react. Luckily Inga's digits remained un-molested.

We went out to the car; got back on the 101 and headed north back to the city. As Inga concentrated on driving the Plymouth, I took my chance, pulled my hat down over my eyes, and did some serious thinking. Here's how that went:

It was clear that an explosion brought down flight 402. Was it a deliberate act of sabotage or a catastrophic accident? If it was a deliberate act who was the target? All the people on the plane? A crew member? A particular passenger, like Mrs. Constance Brady? Maybe Howard Hughes? If someone had heard the rumor, and he was supposed to be flying on the Connie that day…

These questions and more bounced around my head like a six-week-old puppy in a Safeway pet-food aisle. As we got closer to the city, I asked Inga to find a coffee shop. I figured two heads were better than one and I thought maybe she might open up to me a little and share a little background on her employer. She left the 101 and turned onto Potrero. Soon we were pulling up on the corner of 24th and York. We walked into the St. Francis diner and grabbed two stools at the end of the counter near the door.

"You hungry?" I asked. "My treat."

Inga scanned the menu behind the chrome counter.

"I'll take a Rueben and a coffee. And some fries."

I turned to the young guy behind the counter.

"Sounds good to me, I'll have the same, hold the fries."

The coffee came in seconds, it was good and strong, just the way I like it. As we waited for our sandwiches we talked: about her moving from Iceland in 1942, about her parents and family back in Keflavik which is a tiny town on the coast about thirty miles west of the capital Reykjavik. She was the youngest of three kids. Both her brothers were fishermen before the war.

Inga's journey to the States sounded like something from an adventure novel. She's got herself a trip on a west-bound freighter that had stopped in at Reykjavik for repairs. She'd promised to marry the skipper if he got her safely to New York. She told of one night when the convoy they were in was targeted by U-Boats. They'd lost three ships, all of them going to the bottom in a matter of minutes. The captain had been ordered not to stop and pick up survivors. Inga didn't think he would have done it anyway.

Of course, she'd jumped ship the second they had tied up. She'd made her way across the country, working as a waitress, dancing in two-bit sleazy dives…whatever it took to survive. Inga brushed over this part of the journey fairly quickly. I didn't ask any questions. She talked about moving to the bay area and struggling to find work that didn't involve dancing around in skimpy costumes in front of lecherous men.

"So how did you come to be working for Paddy Brady?" Our meals arrived. Inga dug in straight away; she took her time before answering me.

"I was working as a waitress in one of his clubs; The Sinaloa. I had a friend who was a dancer there."

"I know it, on Powell Street. They have flamenco dancers. Was your friend a flamenco dancer?"

"Not exactly, Peggy had a more artistic act."

"Artistic?"

"She was a burlesque dancer, okay?"

"Okay by me."

"Anyhow Peggy was an artistic dancer, I was working as a waitress. One night this guy makes a grab for Peggy as she comes off stage, ripped the top off her costume. He was really drunk, and he and his friends thought it was a great laugh. I showed him otherwise."

"What happened?"

"I guess I beat him up pretty bad, smashed his head on the table a few times. They didn't call the cops and the guy didn't press charges but…"

"Who wants to admit being beaten up by a girl?"

"That might have been it. Anyhow the manager thinks it's best if I don't show my face for a while, like…ever again. Then I got a message from Mister Brady. He'd heard about what happened. I thought he was going to can me or kill me."

"But he didn't."

"No, he offered me a job as a bodyguard and driver for him and Mrs. Brady. Turns out he'd got rid of this driver a few days before. A guy from Mexico called Raul. I found out this Raul guy liked the horses and he was always losing money and the word was he got a little too friendly with Mrs. Brady."

"That doesn't sound like a good career move."

"So, I guess I was a quick fix that stuck around."

"What was Mrs. Brady like?"

"She was a lot younger than Mr. Brady, not much older than me really."

"Any kids?"

Inga laughed. "No, it wasn't that kind of marriage."

"Is there any other kind?"

"She was arm candy, Rick. She was there to look good at dinner parties and banquets, and when they went out. You know the kind of thing."

"Did she ever talk about this Raul guy to you?"

"Never mentioned him."

"Was she happy?"

"I have absolutely no idea. I only know it wasn't a life I would have chosen. I would not have changed places with Constance Brady for anything."

"Did you drive her to the airport?"

"Sure did; I carried her cases in and handed them over at the check-in."

"How was she?"

"She seemed a little nervous about the flight, she looked a little pale. Maybe she wasn't a good flyer."

What Inga had just said seemed to weigh on us both for a while. We finished eating in silence and went back to the car.

"I'll drive," I said. It was getting late. "Can I drop you anywhere?"

"Mona's on Broadway," Mona's was the premiere lesbian hang out in town.

"The infamous Mona's hey? Won't it be a little early?"

"My girlfriend's dancing there now. We kind of meet up before she starts work."

"I'm sure it's a much more civilized place, less chance of getting your costume ripped apart."

Inga smiled.

"Don't you believe it."

Thirty minutes later I dropped Inga off under a sign that read:

Mona's Where Girls Will Be Boys

"Meet you at my office, nine tomorrow. Oh, and Inga; wear what the hell you like."

Inga hurried away to the stage door and I pulled into traffic.

I spent an hour or so at the office, opening mail, writing checks; checking messages…I had several from a Mister Thorpe who was trying to get hold of me. He did not leave a number; said he'd keep calling back. I made a few calls of my own then I headed out. It was 6.15 when I got home, and Josephine wasn't there. I called her office but there was no answer. I grabbed a beer from the fridge and sat outside on the deck watching traffic go by. There wasn't much.

Josephine arrived in a taxi about an hour later. I was on my third Acme by then. Jo paid for the taxi and joined me on the front deck.

"I hope you saved one or two for me."

"Tough day?"

Jo slumped down next to me.

"The worst; you know, if you keep getting these five thousand-dollar jobs I'd be able to quit."

I got up and got her that beer. I shouted out to her:

"Can't guarantee that; I'm not sure working for Big Paddy is good for my health."

I stepped back out of the kitchen and handed Jo her beer. She looked up at me.

"Why? Has something happened?"

"No, not really."

"No, or not really?"

"Nothing's happened; it's just that I don't think there's any way I can give Brady what he wants. I don't have the resources or the access to get him the answers he's looking for. I think we are going to have to disappoint Mr. Brady and I don't think he is used to being disappointed."

"Is there any way you can get out of this job?"

"You mean, send him back the five grand and say, 'Thanks but no thanks'? Again, that's probably not a good career move."

Jo drank some of her beer, stared into space. I asked:

"Have we got any food in the house? I'm starving."

We went back inside and started rooting around the shelves. The phone rang. It was Inga. She told me the barges were in place and they were going to lift the main parts of the wreckage first thing tomorrow. She went on:

"They are going to close the bridge to all traffic. They don't want the press or the public anywhere near."

"Makes sense," I said.

"So, Mr. Brady said he'll pick you up at six from the Berkeley Pier."

"He'll what? He plans to go and watch?"

"I guess so. See you then," Inga put the phone down.

The next day San Francisco bay was shrouded in fog. Like most locals, I'd learned never to take the weather for granted. Even in the middle of summer, this kind of bone-chilling early morning was a regular thing. What was it Mark Twain said about it? Something like: "The coldest winter I ever saw was the summer I spent in San Francisco," For some reason, this quote was burrowing into my befuddled early-morning brain as I stood freezing my ass off at the end of Berkeley Pier.

Brady's boat bumped up to the old ferry terminal about fifteen minutes after I got there. I clambered down some rickety steps and jumped aboard. Inga was there to greet me. She certainly looked the part in faded jeans and a dark blue bulky sweater.

"Well hello, sailor," I said as she held out a hand to help me.

"Hello yourself; coffee?"

"Good call."

After grabbing a coffee, we edged forward until we were standing in front of the main cabin. There wasn't a lot to see. Thick fog enveloped us making everything cold and damp. The only thing we could hear was The Kilkenny's diesel engines and occasionally a distant foghorn. Paddy Brady joined us on deck. I nodded a greeting.

"Captain said this should clear in half an hour," said Brady.

"I only hope we don't run aground on Alcatraz Island."

"He knows what he's doing," Brady proffered a hip flask. I declined. He glugged a shot of whiskey into his own coffee.

We headed west. At least I assumed it was west. There was a gentle, rolling swell. I continued to stare into the fog which had an eerie luminous brightness to it. Twenty minutes later we passed Alcatraz on our port side, the island and prison buildings looming out of the mist like a giant whale breaching. I was beginning to regret turning down the early morning booze. Brady had gone back inside. Inga and I were alone at the bow of the Kilkenny.

"I don't know what he hopes to achieve by this," I said.

Before Inga could comment we heard the Kilkenny's engines slow. We were under the Golden Gate Bridge. The roadway was roughly 250 feet above us and strangely silent, there were no cars crossing. About two hundred yards ahead I could see two large cranes piercing the fog, fog that was (as predicted) beginning to lift. Our engines were idling now as we held our position under the bridge, slightly away from all the activity. We heard the crane's engines crank up and the two arms swung toward each other.

The two large barges carrying the cranes were surrounded by a number of smaller craft, most of them holding their positions, just like The Kilkenny. On one I could see a diving team making final preparations. A police launch was heading our way.

"Wait here," said Inga. She hurried aft to meet the police launch. Three stern-faced uniforms came aboard. Inga led them into the main cabin where Paddy Brady was waiting. I watched through the window, couldn't really tell what was going on. After ten minutes the officers went back to their launch. As the police boat pulled away Inga came back forward and put me in the picture.

"Mr. Brady was expecting that. He threatened to tie the cops up in legal tape if they forced us to move. Then he gave them a major donation for the police widows and orphans fund."

"A little stick and a lot of carrots," I said.

"If you say so," said Inga. I wasn't sure if she understood me.

The diving teams had been down for quite some time when things began to heat up. The noise from the cranes increased steadily as cables were lowered from both barges. After another lull, the cranes were revved up again. Black smoke erupted from their exhaust stacks as the cables were raised, hopefully bearing their precious cargo.

A guy I'd never seen before hurried to my side at the rail. He was holding some sort of hand-held movie camera. He started filming the bizarre scene before us. Paddy Brady joined us at the bow of his boat. Seconds later the cockpit section of the Connie was brought to the surface. As I had suspected the whole front end had sheared off just in front of the wing root. The cockpit was lowered onto one of the barges. Police officers on the barge moved tentatively forward to examine the wreckage. I could just see enough to note that the fuselage was peeled outward on the starboard side. It looked as though I was right about the seat of the explosion. Somewhere close to the seat of Stu Brown, the philandering Flight Engineer. Paddy Brady turned his back on the scene. He told the photographer to stop filming before heading aft. He was muttering to himself:

"Bad idea Paddy, bad idea."

Moments later the Kilkenny turned away from the recovery site and headed north to Sausalito at full speed. Inga went below and came back up dressed in her preferred outfit for the day, her black suit.

"Do you have a hat to go with that?" I asked her.

"Can't get one small enough," she said. Paddy Brady left the Kilkenny after telling the captain to take Inga and me downtown, the Golden Gate was going to remain closed for most of the day; at least that's what it said on the radio. The photographer hitched a ride too. Turns out he knew Inga's girlfriend. He'd worked on a stag film she starred in…small world hey? We were put ashore at Pier 33; we took a Luxor Cab to the office.

We got there just after eleven. I had just enough time to park my rear end before the phone rang. It was Dwight from the D.A.s office.

"How was the boat trip?" he asked.

"Not as much fun as you'd think."

"I'm intrigued, what did Brady think he was going to do out there? And why did he need you there?"

"Damned if I know."

I didn't want Inga to know who I was talking to. She was, after all, employed by the guy Dwight was targeting. So, I kept my answers short. This did not please Mr. Dwight one bit.

"And you were out at the airport too; you've been a very busy man."

"I find it helps to keep busy."

"Anything useful there?"

"Nope."

"Is there someone in the office with you Mr. Marshall?"

"Yup."

"I see, maybe we should speak later."

"Maybe," I put down the phone.

Inga asked: "Who was that?"

"A pain in the ass."

Inga was wandering around the office straightening picture frames, closing drawers.

"Anything I can help you with?" she asked.

"I wouldn't want you to get your hands dirty. And can you stop tidying things? You make me nervous."

"I'm bored."

"You sound like a six-year-old kid."

Inga slinked around my desk then slinked a little more right into my lap. She started twirling my tie in her fingers. Through pouting red lips, she whined:

"Come on Ricky wicky. I'm bored, let's do something. Let's do some more investigating. I like investigating."

I stood up, dumping Inga on her ass; she took the fall in good humor, bouncing back to her feet like a gymnast. She dusted off her pants.

"Ricky wicky?" I said. "Toots, don't ever call me that again, you hear?"

"So, don't call me Toots then…"

I picked up the file we'd collected at T.W.A. and tossed it across the desk.

"If you want to do some investigating why not have a good look through this?"

Inga settled down in my one client chair. The springs creaked.

"What am I looking for?"

"I have no idea. Maybe we are looking for someone with a good reason to commit suicide. Maybe there's someone on there that somebody wanted killed."

Inga leaned back in the chair, straightened out her long legs and rested her feet on my desk. She sighed: "Someone, somebody, something. That's not much to go on is it?"

"No, it's not, and unless the police can work out a way to get the rest of that Connie out of the harbor, we aren't going to get much help from them either."

I sounded like an old grouch. Inga read the T.W.A. files diligently. As she read, she whistled the chorus to 'Ain't Nobody Here but us Chickens.' I started making notes on my blotter. I got through a lot of blotters with that system, but it had worked for me in the past. After a minute of quiet contemplation and a few scribbled thoughts, I realized Inga was no longer whistling.

"What's up?" I asked. She was staring intently at the T.W.A. file.

"It might be nothing," she said.

“What might be nothing?” I asked. She laid the file on my desk and spun it around.

“We didn’t get a chance to look at this at the airport. It’s the boarding check-list.”

I looked it over. The bottom section of the list made interesting reading. The total number of passengers was listed as 48. I started working my way up from the foot of the page. The top section did not make interesting reading at all because it wasn’t there. The first quarter of the form was missing along with passenger names from A to F. Now it could just have been a simple accident, there was no way we could tell until we spoke to Al Grainger. He was the T.W.A. staff member who’d signed off on the bottom of the form.

“All the passengers on the list that we can see have been checked off as having boarded,” said Inga.

“So, one of the people on the list from A to F either didn’t turn up for the flight or didn’t get on board. Brilliant! Well done Inga. I’d kiss you but you’d probably break my neck for doing it.”

Inga did not appear to be grasping what a major breakthrough she’d made. I picked up the phone and started dialing the T.W.A. counter back at San Francisco airport.

“All we have to do is track down this Al Grainger; show him the list, he’s sure to remember who missed that flight.”

“Don’t bother,” said Inga. The call went through, the dame at the other end was shouting:

“Hello? Hello?” in my ear. Inga was pointing to something on the crew list.

“Hello? Hello!”

I looked at the list and slowly put the phone down. Al Grainger was the Chief Steward on flight 402. He was currently at the bottom San Francisco bay with his fellow crew members and forty-eight passengers.

Chapter Five

There had to be a way we could find out who was on the missing portion of the check-list. We knew Constance Brady was one of them. We had to identify the others.

"How many passengers were checked on board from the lower portion of the list?"

Inga ran her finger down the list, counting silently but moving her lips as she did so. For some reason I found this to be very distracting. I waited patiently watching Inga's lips moving. I could have waited all day.

"Forty-Five."

"And there aren't any names on the list you have there that are marked as a no show?"

"Nope. All of them have checkmarks."

"Now we're getting somewhere."

"We are?"

"Sure, we are! We know Mrs. Brady got on board because you dropped her off at the airport. That only leaves two names we have to get hold of."

"And assuming we can get those names what do we do next?"

"We get their home addresses; we speak to their families and friends; we look for anything about them that doesn't fit."

"Doesn't fit what?"

Inga had me there. Unless one of these missing names turned out to have a massive grudge against the airline or maybe Howard Hughes we were going to be no further forward. I leaned back in my chair and steepled my fingers under my chin. I'd seen Basil Rathbone do that in a Sherlock Holmes movie in England, I thought it made me look like I was deep in thought. Saw the movie at the Empire in Cambridge, 'The Spider Woman' it was called.

"Why are you praying? And what doesn't fit what?" asked Inga again.

"Not exactly sure," I said. "Still it's pretty much all we have to go on isn't it?"

I rang Wallace at the T.W.A. office and asked if he would have a copy of the boarding list for flight 402. He said he'd check and call me back this afternoon. There wasn't much else we could do until he called so I suggested lunch.

"It'll have to be somewhere close by as we don't have a car. Getting home later is going to be a bitch, especially if the bridge is still closed."

"I'll be okay, I'm meeting a friend," said Inga.

"Your dancer friend, down at the club?"

"Another friend, I have lots."

"I see," I said.

We had dim sum at a Chinese place a few blocks east. We were back in the office for two. I rang Jo to see if she wanted to meet and catch the Alameda ferry.

"We're going to be working late; Ko is going to give me a ride home."

"I thought he lived in the opposite direction."

"Does he?"

"That's what he said."

"Well, he must have something planned in Oakland tonight. Got to go, a potential client's just come in for a meeting."

She rang off.

Just a few seconds later the phone rang. I thought it was my wife Jo calling back. I was wrong.

"Hi, honey," I said.

A very confused voice came on:

"Err hello, is this Mr. Marshall?"

"Yes, that's me," I said in my authoritative, hard-nosed detective voice. Inga was rolling around in the chair laughing and holding her sides.

"This is Wallace, T.W.A."

"Thanks for calling me back Mr. Wallace. Do you have the list for me?"

There was a lengthy pause. I could hear static on the line and I could hear faint breathing from the other end.

"Mr. Wallace? Do you have the list?"

"I do have the list, Mr. Marshall but I'm afraid I will not be able to share its details with you."

"And why would that be, Mr. Wallace?"

"Two reasons, one: you don't work for the District Attorney's Office in any capacity; in fact, you are currently in the employ of one Douglas Patrick Brady, a notorious bootlegger, and crook."

"I..."

"And secondly, Mr. Marshall I have been instructed by attorneys working for Mr. Hughes and T.W.A. to have no further contact with you whatsoever. Good day."

He ended the call. No sooner had I put down the receiver than there was a knock at the door. Three very large, broad gentlemen in matching suits entered. They were followed by a much smaller guy carrying a brief-case. He was about seventy I guessed, he was practically bald, but he did have the bushiest walrus moustache. He produced a very official-looking letter from the case and placed it on my desk. Then he said:

"Mister Marshall, I presume," I nodded. He pulled a business card from a coat pocket and a pair of pince-nez glasses from his waistcoat pocket. He placed his business card on my desk, the glasses on his nose, and began to speak.

"My name is Elwood P. Thorpe. I represent Trans World Airlines and Mister Howard R. Hughes. I'm serving you with this legal document that states that you have recently knowingly miss-represented yourself as an official of the San Francisco District Attorney's office in order to gain access to personnel and property of Trans World Airlines. The aforementioned plaintiffs request that you refrain from this highly illegal action forthwith. Furthermore; if you attempt to contact any employees of Trans World Airlines you will be charged with harassment and impersonating an officer of the law. Is this clearly understood, Mister Marshall?"

I nodded. The legal bod turned to his companions.

"Duly served and witnessed," The legal bod closed his case with two loud clicks. He put his glasses back in his waistcoat pocket then leaned forward, speaking very quietly.

"A word of advice, Mister Marshall; Howard Hughes is the last person on this planet that you want to mess with. We could have your license right now; we could tie you up in court for the next five years at least. We could take every penny you own Mister Marshall, believe me. Now Mister Hughes knows you served courageously overseas in the war so he's willing to give a fellow pilot a break. This was contrary to my advice."

Howard's legal team left my office. One of the man-mountains took care to slam the door extra hard, almost shaking the glass out of the frame.

"Wow!" said Inga. "I thought for a minute he was going to click his heels like all those Nazi bad guys in the movies."

I scrunched up the letter and handed it to Inga.

"File that under C.S."

"C.S.?"

I held up the wastepaper basket.

"Chicken shit. I get those 'cease and desist' things all the time."

"Yeah but this one's from Howard Hughes."

"Which tells us a lot."

“It does?” asked Inga.

“It does. Although right now I’m not sure what.”

“Idiot.”

Inga tossed the screwed-up ball of paper into the basket.

At the end of the day, I decided to spend the night downtown, sleep in my office. I figured it would take me most of the evening to get home anyway and I needed some ‘alone time’ to think through our next move. Inga left early to meet her ‘friend’ about 5.00. I rang Jo’s office to let her know I wouldn’t be coming home. I was a little surprised when the receptionist said Josephine and Mr. den Hamer had already left for the day. I was sure Jo said she’d be working late. I left a message with reception just in case Jo called in and (in truth) I didn’t give it much thought. I spent the rest of the evening trying to get a handle on the case. At about nine I went down to Rooney’s for a sandwich and a beer. Rooney’s was a not very ‘Irish’ Irish bar (if you know what I mean) a couple of blocks from the office. It’s got all the things an Irish Bar should have: Big Mirrors with Irish Whiskey Advertisements on them, faded prints of farm cottages and hills, beer-soaked bar top, the whole nine yards. But I don’t think there’s a genuine Irish man or woman on the staff.

I got back to the office and attempted to fall asleep on the cot dressed only in my shorts. The place was like an oven so after an hour of staring at the ceiling, I got up, got a drink of water, and opened the window wide as it would go. It was late enough then so the noise of the traffic wouldn’t keep me awake. You could hear the occasional drunk serenading the night and a couple argued for twenty minutes right below the window at about 12.30. After all that solitude and contemplation, I didn’t come up with a smart next move. I didn’t even come up with a dumb next move.

Two days later The Chronicle published the list of the victims of Flight 402. This was an unexpected helping hand and we were glad to get it. The three ‘missing’ names from the top of our boarding check sheet were:

Constance Brady (26) wife of prominent local businessman Douglas Patrick Brady.

Henry R. Dobbs (35) from Portland, Oregon. Henry was Regional Sales Manager for General Electric.

Dorothea Fulton (67) Retired grade school teacher from San Mateo, travelling to Seattle for a funeral.

The Chronicle went on to say that the largest sections of the wreckage were proving to be too heavy for the two cranes currently on site. A pair of larger floating cranes were heading north from The Bethlehem Shipyards, San Pedro, near Los Angeles.

I asked Inga to check the local school boards to find an address for Dorothea Fulton while I phoned newspapers in Portland posing as a reporter for the Chronicle looking for background on Henry Dobbs. Turns out Henry was married and a father of three young children. He had worked his way up to Regional Sales Manager with General Electric in only six years. He was flying up to Seattle to visit key clients and meet with a sales representative. He'd been a keen basketball player in college and coached a local kid's team.

We were still unsure who had missed that fateful flight and we didn't know why they'd missed it. There was a chance that either Dorothea Fulton or Henry Dobbs would still be alive and come forward to explain what had happened.

After three calls Inga had a home address for Dorothea Fulton so we headed out to San Mateo.

We got on the 101 south out of town, eventually passing the airport on our left-hand side. A short while later we ran into dust clouds coming from mile after mile of construction work. Apparently, this was going to be the new 101 Freeway.

We carried on south at about fifty miles an hour, and we were driving into San Mateo in no time. There was a cooling breeze coming off the bay as we slowed to take Third Avenue into the town. Dorothea Fulton lived on her own in a small, well-maintained rancher at Laurel and 9th; close to Central Park, San Mateo. We pulled up right outside the rancher. We both stepped out, knocking the dust from our clothes. Inga ruffled her hair.

"Yuk! I think we should put the car through a car wash, with the roof down and us in it."

"That's not a bad idea," I said.

We stood by the front gate and looked at Dorothea's home. She was a keen gardener; that was plain to see. Mature shrubs offered shade surrounding a well-trimmed patch of grass. Pink magnolia bushes were in full bloom. The white fence was entwined with climbing roses. The place smelled like a summer's day in England.

"She's not in."

A grizzled voice, the kind you get from smoking cigars for fifty years or so, came from the neighbor's yard. The grizzled voice belonged to an old man in a once-white undershirt. He could have been sixty I guess, but they would have been sixty very hard years. If I was a betting man, I would guess he was closer to ninety than eighty. We walked over to talk with him.

"Young Miss Fulton, she's not in."

"We know," I said, although I regretted it that very second. The neighbor grew suspicious; you could hear it in his voice.

"If you knew she wasn't in, why did you come a'calling?"

"I think maybe you might want to sit down sir," said Inga.

"How do you know what I want to do young man?" asked the neighbor. I had to smile. Inga took it in her stride. I took a second before speaking again.

"We have some very bad news about Miss Fulton," said Inga. "We thought it might be better if you took a seat before we told you."

He looked worried now.

"Are you with the police? What's happened?" he asked.

Eventually, we got Mr. Chappelle to step back into the shade on his porch and sit down in a rocking chair.

"Is there anyone else here?" asked Inga.

"Are you the police or not?" asked Mr. Chappelle. I didn't answer directly, so he couldn't say we'd lied to him later.

"We are investigating a recent plane crash, Mr. Chappelle. It was a flight we believe Miss Fulton was on. There were no survivors."

Mr. Chappelle closed his eyes for a long time. He just sat there, rocking slowly in silence. Inga entered his house, looking for the kitchen. She returned with a glass of water and handed it to Mr. Chappelle. He looked up at Inga, his eyes misty with tears.

"Thank you, son."

Over the next hour, Inga and I sat with Mr. Chappelle, who told us he was eighty-six. He talked about Miss. Fulton and seemed to know quite a bit about her. He confirmed that she'd left to fly to Seattle about a week ago and that he hadn't seen her since. If she'd returned home, he would have noticed because he always looked out for her and she always looked out for him. From what we learned to all intents and purposes they were like most elderly couples; they were just a couple who lived next door to each other. He'd help out with the gardening and she'd prepare him a cooked meal at least three times a week.

"Dorothea never married you know, she was a teacher, a bit of dragon from what I heard. She was kind to me after my wife Edith passed on though. That was 1939. We've sort of had an understanding since then, nothing immoral or improper. We just help each other out from time to time; I make sure she's okay, that she's got enough firewood, that kind of thing."

We could tell that Dorothea Fulton's death was going to have a profound impact on her neighbor. Inga asked if he had any children or relatives nearby. Turns out he had a son who lived in Macon, Georgia. They didn't get on. Inga suggested that Mr. Chappelle wrote to his son.

"Did Miss Fulton have any relatives?" I asked.

"She had a sister lived in Seattle, Rose her name was. It was Rose's funeral that Dorothea was heading to."

We stayed with Vincent Chappelle for as long as we could but finally had to say our goodbyes and head back to San Francisco. On the drive back north neither of us spoke. It had been the toughest day I'd ever had since taking up this job. I didn't know it then, but my day was about to get much worse.

As Inga looked so down, I let her drive straight to Mona's where she could forget her troubles for a while in the arms of her lover. This seemed like a good idea to me as I got behind the wheel planning to head home to Jo as quickly as the late afternoon rush-hour would let me.

I got home at six-thirty and recognized Ko den Hamer's bright red Jaguar XK120 parked outside. I figured he must have been heading out this way and given Josephine a ride home. I parked behind the Jag and went into the house. There was a pile of cases stacked by the front door. I lifted the top one; it was heavy, obviously full.

Ko den Hamer and Jo were sitting at the kitchen table. They were both drinking red wine. The bottle in the middle of the table was already half empty.

"I hope you saved some for me," I said. "I've had the worst day ever."

Ko poured me a glass.

"What's in all the cases?" I asked.

Josephine, my wife said:

"Rick, we gotta talk."

Now here's where I give you guys a little free advice. You watch out for those words: 'We gotta talk.' Because nothing good ever came after them. You never hear someone say: 'We gotta talk. You just became a millionaire. Or: 'We gotta talk. I think we should have way more sex, in fact, I'd like to have sex every day of my life.' No, what usually follows 'We gotta talk.' is something a lot like what I heard that evening. Jo was fiddling with her pearls, couldn't look me in the eye.

"Rick, we gotta talk. I want a divorce. Ko and me we've been having an affair for almost a year now. He's left his wife and he's moving in here, with me. I've never really loved you, Rick, I mean. sure, I love you but not in the way I love Ko."

'What the fuck?' Thought I. Then I said: "What the fuck?"

My wife Josephine took a big swig of red wine. She went on:

"Ever since the war we've been going nowhere Rick. You must see that. You must realize I've been very unhappy for a long time now. Your job keeps you out all hours; you come home and fall asleep in the chair most nights."

"Well, please forgive me for working my ass off. I only did it for you."

"Did you, did you really Rick?"

Ko den Hamer opened his mouth.

"Rick, this isn't helping anyone."

"Unless you want to pay for some very expensive dental work friend, I suggest you shut the fuck up."

As you can tell, I wasn't feeling very charitable to the big Dutch fuck.

"How are the wife and kids taking to this new plan of yours?"

"I think maybe you should leave my wife and kids out of this Rick."

At this, I'm across the table reaching to grab Ko by the throat. Josephine jumps in to break us up and somehow my elbow hit's her in the eye. She screams and crumples to the floor. The bottle of wine topples from the table and breaks on the tiles. Ko gets a damp cloth and holds it to Josephine's eye. I cleaned up the broken glass. Eventually:

"I think you'd better go, Rick," she said. "I've packed all your clothes," Now I knew why the cases were in the hallway. I was moving out. I said:

"Well, that's very helpful, but I hadn't planned on moving anywhere," It was the last smart-assed remark I ever made in that house. Remember, Ko den Hamer is a big guy. He got up from the kitchen floor to join me in the hallway and stand behind me as I collected my clothes. I could have taken a pop at him but that would have been cheap, and it wasn't going to solve anything. It might have been satisfying though. Instead, I loaded up the Plymouth. By six-thirty my marriage was over, and I was out of that house for good.

Don't ask me what I did for the next few days because I couldn't tell you. I do remember taking the cases down-town to the office. I don't remember unpacking them. Inga turned up, as usual, the morning after I was effectively evicted from my own house. If she was surprised to see that I'd moved into the office she didn't show it. And I'm sure there are some of you Wisen-hymers out there thinking: *'He's a detective specializing in divorce work; he should have seen it coming.'*

All I can say to that is either a: unprintable or b: irony can be an ironic bitch sometimes can't it?

Should I have read the signs? All the weekend trips away to L.A. and the Napa Valley; all those late night phone calls? The expensive, unexplained but still incredibly sexy underwear? Underwear I only got to see in action once in case you'd forgotten.

Sure, sure I should have read the signs. But to read the signs you have to be looking out for them. You have to feel there's something going wrong before you start looking for confirmation. One thing's for sure; I will never look down on clients who come into my office, cap in hand looking for my help. If all my clients feel half as low as I do when they come to see me, they need sympathy and help, not pity. Shit! That was deep.

I can't remember eating a solid meal of any kind for maybe a week. It's fair to say I was on a liquid diet. The bars in the immediate neighborhood did a roaring trade. One bar-owner booked a trip to Hawaii on the money he made from me. I sank lower and lower into alcohol-fueled self-pity. Hey, what can I say? I was in shock.

After (I think) nine days Inga came into the office with a brown bag from a local drug store and a new shirt. She dumped the bag out on my empty desk and said:

"Right, I think you've had long enough in the gutter, it's about time you climbed back out."

"We are all in the gutter; some of us are looking at the stars," I said.

"That's very deep coming from a drunk at seven in the morning. Who said it?"

"Oscar Wilde."

"Who?"

"Oscar Wilde, English writer, went to jail for loving the son of an Earl, or something. I thought you would have known all about Oscar Wilde."

"Because I'm a lesbian? Is that it?"

"Maybe. Sorry, stupid thing to say. I was just trying to get my brain back up to speed."

Inga wasn't too upset, she said:

"One thing at a time. First, get cleaned up, you look like shit. Second, you start to eat right; I'm taking you for a proper breakfast, it's on Mister Brady."

"He knows about Jo?"

"I had to tell him. He was asking why we hadn't done a thing for over a week. He wants to talk to you."

"He's got my number. He could have left a message with my service."

"Funny, very funny. I have to take you out to Tara for one this afternoon, so you'd better…"

"Tara? As in 'Gone with the Wind?' now that is funny," I said. "In fact, it's the funniest thing I've heard in years."

Inga glared across the desktop at me.

"Let's get this straight Rick. Nobody finds the name funny. Well if they do, they usually don't find it funny for long. In fact, the last guy who found the name of Mr. Brady's house slightly amusing is currently holding up the second span of the Oakland Bridge. Do you follow?"

"I follow. You know I love it when you talk tough. Where is this Tara place anyway?"

"Pacific Heights."

"So, it's not a country estate with servants and stables and cotton fields and southern gentlemen called Rhett?"

"Are we through? Have you got it out of your system?"

"Yes ma'am! I sure have!"

Inga smiled for a second.

"It's on a corner lot on Vallejo Street, near the Presidio. It's a beautiful house and there are plenty of servants. The main dining room looks like the inside of a Tuscan villa. Not that I've ever been to Tuscany…I saw a picture in a book once."

As Inga was telling me all about the wonders of Paddy Brady's town-home I rifled through the contents of the brown bag, now displayed on my desk: Shaving soap and a safety razor, toothpaste and a brush, more soap, even some deodorant.

"Thanks for this," I said.

Inga unwrapped the shirt and I headed into the washroom. She called out to me:

"Let's get you cleaned up and looking halfway respectable. We can talk about our next move over breakfast."

Which is exactly what we did. At the same time, out in the bay, the larger floating cranes were now in position over the crash site. It had been announced on the radio that a lift would be attempted early Sunday morning. Once again, the Golden Gate would be closed to traffic.

"Do you think Brady will want to watch the recovery operation from his boat again?" I asked before shoveling bacon into my mouth.

"Why don't you ask him this afternoon?"

I didn't answer the question; I was too busy attacking three eggs sunny side up, hash brown potatoes, the aforementioned half-pound of bacon, and sourdough toast. When I came up for air Inga topped up my coffee. She sat quietly while I ate, then we talked about the case.

We still had to confirm Henry Dobbs had boarded flight 402. This meant a trip to Portland for at least one of us; I'd prefer to take Inga along with me, she was making herself indispensable. We needed to make sure he hadn't stayed at home with a head-cold or missed the flight for any of a thousand dumb-ass reasons. With a little luck, we would have a dependable body count to work with by the time we returned. I wasn't sure if positive identifications of all the victims would be possible. I was even less confident that we might get a hold of such a list. Maybe my good friend at the D.A.s office could help us with that. He'd want something on Brady in return though. I'd have to keep my eyes open and my wits about me when we got to Tara this afternoon.

During the drive over to Pacific Heights, I put Inga in the picture about my wife cheating on me.

Inga was driving as she knew the way. Once I started to talk it was hard to stop.

"I'm guessing you worked out that my wife left me, well she didn't leave me I guess, in a way I left her; although it wasn't what I wanted to do. She kicked me out of the house. She's been shtupping her boss for over a year. He's left his wife and kids and moved into our house."

"I know," said Inga.

It's a good job Inga was driving. At this point, I could have gone through three red lights without noticing a thing. I said:

"You know? How much do you know?"

Inga signaled and pulled into the side, she turned off the engine.

"I know pretty much all of it."

"What the hell's been going on?" I asked.

"I thought that was fairly obvious. Every time they went away on a business trip, they were at it like bunnies."

"I didn't mean that! I meant how do you know so much about my private life?"

Inga took her time to answer. First, she started with:

"You of all people should know there's no such thing as a private life anymore."

As she went on, I detected a little pride in what she had to tell me. It was the first thing I'd detected in quite some time. She said:

"After the first two days of you living out of your office, I realized something had gone seriously wrong between you and your wife. So, I watched the house for a while."

"My house?"

"I watched the house for the next few nights. He's a good-looking guy this Ko den Hamer; if you like that kind of thing. Josephine seems to think so if she's not faking it."

"Faking what?"

"Sorry, didn't mean to say that. Forget it."

"Faking what?"

"You know, the high pitch whooping noises she makes when they…when they have sex. It sounds a bit like a very excited monkey. Loud too; I'm sure the neighbors have noticed."

"Fuck the neighbors!" I said.

"She might as well, I'm sure they've heard all that's been going on over the last week."

"You're enjoying this aren't you?"

"Rick, I just don't want you wasting the next few weeks, months, maybe years pining after a woman who clearly loves somebody else, or at least fucks someone else very loudly most nights."

"You don't know Josephine."

"I know what she sounds like when she comes," At this Inga began to whoop, louder and louder, her voice getting higher and higher. This went on for an embarrassing minute or two. People walking past looked round to make sure I wasn't stabbing her in the heart. Eventually, I persuaded her to quiet down.

"I also know she likes to be tied up during sex, or is there another reason for the police issue handcuffs on the bed-head?"

"The what?"

"Don't get me wrong, I'm not judging her. We all like a little fantasy every now and then. And before you ask the next question you should really think about getting the locks changed on that house. But (then again) I don't suppose it's going to be your place for much longer so forget I mentioned it."

"If you were a guy, I'd pound the living crap out of you for this!"

"I know," she said. "And if I was a guy, I'd deserve it."

We left it at that. Inga started the car, shoulder checked, and pulled back into traffic.

Chapter Six

We pulled up outside a large house on Vallejo Street. It was a corner lot and to the rear, you could see clear over the city and out into the bay. The house was a dusky rose color and featured three large arched windows facing over a formal garden onto Vallejo. Behind the main building, I could see a courtyard leading onto a second similar building. We climbed Italian marble steps up to the main door. We were greeted by a man mountain in a double-breasted suit. He smiled at Inga, but she did not respond.

"He's expecting us," she said. We were escorted through the main reception area and out into the courtyard between the two buildings. A formal fountain featuring a buxom broad with a very wide ass burbled and sparkled in the sunlight (the fountain burbled, not the wide ass). Paddy Brady came out to meet us a few minutes later. He looked every bit an Irish gentleman farmer. It was a slightly cooler day than the previous few weeks and Brady wore a tan-colored tweed jacket with a light green check in it. His pants were ginger and his brogues (which looked very expensive) matched perfectly.

We sat on iron chairs around a large circular table. Brady got straight to the point, which he had every right to do, having paid $5000 for my skills.

"So, where are we?"

"It looks like the main body of the plane will be recovered in the next twenty-four hours. We should have a confirmed number of casualties shortly after that."

Brady leaned forward and barked at me; spittle-flecked the table between us.

"I can get that sort of bollocks from the bloody papers. I don't pay five thousand dollars for second-hand newspaper articles I can get on any street corner. Where are **we** at?"

I knew that bullshitting Brady would be a very bad career move. I was taking my time; considering telling him about the T.W.A. Boarding list. Would it be a good idea to mention the possibility that his wife was not on the flight? I wasn't too sure; I had to think very carefully about…

"Mrs. Brady might not have got on the flight," said Inga. Obviously, she was having a lot less difficulty in giving her boss what could be false hope. Brady glared at Inga.

"What did you just say?" I stepped up to the plate, or into the breach or whatever the hell you do in cases like this.

"We've checked the boarding list and we think there will be only 48 passengers, not 49, recovered from the wreckage; that's if they find all the err...bodies. The boarding list has three names missing from the top of it. One of these three names did not board flight 402. Constance Brady was one of them," Inga joined in:

"We've double-checked one of the other two, a retired school teacher from San Mateo. She hasn't shown up at her home, so we think she was definitely on the plane. The other passenger is a sales guy."

"Regional Manager."

"Regional Manager for General Electric. He lives in Portland, Oregon."

Brady held up a large hairy hand.

"If Constance did not get on the plane for whatever reason why didn't she come straight home? Why hasn't she been in touch? What the fuck is going on?" Inga had no answer. I kept on talking, something I do when I think I might get shot in the head at any minute:

"There are a number of possibilities: she might have been kidnapped. But we've not received a ransom note. She may have suffered an accident, some kind of medical emergency. Although she was fine when Inga dropped her at the T.W.A. counter. Or she might not want to be found."

Brady was not happy to hear this last suggestion.

"What the fuck do you mean? What are you trying to say?"

Inga came to my defense:

"All this is just theory Mr. Brady; all we know for sure is 48 passengers boarded flight 402 and not 49 as the airline thought."

I backed her up.

"That's right Mr. Brady, anything else is just...guesswork."

"I don't like guesswork. So, what's our next move?"

"We need to eliminate all the unknown factors. We need to make sure Mr. Dobbs isn't at home in the bosom of his family thanking his lucky stars that he missed that flight. We'll drive to Portland and dig around some."

"You still fly a plane?"

"I'm sure I can, why?"

"Let me make a few calls, I'll sort you out a plane. Save us all some time."

I didn't argue. It would be great to be flying again. Brady took Inga by the elbow and led her into the house. Before he did, he turned and pointed a finger at me.

"Wait through there," he said, pointing back toward the lobby. I was glad to get out of the sun and as I waited, I looked over some of the paintings and sculptures placed around the reception area. Some of them seemed very familiar, like I'd seen pictures of them in newspapers. Some were just squiggles on canvas. One wall was covered in a large canvas at least eight feet high. It was covered in what appeared to be drips of paint from a car body-shop, all different colored dots with no pattern or plan. I guessed Brady must have got that one cheap.

Brady and Inga spoke for a few minutes then we were dismissed. On the way back to the office I asked what Brady had said to her.

"What do you think? He asked if I thought you were up to the job, if you could keep focused after the whole…"

"Wife fucking a Dutchman thing."

"Yes, if you like."

"What did you say?"

"I said you'd had a couple of rough days, but you were throwing yourself into your work one hundred percent. You are, aren't you?"

"I'm not stupid Inga, although the evidence over the past week or so might suggest I'm as dumb as a stump. We'll sort this out. You and me."

We got back to the office and I immediately started rooting around in my desk for my Private Pilot's License. I figured if Brady was arranging a 'loan' of a plane the loaner would like to make sure his aircraft would be in good hands; I know I would. The rooting around took longer than I thought and ended up with all three drawers on the floor and years-worth of garbage being strewn around the office.

I finally found my Pilot's License tucked inside a brochure for Ko den Hamer's property development company. Josephine must have dropped it off during her last visit here. I was about to throw the glossy sales material away when the even glossier family portrait on the back caught my eye. The glamorous image featured Ko den Hamer, his incredibly attractive wife, and their two young kids (one of each). It was perfect in every detail. Ko beamed out at us with his arm around a tall blonde starlet-type who wasn't afraid to let the photographer capture all that nature had endowed her with in the chestal department. And let me tell you she hadn't been short-changed when breasts were being handed out. Not that she had more than the usual amount, you understand…just that the two she had were breath-taking. Mrs. Den Hamer wore an orange off the shoulder dress with a broad black belt which emphasized her slim waist. She looked like she'd just won an Oscar. The two kids smiled angelically, and their matching outfits were dazzlingly clean. Just out of the wrapper no doubt. The whole scene made me want to puke.

Then something else made me look a little closer. The den Hamer's were posed on a picture-perfect lawn in front of a very expensive house. It was just as big as Paddy Brady's place with at least four bedrooms facing the front. On the ground floor, there was a wrap-around porch decorated with black ironwork. The bedroom windows had Juliet balconies painted the same color. It reminded me of The French Quarter in New Orleans. The house was painted in a magnolia/cream combination which enhanced that impression.

The view to one side of the house showed a steep hillside leading away toward the city. In the distance, the bay sparkled in heavenly sunlight. This view looked very familiar. It was almost identical to the view from Tara, Paddy Brady's townhome. Were they neighbors? It certainly looked as if Ko den Hamer lived on the same block as Paddy Brady. Well, he used to until very recently. I handed the brochure over to Inga, who was on her knees clearing away all the crap I'd just thrown out of my desk drawers.

"Does this place look kind of familiar?" I asked.

"Should it?" she asked, throwing it back at me. Patiently I passed the brochure back.

"Don't look at the people, look at the house, and look at that view."

"Nice place."

"And?"

"Oh, I see what you mean. This is up on Vallejo, near Tara; so what?"

I didn't say any more. An idea was forming. Maybe even the beginning of a plan, a plan that Inga would not approve of. Still, she didn't have to know everything I did; did she? And thankfully Inga chose not to pursue the matter. She had a hot date that evening and spent most of the late afternoon getting ready. I must admit she looked stunning when she returned from the washroom already to go. She had on a white dinner jacket and black dress pants, patent black leather shoes, a dress shirt, and a black bow-tie. Her hair was slicked down with some kind of gel and she had painted in a pencil-thin moustache over her strawberry red lips.

"A night on the town?" I asked.

"Something like that. Can you give me a ride to Mona's for seven-thirty? I don't want to take the street-car."

"No problem, I'm heading out myself shortly."

"Anywhere special?" asked Inga, suddenly interested.

"Nothing for you to worry about, ready to go?"

Inga checked her watch, a large man's wristwatch with a gold band.

"We'll be a little early but that's okay."

"I'll buy you a drink while you wait," I offered.

"In Mona's? Are you sure?"

"They take U.S. Dollars, don't they? Don't worry; I'm not going to hit on any of your friends," Inga laughed out loud.

"I'd like to see you try."

"Maybe some other time; do you want that drink or not?" We headed for the door.

"I'll drive," said Inga. I locked up and we headed downstairs, out the back to collect the Plymouth.

We were the first customers in Mona's that night. I had a beer and Inga had a Singapore Sling. We sat at the bar and talked like any ordinary couple in any ordinary bar in the United States. Except that I looked like crap and she looked like Fred Astaire's much taller, much better-looking baby brother. Inga's friend Peggy would only be on much later. I told Inga I'd catch her act another time. I left Mona's at about eight. I didn't want to be too late getting to the house on Vallejo.

I drove back to Pacific Heights. Once on Vallejo I slowed right down and cruised along looking down every cross-street trying to find the view that matched the picture on my lap. After three journeys up and down Vallejo I found it; three blocks east of Paddy Brady's place. I stopped, turned off the engine, and sat looking across the street at Ko den Hamer's house. It would be another hour before daylight really began to fade but I could see lights being turned on in rooms upstairs, probably the kid's being taken upstairs to bed. I waited a few more minutes then I walked across the deserted street and up to the front door. I rang the bell.

Eventually, the door was answered by a small round lady, probably in her late sixties. Her thinning grey hair was pulled back tightly in a bun. She had a kind face, pale with thin lines around her mouth and eyes. She wore a flowing flowery dress that touched the floor. She looked up at me suspiciously. I guessed this would be Mrs. Den Hamer senior. She would be roughly the right age, not very tall though…for a Dutch lady.

"Can I help you?" she asked.

"Mrs. Den Hamer?"

"Never heard of her, good evening," She began to close the door.

"This is the den Hamer residence?" I asked.

The door stopped closing.

"Certainly not," said the old lady. "It's my residence," The door began to move again. Luckily, I had the brochure rolled up in my jacket pocket. I pulled it out, flattened it quickly, and passed it through the (once again) closing gap.

"I'm really sorry to bother you at this hour ma'am but would you mind looking at this picture?"

The old lady took the brochure and leaned in close to peer at the image.

"As you can see, this picture was taken right here on your lovely lawn. Could you take a look at the family in the photograph…do you recognize them?" The old lady took her time. Then she handed the brochure back.

"Never seen these people before in my life; now I'd like you to tell me who you are and what exactly is going on here. Then I think I shall call the police."

"No need to be alarmed Mrs.?"

"…I'm not going to tell you my name young man until you tell me yours," I handed over one of my few remaining business cards.

"My name's Rick Marshall, I'm a private investigator. I was under the impression that this man lived here with his wife and children until very recently."

"…and he is?"

"He's a Dutch property developer called Jacobus den Hamer."

"As I said, I have never heard the name, and it's not a name you'd forget now is it?"

"You got that right. And you've never seen any of these people in the picture?"

"Why do you keep asking me the same questions? Do you think I'm not of sound mind? Because I can assure you, young man, I'm as sane as you are," I folded the brochure and put it back in my pocket.

"That wouldn't be saying much, ma'am. I don't know about you, but I think this guy den Hamer has been on your property at least once and I'm a little worried that he might be using your lovely house and gardens to commit some kind of fraud."

"Do you really think so?"

"I do and if I were you, I'd have someone check all your doors and windows, just to make sure they are secure, and they haven't been tampered with. Mister den Hamer might come back with some accomplices; maybe he plans to rob the place."

"Oh my."

"Don't be alarmed, you're perfectly safe for now…I could give the place the once over if you like, free of charge of course. I'd like to apologize for upsetting you earlier."

"Well, I don't know about that young man," said the old lady.

"I'm perfectly willing to wait out here if you wish to call the police."

"I don't think that will be necessary. Would you like a cup of tea, Mister Marshall?"

"Now that you mention it; that sounds like a very fine idea."

"Come in; let's go through to the kitchen. I'll get Emma to put the kettle on."

After a quick circuit of the house, checking windows and doors, I spent the next two hours in Mrs. Eleanor Epstein's kitchen. We drank copious amounts of Earl Grey tea and I ate almost a whole apple cake. I told her all about Ko den Hamer seducing my wife; she told me all about the late Marius Albert Epstein, who for a number of years had been the most successful gold bullion trader on the western seaboard. Marius Albert Epstein had gone to meet his maker fourteen years ago leaving his grieving widow 'particularly well cared for' in the financial department.

Eleanor Epstein had lived at this address for over twenty-five years. Every summer she spent a month at her younger sister's in Boulder, Colorado. Eleanor thought the photograph I'd shown her must have been taken last year during the time she was out of state.

This didn't make any sense to me…unless Ko den Hamer was a bigger and better con man than even I had given him credit for. What it did tell me was this: he'd probably been lying to Josephine from day one. The downtown office and the perfect family (as featured in the rigged photograph) could be just window dressing; a front to make this Dutch ass-hole seem way more successful than he actually was. He was running a long-con. That was it! He was doing the old gold rush con, only with vineyards…buying up worthless land from unsuspecting owners and selling it on at a massive mark up to greedy saps who should know better. The big question was: how much of this was Josephine aware of?

The second question that came to mind was equally important to me. The house was fake I knew that now. What about the wife and kids? I couldn't know for sure. I could check the hall of records, see if there was a marriage recorded or the birth of a child or two but that would not be conclusive. The den Hamer's could have been married in Holland before coming to the States. The only way to be absolutely certain about whether this picture-perfect family actually existed would be to track down the hot dame in the photograph. How the hell was I going to do that?

As I waved a fond farewell to Mrs. Epstein, I was determined to find out all I could about Mr. den Hamer and his family…this left me only one course of action. I was going to have to break into his office.

The next morning, back at my office I charged Inga with checking through all the local phone books looking for any den Hamers. There were none to be found. Inga tried calling the operator, had no joy there. Inga was far from happy doing secretarial work on a personal case that had nothing to do with her employer.

"Mister Brady is going to shit all over you if he finds out what we are doing right now."

"But he's not going to find out, is he?" I retorted. "Because you are not going to tell him…besides, we can't really do much until the plane turns up."

"We could drive instead."

"It's over six hundred miles to Portland; that would take us maybe eleven hours solid driving or two days with an overnight stop. A small plane will cruise at maybe 130 miles an hour. We'd get there in under five hours, check up on Dobbs and be back home for happy hour the same day. What would you rather do?"

"I'd rather be doing anything but this," And just at that moment the phone rang, it was Brady. We were instructed to be at the ferry building, adjacent to Pier Two at seven tomorrow morning.

"You'll meet a guy called Pete, he'll hand you two hundred dollars for fuel and expenses and he'll show you around his plane. It's a Canadian plane, a single-engine. Should be a piece of cake for an experienced pilot like you Rick."

"It's a De Havilland Beaver?"

"Do I look like a plane spotter? The guy said it was built in Canada for bush pilots, whatever they are…and it's tough as old boots."

"It's a float-plane?"

"I guess so; it's being tied up at Pier Two so I would guess it's on floats. Is there a problem?"

"No Mr. Brady, there's no problem."

I'd only ever flown a float plane once before, but I wasn't going to tell Brady that. This meant I would have to get into den Hamer's office that night. The afternoon passed slowly. I kept myself busy checking charts for the flight north to Portland. Just before we left the office late that afternoon Elton Dwight from the D.A.'s office checked in. I didn't have much more to tell him about the investigation. Dwight said:

"Tell me about the interior of Mister Brady's townhome," I told him about the layout in general and I told him about the paintings.

"Did you see his Pollock?"

"Did I what?" I asked.

"His Jackson Pollock, it's quite a big piece, said to be worth close to a million dollars."

"The only big painting I saw was covered in dots and spills of all different colors."

"That's the one. It's good to confirm where he's keeping it. This information will be very worthwhile when we start seizing his assets."

"And it's worth what?"

"It's estimated to have cost Brady $990,000 two years ago."

"I'm in the wrong business."

"I hope not Mr. Marshall," said Dwight from the D.A.'s office. I put the phone down.

KDH Developments had a suite of offices facing Union Square. They were on the third floor at Geary and Powell above The Golden Pheasant Restaurant. I walked a few blocks from my office and jumped aboard a cable car, jumping off a short while later at Powell. I took a few minutes and wandered around the square, past formal gardens and trees, past the Dewey Monument in the center, all the time looking up at the third floor of Geary and Powell.

I stopped across the street from The Golden Pheasant. I was hungry, maybe I should wait inside, grab a bite to eat? Not a good idea, knowing my luck Ko den Hamer and the good lady wife, my good lady wife might just call in there for dinner before heading home to my house. If a cat had walked across my path at that precise moment, I might have kicked it clean across the bay. I took a long, calming breath and decided to wait exactly where I was; in the shade of a palm tree with a great line of sight on the office building. I pulled my hat down over my eyes a little, did my best Humphrey Bogart.

Ko den Hamer and Josephine Marshall left the building arm in arm at 6.22 pm. They did not see me. I gave them ten minutes to clear the area, just in case either of them had left something at the office. Then I crossed Powell and went in the main entrance. Up on the third floor, I found KDH Developments next door to a travel agent. Everything was quiet. I waited another few minutes just to be sure; then I stepped forward to the half glass door with KDH in large gold leaf lettering. The lock was embarrassingly easy to open; it took me less than twenty-seconds to break in.

I closed the door behind me. The blinds were half-closed; there was plenty of natural light. The office was as I remembered it; Josephine's desk was to the left in front of a three-foot tall divider. Two straight-backed wooden chairs stood against the wall opposite. Ko den Hamer's much larger desk was beyond the divider along with two burgundy leather wing-back chairs and a low coffee table. I looked over Josephine's desk again. Something was different. She'd changed the nameplate that sat at the front of the desk. It now read Josephine Hill (her maiden name). I wondered how long ago she'd made that little attitude adjustment.

I pushed open the little gate in the divider and moved to Ko's desk. It was very ordered with stacks of files in a tray to the right and an array of silver-framed photographs to the left. There was a copy of the family portrait taken in front of my friend Mrs. Epstein's house. There was a formal portrait of the two kids. The largest picture featured the delectable Mrs. Den Hamer wearing a low-cut dress.

The lighting made her look like a forties film star, the photograph had obviously been done by a professional. I took the picture out of the frame checked the back and made a note of the studio's name and address.

STELLAR PHOTOGRAPHY
Raymond Starkey
4th Floor
201 Powell Street

I sat in Ko's chair and started going through the drawers beginning with the one right in front of me. Nothing much there, the usual junk that you'd find in any desk: notepaper, pens, pencils, a pipe...did not know he smoked.

I moved on. The drawer to the right was locked but the one below it wasn't. I pulled out the bottom drawer and reached up to release the locking mechanism. The top drawer slid out revealing a diary, a large envelope full of twenty-dollar bills (possible a thousand dollars in total), and a snub-nosed 38 Colt revolver. *'Interesting, why would Ko den Hamer need a cannon like this?'*

I put the Colt on the blotter, put my feet up, and started working through the diary. I didn't come across anything about seducing my wife, but he didn't need to diarize that. He'd managed that all too easily. I did come across the names and numbers of some prominent people in Hollywood. I wrote down the details in my handy dandy detective's pocketbook.

He had details of three farms east of Sonoma. I figured these would be the center-piece of his property scam, if he really was running a scam. Or they were legitimate land deals he was working on. Either way, I guessed I might have to take a little trip up there in the very near future. I was putting the contents of the locked drawer back in place when I heard footsteps in the tiled hallway outside. I closed the drawer quietly, slid out of the chair, and crouched behind the desk. *'What was that smell? Gasoline?'*

I peered around the edge of the desk just in time to see a wall of orange flame erupt from where the door used to be. In a matter of seconds, one half of the office was engulfed by fire. It was being held back momentarily by the room divider. I had to get out and fast. I couldn't get back out of the main door and there was only a small windowless washroom behind the door to my right. Heavy black smoke rolled across the ceiling toward me. The heat from the flames was quickly becoming unbearable. I had to act.

Almost by instinct I took the Colt from the desk and put it in my pocket. I kept low and crawled to the row of large windows behind me. I looked down. There was maybe a forty-foot drop to the sidewalk. Pedestrians below me had no idea of the drama going on high above them. They were about to find out real quick. I grabbed hold of Ko's large leather chair and spun it round toward the nearest window.

With all my strength I lifted it off the floor as it spun around and hurled it at the window. Then I ducked back down below the desk. As the window shattered the in-rush of air fueled the flames which shot over my head. Mercifully the chair fell back into the room. I waited for a few seconds for the flames to die back, pulled my jacket over my head then I stepped through the broken window onto the narrow balustrade outside.

The room behind me was now completely aflame, the windows either side of my escape route were making loud cracking sounds. I looked down. People on the sidewalk were staring up at the flames. One guy in a straw hat pointed in my direction and shouted something I couldn't hear.

I began to edge along the foot-wide ledge with my back toward the intense heat. I burned my hand on the window behind me. To my left a window blew out, showering glass into the street three floors below.

As quickly as I could I edged further away from the flames, I felt the heat subside behind me as I passed a wall between two offices. I looked around carefully, hoping to find an open window. At that second all the remaining windows in Ko's office blew out with a tremendous crash. Shards of glass shot into the sheet followed by massive tongues of yellow flame. I slipped then, almost going over. With my heart pounding in my chest and my knees ready to give way I inched a few feet further from the fire. I stood with my back to a window and kicked backward with all my strength. After three attempts the window cracked then gave way. I kicked away at large chunks of broken glass before turning carefully and falling into the office.

I was on my feet quickly; I ran to the front door and was about to open it and make my escape. The doorknob burned my hand, not a good sign. I looked down; smoke was beginning to filter under the door. I put my hand to the wooden panel, it was very hot. The fire was spreading fast. This office was pretty much identical to Ko's, so I didn't think there'd be another way out. I was going to have to get back on the ledge and move further along, away from the fire.

I stepped back out; the crowd below was much bigger now and all street traffic had stopped. Over the roar of the flames, I could hear the wail of sirens. The appalling heat to my right ensured I kept moving. I started edging along further away from the flames again. The next office I came to had bars on all of its windows. I was not going to make my escape the easy way. After about twenty feet I came to the corner of the building. Now I had a choice. If I stayed here three things could happen.

1. As the fire spread, I would be burned to a crisp, ending up like some gargoyle perched on the corner of my ex-wife's workplace.
2. The fire department would arrive shortly, rescue me, then start asking what the fuck I was doing on a third-floor balustrade, and hey…who started the fire anyway?
3. The fire department would arrive shortly; rescue me, then hand me over to the police who would ask those questions mentioned in option two.

In short, if I stayed where I was, I was fucked. I looked a little closer at the decorative concrete design on the corner of the building. There were grooves cut across the concrete every foot. They looked deep enough to make hand (and hopefully) footholds. It was time to move. I lay down on the ledge and slowly inched my body round till my feet were dangling in mid-air, scrambling for something to catch onto. I soon realized that this was a very bad escape plan. I could hear women below me screaming, I couldn't look down, but I guessed they were screaming at me. I lost my hold, slid backward, and fell.

I landed with a whump on the sloping balustrade one floor below, bounced straight off it, and fell some more. This was it; I held my breath as I tumbled sideways into space. I threw my hands out, grabbing at nothing but air. With a clunk one hand caught hold of a black metal post. I hung on as best as I could, finally opening my eyes.

I was hanging from a streetlight. I grabbed hold with my other hand and just swung there for a few seconds. People ten feet below me rushed forward to catch me as I dropped to the ground. A young lady in a tan jacket fainted to the ground. People around me started to clap; an old guy shook my hand like I was Joe DiMaggio. I slid to the ground, my breath rasping like an express train climbing a hill.

Three fire trucks pulled up in quick succession. Police officers were moving the crowd back to the far side of the street. The Golden Pheasant had been evacuated, diners, waiters, and cooks mingled with passers-by. In the confusion, I succeeded in slinking away. I needed a drink.

Chapter Seven

Not sure what time I got back to the office, not sure how I got there. What I do know is I was feeling no pain by then. I fell asleep face down on the cot as the room span around me. I dreamed of Josephine and the underwear she wore the last time we were together, five thousand dollars strewn across her body. I woke a few hours later with a redundant hard-on and a headache to beat all headaches. The taste in my mouth led me to believe that I had licked a sidewalk at some point the previous evening, and not a particularly clean sidewalk. There was a calamitous ringing in my ears which I couldn't place. It took me something like ten minutes to work out it was the phone.

It was Inga.

"Why are you still at the office?" she asked.

"I live here now," I answered.

"I know that, but aren't we flying to Portland today?"

This might be a trick question; I considered my options then said.

"Yes?"

"So why am I the only one at the pier meeting Pete and his plane?"

This was a good question. One I had no real answer to.

"Can you sign for the plane? I'll be there as soon as I can," You could tell Inga was having trouble keeping her temper in check. You could almost hear her teeth grinding at the other end of the line. She answered slowly:

"I can't sign for the plane because I am not a pilot. Pete needs to see a valid pilot's license before he hands it over, and he's got to show you through something called the pre-flight checks."

"Buy Pete a coffee, I'll be there as soon as I can…get me a coffee too, black no sugar."

I put the phone down before Inga could say anything else. I threw up some, brushed my teeth, changed my shirt. As I put my jacket on the smell of the fire caught my breath…so I hung it over the back of my chair. There was a clunking sound and I remembered picking up Ko's gun. I took it out of the jacket, put it in my drawer. I had a lightweight leather jacket hanging at the back of my closet. I put that on and raced down to the street to grab a cab. I was at the water's edge in twenty minutes. I didn't think that was too bad all things considered.

Inga did not share my optimistic outlook. She hurried over to meet me as I paid the cab; mercifully she was holding a coffee.

"What the hell happened to you?" she asked. "And what happened to your hand?"

"I had a little accident last night. That mine?"

Inga handed over the coffee; it was strong but not too hot. The conversation continued as we walked out along pier two.

"Did you know there was a fire at Mr. den Hamer's office last night?"

Inga looked at my hand again.

"You didn't…"

"Didn't what?"

"Burn the place down?"

"It wasn't me."

"Thank God for that," said Inga.

"Although I was in the office when the fire started."

"You were what?"

"Someone poured gasoline through the mailbox, threw in a book of matches. I was behind Ko's desk when they did it. Had to climb out of the window; that's when I did this."

I showed Inga my new burned up body part.

"Are you going to be okay to fly?"

"I've flown with worse," I said; which was true. What I didn't say was after that flight I spent six weeks in hospital before getting shipped back to the States. Inga led the way down some wooden stairs to a floating dock anchored to the pier. Pete and the Beaver were waiting for us there. It was a pretty little thing, white and yellow. The big Pratt and Whitney radial engine gave it a stubby, no-nonsense look at the front end. It had broad wings with big control surfaces. It should get off the water with a very short run. We were going to find out pretty quickly.

The formalities went the way I like formalities to go…quickly. Pete took note of my pilot's license number and I signed for the hire of the Beaver.

I climbed onto a float and followed Pete inside; I took the left-hand seat as Pete talked me through the instrument panel. Inga stayed on the dock. After that, we were good to go. Pete shook my hand, stepped back out of the cockpit, and climbed down. I slid the side window back and called to Inga.

"Well, are you coming?"

Inga stepped cautiously onto the left-hand float. She looked a little like Bambi on the frozen pond.

She clambered up into the cabin and came forward. Pete slammed the door behind her.

I indicated the right-hand seat. She squeezed her long legs past me and strapped herself in. I handed her a pair of headphones and signaled for her to put them on. I went through the engine start checklist very methodically, taking my time. I checked around the aircraft before shouting:

'Clear' through the side window. Pete returned my call. We were good to go. I set the mixture to 'fully rich' selected the main fuel tank and primed the engine, ignition switch to 'both,' starter switch to 'Starter' position, and fired up the engine. It caught first time as it was already warm. It made a hell of a roar and I felt as if I was riding the engine itself as it was so close to the screen. I throttled back and prepared to taxi. Pete gave the front of the left-hand pontoon a gentle shove and we were edging away from pier two.

I asked Inga to keep a lookout for other craft on the water as I checked over the instruments. I selected a coarser pitch on the propeller, and we moved forward a little quicker. I set the fuel mixture at fully rich, set the prop to 'Increase RPM.' I looked across at Inga.

"All good?" I asked. She nodded. The channel ahead was clear as I turned into wind, put the flaps into the 'take-off' position, and moved the throttle all the way forward. The roar increased again and in a very short distance, I could feel the plane lift slightly on the pontoons. She was tending to pull left as I had expected, this was the propeller wash hitting the rudder. I counteracted this with pressure on the rudder pedals. We were now skating along, out into the harbor. We came up onto the 'step' quickly; I could feel the drag from the water fall away as if it had been switched off.

At 65 mph we were off the water. I throttled back slightly to 2000 rpm, set the flaps to 'climb' and we flew out over Alcatraz. I banked the aircraft to the right as we went over the exercise yard so Inga could look down at the prisoners walking in circles. We continued to gain altitude over the bridge heading west. At one thousand feet, I made a slow turn to the right and we headed north west up the coast. It was good to be in control of a plane once again. It had been a long time.

After a while Inga turned to me with a question, her voice tinny over the intercom:

"What were you doing in den Hamer's office?"

"Snooping."

"I know that! What were you looking for?"

"If I told you, you wouldn't believe it."

"Try me."

So, I explained all about calling on Mrs. Epstein and how the photograph made me more than a little suspicious.

"Like I said back at the office…I think he's a con man and he's running a major scam. I just don't want Josephine getting caught up in it."

"Most likely she already is," said Inga. I hated it when she said the things I was thinking. We settled back into silence as the Pratt and Whitney growled away in front of us.

After an hour of smooth flying, I turned due north aiming to pick up Highway 101 northbound. This took us over Fort Bragg. Under an hour later we were approaching Eureka. It was easy to spot as the town is sheltered from the Pacific by a long sandy stretch of sand, broken half-way along by the channel to the harbor. I put her down to the east of this breakwater, it was like landing on glass; the water was so smooth. We chugged up to the nearest dock and found a place to sell us fuel. Inga went into town and bought tuna sandwiches and soda. Thirty minutes later we were back at cruising altitude heading due north. From Eureka, the highway pretty much hugged the coast, so it was easy to follow. We only had light cloud to contend with occasionally, so following the black-top was a piece of cake.

I made mental preparations to use the Eureka fuel stop on the way south. The dock wouldn't be open later that evening so we would have to find somewhere to stay overnight in Portland. I would sleep in the plane, that made sense, but we'd have to find somewhere for Inga. Just before we had taken off from San Francisco Pete had given me a rough idea of how to find a place to tie up on the Columbia River, just north of the city. This turned out to be an outfit called 'Salty's.' He said it was easy to find as it was just north of the main runway of Portland's commercial airport.

As we approached Portland from the south west I cut back on the throttle and set the plane up for a landing. I avoided the airport circuit to the east before doing a low pass along the river.

"Check for floating logs or debris," I said to Inga. I rocked the Beaver from side to side gently so we could check out of both our windows.

"Nothing I can see," said Inga.

"Tighten your seat belt, we're going to land."

I made two smooth right turns, finished my final checks, and made my approach, easing the revs back until the big radial was barely ticking over. We kissed the water once and made a text-book landing. I brought the revs back up a little and taxied into the dock at Salty's.

I completed my shut down checks and secured the aircraft. An ancient mariner kind of guy came out from the small wooden shack at the end of the dock. He had on a large dark brown sweater and waders. He was a heavy man, not very tall. I half expected him to be smoking a corn-cob pipe but no such luck.

"Salty?" I asked reaching out my hand.

"Salty's been dead for years son, I'm Cleveland Smith, bought the place off his widow, couldn't be bothered to change the sign. Besides Salty's sounds way better than Cleveland's don't it?"

'New signs must be expensive in Portland too' I thought. I was about to tell Cleveland I'd done the same with my business, but I thought it might be a good idea not to share too much info.

"Do you need fuel?"

"Sure do."

"You got cash?" I nodded.

"I'll get my boy to fill her up," Salty put two fingers in his mouth and whistled louder than I'd ever heard before. A black youth in overalls hurried down the dock with a drum of aviation fuel on a dolly complete with a hand pump.

"Do you have a phone, Mr. Smith? We need a cab."

"You stayin' in town tonight?" he asked.

"Yup, we should be finished our business tonight, but I'd rather fly back down to San Francisco in the morning. I'll stay with the plane if that's okay with you. But we'll need a place for Inga."

"You betya. You can't go wrong at the Clyde, it's on 10th and Stark, right in the center of town. Nice clean place. The cab driver will know it."

"That sounds fine…thanks."

Cleveland Smith led us down the jetty and into his tiny office. He had a number for Radio Cabs written on his desk blotter. He gave them a call and handed me the phone. The black and white Radio Cab turned up about fifteen minutes later. It was now just after two in the afternoon. I handed the driver a note with the address of the Dobb's residence:

2703 Dunkley Street, Portland

It was in a district called Alameda. I asked Cleveland:

"What time do you close up tonight?"

"We'll be here till about seven."

"I may be back later than that," I said.

"I'll leave a key under the mat. Just make sure you lock the gate after you," We thanked Cleveland for his help and got on our way.

2703 Dunkley Street was another small West Coast rancher; my guess was maybe twenty years old. It was showing its age. Paint peeling from the window frames, the chimney looked in urgent need of some love and attention. There was a blue kid's trike, a baseball glove, and a doll's carriage in the overgrown front yard. As we stepped out of the cab Inga put her hand on my arm.

"How are we going to do this?" she asked. She stared at the blue trike and I could see her eyes welling with tears.

"I'm not sure, but the airline must have been in touch by now. It's not like we are here to break the news."

"So why are we here?"

"You know as well as I do," I said, and I set off down the weed-strewn garden path. Inga hung back as I walked up to the front door. This was the first time I'd witnessed her being afraid of anything.

I knocked. A dark-haired girl, maybe six-years-old opened the door. She looked up at me; she was holding a Raggedy Anne doll behind her back. From what I could see of the doll it was as old as the house at least.

"Hello, sweetie," I said. "Is Mommy in?"

A harsh woman's voice called out from the rear of the house:

"Who is it, Sally? I told you not to go opening the door to strangers."

"I didn't know they were strangers till I opened it," replied Sally. I liked Sally already, which made what we were about to do even more difficult. Mommy didn't think she was so cute.

"Don't you sass me, young lady, get in the house!" Sally ran back along the hallway leaving the door open.

"Are you gonna get that or what?" asked the voice from the rear. A gruff new voice answered:

"I'm reading the newspaper."

"Does the paper tell you who's at your front door?"

"Nope."

"Then why don't you put the newspaper down and go find out?"

We clearly heard a newspaper thrown to the floor; chair springs creaking followed by heavy footsteps. Then there he was Henry R. Dobbs, the dead man alive and well. I was thinking to myself: *'He sure looks good...for a corpse.'*

"Yes?" said the dead man.

"Henry Dobbs? Henry R. Dobbs?"

"Right on both counts, who wants to know?"

"Mr. Dobbs, weren't you supposed to be on the TWA flight out of San Francisco on the 4th of July?"

"The one that crashed?"

"The one that crashed," said Inga. Dobbs looked Inga over for the first time. It was like watching a hungry dog looking at a juicy bone.

"Missed it by fifteen minutes; got stuck with a client downtown, just couldn't get away. The cab driver drove like a madman to get me to the flight on time, but I was too late…lucky really. I took another cab back into town and got on the train two hours later. I was pissed for a while; I like to fly. Then I read what happened…like I said, lucky really; you from T.W.A?"

"Not exactly…can we come in for a second?"

"Sure buddy, Miss…you don't look so good. Can I get you a glass of water, or a drink maybe?"

"No; I'll be fine," Inga said, although she did look very pale. I took off my hat and we followed Dobbs down the hall which was decorated with a number of crucifixes and cross-stitch quotations from the good book. Mrs. Dobbs was a tall angular woman with a sallow complexion and cheekbones you could slit your wrists on. She was dressed in a somber patterned housecoat that hung from her square, bony shoulders like a lifetime of disappointment.

She had been peeling potatoes at the sink. She snapped her head around like a chicken, surprised to see visitors in her kitchen. She wiped her hands on a washcloth and came forward to greet us. We sat down at a small, square table. Everyone looked around at everyone else not wanting to be the first person to speak. Eventually, I took the plunge:

"Mister Dobbs I'm sure you've come to realize you've had a lucky escape. I've been employed by a prominent San Francisco businessman to find out what happened to flight 402…and to confirm whether his wife was on the aircraft. Meeting you here today pretty much confirms that this unfortunate woman was on flight 402. You see, we discovered there was one person short on the boarding checklist. This missing person was either you…or my client's wife."

Dobbs' face showed his confusion. He was trying to find the right thing to say.

"It's a hell of a thing," he said. Mrs. Dobbs crossed herself furiously.

"Jesus Mary and Joseph," she said. "Please tell your employer we'll say a prayer for him at Mass on Sunday."

"I'm sure that will be a comfort," said Inga. Mrs. Dobbs looked at Inga, really looked at Inga for the first time since we'd entered her house. Her demeanor became a lot less saintly in double-quick time. She pursed her lips and made a noise like a snake sizing up a field-mouse. Mrs. Dobbs said:

"It was surely God's work that saved my husband from a terrible fate." I could see Inga was ready for a fight. I stood up, planning to get out of the Hobbs house as quickly as possible. Inga said:

"If it was God's work that saved your husband was it also God's work that condemned everyone else on flight 402?"

"The Lord works in mysterious ways, His wonders to perform."

"I've seen the wreckage of that crash and I've seen what happened to the people inside. It didn't look too wondrous to me," snapped Inga

"We've taken up way too much of your time," I said. "We'll leave you good people in peace." Mrs. Dobbs said to me:

"God be with you." She didn't say anything to Inga. Mr. Dobbs followed us to the door.

"I guess your boss will be disappointed I'm not at the bottom of the bay." I nodded sheepishly.

"I wouldn't say that...but it's going to be a tough few days, that's for sure."

I put on my hat. We all shook hands then Inga and me walked away. Dobbs picked up the trike and took it inside. We walked to a cross-street and were lucky enough to flag down a passing cab after a few minutes. I took Inga to her hotel where she checked in. I made sure she had enough money for the bill and cab fare in the morning. We ate at a nearby diner. I told her I'd be up early in the morning doing pre-flight checks...

"So, grab a cab and get out to Salty's as soon as you can. We need to get back to see your boss."

"Suits me." She said. "I'm pretty tired; I guess I'm not used to all this high-flying excitement."

"Stick with me kid." I joked. "It's high flying excitement all the way."

We finished dinner and I walked her back to the hotel. We had one drink at the hotel bar then I got reception to call me another cab and we said goodnight. On the way back to the plane my head was full of plots and schemes.

I tried to concentrate on this job but after a while, I started to think about Josephine; how she smelled after a bath, how her skin felt cool and smooth when I woke her in the morning. How she used to laugh at my corny jokes. For a moment I thought about asking the cab driver to find me a liquor store, but they'd be closed by now...I could always find another bar though.

Salty's was in darkness when I got back there but I succeeded in not falling off the dock. I climbed aboard the Beaver and made a bed on the floor in the passenger compartment. With the gentle rocking of the water and nothing to hear but crickets, I fell asleep pretty quickly.

Chapter Eight

At around seven-thirty next morning I was finishing off my pre-flight checks when I heard Inga's cab pull up next to the shack that served as Salty's office. The sky was overcast but I'd phoned the weather guys at Portland's civil airport and they said the weather further south was set to clear. I figured if we got on our way early enough, we'd dodge any potential problems. Cleveland Smith arrived in a battered 46 Ford Pick-up at eight. He'd brought some donuts for us to share.

"Won't be a minute, I'll get the coffee on." He said and hurried away to the office. In a short while I followed him back down the jetty, thanked him for all his help, and paid him for the fuel. He didn't want a penny for the overnight moorage or my room and board. We squeezed into the shack and drank a quick cup of joe. After that we said our goodbyes and headed out to the Beaver. Cleveland shouted to us from the dock:

"Drop by any time." Inga waved to him. I told Inga to take her seat in the cockpit, untied the last mooring rope, and hopped onto the pontoon. A gentle current nursed us out into the river as I started the engine. I watched all the gauges carefully as the big radial warmed up. I handed over the pre-flight checklist to Inga and asked her to read it to me. I turned into the wind, set the flaps and propeller pitch, and opened up the throttle.

After only a few seconds at full throttle, the Beaver practically leaped into the air. We climbed out north of the civilian airport. I checked in with the tower and was given clearance to traverse the city at one thousand feet heading south west. We picked up the coast and Highway 101 in less than thirty minutes. I turned due south and kept the coastline under the port wingtip.

We made the refueling stop at Eureka just as I'd planned. Inga persuaded the manager of the dock to let her make a call to Paddy Brady. Before I restarted the engine, Inga turned to me and said:

"Mister Brady wants you to fly into Sausalito Harbor. He's arranged for the plane to be collected from there. He wants to meet us at the hotel."

"He's the boss," I said as I fired up the engine once again. After take-off, I had some time to think as we cruised south to San Francisco. I realized he wouldn't be my boss much longer. We'd pretty much confirmed that Mrs. Constance Brady had perished in the crash of the T.W.A. Lockheed Constellation on the 4th of July 1952. Any doubts would be removed when and if the bodies were recovered from the wreckage and officially identified. I believed the aircraft had suffered an in-flight explosion of some kind, but I had no way to prove that conclusively; I was no closer to learning what had caused the explosion. I was going to have to tell Paddy Brady I couldn't do any more for him. Maybe I should offer him a refund on his $5000? A very small refund...

I ran over different versions of this conversation in my head for a few minutes...did not find a version I liked. Inga interrupted my deep thoughts.

"Are you okay? You've been in a world of your own for over an hour, which is okay except you are meant to be flying the plane."

"I was thinking about what we tell Mister Brady?"

"What we tell him?"

I flew south for another hour; I was looking for Dillon Beach which sits at the end of a long spit of land pointing north west into the Pacific. At this waypoint, I turned to the east, heading inland and climbing back up to two thousand feet for the final leg of the trip. Twenty minutes later I picked up the northern end of San Pablo Bay. I lost height over water and followed the western edge of the bay south to San Rafael and eventually Sausalito. I did the required low pass over the bay near the town of Sausalito and confirmed wind-speed and direction. Inga checked for surface vessels or debris. Then I swung the Beaver out over the water to set her up for landing. One more pass confirmed there was no traffic to worry about. I lined her up into wind; prepared to land. Adjusted the trim, throttled back a little; changed the pitch on the propeller. I pulled the throttle right back to idle and let the plane sink slowly toward the water.

A tiny bow wave on the floats told me we were down. I turned to the left and taxied in toward the main pier on Sausalito Beach. I opened the side window to get some cool air flowing and I could hear the bark of sea lions sunbathing on rocks nearby. Every now and then a pelican dove vertically into the water, coming up with its prize seconds later. People were working on houseboats along the shoreline. Sausalito looked like a great place to live. I wondered if there were any apartments for rent...then again, maybe it was a little too far out of town.

As I nudged the left-hand float up against the dock a reception committee came out to meet us. Pete, the owner of the Beaver was there; he tied off the plane and began a quick inspection for any damage. As I climbed down out of the cockpit, he was there to give me a hand stepping onto the dock.

"How was she?" he asked.

"Great little plane, really short take-off runs, no problem at all," I replied. "Do I need to sign anything?"

"No, no, you're good to go. Glad you enjoyed her." We shook hands then Pete went aboard to check fuel levels (I think). Inga was talking to two more very large guys in black suits. They may well have been the two guys I'd seen before. You know how it is; after a while when you keep seeing them…all large guys in suits tend to look the same. Inga caught up with me as I walked along the pier.

"He wants to see us now."

"How did he know we'd landed?"

"Dino and Brendan have been keeping an eye out for us."

"Dino and Brendan?"

Inga nodded toward the big guys in suits who were walking either side of us. We made a very strange group of four as we strolled along Sausalito Pier.

Brady's 1952 Cadillac Fleetwood sedan was parked illegally at the entrance to the pier. Two beat cops walked past it without a second glance. The driver stepped out and opened the rear doors as we approached. Inga and I got in the back, Dino and Brendan had to squeeze in next to the driver. The big sedan moved away silently. It was only a few minutes before we pulled up out front of the Sausalito Hotel.

The hotel was a Spanish style building on the corner of Bridgeway and El Portal; just two floors high and painted a very pale yellow; it had fancy brickwork on the roof which made you feel you were south of the Border, down Mexico way…One side of the hotel looked out on a park with very large palm trees offering shade from the early afternoon heat. We went inside. Dino and Brendan took us to the hotel bar which was closed. Paddy Brady sat alone in a booth on the back wall. He had some papers spread across the table in front of him.

Inga kind of melted into the background and I was left alone in the empty bar with one of the most powerful crooks on the western seaboard. I had to tell him his wife had been on flight 402 after all and had died in a horrendous explosion and crash. I swallowed hard and walked across the bar on rubbery legs. Brady looked up from the papers on the desk.

"Well?" I sat down opposite Brady.

"As far as we can tell Mister Brady your wife Constance was on the flight. I'm afraid we have to accept she's dead…"

"We do, do we?"

"Well, it's not going to be 100% certain until all the...errr, bodies are recovered. Even then there may not be the possibility of positive identification."

"You think she might have been blown to bits?"

"I didn't say that Mister Brady..."

"No, but you were thinking it."

"Mister Brady, I think I've done all I can for you on this..."

"You think you've earned your $5000?"

"As I said, Mr. Brady, there's not much else I can do personally. The police will know much more about this before I do. I'm sure they'll keep you informed."

"Aye, they'll keep me informed all right...the bastards! And they'll take great fucking joy doing it."

"You're probably right."

"I know I'm fucking right! Listen, I want you to find out why the plane blew up..."

"I..."

"I'll pay you another five grand if you can prove what happened before the police do. I have to know if someone targeted Constance because she was my wife."

I stood up slowly.

"Mister Brady I..."

"...You weren't thinking of saying no to me were you son?"

I agreed to keep working on the case, which meant I agreed to wait around for the body count and identification procedures to take place. I had nothing else to go on. This was lucky in some ways because I could keep busy on other matters, a lanky Dutchmen screwing my wife being top of the list. If only I could find a way to occupy Inga with something related to the Connie explosion; I could then concentrate on KDH Investments.

I was dismissed and given a ride back into town. As usual, Inga tagged along. As we crossed the bridge I couldn't help looking out to sea to the point where Connie had hit the water. Inga caught me staring. I said:

"Look, Inga, despite what I just told the boss there is nothing else I can do for him. So, you will be wasting your time if you continue following me around."

"It's what Mister Brady wants..."

"But there's nothing to see, there's nothing more to report."

"I know that, I'm not stupid."

"So why are you still tailing me?" And we both said the next sentence at the same time.

"It's what Mister Brady wants."

The next morning Inga was at the office door at seven-thirty, which is unfortunate because I didn't wake up till nine. As I got washed over the tiny sink Inga went out for coffees and donuts, the breakfast of champions. I was at my desk looking at the 8x10 glossy of the den Hamer family, I reached for the phone book, I'd find the photographer's studio and pay him a visit; maybe he could tell me something about the mysterious Mrs. den Hamer, whoever she was. Inga put breakfast on the desk and came round behind me to look at the picture.

"She's cute," she said.

"If you like that kind of thing."

"What's not to like? Great smile, great tits, and a great figure."

"So, we both agree, she's great, but the real question is who is she?"

Inga went back round the front of the desk, took the lid off her coffee and gave it a cautionary sniff. Then she asked:

"Has this got anything to do with Mrs. Brady?"

"Possibly," I answered.

Inga gave me a look like an angry school ma'am catching her favorite pupil cheating on a test.

"Okay not really," I said, raising my hands in submission.

"Well, I won't tell him if you don't. What are we looking for? What do you think this den Hamer guy is up to?" I told Inga I wasn't one hundred percent certain, but I knew for a fact he didn't live at the house in the photograph and I suspected the nice busty blonde lady on his arm wasn't his wife.

"She looks like an actress," said Inga.

"Yes, we both agree she's a stunner."

"No, that's not what I meant. She looks like a local actress; I think I've seen her at a few auditions for stage plays."

"You're an actress?"

"Not me you idiot, a friend."

"The dancer?"

"The dancer; and her name is Karyn with a Y. I sometimes keep her company when she goes for auditions; believe it or not, there are some real nasty types out there."

"Oh, I believe it, do you know where we might find Karyn with a Y?"

Inga did know where we might find Karyn with a Y. Like most actresses, Karyn with a Y worked week-days as a waitress as well as the odd gig as an exotic dancer at a lesbian club. You had to admire her energy if nothing else.

We caught up with her as she came off shift at an all-night diner on Mission Street near the Transbay Terminal.

The diner was built in a converted Pullman railway car, now standing on sleepers. Karyn finished her shift at 9.30; we waited for her outside, sheltering from the drizzle under a tree. Inga waved her over as she stepped down from the diner. Introductions were made and I offered to buy Karyn some breakfast. She looked back at the diner.

"Not this place, the owner's wife is working the griddle today. She can't cook eggs for shit!"

"Good to know," I said.

"I know a good Mexican Cantina, it's not too far," said Karyn and she set off walking down Mission toward the water. Inga walked alongside her, occasionally bending to whisper something in her ear. I followed behind like a third leg. A couple of blocks later we came to El Corazon, a tiny café filled with dark-skinned locals. The walls were crowded with paintings of tattoos and decorated crosses. The food smelled fantastic! We joined the line-up and placed our orders. The morning rush was over now so we only had to wait a few minutes to get a table by the window. Our food arrived just a few minutes later.

I knew Karyn would be hungry, so I let her eat breakfast before showing her the photograph of the supposed den Hamer family.

"Inga thought you might recognize the lady in the picture."

Karyn smiled.

"That ain't no lady that's Rhonda Pearlman," she said. "She's quite the girl is Rhonda."

"You don't say..." say's me.

"I do say. What do you want with Rhonda?"

"I just wanted a word about the guy in the picture."

"It'll cost you a few drinks."

"Not a problem, where do we find her?"

"Not sure where she's living at the moment, you could always try her agent. She's in the same building as the photographer who took this; they do a lot of business together. It's right where the cable car starts from."

The rain had dwindled to a few drips and drops as the sun came out, giving the streets and sidewalks that 'just washed' sheen and the smell that only comes just after a shower. It was a few blocks to Powell and O'Farrell, but I figured I, for one, could do with the exercise. The walk would help me digest the massive breakfast I'd just eaten. Inga and Karyn hugged on the street corner and we said our goodbyes.

Inga asked me a question as we walked:

"If you do prove den Hamer is a crook do you think she'll come back to you?"

"I don't see why not. If he is a crook it will mean he's been lying to her all along."

Inga was quiet for a few steps.

"You don't know much about women, do you?"

'What was that supposed to mean?' I thought, but I did not answer her. Because I knew what she was saying; she was right, I guess. If I'd known anything about women, I would have spotted that my wife was fucking her boss…I was still deep in these self-pitying thoughts when we reached 201 Powell, an impressive office building with a large list of clients in its marble-floored lobby. We took the elevator to the fourth floor; I'd had plenty of exercise by then.

"Which office do we try first?" asked Inga.

"Let's try the photographer, he'll be easier to get on his own and I have a little idea I want to try on him."

Stellar Photography had a small reception area with a large receptionist in it. She was a young girl, not even twenty I guessed but she was the size of a small sedan. She wore a pea-green dress which looked like it had been spray-painted on her. Everywhere you looked across that green landscape acres of fat bulged, stretching the stitching to breaking point. She looked up as we entered the office but soon returned her attention to a sandwich that I could have lived off for a week. Spitting breadcrumbs and (I think) salami with mustard she acknowledged our entrance:

"Yeah?"

"Ray in?"

"Who shall I say is calling?"

"Rick Marshall, Daily Variety."

The poor girl almost choked on her sandwich; her face went a striking plum color until she coughed violently sending a tidal wave of crumbs over her desk. She squeezed herself from behind her seriously tiny desk and waddled into the rear office, closing the door behind her. We heard a muffled conversation which ended when Ray Starkey instructed his receptionist to:

"Get your fat ass out there and send him in." This she proceeded to do. I went into my act, trusting that Inga would have the good sense to roll with it. I bounded across the threadbare office carpet and grabbed Ray Starkey by the shoulders.

"Ray Starkey, the Ray Starkey! Long-time no see. How the hell are you?"

Ray remained standing by his desk.

"Don't say you've forgotten me already, you son of a bitch!"

Ray blabbed something that might have been:

"Of course, not…I err," I pressed home our advantage; turning to Inga I brought her into the play.

"You see? You See? I told you he was the guy for us," Inga joined in (God bless her).

"If you say so…"

"If I say so? I tell you Inga baby, this guy is a genius. He's just the man we want for the Gene Kelly shoot. Sure, we could use a local guy but this man here…this man here is the one Mr. Kelly wants."

"Gene Kelly wants me?" said Starkey flopping back into his swivel chair.

"Sure, he wants you, sure he wants you. And what Gene Kelly wants…"

"…Gene Kelly gets," said Inga, right on cue.

I turned to Ray Starkey.

"You available to fly to Hollywood for a few days, end of the month?"

"I…I…I'd have to check."

"You do that Ray and while you're at it tell me where I can find this young lady."

I handed over the 8x10.

"Rhonda Pearl? She's one of my best. Very flexible, can do any number of looks. And she's always very grateful for the work…if you know what I mean."

I could hear Inga's fists tense as Ray said this.

"You got an address or phone number?"

"Miss Seidelmann will have it on file… Miss Seidelmann?"

The door to reception opened.

"Can you get me Rhonda Pearl's contact details?"

"Right away Mister Starkey."

"Why don't you write them down for us Inga? I need a quick word with my pal Ray here."

Inga hurried after Miss Seidelmann.

I took the 8x10 back and looked at it casually.

"Can you tell me anything more about this shot Ray, old buddy; old pal?"

He could. The photograph had been taken about a year ago. The client had requested a 'stunning, exciting lady, preferably blonde, in a cocktail dress plus two children under the age of five.' The hard part had been getting the two kids. The client had arranged the location shoot and the whole thing had taken 'maybe two hours' from start to finish.

"I guess this wasn't the only photograph taken. Do you still have the contact sheet?" He did. My good buddy Ray checked in his files and handed me two contact sheets with twenty-four pictures on each. I put them with the 8x10 and said.

"Okay if I take these for a few days? Inga will get them back to you."

Ray wasn't too happy with this development, but his latent greed overcame his slightly more latent suspicious nature. It was time to leave. I said:

"We've got your number Ray; we'll be in touch with the travel and hotel details. Beverley Hills Hotel okay for you?"

We were out of the office and into the elevator before Ray Starkey could draw breath. Inga pressed the button for the 2nd floor and we headed down to speak to the talent agency.

Before we entered the office, Inga took a hold of my elbow.

"What's the point of going in here? We've got all we need, don't we?"

"I just want to get as much background on Ko den Hamer as I can. Every little bit of information helps build up a picture of him."

"Wow, good thinking Sherlock."

"Here's what we do when we get inside. We'll tell them you're looking for representation…"

"And who are you?"

"I'm your ever-loving boyfriend."

"Really? You think you can pull that off?"

"Sure, I can," I said. Inga leaned over and gave me the lightest kiss on the cheek, she smelled of watermelon and strawberry.

"Let's see, shall we darling?" she said.

The Lena Lawrence Talent Agency was run by (surprise, surprise) Lena Lawrence. She was an ex-Fox Starlet who never made the big time. Her office walls were covered with photographs of a younger Lena standing next to or at least fairly close to almost every male movie-star from the last decade. Clark Gable, Cary Grant, James Stewart, they were all on the wall. John Wayne, Bing Crosby, Danny Kaye… On closer inspection none of these luminaries appeared to be with Lena Lawrence, they just seemed to be standing in the same general area, like Brits lining up for a double-decker bus in London.

Lena had a slightly shop-worn air, a sadness borne of bitter memories and disappointments. She paid me very little attention as we sat down, but she looked long and hard at Inga. I couldn't blame her for that, Inga was a striking young woman, there's no doubt about that. Finally, Lena looked at me:

"She's a little too tall for movie work. She'd tower over most actors; they don't like that. But she'd do well as a photographic model. She's got great skin, lovely face. What are her numbers?"

"Huh?" I said.

"What are her measurements?"

"I...err, Inga, darling?"

"34.24.34. I'm six-foot-tall in my stockings."

Lena looked at Inga some more.

"Is that an accent I hear, my dear?"

"I'm from Iceland."

"That's very...exotic. I don't think I've met anyone from Iceland before."

"Me neither," I said. "It's a very small island."

Lena reached in her desk drawer and pulled out a compact 35 ml camera, a Zeiss-Ikon I think, I had the same camera in my desk drawer.

"Can you come over by the window dear? I'd like to take a few quick snaps if that's okay."

Inga moved into the light. As Lena snapped away, I started digging.

"We were given your name by a friend of mine, a Dutch guy called Ko den Hamer."

"Really?" said Lena as she moved Inga around like a mannequin in a shop window.

"Great guy, have you done much work with him?"

Lena put the camera down and returned to her desk. Suddenly stony-faced she asked:

"What's this about?"

"I don't know what you mean?"

"Why are you asking about Ko den Hamer?"

"I wasn't, I was just making conversation, he was the guy..."

"I think you should leave before I call the cops."

I played up the innocent party bit and said:

"There must be some kind of mistake."

"There is and you just made it, now get out!"

We got out. Back on the sidewalk, we stood on the street corner for a moment or two.

"You see, it was worth making that second call. She told us way more than the photographer."

"She did?" asked Inga.

"Sure, she did, and I'm beginning to think Ko den Hamer is up to something way more interesting than faking a few family portraits. I knew there was something dodgy about that guy and Miss Lawrence has just confirmed it."

"I don't see it," said Inga.

"That is why I'm the detective," I said feeling way too smart for my own good. But if I'm honest I was only going on a gut feeling...a gut feeling that might have a lot to do with the previously mentioned 'screwing my wife' scenario. I wanted this guy to be up to his neck in something diabolical. Something I could put an end to. Something that would get him the chair…twice!

"What next?" asked Inga. I looked around for a call box. I said:

"We talk to Rhonda Pearlman obviously."

"Obviously…I'm just thinking out loud here, but it might be a good idea if we can (at least) make this look as though we are investigating the crash, just in case we get asked."

"That is good thinking Inga. I've got an idea about that…it should work."

"Are you going to share that idea?" she asked.

"If Mister Brady asks, we say Rhonda was one of the flight engineer's recent conquests…what was his name again?"

"Brown, Stu Brown. Do you think that will keep Mister Brady off your back?" It was interesting that Inga said, 'your back' and not 'our back.' Maybe she wasn't as on board with the investigation as I'd hoped. I made a mental note of that then said:

"I don't think he'll bother to check, to be honest. But if he does, we can say she made threats against Brown, Stu Brown and we are just being thorough. Clients like thorough."

There was a coffee shop on the corner of Powell and Geary. There was a public phone at the rear next to the washroom. Inga ordered two coffees to go and I made the call to Rhonda Pearlman. There was no answer.

Back on the street, I realized we were only a block away from Union Square, the scene of my recent close encounter with a burning office. We took a stroll to see how the place looked. The Golden Pheasant was boarded up and the windows above it were still out, gaping like broken teeth in an alcoholic's smile. Broken blinds swayed in the breeze. The smell of burning timber had died away a little but it was still a long way from pleasant. I looked up at the street-lamp that had saved my life. I finished my coffee and said to Inga.

"Let's try Rhonda again, maybe she's home now."

"I'll make the call; she'll feel less threatened if it's a woman trying to get in touch out of the blue."

"Good thinking," I said. "I know a place where we can make the call and get a decent drink."

Chapter Nine

The Sir Francis Drake Hotel was back on Powell Street, 450 Powell to be exact. Inga made the call to Rhonda Pearlman from a phone in the grandly furnished lobby. I waited for her by the elevators. I wouldn't normally go into Sir Francis; it was way expensive and classy for a low life like me. Though I did like the guys dressed as 'Beefeaters' in their fancy red uniforms and funny hats guarding the entrance, they kind of reminded me of London. Maybe I'd go back there one day.

I figured Inga deserved a reward for all her hard work and the view from the rooftop here was spectacular. I remembered bringing Josephine here for the New Year's Eve party, 1941, less than a month after Pearl Harbor. But that was a long time ago when I was a fresh-faced fly boy ready to go save the world from Fascism. In the elevator, Inga said she'd spoken with Rhonda Pearlman and they'd arranged to meet at a bar close to her apartment that evening. I asked:

"Where does she live?" Inga double-checked the address she'd been given at the photographers:

"423 Buchanan Street, she shares a basement with two other girls; sounds like my kind of place."

The elevator jockey was a small bald man maybe in his sixties. He stared at Inga as she spoke; he was quickly getting a little hot under the collar. She seemed not to notice although I'm sure she knew the effect she had on poor saps like the elevator guy and me.

We had a beer and a chaser at the rooftop bar, took our time over the drinks and looked over the city for a while. I realized then how much I loved this city, with all its faults and the fog and the rain it was still a great place to live. After an hour or so we took a cab out to our rendezvous, The Lamplighter Bar on Bush Street.

Rhonda Pearlman was late. We had another drink in the Lamplighter, but she still hadn't shown thirty minutes after the time Inga had arranged. I decided we should walk round to the basement at 423 Buchanan, ask a few questions there, if anyone was home.

We found the door to the basement at the rear of the building. Inga knocked. There was no answer.

I stepped forward, put my ear to the door. I could hear voices, male voices. Inga leaned into the door too. She looked across at me with a puzzled expression on her face. She held up two fingers and whispered:

"Two guys?"

"That's Dragnet, on the radio," I said. I knocked this time, real loud. The sound echoed down the alleyway. I remembered Ko den Hamer's gun sitting all alone in my office desk and cursed my own stupidity. I tried the door; it wasn't locked. I told Inga:

"Wait here," I opened the door slowly and went in. I scanned the kitchen. Clean dishes were stacked next to the sink. A coffee pot was bubbling away on the stove. There was toast in the toaster. Everything was in its place. There was no sign of struggle. I called out Rhonda's name. There was no reply. I turned off the radio. I turned off the coffee. The orange linoleum floor was worn and faded with a darker geometric pattern. I thought I could see black scuff marks in the doorway leading out of the kitchen; maybe to a bedroom? Inga peered in from the alleyway; then stepped forward into the kitchen.

"I can't see a thing from out there. What's going on?" I said:

"Don't touch anything and be careful where you step." I turned around and went into the bedroom.

"Inga, can you hear me?"

"What's wrong?"

"I want you to do something for me okay?"

"What's happening Rick?"

"I want you to turn around, be careful not to touch the doorframe, and go outside. Go to the end of the alley and look around for a phone. If you have to go, back to the Lamplighter, they have a phone at the end of the bar. Call the police, give them the address and tell them there's been a murder…two murders. Then come back here but don't come into the apartment. Do you understand?"

Inga was right next to me, looking over my shoulder into the bedroom she saw what I'd just seen. Without a word she turned away and left the apartment. After a few seconds, I heard her throwing up in the alley.

There were two bodies on the bed, laid out side by side. Neither of them wore much in the way of clothes but it didn't matter to them now. One was a young Asian girl of maybe twenty. She had knife wounds to her chest and stomach. There were vicious-looking cuts on her forearms, and she'd had a couple of fingers cut off. Defensive wounds I guessed. There was a great deal of blood soaking into the bedclothes. She was wearing only a bathrobe that had either fallen open or had been opened to reveal the murderer's handiwork. She was only small…probably just over five feet tall. A pink shoe hung from her left big toe. Her dark brown eyes stared vacantly up at the ceiling. Her left hand was holding her friend's right. Both the victims wore the same glossy red lipstick. They had obviously been posed.

The second victim was taller, heavier, and maybe a little older. She was olive-skinned but she had long wavy blonde hair, it must have been dyed. She was naked apart from a pair of sheer red silk panties and one stocking which was rolled down her left leg. She had been stabbed in the throat only once. A lot of blood had spurted from an artery. Red spray covered her breasts, her tanned shoulders, and her neck. She would have died in seconds. Her red silk dressing gown and slippers were placed meticulously on a large blood-soaked towel at the foot of the bed.

The bed was awash in blood, still wet. I figured we'd missed this blood bath by less than an hour. My guess was the older victim had answered the door and been killed instantly. Then the killer or killers had discovered a second person in the basement suite. It struck me that the second murder had been a much more frenzied attack, maybe in panic. The defensive wounds on the young Asian girl's arms showed she'd fought for her life. But this whole thing did not strike me as an opportunistic crime by some crazy guy. For a start there didn't seem to be any sexual assault, not that I could tell; I didn't look too closely. And how many mad-men take the time to clean up after themselves? True the two victims had been posed and that could have been part of some pervert's modus operandi, but it could easily have been done to throw the police a curve.

There was a light on, and I could see into the tiny bathroom to the right. There was a small sink on the wall. It looked as if someone had thrown up in the sink then wiped it clean with a hand towel. There was a streak of red on the towel that had caught my attention. Was that lipstick? Assuming the mess in the sink came from the killer it told me that whoever did this was not a professional. Something went horribly wrong here, whatever the killer had originally planned…

I don't know how long I stood there. If my brain was sending signals to my feet about 'getting the hell out of this place' my feet weren't receiving those signals. After maybe five minutes I heard movement behind me.

"I thought I told you to stay outside," I said. But it wasn't Inga. It was Rhonda Pearlman. Finally, my feet got the message. I turned to block Rhonda's view of the bedroom and get her out of the apartment. I was too late. She was frozen where she stood. Her face looked like she was looking into hell. All the color drained from it, her eyes rolled back, and she crumbled to the floor. Inga appeared at the doorway to the apartment seconds later.

"The police are on their way…who's that?"

"It's Rhonda Pearlman. Help me get her out of here."

We picked Rhonda up between us; Inga took her legs; I lifted her body from behind. We took her outside into the alley and we were putting her carefully down when a black and white arrived, all sirens and blue lights and screeching tires. Of course, the first thing they do is pull their guns and tell us to put our hands up.

"Can't do that officer," I shouted. "We don't want to drop the lady."

More shouting and pointing of guns. I suggested:

"Why don't you let us put the lady down, then put our hands up? We are the folks that called this in."

He called to his partner in the black and white.

"Hey Johnny, get a blanket, will you?"

Johnny opened the trunk and hurried over with a coarse grey woolen blanket which he held ready for Rhonda.

"Okay, put the lady down then put your hands up."

We did as we were ordered. Johnny wrapped Rhonda in the blanket; she mumbled something but did not come round. Two more black and whites arrived followed by a Light Grey Ford Tudor.

A tall grey detective in a tall grey suit stepped out of the Tudor, put on a grey hat, and came over to join in the fun. This was becoming one very crowded alley. I guessed this guy must have been listening to the same radio show as the victims because he certainly thought he was Joe Friday in the flesh.

He left us standing in the alley with our hands in the air and an unconscious woman at our feet. He spoke to the cop on the door of the apartment before going inside. He emerged only a few minutes later and came over to us. He waved for us to put our hands down. He spoke to Inga first.

"You call this in Miss?"

"Yes, we were…" Detective Friday cut Inga short, turned to me.

"And you are?"

"Rick Marshall, I'm a private detective…" Friday's whole demeanor changed, he suddenly looked weary, resigned. He held up a hand the size of a dinner plate.

"License?"

"Okay if I reach into my wallet?" He nodded. I pulled my license out of my wallet and handed it over. Rhonda was waking up. Johnny from the black and white helped her get to her feet.

"And why were you here in the first place?"

"We had arranged to meet Miss Pearlman. This is Miss Pearlman."

The detective addressed Rhonda.

"You live here?" She nodded.

"With the other two dames?" Rhonda nodded and asked:

"Lilly and Anna…are they?"

"Dead? Yes, they're dead." Rhonda burst into hysterical tears. Inga held her close. The detective waited for Rhonda to catch her breath.

"That true, they were here to meet you?" Rhonda nodded, wiping at her nose with the back of her hand. The detective turned back to me.

"So, what happened?"

"We knocked a few times, no answer. I was a little worried that no-one was answering, and we thought we heard male voices, so I tried the door. It was open…"

"Voices?"

"It was the radio, Dragnet."

"Dragnet? Never heard of it." So much for my Joe Friday theory.

"Did you touch anything?"

"Door handle and the radio on/off switch, nothing else."

"We're gonna need you both to come down to headquarters, fingerprints, you understand…"

"Anything to help detective…" I turned to Rhonda.

"After we've all been downtown, do you have somewhere to stay? You won't be coming back here for a while."

In a voice so slight I almost didn't hear she said:

"I won't be coming back here ever again. I know a guy; I can stay with him."

"Do you have his number?"

Rhonda told me the number and once again the handy dandy notebook came out to play.

"You finished?" asked the detective gruffly.

We got to ride downtown in the detective's brand-new Ford Tudor. The detective, who was in truth called Joe…Joe Grunwald took us to 750 Kearney Street, Police Headquarters. It was an imposing stone building (as you might expect) facing out onto Portsmouth Square Plaza; it had five high arched windows along its front stretching almost to the flat roof.

We had our prints taken down in the basement then a uniform walked us up three flights of stairs to an interview room. Joe Grunwald arranged for coffee then we all sat around a small wooden table in the windowless interview room. Joe had a pad of lined paper and he began writing notes even before he asked his first question; which was:

"Why were you meeting with Rhonda Pearlman?"

"It's part of an on-going investigation," I replied, sounding very official and efficient (I thought.)

"And your client is?"

"You know I don't have to tell you that Detective."

"It might be a good idea for you if you did."

"How come?"

"Well, it would lessen the chance of me having the both of you thrown into the drunk tank for the night."

"And why would you do that?" asked Inga.

"First; because I can and second because I don't like sleazy divorce-snoopers and window peepers like your friend Mister Marshall here."

"If it's going to be like that Detective, I think I'd like to have a lawyer present."

"Do you have a lawyer, peeper? Cos you're gonna need one. I've got you at the scene of the crime, I've got your confession that you were there, and I've got your prints to prove it..."

"I told you about the prints and I told you we were there to meet Miss Pearlman; she's corroborated that fact..."

"And you've got a history of following women and you admitted you're a peeping Tom..."

"The hell I have! You know I only follow women when I'm working for a client."

'That didn't come out right.' I thought. At that point the door to the interview room swung open, revealing Elton Dwight in all his sartorial splendor. In this case, a mustard-colored suit topped off with a dark blue bow-tie. He was flanked by two more somberly dressed assistants.

"You won't be needing a lawyer, Mister Marshall, you're both coming with me."

Detective Grunwald leaped to his feet, his chair made an angry screech on the tiles.

"What the f..."

"Sit down Detective," said Dwight, walking into the room.

We finished off our coffees, got to our feet. I couldn't resist having a parting shot at the detective. I held out my hand.

"Well, that was fun, let's do it again some time..." Grunwald threw his notepad at the wall and pushing past Inga and Elton Dwight he stormed out of the interview room.

"That smart mouth will get you into trouble Mister Marshall," said Assistant District Attorney Dwight. He was right about that. I should have listened to him.

Back on the street in front of Police Headquarters I turned to Inga and joked:

"Free at last!"

A straight-faced Elton Dwight directed us to the waiting Packard.

"We can talk in the car. Where can I take you?"

"Clement Street will be fine."

"The office? Planning on working late Mister Marshall? Is there a reason you are less than keen to go home to your beautiful young wife?"

"Don't push me, Dwight!" I snapped.

"I wouldn't dream of it. Maybe we should take your companion home first. Where to Miss Bjarkardóttir?"

"I'll go with Rick to the office; I've got nothing on tonight."

"I find that hard to believe, a delectable young lady such as your-self without a suitor."

The more this guy spoke the more he sounded like a Southern Gentleman from Margaret Mitchell's book. I was pissed. Dwight went on:

"And I'm afraid that I really have to insist on speaking to Mister Marshall here, alone…in private."

Dwight leaned over Inga's thighs and opened the door.

"So, if you don't mind…" Inga got out of the Packard. Much to Mister Dwight's annoyance, I skipped out too.

"We'll take a cab, Mister Dwight. If you want to speak to me call the office in the morning and make an appointment with my secretary," I slammed the door. The Packard pulled away quickly causing a passing cab to slam on his brakes. As the cab driver yelled a stream of very inventive obscenities we jumped into that very cab. We went back to the office by way of a liquor store and a Chinese restaurant, the Nam Kee Noodle Box on 7th.

Over noodles and lemon chicken, special fried rice, and beer we reviewed everything we knew about the double murder. In fact, it was Inga who brought up the subject. I thought she might want to forget all about what we'd witnessed that evening.

"So, do you agree with Grunwald? It looks like he thinks it was a psycho who just tricked his way into the apartment and went nuts?"

"It's a theory, but that's all it is. Any number of things could have happened."

"Like what?" asked Inga. I slurped some noodles a little too noisily.

"…Sorry. I don't know, maybe one of the girls had fallen out with a boyfriend, he comes round, things get rough and he pulls a knife, kills the first girl, then the second hears the commotion, comes out of the bedroom and he has to kill her too…"

"…Then he strips them both and calmly lays them on a bed, side by side like a peep-show Hansel and Gretel? I don't think so," said Inga.

"Neither do I, even as I was saying the words it didn't ring true."

Inga began to pack up the empty food cartons.

"There is something we haven't considered. We were going to meet Rhonda, right? What if someone wanted to make sure we didn't speak to Rhonda? So, they went to kill Rhonda, or paid someone to kill her…"

"But Rhonda wasn't there…"

"…The killer wouldn't know that. He'd have an address and a young lady to kill. When a blonde answered the door, he killed her where she stood," Inga sat in silence for a long time. I finished the last beer. Inga asked:

"But who would be crazy enough to have Rhonda killed just because you were going to talk to her about this den Hamer guy? It's not like he's a war criminal or something. Maybe…just maybe he's involved in land fraud and of course, he's fucking your wife but that's not the kind of thing you kill two girls to cover up…is it?"

"Exactly, so if it is Ko den Hamer behind the killings, he's got to be involved in something really big. Way bigger than we thought. Don't forget the fire at his office. That was no accident. That was meant to kill me."

"We should go to the police," said Inga.

"And tell them what? We don't have proof of anything yet and Grunwald is itching to throw me in the slammer and throw away the key."

"Yeah, it's funny how he took an instant dislike to you…"

"…And me being such a likeable guy."

Inga nearly choked on her last fork-full of noodles. Eventually, she stopped coughing, took a sip of my beer.

"What are we going to do?"

"We aren't going to do anything. I'm going to find Ko den Hamer and I'm going to follow up till I find out what the hell is going on. You can't get involved in this Inga; Brady might let it slide if I do a little moonlighting…but not you."

"How are you going to find den Hamer?"

"Well, he won't be back in his office for a while, but I do know one place he'll be on a regular basis."

"Your house?"

"My house. I'll watch the place for a few evenings. He's sure to show up. It would be stupid to get a woman's husband kicked out of the house and not enjoy the prize you won."

"I'd like to come with you. I don't want you doing anything stupid and getting yourself hurt…or killed."

I was touched.

"That's very nice of you to say so, I'm touched."

"Yeah, I'd hate to go back to driving Mister Brady around."

"Funny, very funny."

We moved on to discuss what we had on The Connie explosion. After all, it was the case I was supposed to be concentrating on. I was looking through the crew list when I noticed something that might be of use…to me, it was of no way relevant to the Constance Brady case but (I must admit) by then I was a man obsessed.

The Flight Engineer's home address was in a small town called Napa; I think it's a farming community about fifty miles north of the city. I figured a trip up there to talk to his widow might be a smart move and it might allow me to check out those properties that Ko den Hamer was talking about to investors. I didn't expect to get much more than the time of day from the widow Brown but after talking to her I'd have the rest of the day to try find out what the hell was going on in this Napa place. It was nearly ten. Inga looked at the clock on the wall and said:

"I'm gonna head out. What are we doing tomorrow?"

"We're going on another little drive, north this time. I want to talk to the flight engineer's widow."

Chapter Ten

We set off north over the Golden Gate sometime after nine. The weather was improving, and the usual early morning fog had lifted from most of the bay by then. There was a cool breeze off the Pacific, but I still had the top down on the Plymouth.

We stuck to the highway heading north, passing Sausalito on our right, went through Marin, and pretty much followed our noses for a while. We passed the road leading to San Quentin and a short drive later we turned off the highway at Black Point. We headed north-east until we reached a small town called Schellville. We turned right at Schellville and followed the signs for Napa. We were in farming country now; the wide valley bottom was planted with all kinds of fruit, row after row; mile after mile right up to the town of Napa.

We cruised down (what I guessed) was Main Street until we came to the Fox Movie Theatre. We pulled in close to the corner and took a while to stretch our legs…thinking maybe we would find someone who could give us directions to the Brown residence. We stopped in a drug store and grabbed a malt shake each. Inga turned on the girlie charm and got the help we needed in finding Mrs. Mable Brown. She lived in a small-holding on the very edge of town, out on Sonoma Road. The old guy behind the counter said:

"Can't miss it; the last house on the right looks like it hasn't seen a lick of paint since before I was born."

He leaned across the counter and whispered to Inga:

"And that was way into the last century." He smiled a gap-toothed smile at Inga. With twinkling eyes, he said:

"You have a nice day now Missy." And he hurried off to mix potions, count out pills or whatever it is pharmacists in a small town drug store do when they aren't pulling malt shakes. Back on the street, Inga shivered:

"Ugggh, I feel like I need to take a bath."

"He was just a harmless old guy being pleasant," I said. Inga replied:

"Let's just find this place and get out of here. I hate these small back-woods towns, they give me the creeps."

We found Sonoma Road easily enough and turned left onto it. In less than a minute we were on the edge of town and looking at what (we guessed) must be the Brown place. It was a small shack, even smaller than your average small shack, maybe three small rooms. The roof was patched in a number of places; the front windows were missing a shutter or two. It stood on a patch of bare sandy earth which looked like it was working on its very own dustbowl.

It was difficult to tell what color it had once been painted as most all of the paint on the walls had long since faded or peeled. I guessed shitty brown, but I could have been way off.

We got out of the car half expecting a prospector with a shotgun to come out and tell us to 'git while the gittin' was good.' We crossed the dustbowl successfully and stepped carefully onto the front porch. It creaked like a Spanish Galleon in a storm. I did not dare take another step, so I stretched out to knock on the door. I nearly knocked it off its hinges. There was no answer.

"Nobody home, oh well time to head back to civilization," said Inga cheerily.

"Let's try round the back."

"You think she might be out back feeding the polo ponies or swimming in the pool?"

We went around the back. It took us two minutes to walk around the place and find nothing apart from a stack of army surplus items stacked against a fence. Some shovels and picks; some empty ammo boxes and what looked like a Jeep engine covered in a tarp. As we came back around the front, we saw a heavy-set woman in a shapeless coat walking up to the front door. She didn't seem too surprised to see us.

"Mrs. Brown?" I ventured.

"Well, what do you think? Is it worth saving?"

"Worth saving?"

"The house, the house. Can we repair it, or would it make more sense just to knock it down and start again?"

"What do you think?" I asked.

"What do I think? What kind of damn fool question is that? You're the carpenter. Can you save the place, or should we start again?"

Inga was quicker to grasp what was happening here.

"Well, Mrs. Brown it all depends on the money available."

"Don't you worry about that. When my husband's insurance pay-out comes through there'll be plenty to go around. The smartest thing I ever did was increasing the coverage on the old fool… dangerous business, flying," For some reason, my left ear began to itch like hell. Mrs. Brown appeared to be much happier than a recently bereaved middle-aged woman should be.

I decided to test this. I put on a very somber voice, a bit like an undertaker when he says: 'do you want to see the body?' I said to Mrs. Brown:

"We'd both like to offer our condolences on your tragic loss Mrs. Brown. It must have come as a great shock."

Mrs. Brown ignored my heartfelt sympathies.

"Yeah sure, thanks…thanks a lot. So, do we knock it down, build a bigger place? I'd like more bedrooms and a big kitchen, a gigantic kitchen. I want my sister to be green." She stood in silent contemplation for a moment then she said, "Hell, let's knock it down. You only live once, as my husband used to say."

"Then we shall put some ideas on paper for you Mrs. Brown. We'll get back to you real soon."

And with that Inga and I beat a hasty retreat back to the car. As we pulled away a guy in a brown Chevy pick-up with a sign on the door saying: **'Fred Belmont Construction'** stopped by the property and jumped out carrying a large tape measure and a notebook. He put a pencil behind his ear and walked toward the house. I put my foot down. As we drove away in a cloud of dust Inga turned to me and said:

"What the hell was all that?"

"Not exactly the heart-broken grieving widow hey?"

"Now that was…weird," said Inga. I said the next few words as casually as possible:

"While we're up here we might as well look at one or two of the properties our friend Ko den Hamer has been foisting on unsuspecting investors."

But Inga looked at me as if I had my hand inside her bra, and she didn't want it there.

"Just how dumb do you think I am Rick…"

"…I don't know what you mean; I don't think you're dumb…"

"…Then stop treating me like I just came in on the last Herring Boat."

"Herring boat?"

"Herring boat."

"I just thought that as we were up here anyway, and I just happen to have a note of two or three addresses."

"Don't tell me anymore. Just drive."

I drove. I drove back into town then turned, heading north again. After maybe fifteen minutes we came to the first address on my list. Yountville Farm lay to the west of the highway just before the town of Yountville. The property made Mrs. Brown's place look like San Simeon, William Randolph Hearst's pile of bricks…you know the place, it was the inspiration for the big castle in

Citizen Kane…don't tell me you've never seen Citizen Kane? You ought to get out more.

Where was I? Oh yeah, Yountville Farm. The place was a mess, row after row of dead fruit trees. The place was overgrown with weeds and creepers. We couldn't see any farm buildings left standing. We couldn't see any **for sale** signs either. I got my handy dandy detective's camera out of the glove box (you remember, the CMC Miniature camera) and took a few pictures; I even took one of Inga when she wasn't looking.

We walked around the place for half an hour, hoping to find someone to talk to about Yountville in general and what was left of Yountville Farm in particular. Then just as we got back into the car the local sheriff makes his entrance, skidding up behind the Plymouth in a cloud of dust and gravel. He took his time putting his funny hat on, then his dark glasses. I saw him check himself out in the rear-view before he got out of the car.

He was a tall gangly young man, he looked about nineteen, but I guess he must have been a little older. His sandy grey sheriff's uniform had sharp military-style creases; his shiny sheriff's badge blazed in the mid-day sun. His revolver was oiled and ready for action. This guy meant business! I tried to keep things light.

"Afternoon Sheriff! How can we help you today?" The sheriff slid his aviator glasses slowly down his long aquiline nose. He spat tobacco through his equine teeth missing his own shiny boots by inches.

"You folks ain't local," He said like it was a crime.

"Nope, we're from San Francisco," I thought about saying: it's a big city about an hour's drive from here with lots of tall buildings that folks live and work in. But I didn't. Still…thinking it made me smile, that was a mistake.

"Sumthin' funny?" He asked, resting his right hand on the butt of his gun.

"No sir, nothing funny here."

"This here is private property, you were trespassing, I should write you a ticket."

"We were wondering if the place was for sale."

"What? This old dump? Can't grow nothin' here 'cept weeds."

"It does look a little run down."

"Ain't nobody farmed here since before I was born. It's owned by the town of Yountville on account of nobody's paid taxes on the place since…"

"…before you were born?" I ventured.

"Right. You'd need to speak to the Mayor if you wanted to buy the place."

"My wife and me, we'll think about it," I said. "Thanks for all your help Sheriff," The sheriff tipped his hat to Inga; just the same way James Stewart does in all his westerns.

"Ma'am," he said. Then he climbed back onto his horse and rode off into the sunset (scratch that...he got back into his car and drove slowly back into town).

"Not the hottest bit of real estate on the market. I wonder what KDH Investments is up to."

Inga was stuck in western housewife mode. She said:

"Hon' I'm kinda peckish. Can we head back into town for some vittles?"

"Sure, if you promise not to call me hon' ever again."

"Deal," I turned the Plymouth around at the side of the road and we drove back into Napa to grab a bite. After lunch, I filled up at a gas station on the edge of town and bought a local map. I had a second address (Humboldt's Orchards) in my notebook and I didn't want to waste the afternoon driving all over Hicksville trying to find it.

South of the town I followed the road for Vallejo. We passed a large stone archway which was the entrance to the State Insane Asylum. I didn't turn in; hey why make things easy for the guys in white coats? I put my foot down a little as we passed. On the map, I had marked where I figured the second property should be.

I drove straight past it, didn't realize my mistake until we came up to the turn for Napa Army Airfield. I knew of this place, it used to be an emergency landing strip for trainee pilots. It looked like it was now in civilian hands. I took the turning and drove up to the airfield. I needed a place to check my map, I hated getting lost. I spotted a sign for Jonesy's Restaurant and figured we might as well get out of the sun and be comfortable while we asked about this mystery property. Inga went to the washroom and I ordered coffees and two slices of Cherry Pie which looked delicious.

The redhead behind the counter came over to the booth with the coffee and pie. She was a looker, curvy, and cute. Just the way all waitresses should be. She wore a pale pink overall that was tight in all the key places, made a nice swishy noise when she walked. Her luxuriant red locks hung over her shoulders. As the place wasn't busy, I took the chance to ask if she knew where Humboldt's Orchards was.

"Ain't round here."

"Are you sure? I've got an address just off the highway."

"I'll check in the back. The cook's been here since before the war. He'll know where it is...or was."

I thanked her and she sauntered back into the kitchen. The view from where I was sitting was uplifting...if you get my drift. My favorite waitress came back from the kitchen, but she stayed behind the counter and shouted:

"Hymie said ain't no orchards around here, used to be a hundred years ago, but not since the twenties. Lot's further north in Napa and Sonoma though."

"Thanks for your help, much obliged," I said. Inga sat down in the booth.

"Are we getting any further?" she asked.

"Not really, although this local is much friendlier than the sheriff."

"That wouldn't be too hard."

"True." We both took big spoonfuls of the cherry pie. I thought about Josephine, she would love this. There's nothing she liked more than a good cherry pie. Apart from getting fucked by tall Dutchmen.

"Are you okay?" asked Inga. "For a second there you looked like you had all the cares of the world on your shoulders."

"What me?" I bluffed. "I'm fine, never better."

We decided to head back to town. There was very little else we could do in Napa. As I drove away, I looked to my left. The airfield had several mothballed B17's parked at the edge of the tarmac. Some were missing engines, rudders; some leaned drunkenly on flat tires. The place felt like it was full of ghosts, even though it was being re-invented and light aircraft flitted around it constantly. I could not get the memories out of my head when I saw those beautiful silver giants being left to fall apart where they stood.

As we were driving back news came over the radio that the main fuselage of the wrecked Connie had been recovered and was being moved to the naval base at Treasure Island. The announcer said several bodies had also been found. After that news report, we thought it best to pull over in the next town, find a phone and check in with Paddy Brady. Inga did the phoning and I stayed in the car. She had a concerned look on her face when she got back to Plymouth.

"He asked me what Constance was wearing when I drove her to the airport. The police have been on; they have a body kinda matching Mrs. Brady's description. They want Mr. Brady at Treasure Island tomorrow morning, nine' o'clock. He's going to take his boat over. He wants both of us there."

There wasn't much to say after that. It looked like one half of the mystery was going to solve itself tomorrow morning with the positive identification of Mrs. Brady's body. I dropped Inga close to another lady friend's apartment in North Beach. I arranged to pick her up at the same corner tomorrow morning at eight. After that, I drove out to see Mrs. Georgeopolous. I stopped off at a bakery and bought her a couple of cream horns. She had a soft spot for fancy desserts. I rang the bell to her apartment, and she buzzed me up. She was waiting in her doorway to give me a hug that made my eyes bulge.

We talked for about an hour. I thanked her for mentioning my name to Paddy Brady, getting me the biggest pay-check I'd ever received. I said if I got the bonus at the end of the case, I might be able to buy her out. She said not to worry about all that. I got the feeling she wanted to know all about the case but was too polite to ask. I promised to tell her the whole story once I knew the whole story and when the case was closed.

Mrs. Georgeopolous forced me at knifepoint to eat a massive pot roast dinner with two kinds of potatoes and three vegetable dishes. All of it washed down with bitter red wine and two shots of ouzo. I managed to waddle out of her apartment under my own steam but only just. I staggered down three flights of stairs and out into the street. I made it to the car and collapsed behind the wheel then drove back downtown with an ache in my heart and a bigger ache in my gut.

After my meal with Mrs. G., I didn't have far to go for my next waypoint. I drove to my old neighborhood, parked the Plymouth two blocks away, and walked to my house. It was dusk, just gone nine'o'clock but I couldn't park the Plymouth across the street from the house. Josephine would recognize it instantly…if she was there.

Harry Loomis lived across the street from us. He was in his sixties, worked as a guard on the Union Pacific Railroad. So, I knew he was away a lot. I also knew he drove a beat-up 1940 Chevy Sedan. This car was never locked because a: no one in their right mind would want to steal it and b: you could open it with a pen-knife if you wanted to.

At nine-fifteen it was dark enough for me to saunter down the street, try the lock on Mr. Loomis's Chevy, open the door, and slip inside. I had a good view of the house from this vantage point. I rolled the window down a little, so the car didn't steam up and began the surveillance. The house was in darkness, so I didn't know if I was in for a long uneventful stay.

I was in luck, just after ten Josephine and Ko den Hamer rolled up in his little red Jag. I knew it was them from a block away. There aren't many cars in the bay area that sound like a Jag, only other Jags.

They got out of the car and walked arm in arm up to my house. Ko was carrying a small leather briefcase. I needed to see what was in that case. I still had my house keys so I knew I could get in easily enough unless they had changed the locks…still, I knew a couple of loose windows that I could slip through if need be. I waited.

I didn't have to wait long. The happy couple turned off all the lights downstairs and hurried up to bed inside ten minutes. I saw the lights in our bedroom come on and through the blinds, I saw two figures move together. I wondered if anyone on the street had ever watched Josephine and me go through just the same motions. That didn't help. That didn't help at all. I waited a few more minutes then I crossed the street, checking there was no-one else around. I unlocked the door with my own set of keys and stepped quickly inside, closing the front door behind me quietly. I needn't have bothered being so careful. I could have driven a Sherman Tank up the driveway and our young lovers would have been none the wiser. There was so much noise coming from the bedroom I could hardly think straight. And Inga was right, Josephine really did make some very strange whooping sounds when she was, you know, getting nailed in our marital bed by the Flying Dutchman.

For a few seconds, I had fantasies of grabbing the biggest kitchen knife in the house, storming upstairs, and putting an end to the whooping, once and for all. I also thought about turning around, walking out the door, and never seeing or hearing Josephine again. But I was a detective now, maybe not a very successful one but nevertheless...This house contained answers I was looking for and the answers weren't upstairs in the bedroom. They were in the briefcase that had been conveniently left in the hallway. I picked up the briefcase and took it in to the kitchen which was at the rear of the house. I closed the kitchen door and turned on the light.

The case was stuffed with papers, some hand-written notes, and legal documents. The three addresses I'd noted down in Ko's office were part of a much more extensive list of land parcels. They all seemed to be located in the Napa and Sonoma valleys. One name featured on at least three deals: M. Cohen, Las Vegas, Nevada. It looked to me as if Mr. Cohen was ready to finalize deals on a number of farms.

I made a few notes in my handy dandy detective note-book (I'm never without it) then I packed everything back in the case, turned out the light, and went back into the hallway. Things appeared to have cooled down a little upstairs; at least the whooping had stopped. I figured I should leave just in case one of them came down for a drink after their exertions.

I needn't have worried, as I headed toward the front door the thumping noises and the whooping started up again. I put the briefcase back. I could hear my wife wailing in ecstasy a few feet above my head, she sounded a little like a steam train going through a tunnel, or was that just an image that came to mind?

I left, but I'd already decided to come back another night, equipped with my camera. I wanted a full record of all these proposed deals. I also needed to find out more about this Cohen guy in Las Vegas. I thought the assistant D.A. might be able to help me there. I walked the two blocks back to the Plymouth and drove back across the Bay Bridge. I slept in my office, my head full of images of my wife and Ko den Hamer going at it like randy chimps in a zoo. I could not get the 'whoop, whoop, whooping' out of my mind.

Treasure Island sits roughly halfway between San Francisco and Oakland under the Oakland Bridge. Alcatraz Island and its famous penitentiary sit a little over a mile to the west. Inga and I arrived on time at the Naval Base on the exotically named Treasure Island. We signed in at the main gate and were directed to a disused hangar which had been commandeered as a holding area for the wreckage of flight 402.

The two main pieces of the fuselage had been placed in the center of the hangar. Smaller pieces of wreckage were carefully displayed all around this silver ghostly apparition, the wreckage spreading over nearly all the hangar floor. The whole scene was lit by arc lights which gave it a theatrical, menacing look. Investigators moved carefully through the pieces of the aircraft making notes on clip-boards, flash-bulbs froze the scene every few seconds. The most unnerving thing about the whole thing was the silence. Apart from the flash-bulbs sounding like popcorn in a pan, there was no sound at all.

To the rear of the hangar was an industrial-sized cold store, originally used to house frozen meat to be loaded on supply ships for distribution to the Pacific Fleet. This cold store was now a temporary morgue.

We stood at the entrance to the hangar with armed guards for company. The large doors were open about twenty feet wide. Brady was late. We waited some more. Eventually, a knot of people marched toward us from the water's edge. Inga ran over to see what the problem was. Brady was taken to a nearby office, probably to have the whole process explained to him. Inga came back over.

"Some stupid rating wouldn't let them moor The Kilkenny on Naval property. I've never seen Mister Brady so angry…" I said:

"That might be a good thing; it might help him get through the next half hour."

At that point, a familiar car slid up behind us. Elton Dwight, Assistant District Attorney stepped out of the rear, resplendent in a Burgundy colored jacket; charcoal slacks, and black and white wing-tips. He had the sense to ignore me completely although I could see he was surprised to see me. A slim, stone-faced woman in her fifties…I guessed maybe a stenographer, followed him into the building. She was carrying a small black case and a yellow purse.

I stayed outside the hangar with my armed guard. Inga accompanied Paddy Brady into the rear of the building. I don't know what I expected to happen but one thing I did not expect was Inga rushing back from the temporary morgue in a matter of minutes.

"He wants you to see this," she said as she ran to collect me from the entrance to the hangar. The armed guard didn't seem to object so I walked with Inga to the morgue.

"There's something weird going on here," she said.

"Tell me what happened," Inga was practically running back to the morgue, she said:

"Before he looked at...you know; the body. They showed him some clothing. He asked me to look at it too."

"At what?"

"Mrs. Brady's coat, it's definitely hers, it's the one she wore when I dropped her at the airport, you can't mistake it. It's a designer piece, made to measure; black with a fox fur collar. It's even got her name sewn into the neck-line."

"Okay, I get it. It's her coat. Why is that such a big surprise? What's the big deal?"

"I've not got to the good part yet," said Inga. We were now just outside the swing doors leading to the morgue.

"You are not going to believe this."

Chapter Eleven

"It's not her! It's not Constance!" Paddy Brady barged through the double doors from the makeshift morgue, charged over to us, and lifted Inga off her feet.

"It's not her! I told you it wasn't her when I saw the body," he repeated. "Now I know for sure…she's alive! All we have to do now is find her."

Brady stood in between Inga and me; he put his arms around us and led us into the morgue.

"Let me show you what I mean. This way…"

We passed Elton Dwight on the way down the corridor to the examination suite. He didn't pay us any heed. If Paddy Brady had words that morning with Mr. Dwight, he didn't seem too worried about it. The first thing I noticed when we walked into the morgue's examination suite was the smell. It was something I'd never experienced before. There were three bodies on separate metal tables, covered in white sheets. Two attendants in light blue lab coats and combat boots stood around looking slightly embarrassed. The County Coroner was a very busy man and had moved on to another viewing close by.

We all stood around wondering what to do, waiting for Paddy Brady to come back. We heard a desperate wail of anguish from the room next door. I guess the coroner had been able to confirm one victim's identity this morning. After a few more awkward minutes spent staring at everything but the three sheets on the slabs Paddy Brady burst into the room with two official military types.

The first military-type spoke to Brady:

"Just so we've got this clear; you can confirm that exhibit 'A' is, in fact, your wife's coat?"

Brady snapped: "Yes, yes, get on with it man!"

"And we've already told you that said coat was being worn by the deceased person on this table?"

The military type moved toward the closest table.

"Yes!" said Brady, practically shouting. The military type folded back the white sheet to the waist. The head area was covered by a separate smaller sheet, there had obviously been some serious damage done in this area. The smaller sheet just didn't lie right. There looked to be a large part of the head missing. I for one was glad the small white sheet was doing its job. A few strands of blonde hair, still wet from when the coroner washed the body, were visible on the intact side of the skull.

The rest of the body (that we could see) was complete; a woman in her early twenties with full proud breasts, the skin terribly pale, almost jade in color. There were mottled patches all over the lower half of the body where the blood had pooled. Beneath the right breast, on the rib cage was a small tattoo. It looked a lot like a butterfly, but I didn't move forward to check. Military type finally got to the point.

"But you are telling us this is not Constance Louise Brady, your wife."

"No, it's not."

"How can you be so sure? As we mentioned there is considerable damage to the skull and face. There's no way you could identify anyone from...from that."

Brady stepped forward.

"You see that butterfly tattoo?"

"Err yes?"

"My wife, Constance Louise Brady, did not have any tattoos."

The second military-type joined in.

"Are you certain? Could she have had the tattoo recently?"

"If she'd had a tattoo I would have known," said Brady. "Are you saying I don't know what my wife looks like naked?"

Military type number two had the good sense to back down.

"I...certainly not Mister Brady, I errr. We have to be one hundred percent certain, I'm sure you understand."

"Look, sonny," said Brady. "Understand this. I'm telling you this poor thing is not my wife. So, let's sign all the forms and documents and we'll get the fuck out of here and you can try find out who the hell this is."

The personal effects of this poor creature were laid out on a metal table on the far wall. The coat, Mrs. Brady's coat was put back with a small pile of clothes and a red wig. I collared one of the mortuary attendants, slipped him a ten spot.

"She was wearing a red wig?" A nod.

"She wasn't a natural red-head...and she wasn't a true blonde either."

Just for my benefit, he lifted the sheet covering the body again. Dark brown pubic hair gave the game away for our mystery lady.

I thanked the attendant for his time and rejoined the entourage as it swept from the examination suite and eventually out of the hangar and into the welcoming warmth and fresh air. Everyone took a few deep calming breaths. At, that time more and more questions came to life in my mind.

1. If it's not Constance Louise Brady, who the hell is it?
2. Why was she wearing Mrs. Brady's coat?
3. If Inga delivered Mrs. Brady to the airport how and when was the switch made?
4. Why was this done? and…
5. Where was Mrs. Brady now?

Another question trumped all those I'd just run through, it was this: Could Mrs. Brady be desperate enough or evil enough to fake her own disappearance and cover it up by arranging to have an aircraft blown out of the sky? I dismissed this train of thought just as soon as it left the station. The whole thing was too fantastic to think about…wasn't it? None of these questions appeared to be troubling my employer, Mr. Brady.

"Let's piss off back to Sausalito…we can have a knees-up on the boat!" said he. "We've got lots to celebrate. Inga, Inga! You bring Rick's car to Sausalito. He's coming with me."

Inga whispered in my ear.

"Wow, what an honor. He must think the world of you…then again he might just throw you over the side for a laugh."

"Hope to see you later," I said. "And if I do get to go for a swim in the bay you can keep the car."

"You'll be fine," said Inga. "Just don't mention all the questions about his wife you were just thinking up," I thought: '*How the fuck did she know that?*'

Inga took the keys to the Plymouth and walked off to collect it. The rest of us went down to the dock and boarded the Kilkenny. We were hardly untied before the whiskey started flowing. We sailed directly for Alcatraz Island where we did a circuit of the prison. The Captain was smart enough to stay far enough away from the rock not to bother the guards. That way no-one felt the need to dispatch a boat to keep us at arms-length. Paddy Brady handed me my third whiskey and said:

"I like to do a lap of the island every now and then. I have a number of close friends there. I like to let them know I'm still doing okay."

I wasn't sure if prisoners would be able to see the Kilkenny from their cells and I didn't want to find out. Brady was obviously in a good mood, so I took the chance to clear up a few things with him. I wanted to make sure he didn't think I could find his wife without considerable digging around in his private affairs and asking some very awkward questions. We stood by the bow; Brady had calmed a little; maybe he'd had time to reflect on what we'd just discovered. I steeled myself and launched into the first question.

"Mister Brady, I think we have to be asking ourselves a few difficult questions about your wife…"

"You mean like: why did she arrange the switch with that poor bitch in the mortuary, whoever she is?"

"That would be a starting point yes. Is it okay to ask you about it?"

"Why wouldn't it be?"

"Well to be frank…"

"…I wish you would be, for fuck's sake."

"To be frank, it looks to me as if Mrs. Brady set this whole thing up. It looks like she wanted to disappear and not be found. Why else would she fake the flight to Seattle? Now the bad news is she could be anywhere by now. And if someone doesn't want to be found then it's very hard to find them. She most likely has enough money and help to be…"

"…How much?"

"I don't get it, how much what?"

"How much do you want to find her? Ten Grand?"

"It's not a question of what it's gonna cost, Mister Brady."

"It sure sounds like it to me."

"I'm just saying, trying to find someone who is actually hiding, covering their tracks…well it's a lot harder than a normal missing person's case."

"Have you done this kind of thing a lot?"

"I've never worked on a case as complicated as this before."

"Then how do you know how much harder it's going to be son?"

I finished my fourth Irish Whiskey.

"Good point Mister Brady…"

"Call me Paddy, look…you and Inga carry on what you're doing. Just keep me in the loop, keep me up to date on any developments. I'll arrange for another ten grand to be delivered to your office. We'll talk again soon."

And with that Paddy Brady took my empty glass and made his way back to the cabin. I started making big plans to buy out Mrs. Georgeopolous and start an agency under my own name…maybe even have a new sign on the door and a fancy nameplate on my desk like Josephine's.

We swung north and were tying up at Sausalito for mid-day. By then I was in no condition to drive so I was more than happy to let Inga chauffeur me back over the Golden Gate Bridge into town. I slept like a lamb all the way back. Back at the office, Inga made strong coffee and we both took some time to work out our next move.

"Do you think there's any way they will identify the headless lady with the nice tits and the butterfly tattoo?" asked Inga.

"We could ask around the local tattoo shops but there must be hundreds of women in the bay area with butterfly tattoos and maybe some with nice tits too. Sorry…I was just thinking out loud. Maybe I'm still a little drunk."

"S'okay."

"I think we'll be spinning our wheels trying to find out who the poor woman is…was. Even if we did get an I.D. it wouldn't get us any further finding Mrs. Brady. Quick question: could Constance Brady drive?"

"I don't think so."

"Good, that cuts down her options."

"I don't follow," said Inga.

"Well, it's like this…she had to have some way of getting out of the airport after the switch. If she couldn't drive, she has three options: she gets another flight, she gets a cab or some else picks her up. So, we're starting to narrow things down…I suppose she could also bum a ride."

"Not Mrs. Brady; no way."

"So, here's what we do. You get onto the cab companies that cover the airport and ask them about fares around the time of the flight on the 4th. They will all have been short-staffed because of the holiday so it's likely they'd remember. I'll check if there were any flights in the next…say an hour and a half after flight 402. She wouldn't risk waiting at the airport any longer than that."

"That just leaves being picked up by an accomplice."

"Yeah, that's a tricky one. Why don't we concentrate on the possibilities we can check and worry about the accomplice if we don't get a bite."

"Work's for me," said Inga. "I knew you were good at this."

"Did you ever doubt me?"

"Only when you were too drunk to stand after your wife threw you out," she joked. My face must have clouded over at that point because Inga came toward me and took a hold of my hand. She said:

"Sorry Rick, I didn't mean that," I made a brilliant attempt at laughing it off…I think.

"No, no you were right to say it. Okay, you stay here, call round the cab companies. I'll head back out to the airport. I should be back by five."

I finished off another cup of black coffee and went downstairs, out into the alley to collect the Plymouth. The short trip out to the airport took a little longer than I expected. The construction work we had encountered when we traveled to San Mateo had moved further north. I crawled past it before my turn off.

When I got to San Francisco International Airport I went straight to the T.W.A. counter. I was lucky, Miss Harper; the buxom red-head was on duty. I breezed over to her smiling my brightest smile.

"Miss Harper, it's great to see you again, how are you?"

It was obvious she was having trouble putting a name to my face.

"I'm fine thanks, can I help you?"

"Well, it's funny you should ask because I do have a quick question or two that I'm sure you can help me with. Remember flight 402, the one that crashed into the bay?" Now she recognized me, she reached for the phone.

"Were there any flights that took off within…oooh, let's say an hour after 402? No need to call the boss, Miss Harper. We wouldn't want to tell him all about your affair with the flight engineer on 402, Stu Brown."

Miss Harper put down the phone; she had a very sour look on her freckled face.

"What did you want to know?"

"Flights that took off after 402?"

Miss Harper knew the answer without checking any paperwork.

"There was only one. We stopped all Lockheed Constellation flights as soon as we heard about the…the accident. But there was one that took off thirty minutes after 402. Flight 312 to Lindbergh Field, that's San Diego."

I knew where Lindbergh field was, but I let her have her moment in the sun.

"Would you have a boarding list for that flight please?"

She hesitated, I guess weighing up the kind of shit she would get in if anyone found out she'd been helping me versus the mountain of hurt she would get if I told her boss about her affair with Stu Brown (which I'd only guessed had happened).

"Wait a minute," she said, and she walked into the back office. She came back a few minutes later.

"The list is missing," she said. "We keep boarding confirmations for six months, that's T.W.A. policy but something's weird. Flight 312 on the 4th of July is missing completely. Must have been miss-filed; sorry."

She said: 'sorry,' but I heard, 'go fuck yourself' funny that.

"No matter," I said, all breezy and carefree. "See you around," The look on Miss Harper's face said: 'Not if I can help it.' On the trip back from the airport I hit the construction delays again. The northbound lanes looked to be completely blocked. Traffic was being diverted down what looked like a farm track. The track led away into the distance for a mile or so. As I set off down the track the cars behind me were held up by the flag-guy. *'That's lucky.'* I thought. *'Looks like I'm the last one through for a while.'*

A few hundred yards away from the main road I was stopped again by another flag-guy. I watched as the cars in front of me drove away into the distance. I waved the flag-guy over, thought I'd ask him what was going on and how long I'd be held up. He didn't look too keen to talk. He kept looking around nervously. Then after half a minute he dropped his yellow flag, jumped across a ditch, and simply high-tailed it across a nearby field. I got out of the car and watched him go for a while. It was the weirdest thing.

I turned to get back in the car and get back on my way. Just as a Mack truck slammed into the back of it. There was a noise like the doors of hell slamming shut and my Plymouth flew away from me and into the same deep ditch the flag guy had hurdled a minute earlier. The Mack truck didn't seem to be too damaged; it had some over-sized fender welded across its front end. The driver didn't look at all surprised by what had happened. He just sat in the truck looking at me.

A big Buick pulled up behind the truck and four guys jumped out. I couldn't tell you much about what they were wearing but they were all carrying Thompson sub-machine guns. It's funny how those little details stick in my mind.

I followed my car into the ditch. I dove full length to try get the car between me and the four machine guns. I landed awkwardly in the ditch and I think I broke my right elbow. When I got to my feet my arm just kinda hung there like a big wet noodle. I didn't have any time to worry about that because at that moment the four guys from the big Buick thought it might be fun to let rip with their toys.

They stood in a semi-circle at the edge of the track and started shooting my car up. Bullets flew in all directions, smashing the windscreen, thudding into the body-work and the seats. The clatter of the four machine guns brought flashbacks of fighter attacks over Europe, but this was way closer, way louder.

Several bullets clunked into the trunk, I guessed it would only be a matter of seconds before the fuel tank was ruptured and the whole car went up in a fireball.

I don't like fireballs; I've been too close to one to ever wish for a repeat of the experience. I had to find a way out of this, and I had to do it fast. The bullets kept on coming, the smoking Thompsons bucked in the hands of the four hit-men. I was crouched low behind the hood so the engine block would shield me from anything but the luckiest shot, but this wouldn't last long. In a matter of seconds, the fuel tank could go up and take me and car with it. Or the four hoods would split up, move to different sides of the car and I'd be surrounded and heavily outgunned.

I looked back up the dried-out irrigation ditch. There was a conduit about twenty feet away from me. I threw myself to the ground and started crawling in the dust and dirt. Every time my broken arm hit the ground, I felt like screaming. Waves of nausea threatened to drown me in pain. I kept low, the noise above me kept on relentlessly. Every second or so a ricochet sang past me and plopped into the earth by my head. And then (as I expected) the fuel tank caught fire. In a matter of seconds, the Plymouth burst into a house-sized ball of orange and yellow flames. I felt the shock wave and the heat pass over me. Large pieces of body-work rained down around me, a complete door flew over my head before cart-wheeling into the field. Another bullet rang of a piece of metal and came my way. I'd just turned to investigate the source of the ding when that source (i.e. the bullet) cut a crease across my forehead narrowly missing my eye. That shook me a little, I must admit. Blood began to run into my eyes.

I gambled that the four shooters would have been forced to take a few steps back by the explosion. I was right. The shooting stopped for a few seconds. Maybe they were re-loading? I took my chance, got quickly to my feet, and dove into the piping. My right hand hit the base of the pipe with a clunk and I must have passed out with the pain.

I don't know how long I was out but when I came to the wreck of my car, still smoldering, was surrounded by construction workers and cops. I could see uniformed legs milling about the wreckage. Warily I stuck my head out of my hiding place and got slowly to my feet. I took a couple of faltering baby steps then everything faded to grey and then in time-honored tradition...black.

I woke up in a hospital; my right forearm was in plaster. My head was bandaged. It was just like old times. I figured I might as well keep the bandage on my head all the time, just think of the money I would save on fashionable hats I was always buying, and it would save so much time when I got hit over the head or clipped by a ricochet like today.

All the bright white in the room hurt my eyes. I tried to get out of bed, take a look out of the window; see where I was. Not a good idea. The room did a barrel roll and I lay back down on the very comfortable bed for a while longer. When I woke again, I was being poked and prodded by a thirteen-year-old boy in a white coat. He must have got a Doctor Dress-Up Kit for his birthday because he had a stethoscope around his neck...it was cute, his mom had even put a tie on for him.

The thirteen-year-old spoke in a very upbeat, happy-clappy kind of way which got him on my bad side straight out the gate.

"Well, we have been in the wars, haven't we?" he asked.

"I have certainly. How many have you been in sonny?"

"I just missed the last one; I was in med school till '46."

"They let ten-year-olds into med school?"

"I think we might need to lower the dosage on the painkillers Nurse. Mister Marshall is hallucinating."

I looked at the nurse.

"You leave the painkillers right where they are nurse; I'm just messing with the Doc."

The doctor was studying an X-Ray.

"How's the arm, Mister Marshall?"

"Hurts like hell to be honest Doc."

"Well, it was a clean break."

"Doc, would you level with me? Will I be able to play the piano?"

"I don't see why not," said the Doc.

"That's great! I couldn't play a note before!" said I.

The nurse giggled; the doc blushed a little, I think.

"I think Mister Marshall will be just fine, we'll keep him in overnight, just to make sure there are no after-effects from the head injury…oh and nurse…do not forget the enema."

"The what?"

The young doc was laughing fit to beat the band as he moved on to his next victim. No-one came to visit me that evening. I'm sure no-one knew I was in the hospital, and if they did know, I'm damn sure nobody cared.

The next morning, I was getting ready to head back to the office. This took some time…have you ever tried to get dressed using only one hand? (Don't answer that.) It's like sex if it's done right…it takes a long time and involves a lot of wriggling and rolling about. After about thirty minutes of this, I was upright and pretty much decent. That was the time the Elton Dwight from the D.A.'s office chose to show his smug face.

"I hear you were involved in a shoot-out with a gang of thugs…"

"Not exactly a shoot-out, more of a shoot at. I didn't have a weapon."

"Have you spoken to the police?"

"Not yet, I wasn't in a very talkative mood when they brought me in, I was unconscious."

"You've had a lucky escape," said Dwight, sitting down at the foot of the bed.

"Yeah, that's me, lucky all over."

"Do you know who they were?"

"Nope."

"We do, they were working for a Las Vegas high roller called Micky Cohen; he's purported to own two casinos."

"That's a five-dollar word, Mister Dwight. Can you explain what you mean in dime-sized bites?"

"Micky Cohen doesn't own the casinos, the mob does. Micky runs them for the Chicago Syndicate. Now, why would four torpedoes from Las Vegas drive all the way up here to shoot holes in your car?"

"That's a damn good question Mister Dwight and I wish I had an answer for you. But I'm completely in the dark on this one so if you don't mind, I'm checking out of this roach motel and heading back to the office."

I headed for the door.

"Do you have a ride?"

I didn't and as beggars can't be choosers, I was happy to accept the ride in Dwight's Packard. The assistant D.A. asked me questions the whole journey:

"Was I sure I'd never heard of Micky Cohen?"

"Had Brady ever mentioned Micky Cohen or Las Vegas?"

"Where did I think Mrs. Brady was now?"

...That kind of thing. It was a very one-sided conversation. Not for the first time in my life I had no answers; none that made sense. I thanked Dwight for the ride and promised to keep in touch. Dwight couldn't resist a parting shot as I clambered clumsily from the Packard.

"You might want to look into life insurance Mister Marshall, or maybe a bodyguard or two."

'Life insurance?' I thought: *'why did that suddenly seem very important?'*

Back in the office I lowered myself carefully onto the cot. I planned to sleep for most of the day then find a way to feed myself a decent steak. I might have to get the waitress to cut it up for me. Now, where could I find a waitress to do that?

Chapter Twelve

The office phone rang at mid-day, putting an end to my plans for some R&R. It was Inga. I told her all about my little adventure yesterday and she said she'd be right over.

"Better bring a car with you; mine got shot to shit."

Inga said she'd talk to Paddy Brady and put him in the picture about my sudden lack of transport. About an hour later Inga appeared at the office door.

"Mister Brady is outside; he wants a word about yesterday."

Outside on the sidewalk, I was surprised to see two cars, one much smaller than the other. Brady was in the rear of his usual Cadillac but almost hidden behind it was a very small two-seater sports car, bright red. I'd seen similar cars in England when I was stationed there. R.A.F. officers drove them all the time. I didn't remember them being so small though. Sitting in the giant shadow of the Cadillac this bright red MG looked more like a toy car that had fallen out of the caddy's trunk.

Brady called me over. I climbed into the back-seat beside him.

"The shooting yesterday…four guys?" I nodded.

"Machine guns on a deserted piece of highway?" I nodded again.

"No witnesses?"

"None, or none that want to talk to the police," Brady looked momentarily concerned.

"Sounds a lot like a mob hit." I knew that already, but I couldn't tell Paddy Brady that.

"Who could you have pissed off so much that they fly in four shooters to take you out?"

"That is a question I've been asking myself all night and all morning," I said. "I didn't get an answer."

"I'm glad you think this is funny."

"Believe me Mister Brady; I take this kind of thing very seriously. In fact, I think maybe we should call the whole thing off…call it quits. You've been very generous Mister Brady but if I'm full of holes I'm never going to get to spend the money you paid me."

"What makes you so sure that our arrangement has got anything to do with the hit?"

He had a point there…I told him so. Brady went on:

"I think we'll carry on with our arrangement, but I do think we will have to keep a closer eye on you. So, I'm going to ask Inga to stick with you 24/7. You are going to need a driver for a while anyway. Your new car has a stick shift."

"What new car?" I asked. Brady waved toward the rear of the Cadillac.

"I'm giving you this red sports job from England; latest model MG something or other, one of the first on the West Coast. Ordered it for Constance but she didn't like the color of the seats. Last few weeks it's just been sitting around at the back of the garage. You might as well use it."

Brady shouted instructions to his driver, which was my first clue that the conversation was over. I stepped out of the Cadillac and it swept away from the sidewalk seconds later. Inga towered over the little red car like a giraffe looking down at a fire-plug.

"Aren't you the lucky guy?" she asked.

"Am I? I guess so. Can you drive a stick?"

"I'm amazed you need to ask," said Inga.

"Well, put it in the elevator, take it upstairs and park it in the office next to my bed."

"You don't like?" asked Inga.

"It's going to be very easy to spot if we have to follow someone, unless we hide behind trash cans and dogs as we drive down the street."

"You are the funniest man," said Inga. "Now what do we do today?"

"Let's go find Sammy Kirk. See what he's going to do with his pictures. He'll be down at the Hyde Street Pier on a nice day like today," I lowered myself slowly into the tan-colored bucket seat. Inga slid in beside me and started up the MG. She hit the gas and we were launched out into the street with a 'roart' of exhaust noise right behind my ear. We jinked and dodged between cars, trucks, and trolleys like a running back breaking into the backfield. We were skidding to a halt by the pier in no time at all. Inga gave the throttle a healthy blip and turned off the engine.

"I could get used to this; can you have a broken arm all the time?"

"I'll see what I can do," I said. We found Sammy in his usual spot near the end of the pier. He finished with a client and stepped over the say hi. He saw my broken arm.

"What the hell happened to you?"

"Cut myself shaving."

"Yeah right…who's this?"

"Sammy this is Inga…she's my…assistant."

"Wow Ricky, coming up in the world. How the hell can you afford to pay for such a lovely young lady to…what does she do, exactly?" I could tell if we carried on with this conversation Inga was likely to throw Sammy and me into the bay. I changed the subject.

"Listen, Sammy, I've been thinking about those pictures of the crash. Have you decided to publish or not?"

"Funny you should ask me that Rick because I have had some offers…"

"… From the papers?"

"All the papers…they all came knocking, don't know how word got out or how they found me, but they all came a'knockin'. Your friend Melvin was a great help."

"So, you sold them?"

"Last week…to The Hughes Corporation of Dallas, Texas."

"It figures. Did you keep the negatives?"

"That would have been strictly against the terms agreed between my lawyer and the nice gentlemen from The Hughes Corporation of Dallas, Texas."

"So, you kept them?"

"Sure, I did."

"I'm gonna need a look at all of them. Can you run me off a set of prints?"

"Who do you think I am, Kodak Labs?"

"I can pay for your time."

"I'm just messin' with you, Rick. Come by my place tomorrow evening. I'll have a set ready for you. But strictly for your eyes only. I wouldn't want The Hughes Corporation of Dallas, Texas hearing about this."

"For my eyes only…how much did you get anyway?"

"I can't tell you, Rick. I had to sign some papers…a promise not to talk to anyone about it. But I will tell you I'm going to be leaving the city soon and quitting this racket. Its hell on the leg, all this stomping around, great for meeting dames but hell on the wooden leg. I'm buying a place north of here, put down a deposit and everything. Melvin's handling it."

I told Rick I was really happy for him. We shook hands and I said I'd drop by some time after six tomorrow. It was a warm day, so we grabbed a soda from the stand by the entrance to the pier. Inga had a question:

"When are we going to be talking with Rhonda Pearlman? And how are we going to find her again?"

"You haven't forgotten who you're working with?" I asked as I pulled out my notebook and showed her the number for Rhonda Pearlman's male friend. I nodded to a nearby payphone.

“Why don’t you finish your soda then give this number a call.”

“Gee it must be great to be so smart,” said Inga. I watched heads turn as Inga walked over to the payphone. I was sure she knew the effect she had on poor saps like me. I wondered if she pitied us, I wondered if she liked the attention even though it was miss-placed. Could she enjoy feeling attractive to the opposite sex even if she wasn’t attracted to the opposite sex? As my dad used to say, ‘That is a two-pipe question.’

The sun was getting hotter; I tilted my hat back and lifted my head, feeling the warmth on my face. I thought about Josephine. I wouldn’t be able to drive across to watch the house tonight; it would be a few weeks before I could manage the stick shift on the MG. Should I ask Inga to watch the place for a few hours each night until Ko den Hamer turned up? And if he did turn up while Inga was watching what would I want her to do?

“There’s no answer,” said Inga.

“We’ll try again later.”

“What now?”

A large hand clamped down on my right shoulder making my broken arm zing with sharp pain.

“You are clearly the guy in this town that things happen to,” It was Detective Grunwald.

He was wearing the pants from a dark brown pin-stripe suit and rumpled shirt with a sardonic sneer on the side.

“I heard about the shooting. What can you tell me about it?”

I answered slowly.

“I’ve already spoken with the D.A.’s office about this. Mister Dwight.”

“… So, it won’t be a hardship to talk to me,” I was going to walk back to the car. Grunwald blocked my path and his wing-man was already moving Inga out of earshot. I heard him say:

“Why don’t you cool your jets blondie?” which I knew was not the best way to get Inga on your side. I looked across at her; saw the angry fire in her pale blue-grey eyes. I gave her a very slight shake of the head. I didn’t want to give the cops any reason to go all ‘justifiable force’ on our asses. I was beginning to miss my regular gig…you know, divorce work. I have never been shot at doing divorce work (I have been spat at, but that’s to be expected) I have never been threatened with jail time by a cop, uniformed or plain-clothes. I have never been in the employ of a known gangster and I have never pissed off one of America’s captains of industry.

“Are you listening to me?” asked Grunwald. Obviously, I wasn’t.

“I’m hanging on your every word Detective Grunwald.”

"Hang on this smart-ass!" Grunwald (who must have slithered out of the wrong side of the bed this morning) grabbed my elbow…my right elbow, just above the cast. He then proceeded to try lift me off my feet with that elbow…not popular. The previous zing of pain became a fond memory as waves of nauseating, teeth clenching agony zapped around my body like lightning bolts. It was not fun. My knees almost gave way. I caught a glimpse of Inga struggling with Grunwald's sidekick, an oily Mexican with a gold tooth, and slicked back black hair called Hernandez. Then in a second Hernandez was on the floor and Inga was lifting Grunwald's wrist high into the air; as Grunwald was attached to his wrist the rest of the big slob followed. Grunwald pirouetted on tip-toe like a hippo ballet dancing…naturally, a small crowd began to gather. I said:

"Put the nice detective down Inga, he's only doing his job," There was a subdued murmur of laughter from the on-lookers. The laughter died when Hernandez drew his service automatic and levelled it at Inga.

"Get a hold on your pet Grunwald and we'll talk nice and civilized," Grunwald signaled for his partner to holster his weapon. Hernandez did this, all the while cursing under his breath in his native tongue. Now I'm not that good with Spanish but what I think he said was something along the lines of: 'Skinny young lady you will rue the day you ever crossed Manolo Jimenez Hernandez the third, this is not over'…or words to that effect. I said:

"Why don't I tell you all you want to know then we can all get on with our day and no-one needs to get hurt?" Grunwald said:

"You should be in the diplomatic corps." But he followed me back out onto the pier. We strolled along side-by-side and I told him all the things I didn't know. We turned around after a few minutes and walked back. At the end of our little talk Grunwald said:

"You know we could run your girlfriend in right now for assaulting a police officer."

"And you know there's a lot of people who saw Inga kick your ass."

Grunwald stopped walking and said:

"Do you have to keep right on with the wise-cracks? It's not helping your cause."

"I don't have a cause, Inspector. I just want to do the job I've been paid to do, with the minimum of fuss for everyone."

"Okay, okay. So why do you think those two girls were killed in Rhonda Pearlman's place?"

Right here is where I lied my ass off.

"I agree with your inspector. I think we have a psycho killer on the loose, targeting young women who live alone. I only hope you catch him real soon."

"You'd better try real hard not to turn up in anything else I'm working on Marshall, real hard!"

"Happy to oblige Inspector."

Inga led the way back to the M.G. Grunwald happened to be walking the same way. He was mildly amused by our new wheels.

"What the hell is this, a toy? Where did you buy this…Coco the Clown?" His partner Hernandez thought that was real funny.

We drove back to the office where a surprise was waiting patiently for me. Josephine Marshall, soon to be ex-wife of mine had made her-self comfortable behind my office desk. She looked terrific in a tailored skirt and silk blouse. She'd hung her jacket over the back of my chair. It was so quiet and still in the office that I swear I heard Inga's jaw muscles clench and unclench, but I might have imagined that. Inga said:

"I'll make some coffee," and she went into the postage stamp-sized kitchen. She banged pots and cups around for minutes just to make sure we both knew she was not happy with this development. If I'm honest I didn't know if I was happy or not. A lot depended on the first sentence to come out of Josephine's exquisitely painted red lips. I beat her to the punch in an effort to lighten the mood.

"I really must get a better lock on the office door," Jo said:

"I have a key, remember?"

"This must be the one and only time you've ever used it."

"I guess so," she said, with a resigned smile on her face, or was that regret? The whimsical smile turned to a thin straight line then Josephine said:

"I need money for the mortgage," So it wasn't regret then…

I was a little taken aback. In fact, I was a lot taken aback, and pissed.

"Hasn't the new boyfriend got lots of cash to spare? Don't tell me it's all over already…"

What was I hoping to hear in reply?

"No, it's not over, I love Ko and he loves me." Again, if I'm brutally frank, not that.

"So why isn't the big Dutch fuck willing to pay for his fun?"

A perfectly reasonable question in the circumstances, I'm sure you will agree. The look in Josephine's eyes told me she didn't…agree that is. Inga chose this perfect moment in time to waltz back in with a tray of mugs and a steaming coffee pot. Without a word, she slammed it down on the desk and stomped out of my office.

"I can see where all your spare cash is going," said Josephine. Now just for a teeny, tiny moment, my brain thought about instructing my lips to say: 'I wish.' But I caught myself, put a block on that thought and soldiered on.

"Inga doesn't like men, she's my assistant on the Constance Brady case and she's driving me around town for now," I waved my broken arm in the air. Josephine noticed it for the first time (apparently)

"Fell through a sky-light peeping on a cheating housewife again?" she asked pointedly. I was about to correct my wife…err ex-wife…err wife on this fine point but I thought to myself: *'what's the use?'* As I couldn't find a quick answer to this fairly straight-forward question I didn't bother to tell her about the shoot-out, the exploding car, the flying detective, etc. etc.

"How much?"

"If you give me two months mortgage we won't have to meet again for some time."

"Deal," I brushed past Josephine to my side of the desk, unlocked my drawer, took a pile of notes from my little tin box, and counted out some twenties to cover two month's mortgage. I handed it over. I also decided to move the money into my business account right after this little re-kindling of our relationship. But I wasn't going to leave things there.

"You didn't answer my question earlier, how come Mister den Hamer won't stump up for the payments on your little love nest? I know he lives there now."

"Ko still has a big mortgage on his house and he's supporting his wife and kids. He said he wanted to do right by them, make sure they didn't suffer because of of…because of our love."

"He said that, did he? Gee, what a guy…"

"Ko is a very decent man. He's a great father to his kids and he loves his wife…in a way. He doesn't want anyone hurt in this."

"That big place up on Vallejo must be costing him a packet and the wife looks anything but cheap. Are you sure he can afford to divorce her in the long run? Maybe the house is in her name? Maybe it's all her money?"

This was almost fun, and it was (obviously) educational. I now knew for sure that Ko had been lying to Josephine about the wife and kids and the house on Vallejo. What else had he lied to her about? Did she know anything about his property scam in the Napa Valley? I was tempted; I must admit I was tempted to tell Josephine all I knew about her lover. But something made me hold my tongue, which is a habit I should really try and carry on with. As my grand-pappy used to say: Hear all, see all, say nothin'. Wise words, words I planned to live by from now on. Josephine put the cash in her purse and left without another word.

Inga must have passed Josephine on the stairs. I didn't ask the tall Icelander where she'd been. She looked to have calmed down a little. I poured her a coffee and brought her up to speed about the duplicitous Mr. den Hamer.

"So, we really need to find out where he was living before, he moved into my place. His office is burned to bits; we know the house on Vallejo isn't his. We know the wife and kids aren't his either. There's got to be somewhere else. Somewhere we need to get a look at…I'm thinking there are more clues in his briefcase. Are you busy tonight?"

"Nothing I can't cancel."

"It turns out Josephine isn't the only one in our relationship that's hanging on to keys from the past," I twirled my house-key around my little finger on my left hand, before it spun off and splashed into my half-empty coffee cup. Inga burst out laughing. She said:

"You jackass!"

"I'd finished with that," I said.

"If we are going zooming around town this evening you are going to need something to wear. We'll stop off at Mona's they'll have something in the costume hamper," I said:

"It's been a long time since I played dress up," But as usual, when I said something stupid Inga ignored me. So, our first stop was Mona's where Inga skipped inside and came back minutes later with a very large dark blue sweater, the kind of thing the guys down on the wharf wear. This she forced over my head and the cast on my right arm. I slipped my arm back into the sling. It was a long time since this sweater had seen the sea and it didn't smell of fish which would have been bad. It smelled of a very fruity perfume, which was worse. I mumbled:

"Thanks for this Inga…I think."

And so, later that evening, in fact at very close to midnight Inga and I were squeezed into the M.G. in the back alley behind what used to be my house. We were both feeling the cold as neither of us knew how to set up the canvas roof that was tucked behind the seats. I don't think it would have been much use anyway.

It was a clear moonlit night; the stars were out. It was August but already you could see your breath in the night air. The fisherman's sweater was a helping me fight off the frigid temperature, but Inga had chosen to wear some kind of black one-piece stretchy outfit that stretched over all the interesting bits very nicely. She looked like a ballet dancer in warm-up gear. She looked stupendous. Well, the bits I could see in the dark alley looked stupendous. She must have been freezing.

"We're going to have to walk past the front of the house, make sure the lights are off."

"They might just like fucking in the dark."

"Not helping Inga. Not helping at all."

"I'm just saying…"

"Shall we go?" I asked.

"I'll take a quick look," said Inga. "No sense in us both skulking around the neighborhood like cat burglars."

And with that, she stepped out of the M.G. and disappeared into the darkened alley. I was left alone with my thoughts…never a good thing. And naturally, my thoughts turned to the fun and games going on less than fifty yards from my frigid perch. I don't know about you, but I hardly ever just sit and think about things. I guess I'm one of those instinctive; action now, think later types, the perfect pawn for the air force.

They taught me just enough to get a B17 off the ground over the North Sea and on to a target. They didn't give me time to think about what or (more importantly) who was underneath the aircraft when the bomb bay doors opened. They didn't give me time to think of all the buddies I'd seen blown to bits or falling to earth burning like Tiki torches. I remembered one B17 going down over Bremen. The radio operator had his hand on the radio key so the whole squadron heard their screams as the bomber fell to earth in flames a mile long.

"You okay?" It was Inga. I took a second to get a grip on myself.

"This thing stinks like a hooker's closet."

"When was the last time you were in a hooker's closet, Rick?"

"You'd be surprised."

"I doubt it." Once again Inga had the last word on the subject. This was just like being married but without the meatloaf and the sex. I missed the sex, the meatloaf I could take it or leave it.

"Well, they are home; they're downstairs listening to some awful records."

"Not Vaughan Monroe?"

"Could be, I don't know much about oldies like that."

"Oldies?"

"You know…crooners, big bands, swing music. It was all a bit before my time."

"So, what are you into?"

"Most of the time when I want to hear good live music, I go to The Black Hawk on Turk Street or Bop City. I like Jazz, real jazz, modern jazz. You should come with me sometime…when you're not spying on your wife…meet some of the crowd."

For a short while, we talked easily about music in general and jazz in particular. Killing time until my wife and her lover got tired enough or frisky enough to turn off the God-awful music and head upstairs. Apart from knowing Josephine was getting her ashes raked a few yards away from where I sat and apart for the fact that the temperature had dropped alarmingly, it was a pleasant way to spend an hour or so. After that hour Inga once again hopped from the car and hurried away to check the house. She came back minutes later.

"All set."

I clambered clumsily out of the M.G.; my arm was beginning to ache, but at least it was still attached to the rest of me. I decided to count my blessings and get on with it. My cameras were either still in what was left of my car or some light-fingered mechanic had lifted them.

I wouldn't be able to photograph any documents we found tonight. Still, there were two of us so we could split the speed reading and hopefully find what we were looking for in Ko den Hamer's briefcase.

I handed her the house keys and Inga led the way round to the front of what used to be my humble abode. Once inside I looked along the hallway for the briefcase…no such luck. I checked the kitchen, and the sitting room. Nadda, zip, butt-kiss, nothing. The Dutch fuck must have taken it upstairs. I whispered this information to Inga and turned to go. We'd have to try another night. Inga was taking off her shoes. Why was Inga taking off her shoes? She'd get really cold feet when we went outside…

Inga handed me the loafers and started silently up the stairs. There was nothing I could do to stop her now. I stood like a lemon at the foot of the stairs, trying not to breathe. After a few minutes, Inga came back down with the case. She handed it to me, grabbed her shoes, put them on, and walked past me. I followed her outside like a slightly confused, very alarmed lamb. Back in the alley, I hissed at her.

"We can't steal the case! He'll know someone is on to him!"

"I know that!" said Inga. "But we can't stay in the house while we see what's in there. They aren't asleep. They are busy."

"So how did you get the case?"

"It's easy, the bedroom door was open, the case was by the bed, there's only a small bedside lamp on and they were somewhat…preoccupied."

"Well don't be shy. Do tell me what they were doing. Please tell me everything in intimate detail."

Inga took a deep breath.

"Well your wife has her hands tied to the top of the bed frame; she doesn't seem to be wearing much. I'm guessing she was wearing some very expensive looking underwear, cream and black silk it looks like. But that's underneath the bed now. He's wearing some kind of leather mask and I saw a jar of petroleum jelly…"

"I was joking! Please shut the fuck up and let's see what's in the case."

And we did. We worked by moonlight, some of the papers I recognized from my previous dig around. We counted five large land purchase agreements waiting for completion; all of them in the Napa Valley, all of them for vast amounts of money and all of them with different companies in Nevada.

In an envelope, we found bank receipts for equally large accounts of money paid into KDH's account. A rough calculation told us we were talking almost two million dollars paid in cash. They looked like full payments on the yet to be finalized land deals. Now, who pays shed loads of money up-front for deals that haven't gone through yet? That didn't make sense. I knew that the land involved in these deals was either worthless, not for sale, or (in one case) the property didn't even exist. Was Ko den Hamer stupid enough to try con the mob? I hoped not because Josephine was either willingly or accidentally very close to this dodgiest of dodgy cons.

We spent close to thirty minutes making notes of bank details, account numbers, and everything else we could get a look at. Then I called a halt and began to put everything back in the case. I handed it over to Inga.

"Look, don't stick your neck out. If you can't get the case back up-stairs just leave it in the hall. He'll not notice the difference."

"We can't be sure of that," said Inga; then she was gone. I shouted after her in that loud whisper voice we all use when we don't want to be heard. She didn't turn around. She was back in a few short minutes.

"Piece of cake; they are sleeping like babies. By the way, your wife snores like a band-saw cutting wood."

"I did not know that," I said, hoping that my sarcastic tone was audible over the M.G.'s exhaust note. As Inga drove us back into town, I tried to summarize our next moves. I was still a little wary about spending so much of our time on a personal case. So, I tried to make sure we were also spending time finding out what had happened to Constance Brady.

"I think we need to talk to a lawyer. I'll give Melvin Hammerstein a call. We need to describe everything we saw in the briefcase, see if he can make any sense of it. And then we need to get back in touch with the modelling agency. See if they are down a blonde."

"Down a blonde?"

"The lady on flight 402; the one who was paid to take Mrs. Brady's place, the one in the morgue missing half her head, the one with the tattoo. It won't tell us why the switch was made, and it won't tell us where Mrs. Brady is now, but it's a loose end and the girl on the slab has probably got family somewhere. We need to find out who she is…err was. First thing tomorrow we'll speak to the modelling agency and then I want you to start calling round Tattoo Parlors," Inga sighed theatrically.

“Really? You really think someone will remember doing a butterfly tattoo on a blonde who we can’t describe from the neck up. Apart from anything else these places must do hundreds of butterfly tattoos on women who might just match our blonde’s description. Even if they did recognize their handiwork what if the client paid cash and didn’t leave a name?” I said:

“Hmm, you know you’re right. It is a very long shot; it might be totally hopeless.”

“I’m glad we agree,” said Inga.

“Do it anyway,” I said.

Chapter Thirteen

"So, Rick, how's that lovely wife of yours?"

"She's been having an affair with her boss for over a year and two weeks ago she kicked me out of the house we own so he could move in."

"Ouch!" exclaimed Marvin. "And what happened to your arm, you didn't get into an altercation when she kicked you out of the family home?"

"No, no, that was much later when someone decided to shoot the Plymouth full of holes." Melvin looked perplexed, but that was the way he looked most of the day, so I wasn't too worried. I went on:

"If I'm honest I think they were trying to plug me full of holes, but the car got in the way."

The meeting with Melvin Hammerstein had got off to a shaky start. It had just gone ten the day after my second nocturnal visit to my recently vacated home. Melvin met us at the empty receptionist's desk. After the awkward questions about my crumbling personal life and damage to my personal property and my actual person, he directed us through to his office. I attempted to introduce Inga who was back wearing her favorite man's suit. That is to say her favorite suit; cut for a man that she had bought for herself, not the suit that belonged to her favorite male human being…oh shit, you know what I mean!

"Melvin, this is Inga she's…err," Inga chimed in:

"…I'm his new assistant," She shook Melvin's hand. He took out his half-moon glasses, wiped them on a silk handkerchief, put them on then looked her up and down.

"That is a very striking outfit my dear and so practical."

"Glad you like it," said Inga looking across at me in an attempt to score some kind of point. Melvin turned to me also.

"I'm sure you've spoken to your friend Mister Kirk, so you'll know all about the agreement we came to with Mister Howard Hughes and his legal team," I nodded.

"Looks like Sammy is set for life, thanks to you Melvin."

Melvin Hammerstein waved off my compliments modestly.

"I was only doing my job, Rick. And speaking of which, what brings you in to see me today? I don't normally do divorce work you know, but for you..."

"I'm not looking for a divorce Melvin I need to talk to you about a possibly massive fraud we've come across in the course of an investigation," Melvin tore a sheet off a legal pad, picked up his pen and said:

"I'm ready, tell me everything."

So, I pitched right in and told him all about this mysterious guy who was getting very large sums of cash paid into bank accounts supposedly to buy property north of the city. None of the sales ever looked to have been completed and we knew for a fact that at least one of the properties meant to be for sale didn't exist.

I didn't mention Ko den Hamer, but I did fill him in about the town all this dough was coming from, Las Vegas. It was when I said 'Las Vegas' that Melvin really began to pay attention. He asked:

"Do we know which organizations or companies in Las Vegas are sending the money here?"

I told him I'd heard the name Micky Cohen mentioned. Melvin put down his pen. He took off his glasses and drew a long breath before speaking. He said:

"I think you should think very carefully about your next few steps here Rick. I think you should speak to the F.B.I. or the district attorney's office right away. What you have uncovered here is decidedly illegal. This will most certainly put you and this lovely young lady in great personal danger if certain parties become aware of your interest."

"What's going on here Melvin?"

"It's quite simple Rick. This is most likely money laundering, money laundering on a massive scale. Here's how it works...The Chicago Mob owns several casinos in Las Vegas. These casinos make a great deal of money, most of it in cash. The mob also uses these casinos to 'hide' profits from other activities: prostitution, drugs, extortion, that kind of thing. But they have a major problem...too much cash. If these casinos are ever raided, they would have no way of explaining where all the extra cash had come from; the cash from the drugs and the prostitutes and the numbers...and we are talking mountains of money. So, they need to move the cash out of state, and they need to clean it. The money has to go through legitimate financial institutions.

"The large deposits of cash 'buy' these mystery properties in the Napa Valley at vastly overpriced figures from a shell company formed just for this purpose. The shell company then pays very large dividends back to its shareholders. In this way, the money will eventually find its way back to

Chicago as a legitimate income from investments. It really is quite ingenious, quite ingenious."

After the meeting, I took some time to try to get a handle on what Melvin had just said. If I'm honest I didn't really succeed. I did know Josephine was mixed up in a scheme that could send her to jail for a very long time if I didn't do something to stop it. How much of this did she know about? I'd seen her signature as 'company secretary' on nearly all of the deeds and documents we'd 'borrowed' from Ko den Hamer's briefcase. Did she know what was going on? How deep was she into this?

It had started raining so the drive back to the office was damp and dangerous. We both got soaked working out how to put the hood up on the M.G. We can't have got it right because it was no use at all keeping the rain off us. Genius at human relationships that I am I chose this time to ask Inga about her preferred choice of dress (or not dress) if you catch my drift. I had to shout over the rain drumming on the hood just beyond the tiny windscreen. I was terrifically diplomatic:

"Inga…just out of interest…why did you start wearing men's suits? I mean, I know you like girls and hey, I'm fine with that but don't you think dressing like a guy might be more trouble than it's worth?" Inga took two city blocks to answer.

"You really want to know?" I said:

"Yes, I really want to know."

"And it's got nothing to do with my preference in sexual partners?"

"Absolutely nothing, I couldn't care less who you like to sleep with," I lied. Inga considered her answer for a few blocks.

"Well, if you really must know I started wearing men's clothes back home in Iceland. I have two elder brothers and I was the only girl. We lived on the edge of the village and were pretty much self-sufficient as a family. Being tall I was able to wear my brother's hand me downs without any alterations, so that's how it started."

"But now you wear suits."

"I just find men's suits more practical. I can afford to have them altered now so I like the way they look on me too," Inga stole a glance across at me.

"Go on."

"Go on what?" I asked.

"Ask the next question. The question you've been dying to ask since the day you met me."

"Okay then…have you ever been with a man?"

"Yes."

We pulled up in the alley behind the office.

"And?"

"And what?" asked Inga.

"You'll have to give a little more than that," I pushed.

"It was my fifteenth birthday, he was sixteen, he was called Gunnar and his hands smelled of fish. It was the first time for both of us. He was very nervous; I was a little drunk. It lasted less than a minute. It hurt...satisfied?"

I felt bad for bringing the subject up. For being so weak and sleazy and not realizing how asking the question lowered me in Inga's eyes. I promised not to ask any more stupid questions and got out of the car. I suggested to Inga that she get her head around putting up the canvas hood correctly. I left her struggling with a canvas contraption that was meant to keep us dry and warm. I felt bad doing it, but I didn't want to have to look into Inga's eyes at that moment and see her disappointment in me. And someone had to move the investigation forward.

In the warmth of the office, I prepared a pot of coffee for Inga then phoned The Lena Lawrence Agency to see if they'd had a girl go out on a job on the 4th of July and not return. I might have let the girl on the other end of the phone think I was working with the S.F.P.D. and in a small way, I was. They hadn't lost anyone on a job, ever, which I thought was a good thing.

I was running out of ideas; all I could think of was going through the phone book and calling all the modelling agencies in town looking for a missing model whose hair color could best be described as 'various.' While I was doing that Inga could be chasing around all the tattoo parlors in town looking for the artist behind the butterfly tattoo.

Inga came in, shook her head like a puppy, her blonde pixie hair looked darker.

"There's a towel in the kitchen..."

"I'm not putting that on my head!"

"...and the coffee should be ready."

Inga had succeeded in getting a passing beat cop to put the hood up on the M.G., so she wasn't too pissed at me. We drank our coffees in silence, both of us deep in our own thoughts. If the mystery lady on Flight 402 had been approached in the street or at a bar somewhere...if Constance Brady had paid her cash and made all the arrangements personally, then there was no way we could find out who the body in the morgue on Treasure Island was.

This was seriously depressing, but not half as depressing as the knowledge that by trying to talk to Rhonda Pearlman we had inadvertently caused the grisly death of two of her close friends. And we still had no idea why the Connie had been brought down. It was beginning to feel like we were seriously under-staffed. We needed a whole office full of detectives on this. And then I realized where we could get a whole office of detectives to work on (at least) part of the case. I picked up the phone and called Elton Dwight.

We arranged to meet for lunch at the Buena Vista Cafe on Hyde Street. I took a cab and left Inga back at the office, working the phone, trying to find out who the lady on ice on Treasure Island was. As I stood under the pink neon sign on the street corner, I couldn't help thinking about the last time I'd been there, following Mario Vitali and his under-age niece.

Life was simple then, I only had one case to handle at a time, I followed people who didn't even think they might be followed; I took compromising pictures, took them to the client, got paid and walked away. Nobody got hurt…physically.

Elton Dwight's Packard eased to a stop at the corner of Hyde and Beach just as a full cable car rumbled past, its bell ringing loudly. Elton Dwight was wearing a cream-colored jacket and pants and a paisley patterned waistcoat that looked like it was made of silk. The flowery cologne was just as evident as the last time we'd met. Maybe I was the 'hot date' this time. We stepped inside and Jack the owner led us to a small private table in the rear. He was talking all the time as we walked to the table:

"Good to see you again Mister Dwight, keeping busy?" Dwight nodded.

"Enjoy your lunch, the fresh trout is really good this week and later on I've got something for you to try…on the house. It's a new drink we're working on. I'd value your opinion."

We looked over the menu briefly and placed our orders as soon as the waiter came to the table. I had the Cable Car Meatloaf (I love a good meatloaf) and Dwight had steak, both washed down with a couple of Olympias. We both had a good drink of beer before Dwight started in:

"So, Mister Marshall, what have you got for me?"

"I think we've stumbled onto something you should know about."

"We?"

"Inga and me."

"Ahh yes, Inga, striking young thing, isn't she? How are things going with young Miss Bjarkardóttir?"

"She's a big help. Now, do you want the skinny or not?"

"I most certainly do want the errm, skinny as you call it."

"Okay then, you were kind enough in the hospital to give me a little background on the guy in Vegas that wants me dead…"

"Micky Cohen? Go on…"

"Well, I think I know why he sent those guys."

"Because of your connection to Paddy Brady?"

"Do you want to hear what I have to say or not?"

"Sorry, I'm all ears."

"Before you jump to any more conclusions it's got nothing to do with Paddy Brady…not that I know of. This is all to do with money laundering. There's a guy in San Francisco being paid massive sums of cash to supposedly buy worthless land in the Napa Valley. He's got papers on lots of run-down farms and orchards, all of them not worth a bean. But this guy's clients in Las Vegas are sending him millions of dollars in cash to buy these dust bowls. But the gag is, the sales never go through and the cash that's on deposit here for the purchases somehow ends up as bearer bonds and it makes its way back to…"

"…Chicago?"

"Good guess."

"Not really. The F.B.I. have been keeping us in the loop about this. I still don't see why Micky Cohen would send a team up here to shoot holes in you though."

"Well…I think I might know why. I've been looking at their local broker; I knew there was something fishy about the guy, so I've been doing a little digging. Maybe he got scared and called in some muscle to clean things up. I think he may have something to do with the killing of the two girls in that basement apartment, I think Rhonda was the real target there."

"You are going to tell me this gentleman's name, aren't you?"

"Ko den Hamer. He had an office near Union Square but…"

"Ko den Hamer? The guy currently coupling with your bride? Oh, this is priceless. You cannot be serious. Ha! You couldn't make this stuff up, could you? Ha!"

"I'm glad that I can bring a little ray of sunshine into your dreary life."

Elton Dwight was rolling about in his chair laughing like a side-show puppet. Lucky for me the food came, and he settled down for a while, digging into his steak. I ordered another beer before eating my meatloaf in silence. Maybe this wasn't such a good idea…

"Do you think your wife is mixed up in this?"

"If you'd asked me that a month ago, I would have said 'no way' now…I'm not too sure. She's a signatory on nearly all of the papers…"

Dwight threw me a bone.

"…That doesn't necessarily mean she's a party to the scheme. This den Hamer guy could be using her as a patsy…along with everything else."

He started laughing again and said:

"I'm sorry, I just couldn't resist it." There was a pause, it might have been pregnant; it might just have been retaining water. He went on:

"Okay, okay. Seriously I think your wife…Josephine is in serious trouble. Whatever way the cookie crumbles she could be looking at some serious jail time. She's either in it up to her neck or this den Hamer guy has set her up as the fall guy and she's been tied up in a nice little package of evidence with a pink bow on top."

"You have such a wonderful way with words," I said sarcastically. Dwight accepted the compliment at face value. Was I slipping up? Could I not deliver the sarcastic put down as well as I used to? They say that terrible time comes to us all…

As we finished lunch Jack the owner came over with two glasses full of coffee with what looked like whipped cream on top. The cream was settling into the coffee making the whole thing look like the scum that you get on still ponds after six months of direct sunlight. It did not look very appetizing. This was the new drink he'd been talking about to Elton Dwight. It was called an Irish Coffee and (as Jack told the story) he'd discovered it on a recent trip to Ireland.

"It's not quite right yet. The cream is supposed to float on the top. I've seen it done; at Shannon Airport in Ireland they turn these out by the hundreds."

The coffee had a shot of Irish Whiskey in it and it tasted terrific, it just didn't look right. Dwight was polite but none too impressed. He said:

"Let me know when you solve the problem with the cream Jack. You might be on to something here."

Elton Dwight insisted on paying for our meals. I had no qualms about letting him. His Packard was waiting on the corner as we left the Buena Vista. Dwight said he'd be talking to the F.B.I. this afternoon about Ko den Hamer. He could not give me any assurances about keeping Josephine out of it. We said our goodbyes and I got on the next passing cable car, jumping off after a few blocks. I walked the rest of the way back to the office on Clement. I had a lot to think about and sometimes the only way to clear your head is to take a long walk. It had stopped raining by then and steam was rising from the sidewalks as I headed east.

It was late afternoon when I eventually got back to the office. Thinking deep thoughts must make you walk slower, I guess. Inga had checked all the modelling agencies and actors' agents listed in the City of San Francisco phone book. No-one was missing a model or actress after sending them out on a job on the 4th of July. I wasn't surprised to hear this. We could spread the net to neighboring boroughs, but I believed that would be a waste of time and it would most likely drive Inga mad in the process. She was still knee deep in Tattoo Parlors. We were spinning our wheels on this line of inquiry.

Constance Brady had put considerable thought and planning into her disappearance. She would not have used a talent agency to find her stand-in because that would leave a paper trail. Most likely she would have got talking with a young woman who looked like her in a bar or restaurant. I felt in my bones that Constance Brady had not arranged for the explosion on the Lockheed Constellation. That had just been her good fortune.

Inga had succeeded in getting hold of Rhonda Pearlman. We were going to meet her that evening. Rhonda was staying with a male friend who rented a place just off Geary Street.

She had arranged to meet us outside Trad'r Sam's at 6150 Geary. This was only a few blocks from the office, so we walked over. I knew the place well enough, didn't go there too often. It was a little too showbiz for my tastes. The place had been around since the late thirties, it was chock full of bamboo furniture and tropical decorations, it had bunches of bananas hanging from the ceiling and the barmen wore pith helmets for Christ's sake!

We met Rhonda outside under the neon sign. She was with a young guy, maybe in his early twenties. He leaned on a palm tree and looked me over suspiciously before Rhonda convinced him I was legit. The young guy left us, and we went inside. We got a booth against the bamboo back wall. A waiter dressed as a jungle explorer came over and took our orders. Both the ladies ordered Planter's Punches. I had a beer with a whisky chaser. Inga sat close to Rhonda and asked how she was doing. Rhonda said:

"I'm not too sure. I don't sleep too good and I've not been able to go to work, I'm too scared to go out on the street. I'll have to soon I guess…if I want to eat."

"Have the police been in touch?" I asked.

"That big lug Greenwald has phoned a couple of times, keeps asking the same questions over and over again. I'm beginning to wish I hadn't told him where I was staying."

"Do they have any idea why this happened?" asked Inga.

"They don't have a clue. Greenwald keeps going on about sex-maniacs and escaped lunatics."

Our drinks arrived. Two drinks had a pound of fresh fruit salad in them. Luckily my beer and whisky arrived with no vegetation. The jukebox was playing 'High Noon' by Frankie Laine. The movie had just come out in July. I heard it was pretty good. The cowboy song felt a little out of place in this bar. I had the 'happy family' picture from K.D.H.'s brochure folded in my pocket. I flattened it on the table and asked Rhonda:

“Do you remember anything about this job? It was a private commission about a year ago. Do you remember anything the guy in the photograph said to you?”

Rhonda squinted at the picture for a moment then reached into her purse and pulled out a pair of glasses with pink cat’s eye frames.

“About a year ago you say?” I nodded.

“The house in the background is up on Vallejo in Pacific Heights.”

“I remember this big blonde guy kept trying to cop a feel. You can see in the picture, look.”

I looked. Den Hamer had his arm around Rhonda’s waist and his hand disappeared behind her.

“Did he say anything about what the photo-shoot was for?”

“Nope. Kept asking for my home address and phone number though. His girlfriend or assistant or whatever she was…She didn’t like the way he was paying so much attention to me. I was okay, you get used to it on these kinds of shoots, the guy who pays the bill likes to think he’s due a little extra bonus…if you know what I mean. You know I’d forgotten all about this fella. Funny thing is he called me a few weeks ago, right out of the blue; asked if I would go for a drink with him.”

“Did you?” asked Inga.

“Why not? He was cute and he liked to spend money.”

“How many times did you see him?”

“Three times over maybe two months, always the best restaurants, I had a great time. Then his old girlfriend turns up one night.”

“The dark-haired woman from the photoshoot?”

“Yeah, curvy broad, bright red lipstick…say how did you know she had dark hair? I never mentioned that.”

“Lucky guess,” I said. “What happened when this curvy broad turned up?”

“We were at the bar in the Palace Hotel. We’d been out for a meal and…you know things were, err progressing. He’d gone to the front desk to book a room and we were just having a drink at the bar before…”

“…going up to the room?” asked Inga.

“…Before going up to the room. She comes storming into the place and throws a punch at Ko. Right out of the blue! She calls him a whore-monger and a liar and worse. She said she was ready to leave her husband for him…then she lunges at me with both hands…like claws! She was trying to get to my eyes. Ko grabs her from behind, picks her up, and carries her out into the street. She was kicking and screaming and threatening to kill us both. We hadn’t done anything! I didn’t hang around after that. I went out the back entrance and got a cab home. He’s not called since then.”

"When was this?"

"6th of June…it was my birthday, we were out celebrating, you know…"

I flagged down a passing explorer and ordered another whisky. The ladies were still fighting their way past the fruit in their cocktails.

"I don't think there's any way this guy can find you now Rhonda but if he does get in touch, you'll let us know?"

"I'm not worried about Ko. It's that crazy bitch I'm frightened of," I could have said: 'That was no crazy bitch; that was my wife.' But I wasn't sure what Josephine was now.

Chapter Fourteen

It took me a long time to get to sleep that night. I had a lot on my mind, I was learning things about my wife that I didn't want to learn, I was trying to solve three mysteries at once and I was trying to balance on a skinny army cot with one arm in plaster. So, the next morning I wasn't in the best of moods as I walked out to buy a newspaper and a coffee. I took both back to the office, spread the paper out on my desk and thought seriously about adding a shot of whisky to my black coffee, would that make it an Irish Coffee? I wondered.

Inga came in about eight-thirty, I grunted a greeting and she sat in the client's chair on the other side of the desk. I read the paper some more. Inga sat in silence, patiently waiting for me to join the land of the living. I had lifted the paper up between us and I couldn't see her face. I assumed she was looking at the funny pages. I was wrong.

"Raul! That's Raul…that's Raul with Bing Crosby!" I lowered the paper slowly. Inga was pointing to the sports page on her side of the great newsprint divide. She grabbed the newspaper from me, flipped it over, and laid it back down on the desk. She was pointing at a photograph taken at Del Mar Racetrack, in Southern California. It was taken in the winner's circle; Bing Crosby was presenting a silver trophy to a toothy middle-aged woman in a patterned headscarf and a tweedy looking jacket. Holding the horse was a Hispanic guy with luxuriant black hair that shone like polished coal. Inga was pointing at the Hispanic guy.

"That's Raul, Raul Cortez; he's the chauffeur that Paddy Brady fired just a week before Mrs. Brady disappeared."

"Does it say who the owner is?"

"Mrs. Agatha Pendleton, wife of owner Sylas Pendleton the Third, San Diego."

I told Inga we needed to find a phone number for Mr. and Mrs. Pendleton of San Diego. She reached for the phone and spoke to the operator. She had the number for me in minutes. When this was all over, I was going to miss having Inga around. I spoke to someone at the Pendleton household and told them I was an old army buddy looking to catch up with Raul. It was risky but

I knew Raul had only been with the Pendleton's Stable for a short time and I guessed his war record or possible lack of a war record would not be common knowledge with the rest of the staff. The ploy worked well enough, but it didn't get us much further forward. I was told that Raul hadn't been into work 'for the past few days but he should be at the track tomorrow.' That was good news. They also had his address on file; this was also good news. He didn't have a phone (we were back to bad news again). We would have to go to San Diego to try to find Raul Cortez, ex-chauffeur. Inga asked:

"You think Mrs. Brady is with Raul?"

"I think it's a possibility. It's something we have to check."

Inga asked: "You think they were…"

"…Fucking like bunnies? Probably." Inga smiled and said:

"I was going to say; having an affair."

"That too."

"I think you might be barking up the wrong tree there," said Inga. I had no idea why she might say that. I couldn't think of anything smart to say so I just said:

"Woof woof!" That got a brief, slightly confused smile from Inga. We hurried down to Third and Townsend and got tickets on the Coast Daylight Express that left first thing Saturday morning. We'd overnight in Los Angeles and catch the Santa Fe Race Day special to Del Mar. Inga called Paddy Brady to keep him in the picture and most of the afternoon was then spent finding me suitable luggage, and clothes to go in that suitable luggage. As we came out of the third menswear shop, over a hundred dollars lighter I said to Inga.

"You know, I'm beginning to think I should maybe look for an apartment, something close to the office."

"Ya think?" was her reply.

"I can't keep sleeping on the cot…"

"…Get a place with a decent shower, you need it." I got the message; I would start looking for a place as soon as we got back from San Diego.

The next day I met Inga at the station dressed in my new cream-colored suit. The jacket had the right arm tucked inside itself so I could wear it over my cast. I'd also bought two new shirts and Inga had insisted I also bought two ties. I had a '38 tucked inside a pair of socks in my shiny new suitcase. Inga arrived in a pair of wide slacks in surf green, with a white blouse and a navy-blue bolero jacket. Her hair shone in the early morning sunlight. She looked at me over her dark glasses.

"My my Mister Marshall, don't we clean up nicely?"

"You sure do Inga, you look terrific."

"Not too Hollywood?"

"I always say you can't look too Hollywood, especially in L.A. Shall we go?"

We boarded the train and found two seats in the parlor car at the very rear. The seats were much better there. There was even a section with card tables. I'd never travelled on the Coast Daylight; it felt kinda funny to be on the train my wife and her lover had used so often for business and (more likely) pleasure. We left San Francisco at 8.15. A thunderhead of black smoke burst from the locomotive as the black, orange, and red train edged out of the station and began to negotiate the steady incline out of the city.

After an hour or so we moved forward to the dining car for breakfast. We both had eggs, bacon, and a stack of pancakes, coffee, and orange juice. Inga told me about her night bar-hopping lesbian clubs downtown. I was surprised to know there were enough of them to go hopping around for an evening. I didn't say that though.

"How do you look so good on so little sleep?" I asked.

"I drink the blood of virgin girls," was Inga's reply, which was not the kind of thing the old couple sat across from us expected to hear at nine a.m. on a Saturday morning. The old guy, who must have been ninety, began a coughing fit which lasted several minutes and grew in volume and intensity as time progressed. A waiter hurried over to help. The old lady stared across at us with undisguised malevolence. Inga smiled sweetly and asked:

"Is your husband okay? Should we get him some water? Or some of my special pick-me-up maybe? I have a little left." I ate my breakfast way faster than normal; we left the dining car in chaos and headed back to the rear of the train.

"That was fun, let's do that again," said Inga. I did my best School-Marm impression, complete with a wagging finger.

"You are a very naughty girl."

"I can be," said Inga. The growing erection in my pants signified my total agreement with that statement. A deep thought came to me: there's nothing as useless as an erection at the wrong time and/or place. I was thinking this deep thought and Inga must have seen the pain it gave me.

"Penny for them?" she said.

"You do not want to know what I've just been thinking," I said. Eventually, my redundant hard-on subsided, the Coast Daylight rumbled southward and the conversation turned to Patrick Brady.

"Do you figure you'll stay with Brady after all this is sorted out?" I asked Inga.

"I don't see why not; I earn great money and it's not exactly hard work...and Mister Brady does not give me shit because of who I am and how I live my life." I went on:

"But it's hardly a career is it?"

"As compared to what, being a Private Detective? From the way you describe your normal jobs all you do is skulk around in back alleys looking in garbage cans, trying to get pictures of people screwing people they shouldn't."

"Well, if you put it like that." She was right, of course. We rode a good few miles without speaking. Inga watched the scenery go by, I watched Inga. Eventually, I started up the conversation again.

"You do know he's not really a legitimate businessman, don't you?" Inga didn't even bother to answer that one.

"It's just that I don't want to see you mixed up with Brady if the whole thing comes crashing down." Suddenly Inga was alert.

"And why should that happen, Rick?"

"No reason, I was just thinking...if it did come crashing down you could get into big trouble."

"For driving cars and knocking a few heads together? I don't think so."

"I just think it might be a good idea to put some kind of distance between Brady's operation and yourself."

"All right, what's going on? What do you know that I don't?" I tried stalling, looking out at the passing fields, changing the subject. But Inga kept after me. I had to tell her something. So, I told her the truth, always the best policy if at all possible.

"I think Brady is under investigation by the District Attorney's office. I think they are looking to bring him down." Inga looked at me for a few seemingly very long moments. Finally, she said:

"That's it? That's all you've got? Paddy Brady plays golf with the D.A. every week through the summer. According to Mister Brady, the D.A. is in the same Masonic Lodge. He spends gentlemen's weekends onboard The Killkenny. And some of the things that happen during those weekends would make your hair curl. I'm pretty sure we have some very interesting photographs in a file somewhere. I don't think you've got that right. If there was anything going down at the D.A.'s office Paddy Brady would know about it." I held my left hand up in surrender.

"Okay, okay. Forget I mentioned it."

The Coast Daylight continued south through San Jose and Salinas. After Salinas, we moved to the Tavern Car where we grabbed two seats at the bar. We had a leisurely lunch of beef sandwiches and beer and watched the world go by from our bar-stools. Later in the afternoon, we passed through Santa Barbara and Ventura.

We pulled into Union Station, Los Angeles right on time at 6.00 pm. It was still very warm as we stepped down from the train. The inside of Union Station looked like a giant library or church, except I'd never seen that many people in either a library or a church. The polished floor had a kind of mosaic in geometric shapes, all browns and creams.

It was impressive, with plush leather chairs dotted around in groups and rows. Bright late afternoon sunlight streamed through large high windows on both sides of the building adding to the ecclesiastical atmosphere.

The outside of Union Station looked even more like a cathedral, a Mexican cathedral. It even had a bell tower. The building shone bright white in the sun. It had very tall arched windows framed in terracotta brickwork. The roof had the same terracotta-colored ridged tile. The place was surrounded by rows of three-story high, dead straight palm trees.

We joined the line up for a yellow cab and when we got our ride, I asked the driver if he could recommend a cheap local hotel. We ended up on the edge of Chinatown on North Broadway. You could see City Hall in the distance as our cabbie dropped us at the Hollywood Hotel. We were opposite the L.A. Times building with its weird castle-like tower and nowhere near Hollywood. The place's run-down exterior only disguised its much more run-down interior. As we stood in the crummy lobby with its peeling wallpaper and threadbare carpets, I thought about going back outside and catching another cab. Inga wouldn't have it. She reminded me:

"You did say cheap."

I offered her a thin smile of apology and dinged the bell on reception. An old Chinaman shuffled out from the backroom…eventually. Now calling this guy old was doing him a dis-service. He was older than the Union. He was about four feet six inches tall; he wore one of those dark blue collar-less smocks all Chinamen wear in Charlie Chan movies and his yellow face was wrinkled like a raisin left in the sun.

"You want loom?" he asked. I held up two fingers.

"Two rooms."

He looked Inga over, licked his lips then asked me again.

"One loom two nights?"

"No two rooms, one night."

"That's what I said, one loom two nights."

"No two rooms."

The Chinaman looked at me with great pity in his eyes. He obviously thought I was maybe suffering from an unspeakable fearful war wound somewhere ‘down there.’ He even stood on his tiptoes to get a better look at my groin. I was reduced to acting out our requirements. I pointed to the keys hung up in little boxes behind reception. Then I held up two fingers. Then I pointed to the calendar on the counter and held up one finger.

“Two looms, one night.”

“That’s what I say, two looms, one night. I give special deal for veterans.” He snapped into a salute and out of habit I attempted to return it. The cast put a stop to that. By this time Inga was practically doubled over with laughter. I paid my new best friend up-front and he handed over our keys. I asked Inga if she was hungry and suggested we drop off our bags and head deeper into Chinatown to find a decent restaurant.

We didn’t have to go far; right on Broadway was the Golden Pagoda. It stood on a street corner and wasn’t hard to spot. It featured a five story-high pagoda lit up in lemon-colored neon, very impressive. The food wasn’t too bad either. We shared a set dinner for two which would have fed four people easily. For one evening at least I was able to relax a little, forget the jobs I was working on, forget the fact that my wife had run off with a Dutch fraudster. I almost forgot the fact that the blonde goddess sitting across from me had no interest in me as a man whatsoever.

We talked about Inga’s childhood in Iceland, about the British occupation of her village during the war, how she learned English from a young man called Geordie Oliver, a corporal in the 10th Battalion, Durham Light Infantry. She said:

“I was only sixteen, but I knew Geordie was falling in love with me. I also knew it would never work out because even though I really liked him, he was funny and kind…I knew by then that I couldn’t feel anything more for him than friendship. Him or any man, as it turned out.”

I told her about how I met Josephine when I was finishing pilot training at Santa Ana. Josephine was a singer with a big band then. We met when she played a U.S.O. show at the base. We danced together whenever she wasn’t on stage. I remember my buddies giving me grief for hogging the hot broad. We kissed just once that night, as we waited by the band’s bus. We discovered we were both from the bay area. She was at secretarial school; I’d been studying engineering at San Francisco State before I enlisted. Josephine was living in L.A. at the time so we started seeing each other whenever I could wrangle a pass.

We got engaged just before I shipped out to Europe three months later. When I returned almost two years later, I had bright pink scarring to my left forehead and forearm, and I was missing most of my left ear. From certain angles, I looked like a monster from a horror movie. We got married my first day back in civilian life. I think back to that time now and I'm beginning to believe she married me out of pity or some kind of miss-placed loyalty. Of course, that thought never crossed my mind at the time. I thought I was the luckiest guy in the world.

The street was virtually empty as Inga and I walked back to the hotel. There were only cabs on the road and only a few late-night drunks on the sidewalk. Back at the hotel, I escorted Inga to her room. Before she put the key in the door she said:

"I had a good time tonight Rick, thanks. It's good just to talk sometimes." Then she kissed me on the cheek, unlocked the door, and was gone in a second. I stood by the door, heard the lock slide into place, and wondered what had just happened. I went to bed with another superfluous erection and slept fitfully.

The next morning, we were back at Union Station to catch the first Racetrack Special of the day. I think we both felt underdressed, all the women wore flouncy, brightly colored dresses and gigantic hats, the guys wore tennis slacks and blazers. Elton Dwight would have fit right in. Inga wore cream slacks and a basic white blouse but with her figure, she still stood out in the crowd. My khaki pants, black shirt, and pale green jacket kind of let the side down. Everyone was having a great time, drinking too much, talking too loud, and looking forward to a day at the races. Groucho Marx would have been very proud.

And I've got to say Del Mar is a show-stopping race-track; bright as a freshly polished new pin. Once inside I took a look at the race card, noted that Pendleton Stables had two runners going today: Fancy Pants in the one' o'clock and Ambling Along in the three. We had plenty of time to look the place over and grab a bite to eat before we needed to be trackside to try spot Raul Cortez.

The place was practically on the ocean and a cooling breeze brought the smell of the Pacific to mix with the scent of horse sweat and hot dogs. There were man-made lakes in the middle of the track with ornamental fountains; this was one classy race-track. Every now and then the crowd around us would part like the red sea and a film star or Hollywood big shot would be escorted past. In the line-up for beers, I heard a rumor that Bing Crosby himself would be presenting the trophy to the winner of the three o'clock.

We had to be close to the winner's circle by the time the one o'clock finished but we had plenty of time, so I decided to place a small bet on Fancy Pants just to make things interesting. I got in line behind an elderly gentleman in a straw boater. He was grumbling at the cashier about his run of bad luck.

His voice was strangely familiar. When he turned away from the wicket, he spoke to me:

"I hope you do better than me son, I've got the witches curse on me today." I smiled meekly, didn't know what to say. It's not every day that W.C. Fields wishes you luck. I joined Inga by the winner's circle and told her all about my close encounter with greatness. She pretended not to know who W.C. Fields was. At least I think she pretended. The horses were on the track for the one o'clock. I handed my betting slip to Inga. She kissed it for good luck then tucked it into her blouse. If I had to retrieve that ticket later things could get very awkward. My mind wandered, I must admit, to thoughts of warming my hands and searching inside Inga's bra for my winning ticket. I needed help. She must have read my mind, not for the first time.

"If you do win, I will be the one getting your ticket back for you," she said.

The one o'clock was run over five furlongs and Fancy Pants was a good bet at six to one. We couldn't see much of the race from our spot by the winners' circle, but we could hear the commentary. Much to my surprise Fancy Pants made a late surge in the last furlong and romped home to win by a length. Inga jumped up and down and hugged me for a while before regaining her composure. Being hugged by Inga was very nice.

Then, with her eyes firmly on mine, she leaned back on the railing and slowly and seductively slipped her hand inside her blouse before very slowly and very seductively pulling the winning ticket out into full view. One guy walking behind me bumped into another guy and spilled two beers down him. The guy in the damp jacket did not appear to notice. He looked at me with genuine envy in his eyes as if to say: 'You lucky bastard.' Funnily enough, right at that moment, I did feel like a lucky bastard.

I didn't have too long to dwell on that thought because the first three from the one o'clock were being brought into the winners' circle. The crowd pressed forward eagerly but we held our spot by the railing. Fancy Pants was the last horse brought into the ring. By then the winners' circle was awash with well-wishers and (I guess) winners. Inga stood on tip-toes to survey the crowd.

"I don't see him, Raul's not here," she said. After the trophy presentation, Inga snuck under the railing and succeeded in getting closer to Fancy Pants and his handlers. She came back to me with news.

"Raul is working today but they don't know if he'll get to handle Ambling Along. The guys say the stable hands take it in turns."

"But he is here today?" I asked. Inga nodded.

"Let's go collect my winnings and I'll buy you a hot-dog."

"Big spender!" said Inga. "How could I resist such an offer?"

So, lunch was a hot-dog and a beer from a concession stand. We found a quieter part of the grandstand away from the crowds and sat down on a concrete step. Between mouthfuls, I asked Inga.

"What can you tell me about Raul?"

"He's nice enough, I didn't know him long. He left not long after I started."

"Do you think he was schtupping Mrs. Brady?"

"From what I heard they were kinda close. She used him as her personal driver most of the time; I remember he made her laugh. She didn't laugh much. But I know they weren't involved that way."

"How come you know that?" I asked.

"I just know." Was all she said.

When the three o'clock started we were back at our spot by the winners' circle but sadly Ambling Along decided to live up to his name. He came in a distant fifth. We did get to see Bing Crosby presenting the winner's trophy.

"What do we do now?" asked Inga

"Let's head to the stables, see if Raul is back there." So, we followed Ambling Along and his handlers back to the stables. It turned out Raul had helped take another horse back to the Pendleton's Estate. I slipped a stable hand a twenty and he told us:

"Spitfire pulled up a little lame, so she didn't race today. If you want to find Raul, you'll have to get up early. He'll be running Spitfire on the beach tomorrow; he usually goes at six. The salt-water helps loosen up tight muscles and the horses love it."

"Good to know," I said. We had a problem. Our overnight bags were in lockers at Union Station and we had nowhere to stay tonight. I asked Inga:

"Any suggestions?" She shook her head.

"Tell you what…we'll get a cab to Del Mar town itself, the cab driver will know a place, there's got to be some kind of hotel or lodging house."

"I'll take you to the best place in town," said the driver. "They'll be busy, it is a race weekend but maybe some folks will be checking out today."

The cab took us to the ocean then turned south, right to the sea-front and the imposing Stratford Inn. It kind of reminded me of some country houses I'd seen in England. It was three floors high, painted white with exposed black wood beams criss-crossing the whole building. We turned into a large oval driveway off 15th Street; the hotel was set in formal gardens. As we pulled up to reception Inga looked across at me with a look that seemed to say: 'Are we really going to stay here?' I shrugged my shoulders and said:

"Hey, you only live once…" There was only one room free and we had to endure some seriously snooty looks from the old bird on reception because we did not have any luggage. But I paid cash up-front and that mollified the old bat. Just to sweeten things I slipped her a ten spot and asked if she could direct us to a pharmacy where we could buy toothbrushes and other essentials.

When I said the word 'essentials,' she got all judgmental on us and pursed her lips like she was sucking a bee. It was at that point that Inga decided to have a little fun with the old dear. She drapes herself over me like a silent movie vamp and 'whispers' in my ear.

"Hurry up big boy, I need you…now."

I must have blushed bright red at that point. I tried to explain that Inga was joking…maybe I should tell the receptionist that Inga was a lesbian and not the slightest bit interested in me? Maybe not.

We ran up two flights of stairs both of us laughing out loud as we went, tumbled into the room, and threw ourselves onto the twin beds. When we'd both calmed down a little, I took a bed-sheet and managed to fashion a 'wall of Jericho' between the beds, just like in that old Clark Gable movie…what was it called again? 'It Happened One Night'…that was it. I didn't bother explaining where I'd got the idea from. It was from way before Inga ever went to the movies.

We found a local pharmacy just down the street, bought toothbrushes and toothpaste. We ate in the hotel's restaurant that night and got back up to the room pretty early. There was a lot of shuttling back and forward to the bathroom individually and a lot of averting of my eyes at certain points. Inga didn't worry about sleeping in her underwear, so I wasn't going to let it bother me. I left a curtain open so the sunlight would wake us earlier enough to get down onto the beach to see Raul Cortez.

Chapter Fifteen

The next morning Inga nudged me awake at 5.30. It was still dark. I turned on the bedside light. She was dressed and ready for the day. I hate people that can get up that early in the morning and look that good, don't you?

"Come on Rick, we need to get down to the beach," she said. I couldn't argue with her but at that moment I wished I could. I would have liked to have said: 'Get undressed right now and get back into bed.' But I didn't. It would have been a waste of time anyway. So, I got dressed grumpily, which is the only way to get dressed at 5.35. My right arm itched like hell inside its plaster cast. The cast didn't make dressing or, in fact, undressing any easier.

Luckily the hotel was practically on the beach at Del Mar, so we were walking along the broad firm sands before six. In the distance to the south, I could make out a group of horses and riders splashing through the surf at the edge of the sea.

"That's got to be them," I said. We walked out toward the water. A few minutes later the racehorses thundered past us going at a steady gallop. They turned by the pier next to the Stratford Inn and trotted back to us. One of the horses peeled away from the group and came closer. A dark-skinned man in a riding helmet and goggles jumped down.

"Inga? Is that you? What the hell are you doing here?"

"I'm looking for you Raul, how've you been?" said Inga. She walked over and started stroking the muzzle of the tall black horse in Raul's charge.

"Is this Spitfire?" she asked.

"Sure is; how did you know that?"

"Guy at the track said she was a little lame."

"You've got a good eye. It's nothing too serious, should be okay for next month's meeting. So, what do you want with me?"

We walked alongside Raul and Spitfire for a while. Inga introduced me and told him all about Constance Brady's disappearance. He didn't look to be the slightest bit surprised by what we told him, but he didn't seem too worried either.

"We were friends; that's all, there was nothing between us. Never was…Sure we got on. I guess you could say we were close but that was all. She was interested in my family, liked me to show her pictures of my children. I'm a married man, got two kids…"

"I didn't know that," said Inga.

"They live back in Mexico. That's why I was glad to get this job. It's much easier to see them. I hope to get them into the States soon…legally of course."

Raul handed the reins to Inga and pulled some small photographs from his wallet.

"This is Guadalupe my wife and this is Elisa and Jose Luis. He's only two."

"Cute kids," I said before passing the pictures over to Inga.

"They live with Guadalupe's mother in a small place called Rosarito; it's about five miles south of Tijuana."

This was getting way too cutesy, and cutesy was getting us nowhere. Inga was still looking at the family pictures. I got the morning back on track:

"About Mrs. Brady…what happened on the 4th of July?"

Raul carefully put the photographs back into his wallet before saying:

"Mrs. Brady had been unhappy for a very long time. Mister Brady does not treat her with respect. He whores around and several times she has caught diseases from him. I think he beats her too. I have seen bruises under her make-up many times. He is (as you know) much older than her and he does not love her. Mister Brady had fired me by then, I was out of work. About a month before the 4th of July she came to see me, somehow, she'd found out where I was staying. She said to me: 'I need to get away Raul. I have to leave Paddy, or he will kill me one way or another.' I said to her: 'But Señor Brady is a very proud man. He will surely kill you if he catches you.'

"'That's why I need your help.' She said. 'I have a plan. I've met a woman who looks a lot like me, same build, same coloring. I'm going to pay her to impersonate me and get on a plane to Seattle as me. She then gets a train back as herself making it look like I disappeared in Seattle. I'll go to the airport with Inga, we make the switch and you drive me from the airport to Los Angeles. Can you get hold of a car?'

"I said, 'Yes, I could.'"

"Where did she go from there?" I asked.

"She flew Trans-Canada Airlines direct to Vancouver, British Columbia."

"Why would she go there?"

"She told me she knew an old school friend who could hide her there. She lives in a place way out of town called Deep Cove. Her friend said it's so out of the way there that no one will ever find her if she doesn't want to be found. As far as I know, she's still there."

"You haven't heard a thing from her?"

"How would she get in touch with me? I didn't have a job for some time after Mister Brady fired me. I did not know if I would still be in the U.S."

"Good point," I said. I was surprised that Inga hadn't chipped in with a few questions of her own. She was surprisingly quiet all the way through my chat with Raul. When we had finished Raul hugged Inga.

"Listen…I gotta go and give Spitfire her rub-down. You won't tell Mister Brady what we did will you?" Inga assured him we wouldn't.

"Are you going to go to Canada, try to find her?" he asked.

"I'm not sure Raul, not yet." We shook hands with our left hands and Inga helped him to get back in the saddle. He rode off south toward the other horses. As we walked back into town Inga said:

"I knew Raul was a good man. I have a sense of these things. You are a good man too Rick; although sometimes things might go easier for you if you weren't."

"Thanks…I think." I said. Looking ahead I hoped that I'd be able to live up to Inga's judgment of my character, I wasn't too sure. We blew the budget and got a taxi from Del Mar to the Union Station in Los Angeles. It was worth it though; we arrived with plenty of time to catch the Starlight departure for San Francisco. It was an overnight train running the same route we'd come south on. Once at Union Station, we were both able to change our clothes and get cleaned up some. I had a shave for the first time in days. This was not the easiest thing to do with one free arm, but I figured it was time to look the part after my promotion to 'good man.'

The Starlight left Union Station dead on time at 7.45 pm. We had already snagged comfortable seats in the observation car at the rear of the train. The porters kindly brought round blankets which would come in handy later. As soon as we settled in our seats Inga turned to talk to me.

"So, what are you going to do? Are you going to tell Brady where Constance is? Are you going to go after her?"

I noticed how suddenly Inga was talking about 'you' and not 'us.' I took my time before answering. I'd been thinking about my next move ever since the conversation with Raul Cortez in Del Mar. The easiest way out was to 'admit' defeat. Tell Brady that we'd spoken to Raul, but he had not been involved with Mrs. Brady's disappearance. If we said that we'd be at a dead end. There was nowhere else for the investigation to go. But if we were going to do that, we both had to be sure of each other. We had to be one hundred percent certain that the other would stick to the story.

And what would happen if Brady found his wife by some other means? He was originally from Canada, wasn't he? Brady might have a network of contacts all over British Columbia. One of them might hear something. This Deep Cove place didn't sound too far from The City of Vancouver and lots of folks travelled to Vancouver for lots of reasons.

Maybe I could go to Canada and persuade Mrs. Brady to return? But if I did that what would Brady do to her when he got her back? On the one hand, he said he loves her, but we were hearing a different story from Raul Cortez. This was really beginning to make my head hurt.

"I need a drink, are you coming?" Inga nodded, as we passed a guard, she asked him to keep our seats, then we made our way forward to the Tavern Car. We took two stools at the end of the bar; we didn't want to be overheard. I ordered our drinks and we waited for them to arrive in sullen silence watching the sun edging toward the horizon over the Pacific. When our drinks arrived, we stared at them in silence for some time too. The only sound was the ice in our glasses as we both toyed with them continually. I cracked first, took a good shot of whisky, and started in:

"Look, this is ridiculous. I've been paid to do a job and I'm going to see it through. We now know where we can find Mrs. Brady and it's not like she's at the North Pole. If we don't go and bring her back sooner or later someone else will."

"If you go to Canada to look for her, I won't be coming with you," said Inga.

"And just how are you going to get out of it?"

"I'll quit if I have to," said Inga. "I'm not going to bring her back to San Francisco where he can start beating on her again."

"You don't know for sure that he beat her," I said.

"If Raul said he saw bruises then I believe him. He is a good man."

"Aren't we all?" I said flippantly. Inga looked at me with what might have been pity, might have been disgust in her eyes.

"I'm not too sure anymore," she said. We finished off our drinks and returned to the observation car to settle down for the night. I could not get the look on Inga's face out of my mind. Why did I care so much about what a lesbian Icelander girl thought about me? It's not like I was in love with her, was it? That would be the most futile, stupid state of affairs, wouldn't it?

Inga fell asleep curled up on a large chair. I found her an extra blanket and with my one good hand, tucked it around her legs and feet. Then I sat next to her staring out at the lights passing by. I must have fallen asleep at some time, but I don't remember when.

We were a little late getting into San Francisco. It was 7.15 in the morning. It was foggy. When I woke Inga had already left her two blankets neatly folded on the chair and gone forward. I guessed she'd gone to get cleaned up, brush her teeth, that sort of thing. As the train came to a halt at the 3rd and Townsend station, I grew a little worried. Inga hadn't returned. I got to my feet and began to walk forward. An elderly guard took hold of my good arm and handed me a note. It said this:

Rick: don't try to catch up with me, I can run way faster than a man with his arm in a sling, even a good man like you. Please don't ask Brady to send me to Vancouver with you. I knew Constance was going to leave Paddy, but I didn't know when and I didn't know Raul was involved. I only pointed him out in the newspaper picture because I thought he would make a good diversion; it was a spur of the moment thing. A stupid mistake on my part. Sorry I could only tell you part of the real story.

Love, Inga
Xxx

I stood on the top of the steps and looked down the platform, but I couldn't see her. For just a split second a saw a flash of white/blonde hair but it wasn't her. I felt like I'd been kicked in the stomach. Eventually, I got a cab and went to the office. I had a lot of correspondence to catch up on, a lot of bills to pay. I kept busy doing this for an hour or so. The phone rang. It was Brady.

"Inga said you have some news for me. She also said she ain't gonna drive you no more. She said you tried to get your end away in some hotel near L.A…" I stammered a few syllables in denial. Brady spoke over me:

"I tell you what Marshall, you got balls I'll give you that, but you don't know much about women. You were wasting your time there my son. She doesn't go for fellas! Didn't you work that out? I'm surprised she didn't cut your nuts off if you tried to cop a feel of her pussy! Not that it might not be worth it, you understand."

Brady was laughing so hard he had a coughing fit. For a second, I thought he might have choked to death holding the phone. That would have solved a lot of problems. He came back on the line.

"I wanna hear all about what happened at Del Mar…including what happened when you groped her box!" There was more cackling laughter and coughing. I held the phone away from my ear for twenty-seconds.

"Get in that little M.G. and get over to Tara for twelve. Can you do that? Good." He put down the phone. I had a few hours free now to work on the Ko den Hamer case; which would have been great, except I had no idea what to do on the Ko den Hamer case. Well, if I'm honest I did have one or two. I had to confirm where he was doing his banking and get a look at his records. My good friends in the District Attorney's office might be able to help me with that. I had to find out where he was working out of during the day. I was pretty sure he wasn't just staying home in my house doing all these deals over the phone. Nobody did this kind of business over the phone.

I had to work out when the next big delivery of cash was coming north from Las Vegas and I had to intercept that delivery. I would need a truck-load of heavily armed F.B.I. agents in tow when that happened. And that was about it; except I had to find a way to do all this and keep my wife out of jail. I figured that was the only way I was going to win her back. After all, that was why I was doing all this wasn't it? I made a few calls, the first one to Elton Dwight at the D.A.s office. He was in a meeting but called me back a short time later.

"How's the arm, Rick?"

"I'm getting a little more feeling in my fingers almost every day, should be out of the cast in two weeks."

"If you say so, I think that's a little optimistic."

"We'll see."

"What have you got for me on Brady?"

"Not sure if you knew this but it looks like Brady is in pretty thick with your boss."

"The D.A? Louis D. Rickenbacker?"

"That's the guy." I could feel the excitement in Dwight's voice when he said:

"Go on."

"I've spoken with a witness that's seen him playing golf with Brady lots of times..."

"...That's not enough; he can always claim it was above board or a random foursome booked by the club."

"They are both part of the same Masonic Lodge."

"... That won't do either, I'm in the same lodge."

"Then how about this?" I said. "The D.A. has attended a shit load of private stag parties organized by Brady and Brady has a film of him in very compromising situations."

For a second, I thought Elton Dwight had dropped the phone or been cut off somehow. After a pause he came back on the line, his voice was shaky with excitement.

"Do we know where Brady keeps these films?" he asked.

"My guess would be one of three places: The house in Pacific Heights, Tara; The hotel in Sausalito or on his boat, The Kilkenny. Listen, Dwight, you are going to have to be very careful how you handle this. If you don't get this just right the whole thing could blow up in your face and a lot of people might get hurt."

"I know that! I will be. Thanks for this Mister Marshall...now, you called me, is there something you need?"

I had my notes from our late-night search of den Hamer's briefcase. I cradled the phone under my chin and scrambled around the loose papers on the desk, finally coming up with what I wanted, a bank deposit slip.

"Can you get access to the records of a business account at The Anglo California National Bank at Fourth and Market?"

"Might take us a few days but I don't see why not." I gave Elton Dwight the account number from the deposit slip. I told him

"I think this is one of the accounts that Ko den Hamer uses in his money laundering scheme for the mob in Las Vegas. Let me know what you find."

"You have been a busy little bee, Mister Marshall...we'll get back to you on this...and the other matter." I ended the call. After all this seriously deep thought I then had to work out how to drive a stick shift with my right arm in a cast. I was getting some movement back in my fingers, so I thought I'd give it a try, maybe drive around the block for a while before heading out to meet Paddy Brady. So, I took off the sling, left it hanging over my office chair, and went down into the alley with keys in hand...my left hand.

I succeeded in banging my hand on the steering wheel as I got in and I got a zing of sharp pain as a reminder not to do that again. With my left hand I gave the engine a little choke and reaching round the steering wheel I turned the key. The tiny 1250 cc engine burst into life with a friendly burbling coming from the rear end. I watched the oil pressure come up then slipped it into gear. The gearshift was very light, and I found I had no trouble selecting gears with my injured arm. I realized there would be a problem if I had to pull on the parking brake, I would have to hold the large steering wheel with my knees and reach over with my good left hand to pull the lever up. I didn't think this would be too much trouble even on the hills in San Francisco. I could always hold the car on the clutch at intersections. The pedals were so close together I could probably be able to press down on the brake pedal for extra sticking power.

I drove around the block twice just to make sure I had the hang of things then turned east on California Street. I was soon nipping in and out of much larger cars heading toward the city. It wouldn't take too long to get to Vallejo and Tara, Paddy Brady's place.

I got there early and parked across the street from the house for a few minutes watching all the activity. I saw Inga drive Brady's Cadillac away from the house, but I wasn't sure if she'd seen me.

I walked across to the front entrance right on time at 12.00 Noon; High Noon. I couldn't help whistling the movie theme as I rang the bell.

To my surprise, Paddy Brady met me at the door. He ushered me through the house to the kitchen.

A solidly built lady with red cheeks and grey hair was stirring a large pan of (I think) gravy. There was a wonderful smell coming from the oven.

"We're having bangers and mash for lunch, I thought you might enjoy that," said Brady. He was right. I'd eaten this British invention a number of times in pubs around Cambridgeshire. The large lady wiped her hands on her apron and reached for a towel. She folded it over several times then used it to pull a pan of sizzling sausages out of the oven. She piled two plates with mashed potatoes, cabbage, and sausages. She plonked them down on the kitchen table and left us to it.

"There's gravy on the stove," said Brady. "Tuck in." All chance of communication was lost for a while as we both set about the mountains of food in front of us. I was getting the hang of eating left-handed by now but I couldn't cut up the sausages, so I just jabbed them in the middle and started eating from one end. It was not the most elegant of recent meals, but it was one of the best. Brady produced several bottles of Guinness from a cooler and handed one over to me. He gave me a glass and gave me a lesson on how to pour the 'black stuff.'

At the end of the meal, Brady wiped his plate clean with a large chunk of soda bread. Then he sat back in his kitchen chair and lit a cigarette. He looked across the table at me, he was suddenly all business.

"So…apart from making a complete arse of yourself with Inga what did you find out down in San Diego?"

There are times in everyone's life when you realize you're at a turning point. When you recognize that decisions made in that instant might send you in a certain direction for the next few years and possibly for the rest of your life. The sad truth is that most people don't recognize these moments. They don't know the momentous changes their next few words might bring about. So, they go ahead and say the next few words that come to mind; words that seem like a good idea at the time. You know the kind of thing: 'Yes I will have another drink, what harm could it do?' Or 'I don't mind, let's invade Poland. No-one will notice.' Or 'Will you marry me?' that kind of thing.

On this afternoon in early September in San Francisco, I did grasp just what could happen following my answer to Paddy Brady's question. I knew all right but I still went right ahead and told him the truth. In my defense I have to point out that Mr. Brady had already paid me ten grand to find that truth. So, I told him.

"Your wife arranged for someone else to take the flight on the 4th of July. Then she tried to cover her tracks before flying to Vancouver, Canada. As far as I know, she is living in a small community north of Vancouver itself. It's got just one road in and out and there are just a few houses there. It's called Deep Cove."

Brady sat perfectly still for a while, the only movement his steady breathing. Eventually, he spoke.

"Deep Cove you say?" I nodded.

"Do you know it?" I asked.

"I never heard of it. I grew up in Ontario, that's the other side of the fuckin country…and let me tell you Canada is a big country. So, tell me…how are you going to bring her back to me?"

"Well, I'm not sure that I'm the right man for the job Mister Brady…"

"Why not? You fly to Seattle, get a car, drive over the border, and get her. It shouldn't take more than five or six hours to get to Vancouver, five or six hours back. You won't need a passport if you are driving over the border."

I was getting a little pissed with being Brady's 'go-to guy.' Maybe I spoke with a little more anger than I should have when I said:

"How do you suggest we get her over the border if she doesn't want to come? She could kick up a hell of a racket as we drive back into the States. I suppose we could tie her up in the trunk, drug the shit out of her, and hope she doesn't wake up or die before we get across the border…It just won't work that way."

Brady scratched his crotch under the table before opening two more bottles of Guinness. He did not appear to be angered by my outburst.

"I like the way you're thinking there Marshall. We are going to have to come up with a much better plan. There's no use going off half-cocked."

I stood up from the kitchen table.

"Mister Brady, I'm grateful for all you've done for me, but I think my work here is done. You wanted to find out why the Constellation exploded which I don't think anyone will ever know for sure. Then, when we found out your wife was not on the plane you wanted me to find her. As far as I can tell I have found her. She's in North Vancouver, Canada. Why don't you just go up yourself and talk to her? Maybe you can work things out between you?"

"Who the fuck do you think you are talking to me like that? Nobody talks to me like that! Who the fuck do you think you are, Ann Landers? If I want marriage advice, I'll talk to Father Mulholland at St. Dominic's!"

"I should go," I said. Brady got to his feet, a bottle of Guinness in each hand.

"Sit down and finish your drink. I've got an idea, an idea you are going to love." I sat down.

"Come with me." I stood up again. We walked through to Mr. Brady's library. He searched around for a moment or two as I stood next to a table in the center of the room. I was trying to guess how many books were stacked covering three walls of the library. Brady came toward me and dropped a very large Atlas of North America on the table.

"You're the flyer, you read maps. Find Vancouver, British Columbia then find me Deep Cove."

I did as Paddy Brady requested and found the relevant page of the Atlas. He pointed to Deep Cove which lay just a few miles north-east of the City of Vancouver. It was about a third of the way up an inlet called Indian Arm, on the western shoreline. Brady looked to be very pleased with himself.

"You see? Do you see? It will work; no bother!" I said:

"I don't follow Mister Brady." Brady pointed with his bottle of Guinness anointing the map of southwestern British Columbia in dark brown beer.

"It's bloody obvious isn't it?"

"Not to me," I said.

"It's in the name, isn't it? Deep Cove, Deep Cove, it's a cove. You can land a floatplane there. All you have to do is fly low over some desolate stretch of the border; find your way into…" He checked the Atlas. "Burrard Inlet, and put her down in Deep Cove. You pick up Mrs. Brady and bring her home, piece of piss!" I waved my cast in the air.

"Bit of a problem their Mister Brady; I can manage an M.G. up and down the hills of San Francisco but I'm not flying a floatplane illegally into Canada on one arm…too many unknowns, too many variables. It's better to be on the ground wishing you were in the air than in the air wishing you were on the ground."

"And just who came up with that gem? William Shakespeare?" asked Brady.

"To be honest I have no idea," I said. "You could send another pilot. How about Pete, the guy who owns the Beaver? He knows the aircraft way better than me. He'll do a great job."

"Pete doesn't own that aircraft anymore; I do. And Peter Reeves is in no condition to fly whether he wanted to or not. He had a little accident."

"Do I want to know what happened?"

"Mister Reeves borrowed the money to buy his plane from…let's say, a financial concern I own. He got behind on his payments and sadly we had to repossess the Beaver. When we went round to see him Mister Reeves got into a little argument with two of my boys…you've met them, Dino and Brendan.

Good boys but they do get a little enthusiastic when they are on a job. That Brendan can be a bit of a handful. I'm told Mister Reeves is currently recovering from a very bad fall. He fell out of a second story window…twice. He's in hospital."

"Which one?" I asked.

"How the fuck should I know?" asked Brady, his face was dark as thunder clouds.

"I was just going to go and see him, maybe take him something to read. Time drags when you're in a hospital bed, I know."

"Are you fucking joking? Are you some kind of saint?" he asked. Then slowly over the next thirty-seconds, an amazing thing happened. He started to smile. He drank some more Guinness and smiled some more. He beckoned me closer.

"Come here flyboy…I am just about to be brilliant. You are going to love this." I got the feeling that might not be totally true.

"I've just come into the possession of a nearly new float-plane I don't want, haven't I? I mean, what the fuck do I want with a float-plane? You are a pilot; you don't have a plane, do you?" I shook my head; then I realized where this was going. I did not like the destination one bit.

"Here's what we are going to do. You can't fly for what, three weeks?"

"About that," I said.

"I'm going to send Inga up to Canada to keep an eye on Constance. Make sure she stays put. In three weeks' time; when you are good and ready, you fly up to Vancouver, pick up the two ladies and fly them back here to me. If all goes according to my brilliant plan, with no hiccups, I give you the papers for the plane. It's yours…free! Now you can't say fairer than that my son, can you?"

I thought about Inga then. What would she say when Brady told her to go to Vancouver and find his wife? Would she quit? That might be a very bad move to make. I don't think many people quit on Patrick Brady…lots got canned, no-one quit. I had to find a way to warn her, I had no way of contacting her by phone. Maybe I should call at Mona's to see if I could get a message to her?

Before I could say another word, Brady was hustling me out of his house. He said:

"Now you just relax, get that arm better, ready to fly. Hey! That's funny…get that arm ready to fly! Let me know if you need anything…anything! But don't go around getting into fights with big blonde Dutchmen, especially not big blonde Dutchmen who are working for the mob…do you catch my drift?" I nodded. I caught his drift all right. We were at the door. Brady practically pushed me into the street.

"We'll be in touch. God Bless!"

So that was it. I stood on Paddy Brady's doorstep and took stock of the situation. If all went according to plan, I could very shortly be the proud owner of a DHC-2 De Havilland Beaver float-plane. All I had to do was get my right arm into working order, fly up to Canada, kidnap a young woman, and bring her back to her husband…simple really.

Chapter Sixteen

I called in at Mona's that evening as planned. Inga wasn't there but her good friend Peggy was. I'd never met Peggy before, but she certainly knew who I was. She had caramel-colored skin and straight jet-black hair cut in a straight line at the nape of her slender neck. She was kinda wearing a silk kimono with a dragon on the back. She hadn't bothered to tie it at the front. Maybe she'd lost the belt; maybe she'd lost the belt at the same time as she lost her underwear. She teetered around on those blocky high-heeled sandals that Japanese ladies wear. I tried to keep my eyes on her feet, but it was difficult with so much on display just a few feet higher. I introduced myself, although she'd guessed who I was. Peggy ignored my obvious discomfort and embarrassment and took me by the hand, leading me back through the club to the dressing room.

There were more attractive bodies of all types in various stages of undress in the dressing room. Some were girls dressed as guys, some were guys dressed as girls, some I just couldn't tell what they were. Everyone was jabbering away, and they all had a great time winding Peggy up about her new straight guy…me.

Peggy took a chair facing a long mirror and an equally long shelf covered in make-up cases, lipsticks, hair-dryers, wine glasses, good luck messages, and flowers. She looked at her face in the mirror and must have been happy with what she saw.

"Perfect!" she said; then she turned to me, a pert pink nipple popped out from her kimono. Peggy didn't seem to notice or care. It was getting uncomfortably hot in the dressing room; it must have been all the lights and mirrors and nearly naked people in the place.

"So, you're the private dick Inga's been working with. What can I do for you?" From further down the make-up table there were girlish snickers.

"Can you give her a message for me? When you see her next?"

"Won't you be seeing her yourself?" she asked.

"We don't work together anymore."

"That's a pity. Inga said she really enjoyed what you were doing…whatever it was."

I could stand it no more. I gently pulled Peggy's kimono back over the renegade breast saying:

"That's better, now I can concentrate."

"I've seen Inga break some guys hand for doing less than you just did."

"I'm just the kind of guy who likes everything in its place," I said with the best disarming smile I could muster.

"It's okay, working in a place like this you get used to not wearing much, you forget how…distracting things can be."

"That's a good word for it…distracting," I said. "So, here's the message. Brady wants me to fly to Vancouver to pick up a package. He's going to send Inga up there to look after the package until I can fly the plane." I waved my cast clumsily around to illustrate my point, nearly knocking a vase of flowers off the counter. Peggy caught it.

"I thought she would want to know about this. Could you ask her to get in touch when she gets a chance?"

"Will do Rick. You should stick around for the show, Inga might drop by later."

"I'll take a rain-check on that Peggy, nice to meet you though." Peggy stood up and gave me a quick hug and said:

"You too, drop by anytime."

I just stood there like a broken tin soldier with my arm sticking into things it should not be sticking into.

Later that night, back in my office I took stock of what was going on in my life, or tried to. In three weeks, I would be flying north to kidnap an ex-gangster's wife and bring her back to him. At that time, I would most likely come into conflict with one of the few friends I had in the world; a six-foot-tall lesbian who I was most likely already in love with; a six-foot-tall lesbian who might very well attempt to kill me whilst in the course of my duties.

My wife was fucking her boss and had been doing so for over a year. Her boss was laundering money for Las Vegas Gangsters and could possibly get them both killed, if I didn't get them both arrested first. I had the three weeks my arm would take to mend fully to solve this problem. I would like to keep my wife out of jail, but I was not sure I could do that.

Someone had killed two perfectly innocent young ladies in a basement apartment, and it was, in all likelihood, partially my fault. The police were stumbling around trying to find a sex fiend serial killer. I did not believe a serial killer had committed these crimes. Therefore, I might be the only guy who could solve this case too. And let's not forget the case that had started it all. I still had to find out why The Connie had gone down.

I hit the hay with faces and places from all of these cases whirling around in my head, mixing together into one gigantic nightmarish vision. I surprised myself by falling asleep as these visions spun.

In the morning I woke early and walked down to the corner for a coffee and a read of The Chronicle. I read all about Charlie Chaplin being refused re-entry to the U.S. and that asshole Joseph McCarthy running off at the mouth. Didn't I fight in a war just a few years ago when the Ruskies were on our side? What had changed? I thought about that for a while, but I figured things would most likely get worse before they got better with this anti-commie thing. I was right.

I was getting more and more use of my arm, day by day. It was getting easier to do basic things like getting dressed, take a piss…that kind of thing. I figured I had three weeks tops to solve the Ko den Hamer money laundering scam, put him behind bars and save Josephine. I would concentrate on that case from now on. And what I had to do was find out when the next big delivery of cash was coming into town, then I had to let the District Attorney's Office and (I guess) the F.B.I. set up a raid to catch Ko and his friends from Las Vegas in the act. The problem was I had to make sure that Josephine (still my wife, remember that)…I had to keep Josephine miles away from the take-down. How was I going to do that without tipping the nod to Ko and his gangster friends?

The big question for the day was this: did Josephine Marshall know she was involved in a money-laundering scheme for organized crime in Nevada and Chicago? I didn't know the answer and I didn't know a way to find out. This would take at least one more coffee. I signaled Molly behind the counter for a refill and at just that second Inga walked in.

"Better make that two new coffees Molly," I said. I asked Inga if she wanted some breakfast, she shook her head. She sat down at my table.

"I guess you saw Peggy…" She nodded. "So, you got my message."

"I got your message," she said. Molly delivered the coffees.

"Are you sure I can't buy you breakfast?" I asked.

"I don't want any breakfast," she said. Something was troubling her, something way more important than me flying to Vancouver to collect Mrs. Brady.

"Rick, there's something you should know, something about Constance Brady." I didn't say a word, but I tried to look all sympathetic and interested. This might not have worked out as I planned, I don't know if I pulled it off. Inga stirred her coffee for at least two minutes, something I had never seen her do before; it was black coffee, after all, just the same as mine. Finally, I put my left hand over hers and stopped the stirring. Inga dropped the spoon and snatched her hand back. Then she took one long breath and started to speak very quietly.

"Constance was having an affair with one of the drivers..."

"...Not Raul?" I said. "I don't believe it, after all that guff about his wife and kids in Mexico, the shifty bastard."

"It wasn't Raul."

"How many drivers does Paddy Brady have?"

"It was me."

We both went back to stirring our coffee for a time.

"So, you knew what had happened at the airport. You were in on the switch?" she shook her head.

"No, absolutely not...I dropped her at the airport just like I told you. Look, I knew she was looking for a way out, I've told you that before. Constance couldn't survive much longer. I thought she might do something stupid...you know, try to kill herself."

"How long were you two knocking boots?" I asked.

"Not long, it wasn't serious; we're not in love or anything like that...it just kinda happened one night when Brady was out of town. Constance doesn't need a lover; she just needs someone to treat her nice every now and then. I guess that's what I'm good at. Think about this...if we were lovers, she would have told me all about her plans, wouldn't she?"

"And now you want me to find some lame-ass excuse not to fly to Vancouver and bring the dame you like to treat nice back to her husband?"

I might have said that last piece a little louder than I intended. The fact that everyone in the café had turned to look at us might have been a clue...more coffee stirring followed. Did I believe her when she said they were 'just good friends'? I wanted to believe every word she said; did she sense that about me? Was she playing me? Inga looked at me with tears in her big grey/blue eyes. She said:

"I told you, we're not in love. Look I'm sorry if you don't believe me Rick, but I'm telling you the truth. I've never lied to you, Rick..."

"No, you just left out some of the facts."

"I'm just doing my job...when the boss says drive this car, I drive the car. When he says help this detective, I do my best to help."

"What about when the boss said: don't fuck my wife?" Again, maybe I said this a little too loud. I felt everybody was watching us, everyone was listening in. I needed to get out of that place, and I needed to get out of that conversation. I left.

I walked quickly back to the office. I was steaming. I could have punched a puppy I was so pissed. I realized now that I'd been played for a complete sap...again. Dames must be lining up to lie to me. All that: 'we're good friends but we might be more.' All those deliberately miss-leading signals all those hints that she might be a switch hitter...they were all just to keep me in my place, to keep me docile and compliant. Like a faithful old bloodhound going about his job, thankful for any small tidbits of affection that got tossed my way.

She knew that if she flirted with me just enough, that if she shared her exotic friends and lifestyle with me just enough, I'd be dazzled by the gay thrill of it all. She knew that I was really a small town; straight-up sort of guy at heart and what she had to offer would surely turn my head. She played me like a cheap accordion. I was going to fly the Beaver, my Beaver to Vancouver and I was going to bring Connie Brady back here if I had to knock her out, tie her up and throw her in the cargo hold. And there was nothing Miss Inga Bjarkardóttir with all her long legs, pixie haircut, and pert tits could do about it.

I threw my hat onto the client's chair and slumped behind my desk, managing to bang my right elbow on my chair's arm as I sat down. I might have cursed some at that point. There was a knock at the door. Inga stuck her head around the door and asked:

"Can I come in?"

"You never asked before. I seem to remember you breaking in the first time we met. But hey come in, come in, sit down. Make yourself at home."

Inga took my hat and hung it up; then she sat down opposite me.

"You're going to go to Vancouver, aren't you?" she said, although she most likely already knew my answer.

"If I didn't go, he'd send someone else," I said, sounding quite a lot like Colonel Paul Tibbets, the commanding officer of the Enola Gay. "You need to be careful what you do when you get up there, Inga. If you warn Mrs. Brady and she disappears again he's sure to know who told her. Then he'll work out why you told her; then he'll send an army to fetch her back and they'll chop you into little tiny pieces as a bonus."

"I'm getting a flight to Seattle at the weekend then I get a local flight into Vancouver. I should be there some-time Sunday."

"And what are you going to say to Constance Brady?"

"I'll tell her everything. It's all I can do. You knew I'd be doing that even before you made the lovely speech about getting chopped to bits."

"Do you still love her?" I asked.

"Will you drop it? I said we weren't lovers, besides that's none of your business."

"It isn't? You know for a short while I thought it might be."

"What's that supposed to mean?"

"Nothing...look Inga it seems to me that we're both caught up in someone else's mess here and we are both going to have to do what we feel is right. If I can do what I need to do without hurting you and yours I'll do it; that goes without saying. But you and I both know Brady will not take no for an answer on this."

"That's a very pretty speech, Rick." She said as she got to her feet. "I only hope you can remember what you said when the shit hits the fan."

"You've got a great way with words Inga...have a safe trip."

"The trip's not the problem is it Rick? It's what happens at the other end."

Inga waved goodbye and was out of my office before I could think of a smart thing to say in return. I hate it when that happens, don't you? I moped around the office for about an hour after Inga left. Then I just had to get out of the place, get my feet moving, and make something happen in at least one case. So, I drove over to the house to see if my wife or her lover were at home. I was in luck...they both were. In fact, they were both coming out of the house when I drove by. I pulled in a few spaces further down the street and watched them walk down the garden path in the small driver's mirror on the dashboard of the M.G. They got in Ko den Hamer's Jaguar XK 120 and drove right past me seconds later. I waited for a car to fill in the gap behind them then I followed.

They went down Telegraph which eventually led pretty much straight to the entrance to the Bay Bridge. Traffic was fairly light as it was close to the middle of the day. I had to hang back at least two or three cars. The Jag wasn't hard to spot though. We must have been the only two British made sports cars heading south over the bridge that day.

Once over the bridge, they took Fremont toward the Embarcadero. They headed toward the water and for a moment I thought they were going to park near the ferry building. But den Hamer did a U-turn and pulled in behind a four-story brick building that was on the city side of the Embarcadero. I waited for a gap in traffic and followed them round to the back of the building. I saw Josephine and Ko walking arm in arm around the side of the building as I pulled into the last parking space in the lot. I hurried after them and got into the lobby just in time to see the elevator stop on the fourth floor. The clock tower across the street struck twelve.

I took the stairs. I was no longer wearing a sling and I enjoyed the heart-pumping rhythm as I bounded up the stone steps two by two. Once on the fourth floor, I did a quick circuit of all the offices. An accountant, a publisher of Pulp Fiction, mainly westerns by the posters showing through the glass partitions, a secretarial agency, and a plumbing supply company's head office.

There was one small office at the rear of the building with no name on the door.

This was the place all right...I could smell Josephine's perfume as I stood by the door. I could hear the sound of a typewriter from inside. Busy, busy, busy. There wasn't much for me to do now but wait. I walked back down the stairs and out to the M.G. I turned it round in the parking spot so I could drive straight out if I needed to. I risked walking across the Embarcadero to grab a coffee and a sandwich from a stand in the ferry building. I planned to be in the parking lot for the rest of the day, unless Ko den Hamer left the office on his own.

He didn't, Ko and Josephine came out to the parking lot just after four. I watched them drive away, they looked to be heading for the bay bridge and I guessed Oakland and home. I gave them ten minutes to be far enough away then I retraced my route up the stone steps to the un-named office. The flimsy lock was no challenge and I was inside in thirty-seconds tops. I went straight to the big desk at the rear of the room and started my search. Most of the drawers were empty and the center drawer only contained the usual crap: pencils, rubber bands, an eraser; some condoms...that kind of thing.

I checked the filing cabinet next. More details of prospective land deals in the Napa Valley and not much else. Finally, I went to Josephine's desk. Placed under the typewriter was a large desk-top diary. Nothing much entered for this week but next Wednesday evening was ringed and a note next to it said.

Candlestick Point. 8.00 p.m.

This was the only diary entry for next week. They weren't exactly rushed off their feet at KDH Developments, were they? I guess that gave them plenty of time to have kinky sex all over the place. Where the hell was Candlestick Point anyway? I had no idea.

I made a note of the date, time and address (you know where) and I locked up the office. I crossed over to the ferry building and found a stand selling tour guides and city maps. I bought one. It turns out Candlestick Point was just a few miles south of here. All I had to do was drive south on Embarcadero, get on to third street, and follow my nose. I got back in the M.G. and did just that. Candlestick Point is a quarry overlooking the bay. It would be a pretty nice spot if there weren't a quarry there. The site was boarded off and F**or Sale,** signs were posted on the main gate. I looked through that gate but couldn't see a great deal. There were plenty of seagulls doing circuits around the empty wasteland but not much else. They banked and wheeled in the thermals coming off the bay and looked like they didn't have a care in the world. One of them took a crap while in mid-air. I heard the all too familiar smacking sound and the white bird-shit splattered my ankles. If I'd got my gun, I might have taken a few pot-shots right at that minute.

Candlestick Point was pretty 'out of the way' so I figured there was a good chance this would be where the next money drop was made. By eight it would be getting dark here and there were no street-lights nearby.

I drove back to the office in a fog. Not a real fog; it was mercifully a clear day. I drove back to the office in a personal fog. I now had a clear choice to make; a clear choice but not an easy one. It all depended on how well I knew my wife. And I was getting less and less sure of that. If I set up the police raid for next Wednesday and I didn't warn her about it she would be going to jail, straight to jail and she wouldn't be collecting two hundred dollars either…no doubt about it. But if I warned her and she was involved, and she told Ko den Hamer…then the raid would be a bust and both of them would get away.

As I probably said earlier; if you'd asked me this question three months ago my answer would have been clear and concise: 'There's no way Josephine knows about her boss's money laundering scheme.' But my problem was this: if (at the same time) you'd asked me: 'Is your wife fucking her boss and does she make whoop, whoop noises whilst he pounds her chained-up body in your bed?' I would have said no and I'd most likely I'd have broken your jaw for good measure. Enough said?

Back at my office I checked the bottom drawer and found out I was out of booze. This could be easily rectified. I spent the whole night getting rectified and trying to find the answer, the ultimate answer to the question written above. That night I did not succeed in doing anything except getting very, very drunk, and somehow breaking out of my cast.

The next day I drove back to my parking spot off Embarcadero, settled down, and waited for the two love birds to arrive. They turned up at nine-thirty and went straight into the four-story building housing their new offices. I had caffeine for breakfast but decided against any food. The coffee was strong and black and steaming hot. It possibly saved my life that day. It was a cold misty morning down by the water and I was glad to be able to wrap my old flying jacket around me. It was the first time I'd been in need of it for months.

The scorch marks on the up-turned sheepskin collar were a constant reminder of how I got my scars, but the coat kept me warm which helped when driving around and sitting around in San Francisco in September.

I hoped, once again, to see Ko den Hamer leave the office on his own. If he did, I was going to go inside and have a few words with my wife. Even at this point, I had no idea what those words would be. After two hours my chance came. Ko came out of the brick building, walked over to the Jag and drove quickly away. I hurried inside and took the elevator to the fourth floor.

Josephine screamed when I walked through the door. I don't usually have that effect on women, certainly not women I've known intimately for almost ten years. It was not a good start. As I walked into the office, I still had no idea how the next fifteen minutes would go.

"Good to see you too Josephine; you're looking well. Extra-marital sex must suit you."

Okay, I admit. I did have that one planned, pretty good hey? And then, just at that second, I thought of a way to see if Josephine was involved with the fraud. It came to me like an epiphany. It was almost biblical in its clarity. This is what I said:

"I came to see if you need any more mortgage money. Unless of course, you get your cut after next Wednesday's meeting?"

"Are you drunk? You smell like booze. Are you?" I carried on with the new plan saying:

"So, you won't take a little off the top after the meeting at Candlestick Point?"

"Candlestick Point? What the hell are you talking about? Where's Candlestick Point?" I had my answer, Jo did not know about the money laundering. She had been kept in the dark. I could speak to the D.A.s office and set up the interception of the money drop. They would lock Ko den Hamer up for a very long time and Jo would come back to me. I'd get the Beaver, start a flying tour company, make a ton of money off rich tourists and we could put all this behind us and get back to normal.

"What the hell are you smiling at Rick?" asked Jo.

"Oh nothing, nothing." I turned around and went back out of the door.

"I'll see you around," I said, just as casual as you like. She slammed the door behind me. I'm sure I heard some kind of framed certificate fall to the floor and break. I went back over to the ferry building, back into the café and ordered a full breakfast. All of a sudden, I was feeling ravenous. After that, I drove back to my office and checked in with my message service. I had three potential clients eager for me to get in touch. I scribbled down their numbers on a piece of paper and stuffed it in my pocket. Then I phoned Elton Dwight at the District Attorney's Office. I was put through and Dwight picked up after one ring and said:

"Good day to you Rick. I'm assuming you have some news for me."

"I know the time and place of the next cash drop," I said.

"Do tell, do tell," said Elton Dwight. I told.

Chapter Seventeen

By the afternoon my arm began to hurt like hell, so I had it strapped up real tight at the first drug store I drove by. I could flex my fingers and there was a little strength coming back in my wrist. If my life depended on it, I could most likely fly a small plane now…if my life depended on it. I decided to play it smart and wait out the full three weeks grace period Paddy Brady had granted me. If I was lucky Inga would get Mrs. Brady to contact her husband and they would sort things out without me having to fly into Canada and kidnap her.

Back at the office, I checked in with my message service. I had a reply from the owner of an apartment to rent on 20th and Castro. This was one of three places I'd seen in the want-ads in the Chronicle and called about. I put the slip of paper into my 'handy-dandy' detective's notebook just in case. But I did not plan to be calling it any time soon. I figured if things went well next Wednesday at Candlestick Point, I'd be moving back into the old homestead with the old 'hot' wife. Maybe she'd let me tie her to the bed as well. This was not something I'd ever done in the past but, hey; if it got Josephine's motor revving, I was willing to give it my best shot…when I moved back in. I was surprisingly optimistic about this.

I made appointments to meet my three new clients throughout the following day. All of them were women who thought their husbands were 'stepping out' on them…my stock in trade. I was about to leave the office to buy some groceries when Inga called.

"Hi, Rick. I'm flying to Seattle tomorrow morning; could you give me a ride to the airport? It would give us a chance to talk; if you're not too busy."

"Believe it or not I do have a client meeting tomorrow at ten…the usual divorce work, you know."

"Oh well, I can always take a cab…"

"No, no I'll move the meeting. I'll take you. Where do you want me to pick you up?" Inga gave me an address in The Castro, strangely enough only a block from the rental place I was supposed to go see. We agreed a time to meet. I called my ten o'clock and moved her back to late afternoon, all of a sudden, I was a busy detective again.

The next morning, I met Inga as planned. I had the roof up as it looked like we might get rain on the way south to the airport. I fastened Inga's case to the luggage rack on the trunk and we set off. For most of the drive out of town, we did not say a word. I concentrated on the driving and Inga concentrated on her bright red finger-nails.

As we passed through Bernal Heights Inga spoke up:

"What's happening with the money-laundering wife and her lover?" I told her all about the planned meet at Candlestick Point.

"And where exactly is Candlestick Point?" she asked. I pointed off to the left.

"Over there, it's on the water, there's a quarry there, not much else."

"Good place to shoot an interfering husband and dump his body."

"I told you, Josephine has nothing to do with the money laundering or the guys from Vegas. She's completely innocent."

"Let's not get carried away here Rick, your wife could be a lot of things but completely innocent? I don't think so."

I know I know...she could be right. I knew there was still a chance that Josephine was up to her pretty little neck in this. She could be playing more than hide the salami with Ko den Hamer. I had so far chosen to ignore this possibility. I didn't want to think about that, so I changed the subject...to one Inga didn't want to talk about:

"So, what are your orders from Mister Brady?"

"Find Constance, make sure she's okay, make sure she's not with another guy (that's a good one) make sure she's not being held against her will. Then I have to check in every other day by phone. Tell him where she's been staying, who with."

"So how does he think you can explain just turning up in the back of beyond and just happening to bump into her?"

"Good question. I don't think Big Paddy has thought that far ahead."

"So, you're supposed to waltz into this one-horse town north of the border, casually bump into Constance Brady, pretend to be just passing through and say something like: 'Oh Hi Mrs. Brady, fancy meeting you here'...it won't work."

"I know that!"

"Which brings me back to my original question: what the fuck are you going to do?" I stole a glance across at Inga at this point, she was crying quietly. I hadn't heard over the engine.

"Rick, I don't know what to do." We were approaching the main terminal building. I said:

"There are lots of things you can do Inga. What you choose to do boils down to one thing really…and it's not as though I'm an expert on this subject so bear with me on this. The way I see it, it all comes down to this in the end: You might not be in love with Constance Brady, but is she in love with you? And if she is what are you going to do about it? Maybe you need to tell her the truth. Let her know how you feel…or don't feel."

Inga kept sobbing as I parked the M.G.

"It's not as easy as that," she said.

"Isn't it?" I asked.

"Brady will have me killed if he finds out Constance was seeing me, and we are together in Canada. He might even send someone with you to do it."

"Then we have to make sure he never finds out."

"And how do we do that?"

"Right now, I don't know for sure. The good news is we've got at least two weeks to work it out."

"Only two weeks?" I waved my right hand in front of her.

"You had to be a fast healer!"

"Can't help it…It's all that clean living and abstinence. It builds up my strength."

"You're saying you're healing quicker because you're not getting laid at the moment?"

"Looks like it, and it's nearly a month now, not that I'm counting."

"I could call my friend Betty; she thinks you're cute."

"That's good to know, but I'm spoken for…you know that."

"You still think that's going to work out?"

"Why not?" I asked. Inga opened her mouth to list a whole schlock of reasons why not, reasons I did not need to hear. So, I put my finger to her lips…

"Don't answer that," I said. We got out of the M.G. I grabbed Inga's case from the luggage rack on the car's trunk and we went inside to the T.W.A. desk. Thankfully Miss Harper was not on duty.

I asked Inga:

"How long before you take off?"

"We made good time driving out here; I've got just over an hour to wait."

"Let's find a quiet corner somewhere and put together a game plan, one that does not involve anyone getting hurt; especially me." Inga gave me a hug. She whispered in my ear:

"Thanks, Rick." She smelled of vanilla and soap. We found a place as far away from the other passengers as possible.

"Let's think this through carefully," I said. "The first option…you find Constance, explain to her what's going to happen when I turn up, then you help Constance disappear again, this time permanently. You either go with her or you say goodbye forever at that point." Inga asked:

"What if she chooses not to run?"

"When I turn up you shoot me in the head and dump my body in the inlet. Personally, I'm not too keen on that one."

"Very funny…"

"The problem with that (apart from me ending up dead) is Brady will work out either you or Constance did it. He'll send more people up to Vancouver to find you and Constance. That could get messy."

"Can't we work out a way where nobody gets killed?"

"Oh, that's easy. You persuade Constance to come back. I turn up in two weeks-time, fly everyone back to San Francisco and move into the float-plane business."

"I can't do that Rick and you know it. I think Brady is sure to kill Constance sooner or later and I can't let that happen. You don't know the half of it. He really is a monster and if he finds out about Constance and me, he'll kill us both."

We sat for a while looking out at the ground crew bustling around Inga's aircraft. After a time, I said:

"We need to have something worked out before you get on that plane and we need to stick to it. Once you get to Vancouver there's no way we can get in touch with each other." After another very long pause Inga finally spoke:

"Rick, this is what I'm gonna do…I'll find Constance, tell her you will be coming to take her back to Brady and there's nothing I can do to stop you. I'll persuade her to get as far away from the West Coast as possible, maybe move to Europe; that might work…"

"…You won't go with her?"

"No, no I won't, how many times do I have to say this? I'm not in love with Constance. I mean we were close for a while, real close but a lot of what I felt for her was pity. I felt sorry for her, wanted to protect her, and help her but that's not love…at least I don't think it is, what the hell do I know?"

"You're sure about this?" I asked.

"I think so," she said. A T.W.A. official walked past announcing:

"T.W.A. flight 402 to Seattle Washington is now boarding. Passengers for flight 402 to Seattle Washington please proceed to the gate."

We hugged again and I kissed her on the neck.

"I'll see you in just over two weeks. Don't do anything stupid till I get there."

"Then can I do something stupid?"

"That works…stay well, Inga." Then she kissed me, the real deal; not a peck on the cheek, not like saying Happy Thanksgiving to your aunty Fanny…a real one hundred percent, no holds barred, smacker, wow!

And then she was gone. I stood by the window and a minute later I caught sight of her boarding the Martin 404 as the pilot ran up the twin Pratt and Whitney 2800's. I waved, she waved back and then she was really gone.

I got back to the M.G. and thought I might as well try to have a word with the T.W.A. crew chief Mike Halloran if he was on duty. I wouldn't get very far if I went back to the T.W.A. desk as I was now personae non grata with them. Not only that but they didn't want me around either. I figured if I swept up to the security barrier in my fancy British sports car and acted like I owned the place I should get access to the hangars. So, I blipped the throttle a few times before racing along the perimeter to the security gate. I needn't have bothered with all the pre-planning. There was no-one on the gate. It was a Sunday and getting close to lunch-time; my guess is the guard had just popped out to get something to eat.

I drove the M.G. straight under the barrier, I had to duck a little as I went through, but no-one came running out, no-one yelled: 'Stop!' so I just drove onto the airfield. Some poor guy's ass would be in a sling if anyone ever found out about this.

I slowed right down and drove calmly out to the T.W.A. hangar. I parked in a vacant slot and headed in toward Mike Halloran's office. As I walked through the main doors a young mechanic, he can't have been seventeen, came up, and asked who I was. I told him:

"I'm with the District Attorney's office; we spoke to Mike Halloran just after flight 402 went down. I need to ask him a few quick questions. Is he at work today son?"

"He's up in his office, you just caught him; he only works Sunday mornings."

I thought the 'son' was a good touch, made me sound all official and full of myself, like I really did work for the D.A. I climbed the stairs, knocked, and entered the office. Halloran was just putting on his jacket, getting ready to leave.

"What are you doing here? How did you get in?"

"I was just dropping someone off for the Seattle flight. I thought we might have a quick word."

Mike Halloran brushed past me and headed for the stairs.

"Well ,you thought wrong, you know you aren't supposed to be here. Besides I have to catch a ride into the city."

I followed Halloran back down the stairs and outside again.

"I can give you a ride, we can talk then." I pointed to the M.G.

"Could I drive it?" He asked. The sky had cleared so working together we quickly had the roof down and stowed behind us. Mike leaped into the driver's seat.

As the crew chief drove the M.G. out past the barrier the security guard did a double-take. Mike knew how to drive the M.G., timing gear changes to perfection. Soon we were zipping north toward San Francisco with the bay sparkling away in the distance. We had to shout a little over the engine noise. I asked him:

"Any progress on the investigation?"

"Some," he said. "I've been splitting my time between the airport and Treasure Island; do you know it?"

"I was out there a short while ago, looking at a hot dame with only half ahead."

"As well as the morgue they are using a hangar to try re-construct parts of the Connie that have been brought up. It's a new idea. It's a pain in the ass if you ask me, takes for-ever to get a clear picture of anything. It's like a giant 3D jigsaw on wire mesh; a jigsaw with millions and millions of pieces. The whole thing will take years. Mister Hughes is paying for it personally."

"Sounds like we'll never know what happened," I said.

"I wouldn't be too quick to dismiss it. There's something you ought to hear about."

"Go on."

"Okay, but it's just an idea I had, I've not shared it with anyone officially." I had an idea of my own. We were getting close to the southern edge of the city.

"Have you had lunch yet Mike?"

"Nope, I usually get a bite to eat when I get home."

"Why don't I buy you lunch?" I gave Mike directions that took us off the highway and down the route I had taken when Inga and I first drove in from the airport. In no time we were at the St. Francis diner, 24th, and York. Mike had steak and eggs; I had a coffee. In between mouthfuls, Mike told me about an interesting find in the cockpit.

"We found small pieces of metal with military serial numbers on. I recognized what we were looking at straight away. It's an ammo box. Lots of guys use them as lunch boxes, I have one at home. We found pieces of this ammo box all over the inside of one piece of the cockpit wall, embedded in the superstructure...on the inside."

"Like the ammo box was very close to the site of the explosion?"

"Or what if it was the site of the explosion? That's what I'm thinking."

"You mean someone took live ammo on a civil flight and somehow it went off?"

"No, that's not what I'm saying. The kind of ammo box we're talking about here usually carried 50 or 30 caliber ammo. It's not the kind of thing you would use to arm a B17, way too small but they were used at sentry posts and all over the bases. I think something else was put in this ammo box."

"You think the ammo box was the bomb?"

"I'm not sure yet. It's not something I can take to the police; I don't have any proof and I have no idea how it was set off. If there was some kind of timer, we'd most likely have found some of the works..."

"What about a barometric trigger?" I asked.

"You mean set to go off at a certain height? I don't think so, she was only at a few thousand feet and she'd been at that altitude since she left the circuit at the airport...it's possible though. I'll keep it in mind."

Mike finished his steak and eggs and he agreed to keep me informed of any further progress. I promised to help him out with any research or inquiries he needed done away from the official investigation. I gave him a business card. Mike lived alone in an apartment just north of Twin Peaks near Haight-Ashbury. After I dropped him off, I found a way back to the office, heading north up Masonic, left on Geary, then right on 4th.

Back at the office I checked messages and wasn't surprised to find only one. It was Sunday after all. Most sane people would be going to Church, staying in bed till noon, playing with their kids, or moping about at the end of a bar, about to finish their fourth scotch. The one message was from Josephine, my wife, which was a surprise. I gave her a call. That was when the real surprises started to happen. She said she wanted to talk to me about Ko den Hamer.

"I think he's mixed up in something that could be slightly illegal and potentially dangerous. I'm not sure if I should go to the police, maybe they'll think I'm involved."

"Do you want me to come over?" I asked.

"Not right now," she said. "He's due home any minute." It stung me to realize that she meant he'd be home to our home any minute.

"When can we meet?" I asked.

"How about Wednesday evening? At eight? Ko's got this big meeting on downtown. You could come over here, I'll cook your dinner. Pasta all right?"

"I'll bring the meatballs," I said; then instantly regretted it. She gave a short laugh then put down the phone. I thought about telling Inga all about this development then I remembered she was on her way to Vancouver now and maybe I'd never see her again. I had planned on tagging along with the strike team from the D.A.s office on Wednesday night but I figured I'd only get in the way. Sure, I wanted to see Ko's smarmy face when they slapped the cuffs on him or (even better) watch him get his dick shot off in a hail of bullets but I now had a hot date with my hot wife, and I wasn't going to miss that for anything.

Monday morning, I got my suit into the cleaners and went out to buy another new shirt. Should I take flowers? I decided not to, thought that might look a bit out of place. After all, I was meant to be going over to help her with a legal problem.

Tuesday I was summoned to the DA's office to attend a final briefing. I had nothing to add to what I'd told Elton Dwight, but it was good to be asked along. I might have said that I believed Ko to be armed and dangerous so they should shoot first and ask questions later…

Wednesday I had a haircut and a shave at Luigi's barbers. Then I collected my suit from the cleaners. As you might have guessed this was not my busiest day at work. I spent most of the afternoon at my desk staring out at the front door. I did decide that it was time to have the name changed on that front door. Maybe I should come up with a new name for the agency?

By seven forty-five that evening I was parking the M.G. behind Mr. Loomis's Chevy before walking across the street. I'd bought a bottle of Sangiovese red wine at a liquor store on the way over. It was Italian, I think. It certainly sounded Italian. Not many people drank wine at home, but I figured if we were doing the whole spaghetti dinner thing, wine should be the drink of choice. It was a fancy bottle with a bulging bottom end, and it came in a kind of fishnet holder. I knocked on the door and I was trying to work out how to say the name of the wine when Josephine opened it. She was wearing a chef's apron that had a bib over her chest and went down to her knees.

"Don't you have a key?" she asked.

"I thought maybe I should knock…I brought wine." She took the bottle from me, turned, and walked down the hallway. She wasn't wearing a dress under the apron. She had that underwear on again, complete with black nylons and a garter belt.

"I didn't put my dress on; I didn't want to get it spattered with tomato sauce."

"Yeah right; that's good thinking Jo. You're looking well." I said. It was a good job she had the bottle by then I think I may have dropped it at that point. We went into the kitchen. Josephine stood at the sink, rinsing the spaghetti with hot water from the kettle; steam billowed from in front of her. I didn't notice. I was looking somewhere else. Her long black hair cascaded down her back and over the straps of her bra. I stood behind her, reached forward, and unfastened the bow holding the chef's apron around her body. She didn't say a word, just stood with her back to me looking out of the window. Thankfully it was pretty dark by now or the neighbors would be either reaching for their binoculars or calling the cops. Jo asked me:

"Are you hungry?" I reached forward and yanked her panties down past her knees.

"Not really, maybe later." I bent her body forward and she parted her legs. I fumbled with my fly and in seconds I was in her. She gasped as I drove deep into her. I reached forward, pulled the apron to one side, and cupped her magnificent breasts in their silky confines. Then I unclipped her bra and reached greedily forward again, all the time thrusting into her, forcing her against the sink. It was messy; it was brutal in a way, not the kind of sex you share with your wife every day. After a time, Josephine eased herself off me and slowly turned to face me. We kissed; then she said:

"I'll turn the sauce off. Maybe we should finish this in the bedroom."

We stumbled across the kitchen and up the stairs discarding clothing as we went. In the bedroom, I remembered the last time I'd had Josephine, the night we made love on the top of five thousand dollars. She led me back to that bed now. Naked in the light coming from the street she was the most tempting vision I'd ever seen. And I never was any good at resisting temptation.

Josephine lay on her back on the bed. I followed her down, licking her stiffening nipples as I reached between her thighs with one hand. Then I was in her again, lifting myself up on straight arms so I could look down at her face and chest. Her black hair spilled across the white pillow.

I loved the way her breasts jiggled with every move of my hips, a hypnotic motion. Josephine's eyes were closed, and she was biting her lip, letting out small groans as we shared our hunger for each other.

It was like the first time we ever made out. It was better than that. There was something different about her, something I couldn't fathom. Afterward, we slept for maybe two hours then we got dressed and went back downstairs. The dinner and the wine remained untouched as we sat at the kitchen table for a while. I asked her a shit load of questions in one sentence:

"What's going on Jo? What do you need me for? You did kick me out, remember? Why am I here?"

Jo took her time, even managed to squeeze out some tears as she said she thought Ko was doing some kind of property deal with some crooks from out of town; claimed not to know anything about it. That she was scared for her life and she needed me to help her.

I knew then she was lying to me. In fact, if I'm honest I knew perhaps an hour earlier that she was just doing what Ko den Hamer had instructed her to do: keep me out of the way while he got the latest delivery of money from Las Vegas. The fact that she would happily whore herself to help her lover made me sick to the stomach. Tonight, would be different though. Sure, I was out of the way but the DA's office and the F.B.I. would have Ko in custody by now. So, the whole charade with the underwear and the apron had been a waste of time.

She thought she was fooling me, and I let her think that. The near-silence as we made love in our marital bed for the last time was the final clue I needed. Josephine was up to her neck in this scheme. She was as guilty as Ko den Hamer. Did I feel guilty about playing along with her little charade? Not really. Things changed between us that evening. It was over. Stick a fork in it and turn it over, it's done.

I left the house just after eleven. Josephine came to the doorway and draped herself over me, telling me how much she loved me. Then she made a big show of saying Ko would be back soon and I should get going. I played along:

"When can I see you again?" I asked.

"I don't know, not for a few days. We don't want to tip him off…"

"What, that you are seeing your husband?"

"That's not funny Rick. Speak to the police for me, will you? Ask them what they want me to do? I could see if I could find out more about what Ko is involved in, look through some of his papers…"

She was a better actor than I originally gave her credit for. When all this did come out in the open, she'd most likely get off Scot-free if she got to talk to the judge and jury. I could imagine her pleading her innocence in front of twelve slobbering jurors…all batting eyelashes and bouncing cleavage. They wouldn't stand a chance.

As I drove away that night, I wondered which station Ko den Hamer and his Vegas cohorts would be taken to. At least that part of the evening would have been taken care of. I guess all Josephine's exertions had been for nothing…pity that.

Chapter Eighteen

The next morning, I was just waking up when there was a knock at the office door. I walked through from the tiny kitchen and opened up. It was Elton Dwight. He wore a hounds-tooth blazer, bright white button-down shirt, and black pants. His bow-tie was a gut-churning mustard color. He was not happy. I walked back to my desk saying:

"Mister Dwight, what's going on?" He said:

"I hope you know just how much trouble you are in. And more importantly, how much trouble you've dropped me in"

"What's wrong?" I asked.

"He didn't show; that's what's wrong. Nobody showed all night! I had fourteen men placed around that site; we all froze our asses off till two in the morning for nothing. Now I've got to explain to the D.A. why I organized this raid and what evidence I was relying on. And all I've got is you. And I don't mind telling you Rick, that's not good for me and it's certainly not good for you."

"I don't know what happened Mister Dwight, honestly. It was all set; Josephine was keeping me out of the loop so the drop could go ahead..."

"Josephine; your wife Josephine was keeping you away from Ko den Hamer? How was she doing that Rick?"

"I don't think we need to go into that right now."

"You'd better find out what happened Rick, and fast. And you'd better find out where this money has gone, if it came into town in the first place. The F.B.I. wants to bring you in."

"What?"

"They think there's a case to answer. They think you were involved in this from the start and you only turned on Ko den Hamer when he started schtupping your wife. They know you can fly a plane and they think you are the guy bringing the money in from Vegas."

"You can't be serious," I said, but I could see that he was.

"They think it's possibly a communist plot to disrupt banking practices on the West Coast. They think you are a sympathizer."

"A Communist plot run by the mob. Dumb fucks!" Elton Dwight did not argue.

"I tend to agree with your assessment Rick but if you don't get this sorted out these dumb fucks are going to have you by the balls."

Not a great start to the day, I'm sure you'd agree. But I was determined to make things go better. I was more than determined to see Ko den Hamer in the slammer, along with my wife if need be. If the drop had gone ahead last night Ko would now be sitting on a shit load of cash. He would have to spread that cash around a little. So, he would be hitting all his favorite banks in the next few hours. It would be a good idea to follow him, make a note of where all these deposits were made and at what time of day. I could then pass on this information to Dwight and his F.B.I. buddies. It was a plan.

So, I cleaned myself up as best I could, threw on a jacket and pants, and headed out back to fire up the little sports car. I left the hood up; a damp fog had settled in, it would be close to lunch-time before the sky cleared…if it did clear. I drove against the morning rush hour, out to Oakland and the good old family homestead. Ko den Hamer's Jag was parked out front, in my spot. I trundled past about half a block, pulled over, and waited. All the time keeping watch in the rear-view. Ko and Josephine came out of the house just after nine-thirty, he was carrying a large leather doctor's bag. Ko put the bag in the trunk then started the Jag. I could hear him revving it up from half a block away. Mr. Loomis would not be happy. They drove past me moments later. I pulled in behind and followed them over the bay bridge again, back into town.

At first, I thought they were heading in to their new office on Embarcadero, I pulled over to the left ready to follow them into the parking lot. They didn't turn left; they carried on past the ferry building and followed the road around the waterfront into North Beach. Eventually, they turned left on Bay Street and almost immediately left again on Stockton. This brought them onto Chestnut Street. They drove west along Chestnut for a few blocks before stopping at a First National Bank.

I noted down the address and the time in and out. Then we were off again. Not too far this time. The next stop was Broadway and Grant in Chinatown, Wells Fargo Bank. Once again Josephine stayed in the car as Ko took the doctor's bag into the bank and came out ten minutes later. All the details went into my notebook. Just before I pulled away to follow the Jag, I happened to check my rear-view and noticed two guys in matching raincoats and hats getting into a dark blue Ford. They could not have looked more like F.B.I. agents if they tried. It was good to know my tax dollars were being put to good use. I was tempted to wave, but I thought I should probably play along. After all, I was showing them what the real crook was up to.

We took nearly an hour to reach the next stop. We were way out in Bernal Heights on Cesar Chavez, another First National Bank; same procedure. It was close to lunchtime, I was getting hungry and I could have murdered a drink, but the chase went on; a Jag, an MG and a Ford schlepping across the city dispersing illegal cash.

We headed east on Cesar Chavez, turned south on Bayshore, and eventually came to the last bank on the run at San Bruno, a Bank of America and Italy. After that the F.B.I. and I followed Ko den Hamer and my wife back to their cozy little office off Embarcadero. When we'd all got settled in the parking lot and Ko and Josephine had gone into the building I wandered over to the blue Ford. The two raincoats weren't too glad to see me even after I offered to fetch them a coffee and a donut each. I said:

"Are you sure? I'm going to be going across the street anyway; I might as well bring something back for you guys." The agent behind the wheel looked as if he thought this was a good idea. His skinny partner looked across at him frowning. Nothing more was said about coffee and donuts. The skinny passenger turned to me:

"What do you think you're doing bub?"

"I'm not Bub," I said. "I'm Rick Marshall, did you not write that down at this morning's briefing? I am the guy you're meant to be following, aren't I?"

"Just keep it up with the smart lip Bub and see where it gets you."

"Is that the kind of threat you learned at F.B.I. school, it's not very good is it?" I turned to the driver.

"Is he new at this?" I asked. "Look I just wanted to check that you guys grasped what we've just witnessed. Ko den Hamer, that's the tall blonde guy in the fancy car, he's just taken a shit load of cash and spread it out over all the banks you've just followed him around…"

"…And now he's up in the office with his hand down your wife's panties," said the agent in the passenger seat. I was quickly going off that guy. I let it slide.

"Very possibly friend, but the important thing is you and I know when and where that money was deposited because…and this is the important piece, that money is from bad guys in Las Vegas, gangsters, no less. It is, in fact, dirty money and we don't want to let the bad guys clean it up so they can spend it on more guns and drugs and naughty ladies. Are you getting all this, or am I talking too fast for you?" I asked.

"That's it!" The skinny agent made to get out of the car. I was leaning hard against his door, so he didn't get far.

"Leave it agent Crosby," said the guy behind the wheel. I stepped away from the car.

"Last chance on the coffee and donuts," I said; no takers. I walked away through the parking lot singing 'Don't Fence Me In' it just felt like the right thing to do.

The rest of the afternoon passed with little to write about. I watched the office, the F.B.I. agents watched me watching the office. The world turned.

Ko and Josephine came out at five-thirty and joined the cars and buses heading back over the bay bridge to Oakland. I let agents Crosby and Hope take the Road to Oakland. I didn't know if the driver was called Hope, but wouldn't it be funny if he was? I decided to think of him as agent Hope. This is the kind of place your mind wanders off to when you sit in a tiny Brit sports car for a whole afternoon, freezing your ass off, dying to take a piss.

The following morning, I took a cab to meet Elton Dwight at Kearney Street. I passed on the locations and times of the money drops. This kept him up to speed with the F.B.I. involvement. My little helping hand looked to have put him in a better mood than the last time we met. He shook my hand and said this was just the kind of hard evidence he needed to get search warrants for my home and Ko's new office. Then I mentioned my F.B.I. shadows.

"They followed you all day? And you spotted them right at the start?" I nodded.

"Don't be too hard on them, I think one guy is fairly new to this, maybe I was his first surveillance job."

"That's not the point," said Dwight. "They are supposed to notify me of any active surveillance details in this case."

"Must have slipped their minds," I said. Then I was brilliant. Make a note of this, because you won't hear of me being brilliant very often. Here's what I said.

"I just thought of something. Correct me if I'm wrong... I'm still the owner of the house on Derby Street. So, if I give you permission, in writing to search the house, then you don't need a warrant, do you?" Dwight beamed.

"That is smart thinking Mister Marshall."

"Brilliant, I thought," says me. "If you are going to search the place, I'd suggest you do it when they aren't there, and try not to make a mess. Don't let them find out the place has been gone over."

"We do this kind of thing all the time, Mister Marshall, don't worry. I'll tell the boys to be particularly careful."

"Hey, I'm not living there anymore. Kick the shit out of the place for all I care, it just might be more useful if we don't tip our hand. Do I sign some kind of release form?"

Elton Dwight said he would get his secretary to put something together for me to sign. Then he had to hurry off to a very important meeting on organized crime, whatever that was. I watched the pretty redhead type out the paperwork, signed two copies, one for them, one for me. Then I went downstairs and out onto Kearney Street. That's where I bumped into Ko den Hamer, much to my surprise. He said:

"Hi, Richard you're looking tired. Can you spare a minute for a little talk?"

"Sure!" I said, all bright and breezy. "Why not? Shall we walk across to the park? How's the wife and kids?"

"Funny, very funny," said Ko. And so, looking to all the world like two good buddies who just happened to meet one morning we walked over Kearney Street and into Portsmouth Square.

We found a vacant bench and sat.

"So, do you want to tell me why you've been following us for the past few days?"

"I've been employed by your lovely blonde wife. She thinks you're having an affair. You've not been home to your lovely town-house for months. And the kids really miss daddy."

"You should be in films Richard; you really crack me up." This guy was Captain Smug, he was King of Smuglandia…are all six-foot-tall, blonde-haired, evenly tanned, extremely fit Dutchmen smug bastards? Probably. Anyhow, I decided to take a little wind out of the Flying Dutchman's sails.

"What brings you down to the D.A.'s office Ko, come to turn states evidence?"

"And why on earth would I do that?" he asked.

"You do know your little money laundering scheme is under investigation?"

"They've got nothing."

"Nothing?"

"And I'll tell you why I know they've got nothing. If they had any hard evidence, they would have arrested your extremely accommodating wife and me by now."

"They could be just building a stronger case, have you thought of that?"

"Do I look worried?" asked the Dutchman. He did not. In fact, his glibly confident answers were beginning to piss me right off. I needed to make something stick. I needed to put a dent in his over-confident demeanor. So, I said this:

"Please thank Josephine for the trip down memory lane two nights back, it was good to get back in the saddle. But I knew what she was doing. I knew she was keeping me out of the way while the money was shipped into town." Ko den Hamer's expression did not change in the slightest.

"You flatter yourself, shamus. I could have let you freeze your ass off at Candlestick Point, just like all the rest of the flat-foots but I asked Josephine if she wouldn't mind giving you a pity fuck. Just for old time's sake. I thought you were looking seriously down these past few weeks, thought it might do you some good. She didn't want to do it at first, she said it was…and I quote: 'gross.' I had to persuade her. And that can be a problem with Josephine. It's very difficult to intimidate a masochist, don't you find? I mean, the more you hurt them, the more they love you. It's pathetic really. The way she looks up at you with those big cow eyes as you half choke her to death or crack a rib or two."

"Laugh it up you clog wearing dip-shit. The only thing you'll be choking is your own dick when I put you in jail." Ko laughed:

"Ha! Good one Richard. But I don't think you've really thought this through. So, I'm going to spell this out for you, just this once. Ready?"

No one ever called me Richard, well my mother did, and she hated my guts. Ko went on:

"Every document in the paper-trail currently being followed by the F.B.I. and the police…every shred of evidence only has one name on it. Can you guess who's name that is Richard? Can you guess who looks like the criminal mastermind behind this whole scheme? I'll give you a big clue…it's not me. If this whole thing falls apart tomorrow Richard, I'll be on a plane back to Europe with a great deal of money and your slutty wife will be giving blow-jobs for cigarettes in a women's prison for the next ten years…maybe she'd enjoy that. Of course, Cohen's men might just want to tidy up a few loose ends so she might not survive long enough to go to trial…"

"You used her all along."

"I'm afraid so Richard, I couldn't resist. She was just so easy to manipulate. All she needed was the teeniest bit of persuasion and she was ready to jump feet first into a life of crime and dishonesty. She was just so desperate for some excitement in her life…I think that was it. And you know the thing she enjoyed most, apart from me fucking her from behind while I choked the life out of her; the thing she enjoyed most was making a fool of you, Richard. She really does think you are quite pathetic, skulking around in back alleys spying on cheating husbands. I tend to agree, it's no way for a war hero to earn a living." I stood up; I couldn't sit there and listen to him talking anymore.

"You're not leaving, are you Richard? We were having such a nice chat. Oh well…I'll say hi to Josephine for you, shall I? Do remember what I said about the little woman. We don't want any harm to come to her, do we? Well not in that way…"

I walked away, there was nothing more to say. I walked up the hill following the diagonal pathway across the square. What was I going to do? I couldn't carry on helping Elton Dwight and the F.B.I. If their investigation was successful my wife would wind up in jail and that would kill her. I thought about ways to get rid of Ko den Hamer and for a short time, I daydreamed about killing the rat with my bare hands. But that would still send Josephine to jail as an accessory to money laundering and fraud.

For the next few days, I went to ground, moved into a flop-house with no phone, kept away from the office. I knew Elton Dwight would search the house in Oakland and the office on Embarcadero. I just didn't want to be around to witness it. After eight days I went back to the office and started checking messages again.

Whoever came up with the term 'swift justice' was talking out of their ass. Days went by before Elton Dwight got up the nerve to search my house, even with my written permission. As the days dragged by, I eventually got busy myself, back in the old routine. I took a job for Mrs. Krupeknik the wife of a sixty-six-year-old owner of a hardware store on Turk Street, not too far from City Hall. It was the easiest money I'd made in a month of Sundays. Mrs. Krupeknik thought her Emil was stepping out with a war widow called Elsie Hall. She was convinced this wicked harlot was seducing Emil, so he'd leave the store to her. She was sure Emil Krupeknik was taking money from the till and giving it to this master criminal, Mrs. Hall.

Elsie Hall worked at a grocer's store one block east of Krupeknik's Hardware. So, I called in at both the stores one day to get a good look at the lead actors in this great romance. Krupeknik was short, stout, and bald as a billiard ball. He wore one of those awful ginger wigs that sit on the top of your head like a pigeon taking a crap. He always wore a brown shop coat even when he was away from his beloved store. He struck me as the least likely adulterer I had ever seen.

Krupeknik was a creature of habit. Every sunny day at lunch-time he left the store and walked one hundred yards to a drug store on the corner of Turk and Hyde. He bought two tuna sandwiches and two coffees, and he took them to a small park. He sat on a bench and watched children play in a small playground with a swing set and slide. If it rained, he only bought one sandwich and he took it back to the store.

Elsie Hall was thin, timid; mouse-like. She never wore make-up and her sallow skin made it difficult to get a good idea of her age. She could have been thirty, she could have been forty-five. Her eyes continually flickered around, making her look perpetually nervous.

I watched Krupeknik's lunch-time routine for a week. It was the only time he was away from the store during the day. The Krupekniks lived in Oakland and I was told by Mrs. Krupeknik that her husband of forty-six years never left the house in the evening.

On two occasions during the week, Elsie Hall sat next to Mr. Krupeknik on the park bench. He would hand over one of the sandwiches and a coffee. They ate their sandwiches, drank their coffee, and talked for maybe thirty minutes before Mrs. Hall hurried back to her job at the grocery. And that was it. After a full week's surveillance, I called Mrs. Krupeknik to tell her the good news; there was no way her husband was 'stepping out' on her. Mrs. K didn't believe me. She insisted I watch him closely for another week.

The following week fall really set in. It rained pretty solid for several days. The one break came on Thursday, so I decided to watch Mr. K much more closely. I didn't go to the park; I went to the drug store, grabbed a coffee, and sat at the counter, waited for Mr. K to come in. Right on time at 12.30 he walks in, orders two sandwiches and two coffees. Then he takes one of the sandwich bags and slips some money in there. I nearly spit my coffee clean across the countertop. I couldn't believe my eyes.

Shaking my head, I followed Mr. Krupeknik out of the drug store and over to the small park on the corner. You can never predict what's going on in someone's head; people will always surprise you, no matter how much you think you've seen.

So Krupeknik sits down and minutes later Mrs. Hall joins him. They sit, they eat; they talk. She takes the brown bag away with her. As she walked away, I hurried in to sit next to Mr. Krupeknik before he could head back to the hardware store. I introduced myself:

"Hello, Mister Krupeknik. I'm Rick Marshall, I'm a private investigator."

Mr. K. got to his feet saying:

"I have to get back to the store." I pulled him back down onto the bench beside me.

"Sit down Mister Krupeknik, I won't keep you long."

"What's this about?" I told him:

"Your wife thinks you are having an affair, she paid me to watch you."

"Me? An affair? That's ridiculous!" He tried to get up again, I pulled him back down.

"What's the money for?" I asked.

"What money?"

"The money in the sandwich bag, it looked to be about twenty bucks. You give Mrs. Hall about a forty bucks per week by my calculations. What's it for, what has she got on you?"

“Nothing, it’s none of your damn business!”

“Come on Emil, I know you don’t want me to tell the wife about this…” Krupeknik grabbed my arm; you guessed it, the right arm. It hurt.

“No! Don’t tell Magda! It would kill her.”

“I gotta tell her something Mr. K. Why don’t you tell me the truth and I’ll see if I can work something out?”

Krupeknik sat on the bench for a minute or so, not saying anything. I was about to nudge him when he finally spoke in a much quieter voice:

“Our son Conrad was in the Marines. He was killed at Iwo Jima along with Mrs. Hall’s husband. They were school friends who signed up together, they’d always been close. Three months after they died, I got a letter from Conrad. Obviously, it must have been posted by someone else in the platoon. I still have the letter, though Magda has never read it. Mrs. Hall has a son, Bradley. In the letter our son confesses to being Bradley’s father. He said they had a brief fling, a one night stand he calls it; that his buddy never knew about it. He said he wants me to help Mrs. Hall, Elsie. To make sure she doesn’t struggle to bring up his son.”

Mr. Krupeknik was sobbing quietly. I helped him to his feet and walked with him back to his hardware store. By the time we got there, he had dried his tears.

“What are you going to tell Magda?” he asked. I had no idea.

“Oh, I’ll think of something,” I said. “Or maybe it’s time for you to tell her Mister Krupeknik. You know there is a plus side to this story. Like so many other people you and your wife have lost a son you loved. But you have a grandson whose life you both can be part of, if you choose.”

I left it at that. I was in danger of sounding like Bing Crosby in ‘Going my Way.’ I walked away smiling. I would make a lousy priest.

Chapter Nineteen

Over the next few days, I started planning the flight to Vancouver, British Columbia. The Beaver had a range of just over 380 miles. This would get me half-way to Seattle. I figured I would follow my previous route to Portland, stopping for fuel in Eureka again. Portland to Seattle was only 175 miles so I would have plenty of fuel after the Portland stop to reach Deep Cove. I was debating whether to make a stop in Seattle to refuel; then I'd be sure of having enough to get back over the border without worrying about getting aviation fuel when I was in Canada.

I marked out way-points and headings on a map and made a copy of the flight plan in my note-book. I had a closer look at my options for the border crossing. I had two potential routes that looked best. On leaving Seattle I could head out over Whidbey Island then drop down to sea level and thread my way through the San Juan Islands. The problem with this route was you entered Canada fairly close to the international airport at Sea Island, Richmond, BC. There was a good chance of showing up on someone's radar at that point, not a good idea.

The other alternative was to head north east and hide the plane between the peaks of the Northern Cascades, crossing into Canada a few miles east of a place called Chilliwack. The rest was plain sailing down the Fraser River Valley before a little hop into Indian Arm and Deep Cove. This route also had problems. If the weather closed in when I was in the mountains there was no alternative than to turn back, that was if I could. I made a note of all possible places I could put the Beaver down if I ran into bad weather. But there weren't that many once I passed Baker Lake and that was nearly thirty miles from the Canadian border.

I suppose I could follow the coast north past Bellingham before heading due north to my destination. I figured this route, although the most direct, would be the one where I was most likely to be spotted and reported crossing the border. I had some thinking to do. I phoned Big Paddy Brady and asked if the Beaver was available for a shake-down. I had to explain what a shake-down flight was but after I did so Mr. Brady said I could drive out to Sausalito and take the Beaver up tomorrow, weather permitting. I did not ask if he'd heard anything from Inga and he didn't volunteer any information. I assumed everything was in hand north of the border, he would have told me otherwise, wouldn't he?

The next morning, a Thursday, dawned with light rain and high cloud. Not ideal but fine for a little jaunt over Richardson Bay. I got to Sausalito just after ten, the rainclouds were thinning out. A goon I'd never seen before escorted me down the dock then lit a cigarette and watched nonchalantly as I began checking over the Beaver.

"You might want to put that out or move a little further away," I called. "I'm going to check the fuel tanks for water in the system."

"Is it dangerous?" he asked. I nodded.

"Why run the risk?" I asked. My smoking friend walked twenty yards back down the dock. I took my time, did all the pre-flight checks. My compadre kept his distance. Eventually, I called him back.

"I'm all done with the pre-flights. I'm going to start up the engine, warm her up then take her for a little spin. Do you want to come along?"

"Is it dangerous?" he asked. I shook my head.

"I'll take good care of you. Look, you either hang about here for half an hour or you come along for the ride, which'll it be?"

The goon dropped his cigarette, stamped it out carefully on the dock then ran back to the aircraft.

"I've never been on a plane." He said.

"Fortunately for you, I have. Climb aboard, take the right-hand seat and strap your-self in."

I started the engine and ran it up a little, watching the oil pressure rise steadily. When we were ready to go, I handed a set of headphones to my new co-pilot.

"Put these on, I'm just going to untie the plane then we'll be on our way. This little button on the control column is what you press when you want to speak to me. Apart from that don't touch anything." He looked across at me and I knew there was a question forming.

"No, it's not dangerous," I said. I untied the plane and jumped aboard, slamming the door behind me. I strapped myself in, got comfortable. And with that, I pushed the throttle forward and we eased away from the dock, the radial engine growling coarsely before us. There was very little wind, so we were okay to take off on our current heading. I selected the correct flap and propeller settings. I looked across at my co-pilot, gave him a thumbs up. He gave me a straight lipped smile in return. I pushed the throttle all the way to the stops and soon we were hitting seventy miles an hour over slightly choppy waters. I eased back on the control column and we climbed into the air.

Up at one thousand feet, I banked sharply to the right and swung the Beaver round onto a reciprocal heading. This would take us back over the Golden Gate. I figured if I was going to be doing guided tours, I should figure out the best routes to take. I imagined myself giving facts and figures to wealthy tourists about the bridge as we flew between the towers. My companion was staring out at the cars on the bridge.

"Jeez mister, this is the tops!" He shouted. I must have smiled that smug smile that all experienced pilots give to people on their first flight. It had been some time since I'd seen someone bitten by the bug.

"Yeah, it's fun isn't it?"

"Could you teach me?"

"This is your lucky day," I said. "Some of these planes only have one control column. This one has two, so if you like I can let you fly her for a few minutes, get a feel for it."

"Would ya?"

"Sure, no problem, let's just get a little further out to sea." I climbed another thousand feet on a westerly heading. Then I gave him a quick run-down of the controls he'd be using. I explained how the pedals worked the rudder and how banking with the control column turned the plane. I said I would handle the throttle for him.

"First we are going to fly straight and level. You won't need to do much at all, just get a feel for the control column. Hold the nose steady in front of you. You see this dial?" he nodded. "Keep the little wings straight on the center-line; that will keep you straight and level." I kept my hands lightly on the column and said:

"You have control." As soon as he gripped the column, I could feel the tension in his wrists.

"Relax, relax. You aren't strangling a chicken. Just hold it like you're driving a car down a straight road."

"Got it," he said. And he did, after a while, he eased the death grip on the controls and managed to keep us straight and level. Then I talked him through the next step.

"Right…now we are heading for Honolulu right now and that's way out of range for this bird. We need to turn her around. So, here's what we do. When I say go you press down a little on the right peddle, the rudder pedal. At the same time, you tilt the column to the right just a little bit. I will tell you if you need to do more."

"Okay, I'm ready," he said.

“One last thing, we need to keep the nose of the plane at the same height it is compared to the horizon. Now you can either judge that by what you see out of the front of the plane or you can look at that same instrument I showed you before. That’s the turn and bank indicator. Got that?”

“I think so.”

“You might need to pull back just a little on the control column; just a touch, that will keep your altitude steady.”

I checked our surroundings and said:

“All clear, let’s give it a go.”

My first pupil started the turn, like all first-timers he let the nose drop a little. I helped him out and pulled back a touch on the control column.

“You feel that? That’s me keeping the nose level, look over the nose. See the horizon?” He nodded. By now we were heading back toward the Golden Gate from the Pacific Ocean side. I took control of the plane.

“Okay you can relax now, I have control.” My star pupil let out an excited whoop which nearly perforated my eardrums.

“If you’re going to do that, don’t have the mic open,” I said.

“Sorry.” We flew over Alcatraz then turned north and did a low-level pass over Richardson Bay before setting up for our approach and landing. I did my pre-landing checks then said to my ‘pupil’

“Follow me through on the controls and you’ll get an idea of what we do to land one of these things on water.” I talked him through every step of the way as we touched down gently before taxiing into the dock. When we had secured the aircraft and turned off the engine, he grabbed me by the hand, pumping my arm up and down for a minute solid. It still hurt a little. I didn’t mention it.

“Gee thanks Mister, you’re a real pal. Wait till I tell Wanda-June, she won’t believe it! Anything I can do for you, you only need to ask. Any time you’re in a pickle yessir, just ask for Dwayne Gibson, I’ll be there!” I had made a friend for life and all it had cost me was one dislocated elbow and temporary deafness in both ears.

The next day I went back to the hospital to have my right forearm checked out. After the usual two hours wait, I was seen by a doctor and given the all-clear in less than five minutes. So now there was nothing stopping me flying north to Vancouver. I didn’t tell Paddy Brady straight away. I needed time to get my head around what I might find when I got up there and what I might have to do before I came back. Eventually I bit the bullet and called on him at the hotel in Sausalito, told him I was ready to go. I took the opportunity to do an engine run up on the Beaver too.

Driving back across the Golden Gate I noticed a black and white slide in behind me. As we came off the bridge, they hit the lights and siren and pulled me over. I had no idea why I was being stopped; I was driving in light traffic doing the same speed as everyone else. I guessed they were going to give me the old 'your brake light is out, here's a ticket' shake-down. When we got to Fort Point, I pulled onto the hard shoulder. I kept my hands on the wheel and waited for the officer to give me the inevitable speech. Nothing happened. Eventually, I turned around in the seat to find myself looking down the barrel of a shotgun. The shotgun seemed to be loosely connected to a very nervous uniformed police officer who was shaking like it was 1906 all over again. In case you aren't up on your history, we had a pretty big earthquake here in 1906, followed by a very big fire, it was kind of a big deal.

I kept my hands on the wheel and tried to speak in a slow calm voice which isn't easy when you have to shout over the noise of cars and trucks passing close by.

"What can I do for you officer?"

"You can keep your hands where I can see them."

"No problem there. Why have you pulled me over?"

"Stop talking and keep your hands…"

"…Where you can see them, got it. Do you normally pull a shotgun for a traffic stop?"

"Stop talking I said."

So, I sat there for what felt like ten minutes, traffic continued to rumble past, seagulls squawked, a steamer passed under the bridge behind me. Eventually, a familiar figure got out of the black and white and strode slowly up to the M.G. Detective Grunwald was wearing the same coat he wore when we first met, a light tan raincoat with a belt hanging loose. It blew about his legs as he came up to the M.G. He held his hat on his head with one hand. I nodded a greeting and reached for the door handle. The cold barrel of the shotgun was pressed hard against the back of my neck.

"I told you…"

"…Stand down!" yelled Grunwald. He opened the door for me. "Let's talk in the back of the black and white. It will be much quieter."

We walked back side by side to the police car.

"Sorry about Mullen, he's only been on patrol twice, he gets kinda jumpy."

"Kinda?" Grunwald laughed as he opened the rear door of the black and white.

"You weren't nervous, were you? A big tough private dick like you?"

"Very funny. What do you want Detective?"

"Get in the car jackass, I want a little word." I got in the car.

"Okay Mister Marshall, Private Detective; can you tell me why you just spent all morning at a hotel owned by a cornerstone of the local criminal community?"

"You mean Paddy Brady?"

"You know damn well I mean Paddy Brady!"

"I was running some tests on an aircraft he now owns."

"Really?" he asked.

"Really," I said.

"I would never have guessed that would be your answer."

"Life's full of little surprises Detective Grunwald; so, if that's all, I'll be getting along."

"In the little red faggot car that used to belong to Brady's wife?"

"If you say so..."

"I do say so! And another thing I say is you seem to be doing an awful lot of work for Mister Brady. And spending a lot of time with his people."

"...I'm just trying to earn a decent living Detective, just like you." For some reason, this short phrase really got under Grunwald's skin.

"You are nothing like me, you two-bit key-hole peeper! I've got my eye on you Marshall. I know you're up to something and I know you had way more to do with that double homicide than you are telling. I'm going to give you just enough rope to hang yourself then I'll have you inside so fast...And another thing, where's the leggy blonde you were working with?"

"I don't think you have much chance with her Detective, but if you like I could put in a good word for you if you're looking for a date."

"With that dyke freak? Get the fuck outta my car!" I got the fuck outta his car as instructed.

"So, you don't want me to put in a good word with Inga, next time I see her?" Grunwald reached over and slammed the door. It was fun to score these little victories against the dark forces of repression. I could not help but smile as I walked back to the little faggot M.G. From that day on 'Little Faggot' became my pet name for the red sports car.

Over the next few days, I continued my preparations for the flight to Vancouver, I calculated the amount of total fuel I'd need, put together a budget to present to Paddy Brady. I assumed he'd hand over cash to cover my expenses on the trip. I thought about carrying a couple of drums of aviation fuel in the bag of the passenger bay. There was plenty of room for them; I'd need a hand pump too. In the end, I decided I wouldn't need them. The extra weight would not be worth carrying for what would, in truth, be just emergency back-up. I knew where I was going to set down for fuel and I had two or three alternatives noted on my maps.

I had heard nothing from Elton Dwight or the F.B.I. about the planned raid on my house. In fact, I'd heard nothing at all about anything from both these twin arms of law enforcement. So, by the end of the week, I decided they could go screw themselves. I was ready for the flight.

I phoned Brady and told him I was ready to go. He suggested that I set off early Sunday morning if the weather heading north was good enough. There'd be less commercial traffic early Sunday morning which would be a good thing. I listened to the weather forecast every night as the weekend drew closer. On Saturday I phoned San Francisco airport and got a more detailed forecast for the next twenty-four hours. I was all set, packed, and ready to go. I planned to get a good night's sleep and then drive over to Sausalito sometime around six in the morning. I went to bed at nine. And then the phone rang.

It was Elton Dwight.

"Good evening Mister Marshall, I'm surprised to find you at home on a Saturday night, or should I say at the office?"

"Whatever." As you might have guessed, I was not happy to get the call. Dwight went on:

"I thought I should let you know, whilst your wife and her lover were at Bay Meadows this afternoon, we were able to gain entrance to your property on Derby Street in Oakland."

"And?"

"And we were able to photograph a number of documents that look to be extremely incriminating. The bad news is they all appear to be extremely incriminating for your wife Josephine, and only your wife. Ko den Hamer's name is not on any document."

"I'm not too surprised to hear that. He told me as such."

"And you didn't think to mention that to me?" asked Dwight, he sounded almost hurt.

"Haven't you got anything on the Dutchman?"

"Nothing that will stand up in court. Most of it is hearsay or circumstantial at best. If we arrest him a half-decent lawyer will have him back on the streets in no time. Your wife is a different matter. I could charge her right now and make it stick. She's looking at ten to twelve minimum."

"What are you going to do?"

"I'm afraid the more relevant question is: what are you going to do Mister Marshall? We are going to have to catch Mister den Hamer in the act, with a substantial amount of Mister Cohen's money in his personal possession. I truly believe that's the only way we can bring charges."

"So why don't you just step up the surveillance, put a tail on the guy round the clock. There's bound to be another drop, and soon I think."

"Would that it were that simple Rick. If I allocate any more man-hours on this someone higher up is going to ask why we haven't already arrested Mrs. Marshall. As I already said, there's sufficient evidence to bring charges right now." I was really ticked, I said:

"Okay, okay. I get the picture. It's all down to yours truly."

"I'm afraid so...and I would be extremely grateful if you could find the time to let us know what you plan to do **before** you do it...Do keep in touch." He rang off. I got back on the cot and tried to go to sleep. The neon signs across the street shone red through my office blinds. The place looked like it was bathed in blood. I wondered if that was an omen.

Chapter Twenty

And so, the next morning, off I went into the wild blue yonder. Except the sky wasn't blue it was dark grey with a hint of orange in the east. I had to do my pre-flight checks by flashlight; that took me back. I had packed my heavy sheepskin flying jacket as I had been told that it got cold in Canada. I also packed vital supplies: a thermos of this new-fangled Irish Coffee and some ham sandwiches.

By seven-thirty I was en-route to my first way-point at Eureka. I watched the dawn brighten the canopy of muscular cumulus clouds to my starboard side. In just under two hours I was approaching my first stop. I put down behind the breakwater just like last time, dead on time. I taxied to the jetty Inga and I had found on the first flight north in the Beaver, had them top up the fuel tanks, took a fifteen-minute break to stretch my legs, hit the john and then I was back in the air right on schedule. Next stop Portland. The clouds above me grew darker as I followed the coastline north and there was a little rain but nothing to worry about. Visibility below the clouds was fine.

I pushed on, in just under two and a half hours at a steady cruising speed of 120 miles an hour I was over Portland. I did my usual low pass before turning into wind for a landing on the river just north of the airport. I'd phoned Salty's a few days ago and, true to their word, they had a drum of fuel at the end of the dock ready for me. I was really beginning to enjoy flying the Beaver; it was steady as a rock and practically flew itself once you got the trim set correctly.

Once I had been tied off Cleveland Smith came down the dock with a fresh pot of coffee to top up my thermos. We shook hands; it was like being met by an old air force buddy.

"Hiya Rick! How are things? Where's that pretty blonde lady of yours?"

"Funny you should ask Cleveland; I'm heading north to pick her up; take her and another lady friend back to San Francisco."

"Is the other lady anywhere near as pretty as Inga?"

"She just might be; I've never met her in person."

"How come you get to fly all over the north-west with pretty women on board and all I got to fly was mail, parcels, and the odd pig?"

"Just lucky, I guess. Hey Cleveland, I'm going to be heading back through here southbound, but I don't know what day yet. Is it okay to give you a call and we set up to do the same thing as today?"

"So long as you keep paying in cold hard cash and you bring the warm soft women in to see me."

"You should have been a poet Cleveland. You have such a way with words."

I would have been happy to stay for an hour or so at Salty's; maybe get a hot meal close by. But time was tight. I needed to keep to my flight plan, or I'd be trying to land on unfamiliar water in near darkness. And that would be stupid. So, I was back in the air in double quick time, following a heading for my next planned stop; the northern end of Lake Washington just past Seattle city-center. This was just under 180 miles north of Portland, it should take me one and a half hours.

I ran into more rain and a slight headwind; it got a little lumpy for a while but nothing I couldn't handle. I lost a little altitude to get a smoother ride. I had flown into Seattle before, to Boeing Field. This was to ferry a brand new B17 down to Santa Ana. As Boeing field is south of the city, I'd never actually seen Seattle from the air. I took the Beaver west of my originally planned heading in order to skirt around the edge of the still busy airfield. Then I flew along the waterfront at a thousand feet. I could easily spot the ferry terminal and a large sign saying: **Port of Seattle** so I wasn't lost.

I gained a little height before turning right over the northern edge of the city itself. This brought me over a large expanse of water, Lake Washington. All I had to do was follow the water to the northern end and a place called Kenmore. Kenmore Washington was the home of Kenmore Air. I'd been given a contact name there by Cleveland Smith at Salty's. He told me:

"This guy Bob Munro knows all there is about floatplanes, Kenmore Air's been around since '46. They service Seabees and Cessnas and pretty much anything that floats and flies. They run charters into the backwoods for hunters and the like. Give him a call and when you get there say hi to Bob for me…he's a good guy. He'll want to have a good look at the Beaver. I hear he's thinking about buying a few."

So right after I tied up at Kenmore's jetty, I go looking for this Bob Munro guy. The place was really busy with floatplanes lined up next to a central hangar, there was a marina to the left and in the distance, what looked like a cement plant. Bob Munro came out to meet me accompanied by a large black and tan Alsatian dog. Bob was a solidly built, athletic-looking man, maybe five years older than me. He had mechanic's hands, finger-nails encrusted with black oil. I mentioned Cleveland's name and his broad face warmed with a wide smile.

"How is the old goat?" he asked.

"He was doing fine when I left him about two hours ago. He said you might want to have a look at the DHC – 2."

"Sure would, if you've got the time."

Bob made sure his dog was being looked after then we walked back out to the Beaver.

"I like the color scheme," he said. "I might use something like that on some of our new planes. If you're working in snow and you have to put down in an emergency all white is not the best color to have your plane painted." We climbed aboard; I let Bob take the left-hand seat. He said:

"I hear she's pretty solid, lots of bush pilots are saying good things about this plane. I'm not too sure about buying a Canadian aircraft though, I'd like to buy local of course but Boeing seems to be building nothing but bigger commercial planes these days."

"Do you want to take her up?" I offered.

"Hell yeah, if you have the time," I said I could spare half an hour. Bob called a guy over who untied us and gave us a gentle push away from the jetty. I talked Bob through the engine start and pre-flight checks were completed as we drifted out a way. The Lake was busy with pleasure craft and the odd speedboat. We had to wait a few minutes for some clear water. I had one final check around the aircraft.

"Okay, you're clear to go."

"Roger that." Bob pushed the throttle forward and we began our take-off run. Once again, the Beaver was up on the step in what felt like seconds and we were climbing into the sky over Seattle equally quickly. Bob made a climbing turn to the west taking us over the expanding suburbs of Northwest Seattle. I could see lots of new subdivisions under construction as we continued our climb out. Soon we were over Puget Sound. Once over water, Bob put the Beaver through some fairly intense maneuvers, tight turns with lots of bank, aggressive climbs. He even tried to stall her out, taking the throttle back to idle and pulling back on the stick. The Beaver stalled as he had planned but he recovered it very quickly.

"That was okay, I've heard that the Beaver can get into a spin fairly quickly…I could feel it might if you stalled in a tight turn."

"Hey if you don't get into a stall in the first place it wouldn't be a problem," I said. Bob agreed:

"Too true…you know I think De Havilland have got a very good aircraft here."

"They made a beauty during the war, The Mosquito. The fastest plane I ever saw."

"Agreed, but not much use for Kenmore Air. I don't think I know any carpenters so airframe repairs would be tricky." I said:

"Still it was a great plane, with those two Merlins it even sounded fast. There's got to be lots of them going cheap now, surplus to requirements. If only I could think of a use for one…"

Bob did a tight right turn and headed back toward the northern end of Lake Washington and Kenmore Air. Five minutes later he made a perfect landing and brought the aircraft back to the jetty. He left the Beaver running and jumped out. I moved across to the left-hand seat and got settled in. Bob shouted back:

"Where are you headed now?" I was ready for this question.

"Blaine; got a client camping out at some-place called Semiahmoo Point, should be heading back down in two or three days. I'll give you a call."

"Don't stray too far north of Semiahmoo Point or you'll be in Canada."

"I'll try to keep that in mind," I said and waved goodbye.

I was back in the air shortly after that, making a sweeping turn to bring me round onto a northerly heading. It was decision time. Where was I going to cross the border? I flew due north over Whidbey Island. Within twenty minutes I was flying over the Strait of Georgia. I tilted the plane and looked down; I could see the inlet guarded by Lummi Island. I was passing a small town called Bellingham. Twenty miles northeast of here was Cultus Lake. Cultus Lake was in Canada.

I set my course. Ahead and to the east, the sky was beginning to blacken. Cloud cover was getting thicker. A curtain of darkening cumulus was blocking my path down to roughly six thousand feet. There was a storm developing. I calculated I had enough room below the clouds to get to my destination. It would most likely be a bumpy ride, but I didn't want to risk flying blind. I'd done it hundreds, maybe thousands of times before but not after the incident with the burning B17. The doctors had warned me they couldn't predict how I would handle instrument flying with the damage to my inner ear.

I was passing over a wide flat plain covered in farms but ahead of me, I could see the terrain rise to meet me as I approached the start of the Northern Cascades. I would have to watch my altitude very carefully. The farmland changed to trees and the valleys ahead of me grew steeper. I saw a river below me. *'That should be the north fork of the Nooksack River.'* I thought. If I was correct, I didn't have far to go. The river flowed through pine-covered hills,

hills I needed to stay out of. The Beaver was starting to jump around in the rough air, rising and falling like a boat in a stormy sea. I had to watch myself, keep the airspeed up but still hold her below the cloud cover. I re-set the trim to help with this.

Out of the left-side window I caught sight of a small lake just a few miles directly to the north. I banked left, turned toward it. This should be Silver Lake. This lake ran north-south, if I flew directly over it, I would be in Canada a minute later. I calculated I crossed the border just after Silver Lake and the tree-covered hills switched back to farmland almost immediately. I was scanning the sky continually at this point but there was no other traffic.

Off to the east, I could now see Cultus Lake, a larger body of water. I flew down a wide flat valley running in a north-easterly direction. Gentle pine-covered hills rose either side of the flatland but there was plenty of room to maneuver. After Cultus Lake, there was a gap in the hills leading out onto a much wider area of farmland. This was the Fraser Valley, I was sure of it.

I turned west before I flew over the town called Chilliwack, picked up the Fraser River, and followed it toward my destination. Things smoothed down a little and I was now heading away from the worst of the growing storm.

With the Fraser below me, I had farm-land and flat valley floors to my left, and a mountain range roughly half a mile away to my right. The light was beginning to fade now. I needed to have this plane down on the water inside half an hour at the latest. It began to rain. I pushed on.

Another few minutes flying west brought me to the last landmark I had on my map, Burnaby Mountain. As the Fraser meandered westward, snaking left and right across a wide valley I saw a prominent wooded hill off to my right. This was Burnaby Mountain. I could make out houses dotted around the base but only the odd trail leading to the summit. I turned north. As soon as I passed Burnaby Mountain, I pulled the power way back and started preparing for a landing. Indian Arm was directly ahead, a long stretch of water, dotted with islands, stretching away to the north-east. I saw three sets of navigation lights on the water, most likely small pleasure boats heading home at the end of the day. In the distance, I could make out snow-covered peaks. The water ahead of me was now in complete darkness.

The water looked black below me as the sun was going down away to my left. I think I saw some kind of bridge with two towers about a mile to the west. I dropped down steeply to two hundred feet or so, the altimeter wouldn't be of much use at this height, I was going to have to judge this myself. From what I could see in the gathering gloom the steep hillsides either side of the inlet were thick with pine trees. They looked as if they grew right down to the water's edge in most places. I flew just over a mile up Indian Arm. I could see house lights dotted along the western shore. Then I made a tight 180-degree turn, carefully watching my airspeed and height, before heading back down the inlet. Deep Cove was basically a cluster of lights at the southern end of Indian Arm.

I could see no boats or obstructions on the water, so I planned to make a landing on my next pass. It was raining heavily now, drumming on the wing above my head like Gene Krupa on speed. I cut the throttle and nursed the Beaver lower and lower toward the inky water. I craned my neck to keep the best look-out possible over the stubby nose. I touched down with the lights of Deep Cove less than half a mile away on my right-hand side.

Then I saw what I thought was a large log floating across my path about a hundred yards ahead of me. I had to move fast. I slammed the throttle forward and pulled back on the controls with all my might. We were still on the water. I pulled back on the stick hard as the revs began to climb. The stall warning buzzed as I got the nose up into the air. I was sure I was going to hit the log. I decided to lift the left float as I went over the log, turning the controls to the right. That might just save me, so long as I could bring the aircraft level again. I flipped the control column to the left seconds later and the right float hit the water, the left float slammed down just after. I killed the power and fought to straighten the plane up. Eventually, I slowed and with the engine back at idle I turned her round to investigate what I'd almost hit.

It wasn't a log. It was a guy in a canoe, for Christ's sake! No lights, nothing, just toodling along in the twilight, not a care in the world. He paddled over to me.

"You okay?" he asked.

"Am I okay? I nearly took your head off. Are you okay?"

"I'm fine…You looking for a place to tie up?"

"Do you know somewhere? I might be a few days."

He pointed toward the lights of Deep Cove. There looked to be one road heading away from the village following the shore northward. Lights appeared on that road at irregular intervals, probably holiday cottages. The guy in the canoe pointed to the very last light.

"That's my brother's place. There's a small dock down on the water there. Follow me." He set off rowing his canoe toward the last light. I let him get twenty yards ahead of me so I could keep him in sight, then I eased the throttle forward and followed him in. After I had tied up and made the aircraft secure, he joined me on the dock. We shook hands and he introduced himself.

"Larry George," he said. I told him my name then I said:

"I'm in from Victoria for a few days, looking to meet up with two women." Larry was a native Indian. He wasn't a tall man; he was dark-skinned and had long black hair with streaks of grey which he wore loose to his shoulders. He joked:

"You looking for two particular women or will any two do?"

"One's from Iceland. She's six feet tall has short blonde, almost white, hair. You wouldn't forget her if you met her. The other one's been staying around here for two or three weeks."

"Well, there ain't a decent-sized hotel on the North Shore, not that I know of. She must be rooming with someone if she's staying in the Cove. Or maybe they're at the Motel."

We walked back up to the house which was a small wooden shack with oil lamps for light. A fast-running stream tumbled over rocks to one side of the shack which looked like it was hanging on to the side of the hill.

Larry asked: "You hungry?"

"Starving."

"I've got a salmon ready to go, do you want some?"

"That would be great, thanks." Larry busied himself prepping the salmon. He got a fire lit in a metal container dug into the ground next to the stream; he threw cedar chips on the flames.

"It'll take a while to warm up," he said. "Grab a couple of beers from the cooler." I did as he asked. We sat out on the small deck looking up at the stars as the fire grew hotter. Eventually, he placed a whole salmon, minus the head, in the embers at the side of the flames. He turned it once after ten minutes or so. The smell was fantastic, I didn't think I could hold out much longer without tucking into this feast. Eventually, Larry carefully picked the salmon out of the flames with some long metal forks then hurried inside to prepare it for serving. He came back out minutes later with two tin plates laden with slabs of fresh salmon and some crusts of bread. He handed me a plate.

"Dig in; I'll get some more beer."

I know I was hungry but that simple meal on my first night in Canada has to go down as one of the greatest meals I've ever eaten. Afterward, we talked for some time, mainly about Larry's life, growing up on a nearby reservation, joining the Canadian Army when he was eighteen, his military service as a sniper in Europe. He told all about what he went through during the D-Day landings and the race to Berlin. I listened mainly. He liked to talk that was for sure.

By ten o'clock I was out on my feet. The long flight had caught up with me a little, so I thanked Larry for his hospitality and made my way back down to the dock. I climbed aboard the Beaver and laid out my sleeping bag on the back-bench seat in the passenger compartment. I laid my flying jacket over the sleeping bag. I was asleep in seconds.

The next morning dawned with low cloud hiding the peak of Mount Seymour which rose to the north of Deep Cove. I walked along the sweeping curve of the bay heading south into the village. Well, when I say village, I mean one street. That's really all I could find. It was called Gallant Avenue and it led from the main waterfront up the hill for maybe eight hundred yards before turning sharply left and heading away, I guess, toward civilization and Vancouver itself. I got the feeling that the City of Vancouver must be many miles away. Deep Cove felt like it was at the end of a very long and winding road.

There was a long wooden jetty pointing out into the bay. Signs indicated some kind of ferry service ran from there, I guess to the city. Turning my back to the water I saw a row of single-story shops including a cafe on the right-hand side of Gallant Avenue ending with an Esso Garage up on the hill, just before the bend. I counted four cars in the whole place. I guess this was good news because if Constance Brady and Inga were staying here one of the locals would know about it. Now all I had to do was find a local. It was a Monday morning and almost ten, but I could not find another living soul in the place. I figured I could either stand around like a spare part waiting for the shops to open or I could walk up to the garage and ask there. It took me all of three minutes to walk from one end of town to the other.

The garage had one pump and one bay. It was run by one man. I guess the one horse was out for a walk when I called. Gus the owner/mechanic/gas jockey wore the regulation oily dungarees. He had the oily rag ready to wipe his hands on. He was a tall, slim, bald man with wisps of ginger hair above his ears. I nodded a good morning and said:

"I'm looking for a young blonde woman…"

"…Aren't we all?" was his predictable reply.

"She's staying with another lady, up from the States. Where do you think I should start looking?"

"And what exactly do you want with these women?"

"I'm supposed to fly them back to San Francisco."

"And you say they are staying in the Cove?" I nodded.

"Have you tried Thornley's Place?" I shook my head.

"What's Thornley's Place?"

"It's a motel, just down the road; turn right, can't miss it." The mechanic pointed back down toward the water, back where I'd just come from. I thanked him for his time and set off toward the water. As I walked down the street the town was coming to life. Shopkeepers were winding out awnings, putting signs out. Total strangers wished me 'good morning' as I walked by. It really was a pretty little place. A lot of the trees by the water were turning yellow and orange and the bay itself shone blue in the September sunshine. And it was so quiet. I could see how someone might want to escape here. I followed the mechanic's directions and turned right at the waterfront onto Banbury. I could see the sign for **COVE VIEW COURT.**

The motel consisted of maybe six log cabins nestled amongst some mature pine trees. It faced Banbury Road on one side and the waterfront on the other. The largest log cabin was the office. I went in, rang the silver bell on the counter.

"Can I help you?" A woman in her early thirties came out from the rear. Her brown hair was cut in a practical style, just to neck length. She wore sensible horn-rimmed glasses. She had a name tag: Reta. I dialed up the friendly manner:

"Hi Reta, I'm hoping you can. I'm Rick; I'm looking for two ladies who have been staying in the Cove for a few weeks. One gal's called Inga, she's very tall, has short blonde hair…the other's not much older, that's Constance; she's a red-head, or she was the last time I saw her. We were supposed to meet up today, but I lost the piece of paper with their address on, I'm such a goof."

Reta looked me over for a while. Not sure what to make of me, I guess. Eventually, she came to a decision.

"They're not in right now. They said they were going for a walk."

"Any idea where?" I asked.

"You just missed them; they were going to walk along the front by the Yacht Club down to the beach. It's only a few minutes away."

"Thanks' Reta, I think I'll wander down there and surprise them."

I walked through the trees to the water's edge and turned left. I could see the Yacht Club at the base of the main street. It wasn't what I expected when Reta said: 'Yacht Club.' It was a just another wooden shack, painted white with a British Flag hanging from the gutter. It looked more like a storage shed than a yacht club. Still, I headed over there. The ladies had walked past the Yacht Club and were actually heading out on the road that would eventually bring them to the Beaver. Were they heading out to look for me? I didn't think anyone in Deep Cove would have noticed my arrival yesterday evening. Maybe my canoeing friend had put the word out?

I picked up the pace and soon I was within a few yards of Inga and Mrs. Brady. I called Inga's name. What happened next will stick with me for a long time. It's not as though anything shocking occurred; it's just that time seemed to slow down so that I would remember every detail. I've read of people saying that kind of thing happens when there's a natural disaster or a car smash. I was fairly close to the two ladies by now and I saw the genuine happiness that lit Inga's face as she turned to greet me. It made me feel terrific.

Then I looked across at Constance Brady. She looked as if she was watching a runaway train heading straight for her. She had just that mixture of horror and resignation in her eyes. I felt as if I stared at Mrs. Brady for five minutes, but I guess it was just a few seconds. She was wearing faded jeans and a large baggy sweater that hung off one shoulder. Her auburn hair was worn loose; she was wearing very little make-up and dark shadows under her eyes made it look as if she hadn't slept well, but she was an attractive woman by any standards.

"Rick!" called Inga. She waved her arms in the air like a schoolgirl who's just seen Frank Sinatra on the street. I ran over and to my surprise, she gave me a bear hug. I'm sure she could have lifted me off my feet if she'd tried.

"Well fancy meeting you here!" I said. Inga laughed, Constance Brady didn't.

"Going far?" I asked.

"Just out for a walk, then we'll head to The Cove Inn, grab a coffee."

"Mind if I tag along?" I asked. Inga looped her arm through mine and the three of us carried on walking out along the track skirting the bay. I told Inga all about the flight up, trying my hardest to make it sound like Lindbergh crossing the Atlantic. Constance Brady didn't say a word. The walk out to the end of the lane and the Beaver took about half an hour. We couldn't walk any further without heading up into the woods, so we turned around and walked back into Deep Cove.

We ordered coffees at the Cove Inn and took a table by the window. We talked about the weather, I told Inga about the ongoing Ko den Hamer investigation and the bungled raid at Candlestick Point. If I asked Constance Brady anything, I got a one-word answer. She was more interested in a paperback she was reading: 'The Simple Act of Murder.' I think it was called. Maybe she was looking to pick up some tips from the master.

I would have to have a word with Inga in private, find out where we stood. I'm sure Mrs. Brady knew why I was there; I just needed to know from Inga how things were going to pan out when I called out 'all aboard the Flying Beaver!' and we skipped this popsicle stand for all points south. I asked Constance how her mother was.

"She's fine." Was the answer.

"What's wrong with her?" I asked.

"Nothing, she's as fit as a fiddle."

"So, the whole story about your mother being ill was just an excuse to get away…" Constance nodded.

"Why not fly to Calgary as planned?"

"Because that would be the first place he looked." Was the answer. "I didn't think anyone would make the Raul connection and I didn't expect him to squeal quite so easily."

After coffee, we walked back to the motel. Mrs. Brady said she was going to her cabin to read. This would give me the chance to really talk to Inga. I suggested to Inga that we leave Mrs. Brady to her paperback. We walked down a few steps at the front of the motel and found a rustic wooden bench looking out over the water. It was a pretty sheltered spot as giant pine trees towered over the scattering of cabins that made up the motel.

"I don't think she'll go back willingly," said Inga, starting the discussion. "In fact, I think she might do something stupid if we try to force her."

"What do you mean?"

"She might do herself harm."

"You mean try to kill herself?" I asked. Inga shook her head.

"No, no I don't think she's the type, but she just might do something that would make it impossible to fly her out of here."

"What can she do? Tie her-self to a rock?" Inga punched me on the arm.

"Idiot!"

"What? It was a logical question! Do you think we need to keep her under close watch? That she might try run away again?"

Inga said she wasn't sure. She'd talked with Mrs. Brady over the past two weeks and she was pretty determined…she was not going back to her husband. My head hurt. This was not going to be easy.

"What happened to the 'flight to Europe' idea? I thought you were going to persuade her to skip town once and for all."

"She doesn't have any money for one thing. Do you think she's the kind of lady that stays in out of the way motels like this? Brady keeps her on a pretty short leash. She can have anything she wants, but she has to ask Brady for it. She's not even got a bank account of her own."

"I thought she was staying here because she was trying to lay low…"

"That didn't work very well did it?" said Inga.

"What do you think we should do?" I asked.

"We?"

"Come on Inga! Don't be like that."

"Like what, exactly? I don't know what you expect from me, Rick." What did I expect from Inga? She was in a worse position than me, if that was possible. I mean if Brady found out she'd been sleeping with his good lady wife then Inga would very likely find herself looking at a freeway concrete support beam from the inside.

We sat on that bench for the next little while. Various boats came and went, people walked dogs to and fro; children came down to the beach presumably to play a while after school. Life in this out of the way backwater carried on around us at its own gentle pace. Finally, I spoke up.

"I think we need to have a straight talk with Constance. Look at her options…" Inga stood up quickly, and threw a pebble into the water, she turned to face me.

"You and your straight talks! This is someone's life we're talking about here! We've got to help her!" I stood up too, I said:

"I know, I know. I don't want her to go back any more than you do."

"Really? Because from where I'm sat you are the only one of us who stands to gain anything if she does go back. How much is he paying you for this job?"

"Nothing…well, nothing in cash."

"Go on…"

"If I get Constance to go back, he's going to give me the plane." For a moment Inga appeared to be speechless with rage. Finally, she whispered one word:

"Whore."

"That's not fair," I said. "I want what's best for Constance just like you."

"So, what are you going to do about it?"

"That's a really good question."

Chapter Twenty - One

There was another pressing matter. I was hungry.

"What do we do for meals here? I'm guessing there's nothing at the Motel?" Inga looked across at me.

"Typical man…if you aren't thinking about your dick you're thinking about your stomach."

"I only asked!"

"There's a barbecue provided by the Motel, guests are free to use it whenever they want and as we are the only guests here at the moment…"

"Okay. Should I get some supplies?"

"Sure. The General Store is pretty much the only place to go. I'll come with, make sure you don't buy just steak, steak, and more steak."

"I can do shopping," I said. "But you're welcome to tag along if you like," Inga called in at her cabin to tell Constance where we were going then we set off for the store.

"Maybe I should get a room at the Motel too, if you think this might take a few days," I said. Inga replied:

"Makes sense."

"I don't suppose there's anywhere I can get a drink, maybe grab a few beers?"

"Are you joking? We're stuck in the dark ages here my friend. You've got no chance." I went to the motel office and booked a room for two days. I'd have to walk back out to the Beaver and collect a few things, but I was thinking my local contact out there might know where I could get my hands on some booze. I walked back to Inga and Constance's cabin, knocked and opened the door and walked in.

Constance Brady was lying back on the bed, eyes closed, legs open, naked from the waist down. Inga was kneeling; her head in between Mrs. Brady's spreading thighs. There was really only one thing to say, which was:

"Don't get up; I'll do the shopping on my own." I stepped back, closed the door behind me, and set off for the General Store. After a few seconds, I heard the cabin door open and slam closed behind me. Inga raced to catch up with me.

"It's not what it looks like," she said breathlessly.

"Really? So that wasn't a blow job?" I replied.

"Rick that's not what I meant, and you know it."

"Right about now it occurs to me that I don't know shit. I especially don't know shit about six-foot-tall lesbian blondes from Iceland."

"That's not fair Rick, and it's cruel," she said.

"Well, I'm sorry if I'm not at my best today Inga, for some unexplained reason I'm feeling a little confused. You see I remember you telling me you didn't love Constance, that there was nothing between you and then much to my surprise here I find you with your tongue inside her. Maybe I just jumped to the wrong conclusions, if so I'm sorry. Maybe she was just sitting on the bed half naked and you happened to trip over the carpet and fall tongue first into her cunt!"

Inga slapped me then; in the middle of the street. The clapping sound echoed slightly. I could hear a high-pitched whistling in one ear for ten minutes or more. I deserved it. I was being an asshole, and not for the first time. Luckily no-one else was around to witness the spectacle. Neither of us talked about what had just happened, we didn't talk at all. We walked to the store, we bought food, we walked half an hour out to the Beaver, we picked up my pack; we walked back to the Motel. Once there, Inga asked:

"What time do you want to eat?"

"Whatever fits in with your plans."

"We'll get the barbecue going around six." I took my pack to my cabin, threw it on the bed then threw myself after it.

Come six I was there to help get the barbecue going. The three of us went about our various food preparations as though nothing had happened that afternoon. I've known bomber crews waiting to go fly to Berlin who were less tense than we were. Sadly, or maybe luckily there was no booze to be had in the whole of Deep Cove. Around seven we tucked into standard cook-out food: burgers, hot dogs, that kind of thing. By eight the light had faded, and the temperature dropped like a stone. I lit a campfire down on the beach and we grabbed blankets from our rooms and huddled close to the flames. The stars came out and a harvest moon lit the bay in an eerie white light. I remember watching embers from the fire dancing out over the silver water. I got talking with Constance Brady.

"Did you hear about your plane blowing up?" I asked.

"There wasn't much coverage here. The local papers tend to lead with local news, you know…councilors with their hands in the till, missing pets, the winner of the biggest pumpkin competition at the P.N.E. that kind of thing. I did read about the crash though, terrible."

"What's the P.N.E?" I asked.

"The Pacific National Exhibition, it's a kind of county fair. It's held in August and September, just across the bridge." Inga chimed in:

"Aren't you the mine of information?" I said:

"If we'd not found Raul that crash would have ended all your problems. Paddy really thought you were dead. I don't know if Inga told you, but we went with him to the morgue to identify your body..."

"Eeughhh!"

"...What was left of it. Mister Brady practically did an Irish jig when he realized it wasn't you."

"That's true," said Inga. "It was quite touching really." Constance Brady scowled at Inga.

"How can you say that? You know what he's like; whoring and chasing women." I said:

"Maybe he's changed, maybe this crash has..."

"...He'll never change!" snapped Constance. She turned to Inga. "And I don't know how much he paid you to distract me and keep me here, but I hope it was worth it!" With that Constance got to her feet and stomped off down the beach to the right.

"Should I go after her?" I asked.

"She'll be back."

"How can you be so sure?"

"The beach ends in about a hundred yards. There's nowhere else to go. She might get eaten by a bear though."

"You're joking right?"

"No, I'm not; there are lots of bears around here. They head up into the mountains for the winter but that won't be for a while yet." I got to my feet and asked Inga:

"Did you bring your gun?"

"Relax," said Inga, and at that second Constance Brady reappeared out of the gloom. She walked past us without a word and went to her cabin. The light from her window shone yellow through the trees.

Inga continued to stare at the dying embers. The water lapped gently against the beach; timbers crackled in the fading orange campfire. Apart from that, there was no sound. Now I'm not one of those guys who can sit in silence for any length of time. I've never been fishing in my life, mainly because there's no way I could sit still by a stream or a lake and do nothing. So, I had to speak:

"Inga, I've got to ask…are you planning on slipping me a Micky and catching the next train back east?"

"Back east? Where the hell is that?"

"Toronto, I guess."

"Why would I want to go there?"

"It's a much bigger city I hear, it would be easier to hide there."

"I told you before, wherever Constance goes…whether she goes back to him or whether she tries to run, I won't be going with her."

"But I thought…"

"Jesus Rick, you are so old fashioned. You're worse than my father. Just because I have sex with someone does not mean I'm with them for life!" Inga stood up.

"I'm going in now," she said. I kicked some sand over the last remnants of the fire and followed her through the trees. She turned to face me and whispered.

"Look…I admit this afternoon was a mistake and maybe it just might have added to the confusion Constance is feeling…"

"Confusion? You mean she's confused about which team she's batting for?"

"If you want to put it like that, yes."

"Do you think there's a chance that she might decide one way or the other in the next few days? Because it would simplify things for me."

"And that's the most important thing to be considered, is it? Making life easy for you?"

"I didn't mean it like that!" I said. "I meant I don't want to have to get rough with Constance." Inga put her finger to her lips.

"Sshhh. It's getting late," she said. "Time for bed…goodnight Rick…and another thing, if you plan to get rough with Constance, you'll have to get past me first."

I got up early next day and walked around the northern end of the bay to have a look at the Beaver, do a little tinkering and make sure we were ready to head out when the time came. An hour later when I got back to the motel Inga and Constance were in the office talking to Reta the owner. Inga saw me and stepped outside and said "hi."

"Have you got any spare cash?" she asked. "We owe them for last week."

"How much?"

"Twenty-five bucks." I handed over three tens.

"That's thirty U.S. that should be more than enough." Inga thanked me and went back inside to pay up. As Inga and Constance came back out of the office I said:

"I guess breakfast is on me too?" The ladies thanked me for my kind offer, and each took hold of one of my arms. We walked off toward the only café in town, looking like The Scarecrow, the Tin Man, and the Cowardly Lion. Dorothy must have been somewhere over the rainbow because she was nowhere to be seen.

As I had paid for breakfast, I figured I had earned the right to start talking about our little problem. On my way back in from checking over the Beaver, I had mentally rehearsed a speech. I was going to make that speech now. I figured I had just as long as it took to drink a coffee and eat fried eggs, bacon, and hash browns. This was my speech:

"Okay ladies, I'm heading back to San Francisco today. You can either come back with me or stay here. I can't afford to hang around in Canada while my wife could get thrown in jail at any minute and I still haven't worked out who blew flight 402 out of the sky. And yes, Inga I do know that Jo will not be coming back to me whatever happens. She is still my wife and I can't let Ko den Hamer send her to jail, not if I can find a way to stop him.

"Now I figure Constance obviously has a choice to make and here's what I think she should do. Come back to San Francisco, see a good divorce lawyer and file for divorce; a good lawyer should also be able to get you protection from Paddy Brady, maybe look at a restraining order. I know a guy I've worked with for years…he's got some strange habits, I suppose you could call him eccentric, but he knows divorce law better anybody.

"And yes, I do know what kind of man Paddy Brady is, but I also know he's going to be having troubles of his own very shortly. Troubles that will make getting a divorce look like chicken feed. So that's it. We may have to spread the journey over two days to make sure we land back in San Francisco in the daytime. But I plan to be airborne by eleven-thirty at the latest. How does that sound to you?"

Having finished my speech, I tucked into my breakfast and waited for the response from Inga and Constance. The silence was unbearable. All three of us concentrated on eating and drinking for a while. Nobody spoke. Finally, Inga put down her knife and fork, they clattered on the plate.

"Rick, would you mind stepping outside for a minute?" she said.

I did as Inga had requested, stepped outside, and hung around by the entrance. You could tell fall was now in full swing. It was much cooler than I expected and for a second, I wished I hadn't left my flying jacket at the motel. I looked through the window as the ladies discussed my ultimatum. I could hear voices raised but I couldn't make out what was being said. Eventually, Inga beckoned me back inside.

"Pay the man Rick; we've got a plane to catch." Neither of my passengers looked too thrilled by the idea. As we walked back to the motel Inga spoke the most:

"I'm guessing your brilliant divorce lawyer is Melvin Hammerstein, if so, I'd have a word with him and make sure he doesn't pull any stunts or jokes on Constance. They won't go down well. He should also know who he's going up against. When Constance files for divorce things are going to get very rough."

"Are you sure we can do this?" asked Constance Brady.

"Sure, we can do it," said Inga. "You said it yourself; you can't go on running away all your life."

"I know, I know," said Constance.

"It's really the only way forward Constance. You'll get a massive pay-out one way or the other. My guess is Paddy won't want things to drag through court, so he'll make you a cash settlement with a non-disclosure clause as part of the deal. And it's what you deserve, remember that."

"I only hope I live long enough to enjoy it," said Constance.

Back at the Cove View Court we split up and went to our rooms to pack. I took all of two minutes, so I was first to the office to check out with Mrs. Thornley. I thanked her for looking after 'my friends.' We said our goodbyes and began to walk around the bay to the dock where the Beaver, what would soon be my Beaver, was berthed. Inga carried both the dames' cases, neither was very large. I carried my overnight bag in my left hand. The right was still giving me trouble every now and then.

Once we got to the dock Inga loaded the cases and then they both made them-selves comfortable onshore while I checked the fuel for water contamination and completed my pre-flight checklist.

When the checks were completed, I waved my passengers forward. Inga clambered into the right-hand seat as she had done previously; Constance Brady strapped herself in behind us. I started the engine and watched the gauges come to life. Everything was in the green so once the engine had warmed up, I jumped down to the dock, untied the ropes, and jumped back onto the left-hand float. I held onto the spar and pushed us away from the dock before climbing in the pilot's door and strapping myself in. Inga already had her earphones on. I checked back to see if Mrs. Brady was strapped in. She gave me a weak smile and a thumbs-up.

It was good to be back in the air and at the controls. It was good to be back in the air and in control of my life. I remembered the feeling of being one with the aircraft, where surprises were generally to be avoided, where certain changes in attitude and throttle input had predictable outcomes. If I'm beginning to sound a little like a control freak here, I apologize. It's just that my life on terra-firma was currently in the mother of all tale spins, metaphorically speaking. And my inability to restore some kind of order was driving me nuts.

I'd made my take-off run heading south down Indian Arm, I made a steep climbing turn over Burnaby Mountain and identified and followed the Fraser River as we crossed over Douglas Island and Barnston Island. We were heading due east at three thousand feet. My plan was to re-trace my route over the border, heading into the hills south of Cultus Lake. As soon as we crossed the border, we would lose height and use the topography to hide the plane as we entered U.S. airspace. And as plans go it was pretty good.

Right up to the point where the National Guard spotted us. The first I knew of it was seeing a streak of silver scream over top of us. This was followed by a thunderous roar and severe turbulence, jet wake I guessed. I watched the silver fighter make a lazy 180 degree turn to the west and come straight back at us. A voice came over the radio.

"Unidentified aircraft entering United States airspace please identify yourself." I didn't answer.

The F86 Sabre shot past our starboard wing-tip, the Beaver wobbled in the turbulent air.

"I repeat, unidentified aircraft entering United States airspace identify yourself." Inga was looking across at me. The voice came over the radio again:

"Unidentified aircraft, this is National Guard fighter aircraft I need you to follow me to the nearest landing strip. Will you comply?"

"What are you going to do Rick?" she asked. By then we were about a mile inside the U.S. I checked ahead, the hills were fairly gentle at this point and I needed to get down into some steep valleys. I could see the white peak of Mount Baker about three miles ahead. The kind of terrain I needed to hide the plane would be in that area. There was also low cloud below the peak. The valleys would have intermittent cloud at this height. That would help. But there was no way I could outrun the F86 to get into the cloud.

"Unidentified aircraft, will you comply?"

And then it came to me. I didn't need to outrun the Sabre. I needed to do the exact opposite.

I eased back on the throttle, almost back to idle speed. I held the nose high and the indicated airspeed began to drop. I put on some flaps. The ride got a little lumpy, but we were holding altitude. Inga's voice had a little panicky warble in it as she asked:

"What the hell are you doing?"

"Just watch," I said. I was watching the airspeed very carefully and I didn't let it drop below sixty. The stalling speed of an F86 Sabre is about twice that. And so, I crawled the Beaver south toward Mount Baker. The F86 flashed by us twice more, but as we passed the summit, I was able to drop the Beaver into some fairly steep valleys which fed into Baker Lake. The fighter climbed out into the clouds. I retracted the flaps and brought our airspeed back up to cruising.

"I suppose you think that was funny? Suppose the guy had shot at us?"

"He'd need clearance from someone much higher up to open fire, that's if he's carrying ammunition, which I doubt. I wonder where he was from..."

I looked back at Constance Brady; she was asleep in her seat. I bet she had no idea what she'd just missed. At the southern tip of Baker Lake, I changed our heading and turned due west. In just over thirty miles on this heading, we would be over Bellingham. We could then turn south again and make our way to Seattle to re-fuel.

Once over Bellingham we made the turn and keeping the highway under our left-wing we were over Lake Washington in just over thirty minutes. The Lake was busy, and I had to do two passes flying south to north before I saw a safe space to put the Beaver down.

As soon as we had tied up at Kenmore Air's marina Constance Brady went in search of a washroom. I asked that the Beaver's fuel tanks be filled and enquired about a pay-phone. I was told to use the office phone.

"I have to call San Francisco and then Portland," I said.

"Don't worry; we'll add a dollar or two to the fuel bill." I was okay with that. I picked up the phone.

"Are you calling Paddy Brady?" asked Inga as she walked into the office. I nodded.

"Tell him I quit," she said. I said:

"Tell him yourself, we'll be back tomorrow." And I started to dial the number in my handy dandy detective's notebook. Did you think I'd left it in the office? No-way. Apparently, Bob Munro was flying some guys to a fishing lodge out past the Grand Coulee Dam, so I told the guys to let him know I called in. We were re-fueled and ready to go in twenty minutes. The next leg would take us to Portland and our overnight stop. I'd told Cleveland to expect us in about ninety minutes or so. That would be around four. I got him to call ahead and hold a room at the hotel Inga had stayed at on our last visit. I would stay with the plane overnight just like our first trip. The flying jacket would come in handy then.

We did better than I expected flying down to Portland. It was three forty as we made our first low pass over the Columbia River. There was a barge being towed slowly downstream as we flew over, so I followed the river upstream for a few minutes, held my position in a tight turn for another two or three then flew back west to make sure all was clear. The windsock on Salty's roof showed a slight westerly breeze so I flew north over Vancouver (another Vancouver, not the one in British Columbia, bet you were confused for a second there) I flew over the town of Vancouver, Washington State, and back around to the east before turning on short final approach. I lowered flaps, selected the correct propeller pitch, and eased the Beaver down onto the water.

Cleveland Smith came out to welcome us as I nudged the dock with my right float. I switched off the engine and shut the plane down. Then I hurried round to help Inga and Constance Brady pick their way across the floats and up onto the dock. Cleveland held out a helping hand for the ladies.

"Travelling in style Mister Marshall, you sure are travelling in style." He shook my hand enthusiastically.

"Good to see you again Cleveland, how's business?"

"Can't complain…are you staying the night on board again?" I nodded.

"The ladies have a reservation at the Clyde, just like you asked."

"Can I call a cab?"

"You know where the phone is, the number's on the wall. I'll get this pretty little thing all gassed up and ready to go for you."

"Let me know what it comes to, we'll settle up in the morning," Cleveland said:

"Sure, thing my friend, sure thing."

Inga had called for a taxi as I spoke with Cleveland. She said it would be with us in fifteen minutes.

That evening we had an early dinner in the restaurant at the Clyde Hotel. As usual flying any distance had made me ravenous. I was beginning to think this was a response learned when I flew B17's. None of my crew ate before missions; I can remember watching the rookies that did hurling at the side of their aircraft just before taking off. The flight time of a sortie over Germany could be as much as eight hours so you were pretty hungry and thirsty by the time you made it back…if you made it back.

Over a steak dinner at the Clyde Hotel that night I kept remembering the faces of friends who I'd lost over Europe. I might not have been the best company. Inga and Constance both had some sort of linguini with seafood. We had a few beers and eventually relaxed a little more. The place wasn't busy, it was still early on in the evening, so we took our time; I had a desert from which the ladies snuck spoonful's when they thought I wasn't looking.

After coffee and a whisky for me, I escorted the ladies up to their room and said goodnight. I had the desk call for a cab, and I was back at Salty's by eleven. I settled down in the back of the plane, wrapped in a couple of blankets and my old sheepskin flying jacket.

Next morning Inga and Constance Brady had breakfast at the hotel then caught a cab out to join me on the river. I had completed all my pre-flights by the time they arrived. We were in the air by ten, once again heading south. We made Eureka in just under four hours, re-fueled, and started our final leg back to San Francisco. In two and a half hours we were coasting into the dock at Sausalito harbor.

Chapter Twenty - Two

At the end of the jetty, we were met by the obligatory limo. Inga and Constance were whisked away, presumably to the hotel. I thought it was a little weird that Paddy Brady didn't come down to meet us personally, but hey…what did I know about relationships? The M.G. had been kept close by and now it was parked by the jetty ready to go. I threw my pack into the passenger seat and jumped in. She fired up the first time and I was soon nipping in between bigger cars and trucks crossing the Golden Gate. Most of the traffic was heading north so I made good time driving back into the city.

Back at the office, I checked in with my answering service. There were four messages from Elton Dwight, three potential new clients. I called the new clients first, explained that I'd been out of town. I took two of the cases offered and arranged to meet my new clients over the next few days. I called Dwight's office, but he'd already left for the day. So, I closed up the office and went down the street to Rooney's. Over several beers and one beef sandwich, I daydreamed about getting the Beaver for real. Every now and then I looked up at my reflection in the large mirror in the fancy frame behind the bar. I didn't look too great. The bar filled up with cigarette smoke and happy drinkers but the tide of revelers kind of washed by me like I was a pebble on a beach.

I wasn't sure if Brady would deliver on his promise about the plane. Still, I was foolish enough to make mental plans on how I'd run the sight-seeing business. It was an idea I'd been toying with as I flew to Vancouver and back. Guys did sight-seeing tours of the bay by boat, why not by air? If seeing sights was what the business was all about what better way than flying? You could do The Golden Gate, Alcatraz, the harbor all in about twenty minutes.

I scribbled some rough calculations on a napkin. Cost of fuel, maintenance, rental of a berth on the pier versus the number of paying passengers per flight multiplied by the number of flights per hour multiplied by hours in the day when flying was possible. There would be times when we couldn't go. San Francisco bay was notoriously foggy even through the summer. And there would be months when the number of tourists would dwindle down to nothing.

Of course, I could do a little detective work then, just to pay the bills. I could do charters too; take guys fishing as Bob Munro did in Seattle.

The more I scribbled figures on napkins the more convinced I became that this would work. Of course, it all depended on Paddy Brady handing over the aircraft. But if he did, I thought I might ask Sammy Kirk to run the ticket stand. He could still do his photography if he wanted to, but the booth would give him somewhere to take the weight off. Or he could quit the photography altogether. He had his nest-egg from the Connie pictures, so he was in clover and didn't really need to work all that hard anyway. If the purchase of that house north of the city hadn't been finalized maybe Sammy could get a place in town, closer to the water. It was just a thought.

It was all coming together; it would work…if Brady came through. Now, what would I call this little enterprise? Again, I started writing down ideas:

Birds-Eye Tours:	Sounded too much like frozen fish.
Rick's Flying Circus:	Maybe a little too much like a barnstorming show.
Rick's Flying Tours:	Not bad.
Ricky's Flying Tours:	Maybe a little more friendly, could I stand being called Ricky…or Ricky Wicky?

I thought back to the one and only time anyone had called me Ricky-Wicky and I wondered what Inga was going to do now she was back working full-time for Paddy Brady. Would she quit, like she said she would? Would Brady let her? I hoped everything worked out for the kid. She was one in a million. I looked in the mirror again, didn't much like the scarred and stubbly face that stared back. I was looking old. Rooney's was beginning to get to me. A three-piece band was warming up in a distant corner. I guessed they'd be singing Irish songs of rebellion and loss. They were guaranteed to do 'Danny Boy' at least twice. I would have to make sure I was out of the bar before then.

I decided to call Melvin Hammerstein in the morning, maybe arrange a meeting. He could brief me on all the legal mumbo-jumbo I'd have to go through to start up my new company, I could also tell him to expect a call from Constance Brady some-time soon. I also decided to start seriously looking for an apartment downtown. Maybe I should speak to Melvin about filing for divorce too? I went back to the office after that, slept fitfully on my cot, dreaming of the day when I had a successful sight-seeing business and a real bed.

The next morning, just as I was coming round, there was a knock at the door. It was Inga; she had her black suit on and had even found a lurid patterned tie to finish off her outfit. She had a large brown envelope to give me.

"What's this?" I ask.

"The paperwork for the transfer of ownership on the plane," she answered. "Mister Brady said you have three days to move the thing off his property. He also said he's very grateful for all your good work in getting his wife back." The second check for $5000 was clipped to the paperwork for the Beaver.

"He certainly is," I said, passing the check over to Inga.

"You must be the richest private detective in town."

"Ex-Private detective soon, I'm going into the sightseeing business." Inga sat heavily into my client chair.

"I'm glad someone got something out of this fuck up. You did okay."

"And all I had to do was get shot at, have my arm broken, and risk my life in a burning building."

"None of that had anything to do with Constance Brady," said Inga.

"I guess you're right."

"You know I am," she said. Then I asked Inga:

"Are you going to quit?"

"That depends on whether I think I can do so and keep this fabulous body of mine in one piece."

"You think there might be trouble?"

"I do," she said.

"Do you want me to have a word with Mister Brady? I could explain that you did all he asked you to do in Canada…I'll tell him you were a great help all the way through the investigation, I couldn't have found Constance without you."

"… Don't remind me, but it's not that I'm worried about," said Inga. "Paddy forbids people to leave the organization. He thinks someone will talk eventually. And there are a lot of skeletons in his cupboards."

"And all over the bay area, I'll bet…Why don't you get away for a while?"

"You don't take a vacation from Paddy Brady." Inga got to her feet. "Gotta go," she said. "I'm driving Constance around today, major shopping trip planned, will take all day."

"Tough life," I said; then regretted the flippant comment. "How is she doing?" Inga was at the door.

"Hard to say…I'll see you around Rick."

I got dressed quickly, grabbed a coffee at the corner store, and drove down to the Hyde Street Pier. I wanted to try get a mooring for my new plane and I hoped to catch Sammy Kirk too. The bay was shrouded in thick fog so there weren't too many people around. Sammy was nowhere to be seen. I found a mooring for rent on a month by month basis. I paid the first three months up-front and told the agent I'd be bringing a plane over as soon as the fog lifted.

"Some-time in December then." He joked. After that, I drove over to Melvin Hammerstein's to put him in the picture about my plans to build a sight-seeing airline. I was going to be the next Howard Hughes…but without the hiding in hotel bedrooms, the peeing in jars and the matinee idol moustache. I did not talk to him about filing for divorce. It was way too soon, and I still thought I could get Josephine out of the jam she was in. And if I did and if I got Ko den Hamer locked up for a good long stretch, then maybe Josephine would come back to me. Later I called one of my two new private detective clients and arranged a meeting at their home for the afternoon. I was a busy little bee, wasn't I?

So bright and early I'm on the road to Daly City, Westlake Avenue to be precise, to the home of Mrs. Lucille Bridger. I thought of Daly City as the place San Francisco shipped its garbage to. And that was in fact true. But things were changing in Daly City, that's for sure. It's very different from San Francisco geographically. It's newer in a lot of places and its flatter too. Most of the City is made up of row upon row of small box-like houses. There's construction everywhere…rancher after rancher after rancher. The place is spreading on all sides like spilled coffee. It was hard to spot any green spaces, no parks or trees, just block after block of new houses springing up.

Lucille Bridger was in her early forties, but she moved like a seventy-year-old woman who's just fallen down a mountain. She had a trapped disc she said, made every day a living hell. After eventually answering my knock on the door, she shuffled slowly back into her living room and carefully lowered herself into a chair. Her mouth was permanently clenched in a thin purple line and it was clear that she'd lost a lot of weight. Her skin hung from her upper arms and her dress was at least two sizes too big across the bust and hips. It had taken me an hour to get out to Daly City and find her, so I didn't want to waste any more of my day. So, I said:

"Okay Mrs. Bridger, what can I do for you?"

"It's my husband," she said. Nine out of every ten of my cases start with that exact phrase. "I think he's messing around with my sister."

"Your sister?" She nodded and pointed toward a wooden framed photograph on the sideboard. Mrs. Bridger was in the photo along with a younger woman who looked a lot like Mrs. Bridger before the trapped disc problem…a long time before the trapped disc problem.

"That's me with Kathleen; she's a lot younger than me… Mom used to say she was a mistake." In the photograph, Kathleen positively shone with vitality.

She had a wide smile and eyes that sparkled with the promise of naughtiness to come. Mrs. Bridger looked like Kathleen's stern-faced mother or grandmother. I looked at the picture for a moment before putting it back in the mark it had left in the dust on top of the sideboard.

"And what makes you think your husband is fooling around with your sister Kathleen? What's his name, by the way?"

"Art, he's a butcher. He's got his own shop in town."

"In Daly City?" she nodded. "And you think he's seeing your sister?"

"I know he is. I followed him." This was hard to believe, I couldn't picture Mrs. Bridger getting to the bathroom without assistance. How could she follow her husband to his alleged rendezvous with her sister?

"You followed him?"

"Are you hard of hearing Mister?" I rubbed my left ear, a reflex I was trying to suppress.

"No, I'm not deaf Mrs. Bridger, this ear might look damaged, but I do okay…and the other one works fine, and so do my eyes and they have noticed that you appear to have a little trouble getting around. I was wondering how you managed to follow your husband."

"Well, I didn't follow him obviously…"

"Obviously."

"My friend Rose did." This was getting better and better. Who the hell was Rose? Did I really want to know?

"And your friend Rose saw your husband and your sister…in a compromising situation?"

"I didn't say that. I said Rose followed them, three days ago. She followed them to a place a few miles south of here on Mission Street, some kind of warehouse in a no-good part of town."

"And this was during the day?"

"Certainly, it was; Art never goes out in the evening."

"Did Rose give you an address?" Mrs. Bridger produced a folded sheet of paper from her purse. She handed it over triumphantly.

"Just so there's no mix-up, Mrs. Bridger, what do you want from me? Do you want evidence for a divorce; do you want me to make them stop? What?" Mrs. Bridger sat thinking for a while then, very slowly she said:

"I want you to scare the shit out of them both. I want that slut to leave Art and me alone. I want her to peddle her big tits and even bigger ass somewhere else." I stood up.

"Okay Mrs. Bridger, if you can write down your sister's address and the address of your husband's shop I'll get to work. You know my daily rate. I'll keep any additional expenses to a minimum. I'll report back to you in a couple of days hopefully, let you know how things turned out…don't get up Mrs. Bridger, if you can write down those addresses for me, I'll see myself out." I passed over my notebook and pen. She scribbled down the two addresses as requested.

I drove into town and found the Butcher's Shop that Bridger owned. I drove past slowly, looked inside. It had floor to ceiling glass at the front and a glass door, so it was easy to see what was going on in the shop. I drove around the block a couple of times before space came up close to my target. Daly City was a really busy place with lots of ladies pushing baby carriages on crowded sidewalks. It was an up and coming place, that's for sure.

Luckily there was a café just across the street from Bridger the Butchers. It was busy too but after a short wait, I grabbed a stool at the counter facing the window and ordered a coffee. I could see across the street into the butcher's shop, no problem. Bridger looked like every butcher should. He was a tall pink-faced man with broad shoulders and a barrel-like build. He had light brown curly hair, receding at the front. His bare forearms looked to be covered in tattoos. I guessed he might be ex-navy. His blue and white apron stretched tight over his stomach showing he was a man who enjoyed the 'fruits' of his labor.

I watched the shop for the rest of that day, nothing much happened. So, I drove back to the office that night and returned the next day, prepared to continue this routine until something got my attention. On that second day Bridger was the only person serving in the shop until mid-afternoon, the place was busy again and obviously doing well.

A stick-thin spotty rat-faced youth with a lank, greasy hair arrived at two-thirty and went into the back of the shop. He came back out minutes later dressed in the same kind of blue and white apron. He started serving customers at the counter alongside Bridger. After a few minutes as part of a tag team, Art Bridger went into the rear of the shop. He emerged wearing a brown, double-breasted suit and carrying a large case. He spoke to his assistant briefly then left. I slurped the last mouthful of my third coffee and hurried into the street after him.

I thought about jumping into the M.G. but I got the feeling that Bridger wasn't going far. I figured if he was going to go any distance he would have got in his van. The van stood resolutely outside his shop. The sign on the side proclaiming:

For the Best Cut's at the Best Prices - Best Choose Bridger

Not a bad slogan really. I would have to think of a similar catchy slogan for the sight-seeing business. Bridger cut down an alleyway away from the main street. At the other end of the alley, most of the buildings were warehouses or industrial units. Maybe we were going to the place he usually met the younger sister? Bridger stopped at a rundown warehouse near the end of the next block. There was no sign outside, so I had no idea what the building was used for. I would not have been able to guess that in a million years. Bridger entered through a side door; the larger rolling door at the front remained closed. I waited and watched for some time. No-one else turned up. Maybe Kathleen was already inside? This place struck me as the least romantic place for a secret lover's assignation I had ever seen.

I decided to head inside. If the door wasn't locked, I'd go in and act as though I was looking for a mechanic or a garage… Bridger didn't know me so I could just wing it. I half expected Bridger and this Kathleen lady to be too busy to notice me anyway. I tried the door, it wasn't locked. I opened it slowly, ready with my cover story in case Bridger was just inside. He wasn't, no-one was.

The warehouse was in near darkness after I closed the door. I could tell by the echo that the large space was practically empty. Maybe there was an office at the rear? A booming voice came from somewhere in the gloom:

"Is that you Lou? Can we get some of the lights working? I can't see shit in here…" Another voice said:

"Hold on a sec." There was a clunk and several very bright lights on metal stands came on, they buzzed loudly. The lights were surrounding a bed standing in the center of the warehouse. Bridger and another man were standing behind a Super 8 movie camera on a tripod. Bridger's case was open at his feet and looked to contain a large whip, some rope, and some kind of gag. A third man came forward from the rear of the building, obviously the man on the lights. Bridger peered over at me as I stood in the semi-darkness by the door.

"You're not Lou," he said. At that point, another door to my right opened and Mrs. Bridger's sister Kathleen came out and walked into the light. She was wearing a see-through robe, a very see-through robe. She was a very eye-catching young lady that Kathleen. You could see she had a future in show business. She certainly seemed happy to show me what she had under the robe.

She was wearing black stockings, bright red lipstick, and a black shoulder-length wig with bangs at the front, nothing else. She looked a lot like a certain lady back east who was making a name for herself in 'photography' magazines…what was her name again? Bettie something…

"You're not Lou," she said. "I usually work with Lou. You're not Lou." Bridger was striding toward us.

"This is a closed set!" he yelled.

"Really? Cos looks like a shitty warehouse being used to make illegal stag movies to me…my mistake."

"Who the fuck are you?" asked Bridger. I pointed to Kathleen.

"Like she said…I'm not Lou." I opened the door and walked back out into the alleyway. Seconds later Bridger burst through the door all bluster and outrage. He grabbed hold of my arm…guess which one? It hurt all right but nowhere near as much as the last time. I took that as a good sign.

"Just a second bub!" barked Bridger. He swung a fist in the general direction of my jaw. I ducked it easily then I spun around and kicked him just under the knee-cap of his left leg. He fell like a hundred-year-old sequoia and lay in the dust clutching his knee and cursing fluently. He was ex-navy, just as I thought.

I thought it best to make a tactical retreat in case Bridger's fellow pornographers came to his aid. They did have that nasty looking whip after all. God knows what else was at the bottom of Bridger's suitcase.

When I got back to the coffee shop I went to the pay-phone in the back and called in an anonymous tip to the local police department. I still didn't know if Bridger and his sister-in-law were having an affair, but I figured that if they were things would cool down for a while between them if their 'studio' got busted. I didn't want to tell Lucille Bridger about her husband's 'hobby' I'm the last person on earth to talk about morals…

I drove back to the office and as I drove back, I couldn't get this question out of my mind. How do you broach the subject to your sister in law that you'd like to photograph and film her having sex with a guy called Lou, who she's never met? I mean, are you all just sat around the Thanksgiving dinner table and you lean over and say: 'Kathleen you have fantastic tits and an ass to die for. I'd like to film you naked having sex and being tied up and I think I can sell the films we make for a shit load of dough…what do you think? Would you like to give it a shot?' And what would you expect your sister in law to say? 'Hey I've got nothing planned for tomorrow, so long as you can find a fit guy with a big dick…I'm game.' It would certainly make for an interesting Thanksgiving, wouldn't it?

The next day I would phone Mrs. Bridger and tell her I wasn't able to take her case after all. I would tell her I was getting out of the private detective racket.

Chapter Twenty - Three

I didn't get a chance to call Mrs. Bridger in the morning. I got a call myself; very early. It was from Inga:

"Mrs. Brady is missing," she said. "We think she just walked away from the hotel in Sausalito in the middle of the night. She's got no money, no passport, nothing...apart from the clothes she has on her. Mister Brady would like you to come over right away. For some reason, he thinks you might be the only man who can find her."

"I'll be over as fast as I can," I said. "What is she wearing?"

"We think a yellow sweater and cream-colored pants."

"Anything else, like a coat or hat?"

"We don't think so."

"Did she speak to anyone; say where she might be headed?"

"No, no-one's mentioned anything."

"Were you with her last night? How did she seem?"

"I didn't see her last night. She went out to dinner with Brady and another couple. They didn't get back till late...Rick, I'm really worried."

"I'm on my way," I said, sounding a lot like a bargain basement Dick Tracy.

I got dressed, ran downstairs to the car, and set off for Sausalito. Low clouds hung over the bay and there was a rumble of thunder from the north. As I got to The Presidio hail suddenly began to clatter down onto the road leading to the Golden Gate Bridge, quickly making it slick and dangerous. The tiny wiper blades on the M.G. struggled to cope. I slowed down as I approached the southern end of the bridge. Up ahead I could see a black and white parked in one of the southbound lanes with its lights whirling. A crowd of people was huddled together looking over the railings. My gut began to do barrel rolls and my ear began to itch. I put my foot down. When I got to the far end of the bridge I skidded to a halt on the hard shoulder.

I jumped from the M.G. and raced back toward the bridge deck. Traffic had slowed southbound as people tried to see what was happening center-span. I looked for anything like a gap in traffic northbound which would allow me to get to the center median. I wasn't having much luck. The hail-stones bounced off the road surface noisily. I saw a gap in the slow lane, so I ran out to the white line. Cars raced past me on both sides soaking me in spray. Everyone started leaning on their horns. I was watching for the next space to appear, dodging passing cars and trucks like a matador with a death wish. Then, as traffic slowed a little a gap appeared. I sprinted across two lanes to the relative safety of the center median.

I held my position there a while and got my breath back. I looked back over my shoulder and turned my attention to the three lanes of southbound traffic. Luckily the cars and trucks on this side were only inching along. I was able to slip between bumpers fairly quickly, only once did I get a friendly nudge from a 51' Buick followed by an even friendlier blast on the horn and some advice about getting my head examined. I was able to keep on my feet and sprint across the slow lane and leap the fence guarding the pedestrian walkway.

I ran to the fast-growing knot of people, my shoes splashing through standing water as the hail turned to solid rain. As I joined the crowd looking down into the water someone shouted:

"Look, they're lifting something out." Everyone pressed forward to the railings. 'It' was a body, a slim body with auburn hair wearing a yellow sweater and cream-colored pants. The body was lifted face down onto the rear deck of a police launch. I couldn't tell for sure if the body was Constance Brady, the bridge deck is nearly two hundred and fifty feet high. Somehow, I knew. I walked back slowly to the northern end of the bridge, the rain getting heavier all the time. I somehow got back across the six lanes of traffic, got back in the M.G. and drove to the hotel in Sausalito. I was on auto-pilot. Days later I couldn't remember one minute of what happened after I saw the body in the yellow sweater being fished out of the bay.

Inga said I just walked into the lobby of the hotel and stood there dripping on the carpet till she happened to come downstairs and notice me. She said she could see in my face that something very bad had happened. She took me into the kitchen and stood me next to the ovens, grabbed a towel, and tried to dry my hair. All the time she was saying my name and asking what was wrong.

After maybe fifteen minutes I registered that someone was talking to me.

"Rick? Rick? Are you okay? What's wrong?"

"Is Paddy in the hotel?" Inga nodded.

"He's upstairs, he's got people phoning everyone Constance knows, he's called the hospitals, he's called all the best hotels...he's even called the police."

"...She's not in a hotel." I said.

"What's happened, Rick? Tell me."

"I can't be sure…I think she might have jumped…I think she's jumped off the Golden Gate Bridge."

Inga didn't want to believe what I was telling her. I said I'd just seen a woman wearing a yellow sweater being picked out of the water below the bridge. Inga said:

"It might not be her; it can't be her. Lots of people wear yellow sweaters. How can you be sure?"

I said I couldn't be sure, but I felt we should tell Mister Brady straight away. Inga let out a long-anguished wail and sank to the tiled floor of the kitchen. I crouched over her, put my hands on her shoulders.

"Come on Inga, let's get you a drink, we'll sit down in the restaurant for a while." I helped Inga to her feet and led her through the swinging doors into the deserted restaurant. I sat her down at a table and went behind the bar to get brandy. She drank it in one.

"Another?" I asked. She shook her head.

"Do you want me to tell Mister Brady?" she asked. I said:

"No, I'll do it." Inga went to the phone behind the bar and told Paddy Brady I was here, and I had something to tell him. Brady said he'd be right down. We sat back down at the table and waited for him. I held her hand. Brady came through from reception at just that point along with three bodyguards.

"You're wasting your time there Mister Detective, I thought you'd have worked that out by now."

Inga pulled her hand away. She said:

"Rick has some bad news, Mister Brady." Paddy Brady sat down at the table and said:

"Well, let's hear it."

"Mister Brady, I think Constance has committed suicide…"

"And why in God's name would you think that?"

"There's no easy way to say this Mister Brady…I think she jumped from the Golden Gate some-time this morning. I just saw a body in a yellow sweater being recovered from below the bridge deck…I came straight here."

"You got binoculars on you?" asked Brady. I shook my head.

"I know it's a long way down to the water from there Mister Brady, but the clothes match what Constance was wearing when she went missing last night and…" Wham! Paddy Brady sucker punched me on the jaw. I think I rocked backward in the chair and fell to the floor. I only think that because I was out cold by that point.

When I came to Inga and me were the only people left in the restaurant. I looked up at Inga as I rubbed my chin.

"He's gone to the bridge," she said. I worked my jaw a little and managed to ask:

"What do you think we should do?"

"I think we should both get the fuck out of here." I thought this was a good idea. So, we got in the M.G. and drove away from the Sausalito hotel. By the time we crossed the bridge a whole lane had been cordoned off. We could see Paddy's limo parked behind four black and whites. We drove back into the city, parked up behind my office, and went inside. Inga made two mugs of coffee, but we didn't touch them. We sat in silence as our drinks grew cold.

The evening paper confirmed that the body of Constance Brady, wife of prominent local businessman and night club owner Douglas Patrick (Paddy) Brady had been found in San Francisco Bay close to the Golden Gate Bridge. Foul play was not suspected. The body had been officially identified that afternoon at the city morgue by Paddy Brady himself. I was reading the evening paper at Rooney's. Inga had left the office mid-afternoon to see a new lady friend. She didn't say if she'd come back. She didn't say if she'd ever come back.

The Funeral was held at the Holy Cross Catholic Cemetery south of the city. As I parked the little red M.G. I couldn't help noticing how out of place it looked against the much larger black limo's and sedans. It looked like a rose placed on a newly dug grave. Holy Cross Cemetery is, as you might expect, a beautifully laid out, peaceful place with mature trees and well-tended lawns. I followed some mourners to the impressive central church, a pink building that seemed to glow in the early afternoon sun. I climbed the steps and went inside.

The place was practically full, only a few spaces right near the back. That suited me, I just wanted to pay my respects and get out of there. I didn't want to join the mourners at the interment. It wasn't my place. As I shuffled along the back row, I saw the District Attorney being directed to a reserved space near the front. An organ was playing quietly; I didn't recognize the tune, never been big on classical music.

I nearly didn't recognize Paddy Brady when he came in. It was only seeing Inga at his side, dressed in a black dress and matching wide-brimmed hat that drew my attention. Brady looked to have aged ten years since we last met. I don't know how, but he looked as if he'd lost ten pounds too. I guess maybe he was on some pretty serious medication, his eyes wandered around the church; he looked as if he didn't know where he was or what was going on. Inga saw me as the entourage walked past, I'm sure of it. But she didn't acknowledge me in any way.

When the service started, I just followed along with the song sheet, stood when everyone else stood, sat down when they did, said: 'Amen' at the appropriate time. In half an hour it was over. I was one of the first out of the big doors and into the sunlight. I was beginning to wish I'd brought a Micky. I really needed a drink.

As the church emptied it looked to me that only a select few invited mourners would be going to the graveside. They included the District Attorney, Louise D. Rickenbacker. I hung around in the parking lot, hoping to see Inga on her own, maybe talk to her, see how she was. Standing by the M.G. I was the first person to see the convoy of six police cars speed into view. Two cars blocked the exit and the rest drove through the parking lot, skidding to a halt by the church steps. Armed police, some in uniform carrying shotguns and some in plain clothes with handguns all got out of the black and whites and ran toward Constance Brady's newly dug grave. I started to follow them when I heard a familiar voice:

"I wouldn't bother if I were you gum-shoe." It was Joe Grunwald. The grin on his face looked out of place in a cemetery parking lot. He was having way too much fun.

"You can't help your boss now. He's going inside for life."

"You're arresting Paddy Brady?"

"Hey, you got it first time! Good guess!"

"He's burying his wife!" I yelled.

"Hmm, I did not know that." He lied.

"What kind of shit-heel arrests a man at his wife's funeral?" I asked. And as if to answer my perfectly reasonable question Elton Dwight climbed elegantly out of the last black and white parked at the church steps. He was wearing a rust-colored suit, white shirt, white bow-tie, and a white Panama hat, Grunwald nodded in his direction.

"That kind." I strode over to Elton Dwight. Grunwald called out:

"Don't try anything stupid, the jail's going to be crowded enough tonight without you stinking the place up too," I yelled at the Assistant D.A.

"You do know Mister Rickenbaker is up at the graveside too?" Dwight was all sweetness and light. He was obviously enjoying himself today.

"I certainly hope so; I've got a warrant for Mister Rickenbaker's arrest right here." He patted his breast pocket.

"I hope you know what you're doing Mister Dwight." He answered me calmly:

"Oh, I think I do Rick. I'd like to thank you for all your invaluable assistance in this matter…"

"I've not done shit!" I shouted.

"Ah but you see, by not doing shit (as you so colorfully claim) and not warning Brady about his imminent downfall you have been one of the key contributors to today's festivities, now if you don't mind..."

Elton Dwight walked away toward Constance Brady's grave. Grunwald grabbed me from behind, pinning both my arms. We were standing like that when uniformed police started to come back into the parking lot with their hands full of irate big-wigs. Paddy Brady and Louise D. Rickenbacker, the current District Attorney were marched to a newly arrived paddy wagon. They walked side by side with their hands behind their backs in handcuffs. Next to appear were several plain-clothes officers who'd clearly been in a fight. Some had bloody noses; some had the beginnings of black eyes forming. Inga came next. She was being restrained by two very large policemen; her dress had been torn at the neckline revealing most of her left breast. She had ugly blue bruising on one side of her face and bloody knuckles. Grunwald drooled in my ear:

"Oh dear, it looks like your freak girlfriend has been resisting arrest. Looks like someone had to teach her a lesson. Still, she'll like it in jail, lots of Bull Dykes to pal up with, she'll have a hell of a party...or they will."

More of Brady's staff were escorted to waiting cars and driven away. The black and whites parked across the entrance had by then pulled aside and the convoy of police cars swept out of the cemetery with lights whirling and sirens blaring. In just a few minutes I was one of the few people left in that parking lot.

I got in the M.G. and drove back into town. I called Melvin Hammerstein, put him in the picture, and asked him to make a few calls, find out where Inga had been taken. I said I would stand bail for her, no matter what it cost. Melvin got to work.

Inga had to spend a night in jail. She was charged with two counts of assaulting a police officer and resisting arrest. She was being held at the county jail on Kearney Street, next to Portsmouth Square, in the same building as the police headquarters I seemed to spend a lot of time visiting...Bail was set at $300 which I posted at eleven fifteen the next morning. Melvin said there was reason for optimism regarding Inga's assault charge as the plain-clothes officer did not clearly identify himself as police. He was less enthusiastic about her chances on the resisting arrest charge.

When Inga was released, we met her at the rear of the building. She shook Melvin by the hand and thanked him for his help. She ignored me completely, walked down the alley across Kearney Street, and into Portsmouth Square. I thanked Melvin, told him I'd be in touch, and then hurried after Inga. I called her name, but she didn't stop so I had to run the diagonal path across the square.

I finally caught up with her at the north-west corner of the square where Grant Avenue meets Washington Street. I called out:

"Inga! Can you wait up a minute?"

"Nope," was her reply. She kept walking west on Washington, heading deeper into Chinatown.

"Can I buy you lunch? My treat?" I called.

"Nope," she said.

"Come on Inga, be reasonable." Inga stopped suddenly. We stood face to face on a street-corner. People tried to listen in as the conversation went from bad to worse.

"Be reasonable? Do you think I'm not being reasonable?"

"I didn't say that."

"You just got my boss arrested…at his wife's funeral! How reasonable is that?" People stopped and stared; a crowd of on-lookers started to gather. A cop on patrol across the street started to take an interest.

"I had nothing to do with that!" I proclaimed.

"Nooo, of course not. You've been speaking with that creep Elton Dwight for months! Did you think I didn't notice? I warned Paddy. I told him this was coming. But he trusted you, Rick! He trusted you!"

"How come you're suddenly in his corner?" I asked. "Up to last week, Paddy Brady was a monster who treated his wife like shit." Inga stared at me with a look of such disgust. Then she put her hand up to hail a cab. As the taxi pulled up, she turned to me and said:

"I never want to see you again."

"Well, just pay me back the bail money and you'll never have to." It was a cheap shot and I regretted saying it the moment the words came out of my mouth. An ancient Chinese man was shaking his head at me.

"What?" I said to him.

Chapter Twenty - Four

The next day's Chronicle had the shocking follow up to the arrest of the District Attorney, but the story had been relegated to page two. Page one proudly proclaimed another successful atom bomb test out at the proving ground in the Nevada Desert, somewhere north west of Las Vegas. A picture of a billowing mushroom cloud filled most of the front page under a banner headline that said one word: **Kapow!**

Page two featured an interview with the Acting District Attorney: Elton Dwight. It also ran a photograph of the ever dapper Dwight sitting behind the desk in his new office. I'm not sure but I think I could have landed the Beaver on that desk…if she didn't have floats. Rickenbacker had been charged with corruption and it was also alleged (by Dwight) that he had been in Paddy Brady's back pocket ever since his election.

Josephine called me as I was reading the self-serving interview with Elton Dwight. Next month's mortgage was due on the house. I said I'd take it over to the house that after-noon. She said:

"I won't be in, just put it in an envelope and leave it in the mailbox."

I planned to take the opportunity to have a look around inside the house, maybe bring myself up to date with Ko den Hamer's operation and future plans. I drove over at three, Josephine would still be working at the new office downtown and that would give me all the time I needed. The street was practically empty of cars. Only Mr. Loomis's old beater was parked on our block. I parked behind it then walked across the street. The front garden was beginning to look seriously overgrown; I thought the Dutch were meant to be into gardening…all those tulips. Maybe he was too busy running his money-laundering operation? Still the overgrown garden wasn't my problem now.

Once in the house, I put the envelope with the money on the kitchen table and got to work upstairs. In the bedroom, I noticed a large new case next to the wardrobe. I knew it was new because it still had the price tag on it from The Emporium downtown. In one bedside table, wrapped in a newspaper, I came across Ko den Hamer's passport and one ticket for the California Zephyr to Chicago and on to New York on the 20th Century Limited to New York. At the bottom of this very interesting pile was one-way ticket to Europe on the S.S. Liberte.

It looked like Ko was planning to skip town. It also looked like he was planning to travel alone. I'd bet my last dime that Josephine didn't know about this. I thought I might have a little fun. I took all Ko den Hamer's tickets, went into the bathroom, and put them in Josephine's make-up drawer. I think young lovers should share everything don't you? In this way at least Josephine would be aware of Ko's plans. What she did with the information was her business now. I would have to call my favorite Acting District Attorney and share this news with him. It wasn't quite as big as a nuclear bomb exploding but it would make a pretty big bang. Maybe the D.A. could persuade the big Dutch Fuck to stick around in California for a while…ten years in Alcatraz would do nicely.

I put the mortgage money on the mat by the front door, went back to the M.G., and set off for town. As I drove, I got to thinking…there was a different way to play this. I could drive back to the house, put the tickets back where I found them, and not tell Elton Dwight about Ko's plans. Then all I had to do was sit on my ass and see what happened when Ko den Hamer skipped town alone. I slowed for a moment or two, thinking this option through. I was crossing the Bay Bridge by then and a trucker gave me a 'friendly' blast on the horn for making him change down two gears. I waved an apology which he must have mistaken for a different message. He crunched a gear, put his foot down and came alongside me and shouted down:

"Get that limey commie fag toy car in fucking gear or I'll run you off the Goddamn bridge!"

American truckers, salt of the earth. I smiled up at him sweetly then gave him a hand signal I'd learned in England. It looked a lot like Mr. Churchill's V for Victory sign, but it didn't mean anything like that. Where did he get 'commie' from? Maybe anyone who upset his delicate sensibilities was a commie? I guessed that most likely it was because the MG-TD was bright red. I settled on that.

Once I got back to the office, I phoned the DA's office and to my surprise, I was put straight through to the Acting District Attorney himself.

"Congratulations Mister District Attorney," I said. "How is life at the top of the shit heap?"

"Rewarding Mister Marshall, definitely rewarding. I have some news for you…"

"…And I have some news for you. Ko den Hamer is skipping town in less than a week. I know his travel plans." I spelled out what I'd learned.

"I think my office will have something to say about that. Do you want to hear my news?"

"Is it good?"

"Not for the people involved. We have uncovered clear evidence that Paddy Brady was also involved in Mickey Cohen's money laundering schemes. It turns out he was the local gentleman who originally put Ko den Hamer and Cohen together. It appears Brady has been a silent partner in KDH Developments from its inception."

"Wow! Small world hey?"

"Small world indeed Mister Marshall…and speaking of which, obviously there will have to be an election for the new permanent District Attorney post…"

"…And you want to know if you can count on my vote?"

"Oh, I don't think it will come to that Rick…no I want to offer you a job as a special investigator for The San Francisco District Attorney's office. You'll have to be deputized of course."

"Of course."

Wow! I did not see that coming!

"We'll be in touch, Rick. Oh, and by the way…it might be better for you if you were to keep your distance from your 'not so' good lady wife. Things are not going to go well for her."

Elton Dwight hit the nail right on the head there. That night a thunderstorm rolled through San Francisco bay. I was sleeping in the office as usual when a massive crack of thunder woke me. A few seconds later the sky lit up light blue as if someone flicked God's bedroom light on and off. Instantly more thunder crackled and boomed and echoed around the bay. The rain was thrown against the office window. I looked at my watch, it was 3.23.

The storm rolled away quickly, and I tried to get back to sleep. But I dreamt of Josephine sitting in an electric chair wearing her fancy new underwear and bright red lipstick. She looked at me, defiant as they threw the switch. Her head snapped back as two thousand volts coursed through her body. Her back arched and her red lips stretched back over white teeth.

"Is that all you've got?" she screamed. Josephine's pearl necklace was suddenly bathed in blood which ran down between her breasts. I saw it all then.

I woke early the next morning needing to be busy. There were lots of elements in my current cases that still needed working out. I'd got nowhere in my search for the bomb maker that blew up flight 402. Sure, I'd found Constance Brady, this had been the reason Paddy Brady had hired me. I'd found her all right…scooped her up like a butterfly in a net and transported her back to the life she'd been trying to escape. And (let's be honest) that hadn't worked out too well for Constance or Paddy Brady had it?

The murders of Lily Fung and Anna Thorne remained unsolved. As I'd feared Detective Grunwald was getting nowhere. That wasn't too surprising. It had all the hallmarks of an unsolvable mystery. It was such a random act; the usual police methods weren't designed to solve this kind of crime. A very high proportion of murder victims knew their attackers. So, the usual predictable plodding policeman would generally follow the victim's husband or lover around for a few days, drag him into a cell on some cooked-up pretext then sweat or beat a confession out of the poor wretch. Once you'd confirmed there were no close relatives or friends involved you were reduced to doing a poor impression of Inspector Renault in Casablanca. Grunwald had given the order to 'round up the usual suspects' and his minions had gone about their task with renewed relish, arresting any man with a history of violence toward women, suspected rapists and perverts, not forgetting the odd foreign national for good luck.

This well-ordered methodology had got the San Francisco Police Department absolutely nowhere. Grunwald and his cohorts had been busy enough, every city has its darker under-side and there were plenty of rapists and perverts on Grunwald's list of targets. He'd methodically worked his way almost to the bottom of the list giving each suspect a lesson in how to take a rabbit punch to the kidneys or how to fall downstairs on their way to the holding cell. He'd actually made three arrests while pounding his way through his suspects but none of them had confessed to the murders of Lily Fung and Anna Thorne. Interestingly no-one had heard anything about the crimes either.

It would have been easy (and tempting) to poke fun at the police but in truth, I had no brilliant insights about The Connie crash coming my way; I was doing just as badly. With nothing better to do, I decided to get a cab over to Sausalito and collect the key to my new life after the detective business. I was going to fly the Beaver back across the bay to its new home by the Hyde Street Pier.

The cab dropped me at the end of the jetty in Sausalito and I walked out to the Beaver, climbed aboard, and started my pre-flight checks. That's when I ran into a little problem, well two big problems really. One was the seriously pissed guy who came running down the jetty toward me and two was the very large Colt Automatic in his right hand. I clambered back up onto the dock and tried to explain that Paddy Brady had given me this fine shiny aircraft as payment for some private work I'd done for him recently. I showed him the documents for the transfer of ownership. He did not read them.

"Do I look stupid?" asked the muscle with the Colt. I resisted the very strong urge to ask if this was a trick question. I took the careful path here and told the big guy with the big gun that he looked anything but stupid…dangerous, maybe…homicidal, possibly, but not stupid. I could think of only one way to get around this pressing problem, well only one way that didn't involve me trying to man-handle a fully trained and very armed thug:

"Is Inga up at the hotel?" I asked.

"The tall dyke who dresses like a man?"

"Yes, that tall dyke." (How many tall dykes did they have?) "Is she up at the hotel?"

"What's that got to do with anything bub?" I took a deep breath, calmed myself before saying (slowly):

"Inga was with me when Mister Brady gave me the Beaver."

"The what now?"

"The Beaver, this aircraft is a de Havilland DHC-2 Beaver."

"You don't say?" I did say, and I went on to say that I was sure Inga would verify that I had been given all the relevant paperwork for the transfer of ownership. I then asked:

"Can we go talk to Inga?"

"We should go talk to Inga."

"That's a damn good idea," I said. I knew when I was licked.

"Come with me," said the mental colossus with the hand-gun. I went with him. We walked back along the jetty; I led the way. There was a phone in a small wooden box mounted on a post. He phoned the hotel, all the time training the Colt on my stomach. There was a short conversation which ended with:

"Inga's sending a car down for you."

"Great. Now we're getting somewhere." I said. Five minutes later Brady's limo arrived. I got in the front next to the driver for the short ride to the Sausalito Hotel. The limo dropped me on the corner. The driver told me:

"Miss Inga is upstairs in the office; she said to go straight up." Miss Inga?

Inga was lounging in Paddy Brady's chair when I walked into the office.

"Did you get promoted?" I asked.

"Kind of," she replied. "Half the men around here are illiterate, and Mister Brady doesn't trust the rest so I'm kind of running the place while he's away."

"Away. He's not gone for a long weekend at the Country Club. He's in San Quentin."

"He gets messages and instructions to me almost every day…"

"…And how long do you plan to keep doing this? The D.A.'s going to make sure Paddy never gets out."

"I wouldn't be too sure of that," she said. "Can I get you a drink, Rick? I know you like Mister Brady's Irish Whiskey, any preference?" I said:

"I shouldn't, I plan to be flying soon."

"About that…I don't think I can let you take the plane, Rick…"

"You don't think you can let me..."

"That's what I said."

"What the hell is going on? You know he gave me that plane and you know why!" I waved all the official documents in front of her. Inga lounged casually in Paddy's big leather chair.

"I've got all the paperwork and it's all official. You know that. You were there!"

"Calm down Rick, have a drink. I don't want to have you thrown out; the boys would surely hurt you. But you're not getting the plane. Paddy may be needing it for his own personal use."

"He's in San Quentin and he's not getting out! What does he want the plane for? Is it going to do fly-pasts outside his cell window? And another thing; who the fuck is going to fly it?"

"Oh Rick, you must know pilots are ten a penny right now. I don't think we'll have any trouble finding another dead beat, burnt out ex-war hero when the time comes."

As you can imagine I was steaming by this time. I'm not proud of what I said next but hey, as I say, I was steaming. I said:

"I wouldn't get too comfortable behind that big desk Inga. Maybe I'll get a message to Paddy Brady myself. Tell him all about how you used to fuck his wife! We'll see who he trusts then." And with that witty repost, I walked out.

I drove back into town, parked the car behind the office, and dove into the nearest saloon. The place was practically deserted, so I sat at the end of the bar and drank steadily for a few hours. At some point, I must have read the paper because days later details of a story on page three came back to me. It was about a Second Lieutenant in the Japanese Army who refused to believe that the war was over. He had hidden out on Lubang Island in the Philippines in 1945 and waged a guerrilla war on the local police and army personnel until his capture three weeks ago.

When his hideout was over-run one U.S. Army officer lost a hand when a booby-trapped ammunition box exploded as he opened it. There was a diagram showing how the ammo box had been rigged with a hand-grenade wired to the inside of the lid. Opening the box had pulled the pin. Major Alan Nesmith (24) had seen the grenade as he opened the ammo box but had been unable to distance himself from the blast and had lost his right hand in the explosion. Major Nesmith had been awarded the Purple Heart.

Second Lieutenant Yuichi Onoda (29) expressed regret for the incident but stated that he thought all notifications regarding the end of the war he had seen had been tricks to get him to surrender. Yuichi Onoda had weighed less than one hundred pounds at the time of his capture. He was shown a film of the official surrender ceremony on the U.S.S. Missouri while recovering from malnutrition and malaria in a hospital in Manila.

All this information must have soaked into my booze-addled brain somehow, like beer soaking into a bar towel. It would become very relevant a few days later. I was thrown out of the bar some-time around midnight. I slept in my suit and woke up the next day feeling like cat vomit.

Two solid days of self-loathing later I got a cab down to Hyde Street to have a word with my old friend Sammy Kirk. Things were quiet in the photography business, but Sammy was still stomping along the pier trying to drum up some trade. It was unseasonably warm for late September but even still there weren't many people around.

"I thought you were giving up this gig Sammy," I said.

"It's a hard habit to break Rick. I like talking to the ladies, you know that." I asked Sammy if he could spare me a few minutes from his busy schedule of chatting up dames. We went to the nearest diner and I stood him breakfast. I had four pints of black coffee; at least I think it was four pints. I told Sammy about my stalled new business venture: Rick's Flying Tours. Sammy said:

"You should take the exchange documents to Melvin. He'll sort things out for you, may take a while…what with Brady being in the slammer."

Now, why didn't I think of that? (The first person to say: 'cos you're a drunken asshole who's losing his marbles' gets a knuckle sandwich.) I asked Sammy:

"If and when we do get this sorted out are you interested in running the ticket booth? You'll have to talk to lots of dames and you can still work the old camera routine if you like." Sammy pretended to think over his options.

"I'm not too sure Rick. I've got a lot of irons in the fire…"

"What irons?"

"I'm shitting ya! Sure I'm in. You just let me know when we get started." We shook on the deal. I said I'd talk to Melvin about the plane and about drawing up a contract between the two of us. As I walked away feeling much happier with myself Sammy called out:

"Rick, this could be the start of a beautiful friendship!" That ass-hole, I thought I was the only one who did quotes from movies. I got a cab to Melvin Hammerstein's office right away. Melvin had found himself a new receptionist/secretary. I don't know what he was paying her, but it wasn't enough! She was a dark-skinned temptress called Lola Cornwall. She was from Shreveport Louisiana and she can't have been twenty-two. She dressed like she was an extra from one of those old swashbuckling pirate movies like Captain Blood, you know the kind of thing, a low-cut peasant blouse, lots of black wavy hair and big (I mean really big) ear-rings. Lola said hello as I walked in:

"Mister Hammerstein is with a client at the moment, I'm not sure how long he'll be."

"I don't mind waiting if that's okay," says me. And I sit down in the chair facing Lola's desk. "You carry on with what you're doing Miss…"

"…Cornwall, Lola Cornwall."

"Miss Cornwall. Don't let me disturb you."

"Oh, you don't disturb me none," she said with a smile that I felt right down in my shorts. Melvin walked out of his office about twenty minutes later, he said goodbye to his client, a tiny wizened woman who looked to be at least ninety years old.

"I'll have the divorce papers written up by tomorrow Mrs. Maltby and don't you worry you'll be looking for a new husband in no time."

Mrs. Maltby kissed Melvin on both cheeks and practically skipped out of the door. Melvin ushered me into his office.

"I see you've been talking to my Miss Cornwall. I can tell by the bulge in your pants and the mile-wide smile on your face. She is an uplifting young thing, isn't she?"

"Melvin Hammerstein she will be the death of you."

"Probably," said Melvin and he didn't look to be too worried by the prospect.

"What can I do for you this fine day, Rick?"

I told Melvin all about the confrontation with Inga at the Sausalito Hotel. He rubbed an earlobe, his left, and said:

"I must admit I am somewhat surprised and saddened by Miss Bjarkardóttir's change of heart. I would not have thought that possible in such a lady. She seemed like such a straight arrow."

"Well it's possible and it happened just like I said. I think they are planning on using the Beaver, my Beaver to fly Brady out of the country, that's if they get him out on bail."

"That's highly unlikely as I see it, but anything is possible I suppose. With regards to the aircraft, possession is often said to be nine-tenths of the law and it's going to be difficult to move any legal proceedings quickly enough to prevent Brady and your aircraft flying the proverbial coop…if he gets out. You should put the new Acting District Attorney in the picture about Brady's access to a private aircraft. He can emphasize the potential flight risk at Brady's upcoming bail hearing. But I should warn you, Rick. It is possible Brady has a judge or two on his payroll. If one of these should just happen to be assigned the bail hearing, well…like I said; anything could happen."

"Could I borrow your phone, I'll call Dwight now."

"Why don't you use the one on Miss Cornwall's desk? The view is so much more interesting from there. And Rick...isn't it about time we started those divorce proceedings?"

I shook Melvin's hand.

"You know Mister Hammerstein; I do believe you might be right." We both walked through to Miss Cornwall's boudoir and were disappointed to find it empty. Seconds later she came in carrying three coffees on a tray.

"I thought coffee might be just the thing you gentlemen could use." I took a cup and asked Miss Cornwall:

"How would you like to work in a sight-seeing company Miss Cornwall? Nice office looking out over the bay, raise in pay; all the free flights you like." Melvin pointed a finger at me.

"Now now Rick." Miss Cornwall smiled sweetly:

"Oh, I'm so happy here, why would I want to move?" I have never seen Melvin Hammerstein look so pleased. He was laughing as he said:

"Well played Miss Cornwall; well played. I think you are going to fit in ever so well here."

After I phoned the D.A.'s office I checked in with my answering service. There were four messages from Josephine, each one asking me to call her urgently. My guess was she'd seen the tickets I'd placed in her make-up drawer. I gave her a call, not knowing how she'd react to my little prank. Ko's tickets were all for the middle of next week. As I dialed, I wondered what could be so urgent. Josephine picked up after one ring:

"He's gone. Ko's disappeared!" she bleated between loud anguished sobs.

"Already?" I asked. Then I realized this would tip Josephine off that I'd been in the house...that I was the wise guy who'd put Ko's tickets in her drawer. Jo didn't make the connection, or if she did, she was past caring. She obviously wasn't thinking straight. I got my act together and said:

"Tell me what's happened."

"He didn't come home last night, and I can't get hold of him at the office."

"And that means he's skipped town?" I needed to know if Josephine had checked her make-up drawer, so I asked:

"Are you dressed?"

"What's that got to do with anything? I call to tell you Ko's disappeared, and you want to know what I'm wearing? You really are a sick bastard!"

"Jo? Jo! Can you calm down for a second? I'm just trying to get a chain of events in my mind. I don't really know what you want from me." I could hear panicky breathing over the phone, Jo was becoming hysterical. I really wanted to know if Ko's tickets were still in the drawer but there was no way to get Jo to check for me. I had to go over and see for myself.

"Jo, I'm coming over. Why don't you go back to bed for a while? I'll be there as quick as I can."

I said goodbye to Melvin and his exotic new employee. I flagged down a cab on the street corner and race back to my office, jumped in the M.G. and did some more racing over the Bay Bridge to Oakland. Jo met me at the door; she must have been peering out of the window, waiting for me to arrive. It was clear she hadn't been near the drawer with the tickets in.

"I need to pee," I said; I brushed past her and ran upstairs to the bathroom. I checked Josephine's make-up drawer. The travel documents were all where I left them. This did not look good for Ko den Hamer. My guess was he'd crossed Mickey Cohen and he'd been lifted by some of his men. Ko was most likely hanging from his ankles in a warehouse somewhere, his balls wired up to a car battery…couldn't have happened to a nicer guy.

Before going back downstairs I remembered to flush the toilet. I pocketed the rail and sea tickets and joined Josephine in the kitchen. Ko wouldn't be needing them now and I didn't want her to know how the Dutch fuck had planned to ditch her after using her for over a year.

"What do you think has happened?" she asked. I shrugged my shoulders.

"I don't have a clue and you don't want me to guess."

"You don't have to be so smug about it. You can hardly keep a straight face you're so happy."

"Me? This is my normal face. I know it's not much to look at…"

"Liar! You're lapping this up."

"I have no idea what you're talking about Jo. I can't say I'm sorry he's gone…wherever he is. Maybe he's been arrested. You should call the F.B.I. or the D.A.s office." Jo was getting very angry. She started patting imaginary pockets in her robe saying:

"That's funny; I had the number for the F.B.I. right here somewhere…I must have lost it."

"They're in the phone directory," I said. "I do know someone at the D.A.'s office. I could check with them."

"Who do you know at the District Attorney's office?"

"The District Attorney."

"Very funny," she said. Without another word I picked up the phone, dialed and asked to be put through to Elton Dwight.

"Tell him its Rick Marshall." I was put straight through. The look on Josephine's face was so funny. She wasn't sure if I was faking the whole thing. She leaned in close to listen to the call. Dwight came on the line:

"Rick…any thoughts on that job offer?"

"Still thinking about it Mister Dwight…I thought you should know Ko den Hamer has not been seen for almost twenty-four hours, he's disappeared. Do you know if the F.B.I. has arrested him?" Elton Dwight had no news about any arrests. He said he'd get someone to check and leave a message with my service. Josephine had calmed a little by the time I ended the call. I suggested we go downtown and check the office on Embarcadero.

"Maybe we'll find some kind of clue there," I said. Jo asked:

"You know about the office?" I nodded.

"Get dressed, I'll drive you. Wear something warm."

"Why?"

"You'll find out." Josephine was ready in ten minutes. It was a good thing I'd taken the tickets out of the make-up drawer. She'd put the rest of its contents to very good use. She looked great considering she'd just lost her lover. She wore a long woolen skirt, a light grey blouse and a fitted jacket in dark blue, almost the same color as her skirt. I took her favorite coat from the hall stand and helped her into it.

"Wait here," I said. "I had way too much coffee this morning…gotta go."

"Again?" she asked. I hurried upstairs, put the tickets back in the bedside table, and hurried back down. When we got to the M.G. Josephine looked down on it…I mean she really looked down on it:

"Where's the Plymouth?"

"Shot full of holes by den Hamer's business partners!" I opened Josephine's door with a flourish.

"Your carriage awaits," I said.

"You have got to be kidding," she said, but she got in anyway. We didn't speak on the ride downtown; Josephine clung to the dashboard all the way. Her knuckles were white by the time I threw the little car left off Embarcadero and into the parking lot behind their office building. I must admit I'd kept my foot down most of the way. When we got up to the office Josephine tried the key in the lock. The door swung open slowly.

"It's not locked," she whispered. Inside Josephine checked the desk drawers and the filing cabinet.

"Is anything missing?" I asked. Jo didn't answer.

"For Christ's sake Jo I can't help you if you aren't going to be honest with me." And I know that was a stupid thing to say considering why we were in that office. Josephine hadn't been honest with me for a long time. She didn't say anything.

"You know what?" I said. "I'm out of here. I don't know why I'm helping you at all. I hope the Dutch fuck is six feet under already…or very soon will be. I don't owe you anything except a one-way trip to Reno and a quickie divorce!" Fancy tough-guy speech hey? If only I had had the balls to mean what I said. Josephine looked at me with eyes rimmed with red. Tears began to trickle down her cheeks. Finally, she said:

"If you must know, there's nothing left about the land deals and the money transfers. Most of the papers in the filing cabinets were here when we leased the office space. We just hid our papers underneath. Now all our important documents are gone. This place has been cleaned out."

"By who?"

"What do you mean by who? How should I know?"

"We need to know if Ko took all the evidence and made his escape or did someone take all the papers when they took him?"

"That's a damn good question," said a voice from the doorway. The voice belonged to one of four F.B.I. agents currently pointing service revolvers at us. I asked:

"Who the hell are you?"

"That's my line and (if you don't mind) can we have your hands where we can see them?" I said:

"I'm Rick Marshall, I'm a private investigator, Elton Dwight can vouch for me and this is..."

"...We know who she is and she's coming with us."

Chapter Twenty - Five

Paddy Brady's ludicrously expensive lawyer had him out of jail two days later. I guess all the talk of 'possible flight risk' was out-weighed by Brady's lack of previous convictions, his charity work, and donations to the Mayor's re-election war-chest. In the end, money talks, and Mr. Brady did have a lot of it. Brady had surrendered his passport which also worked in his favor, I guess. Elton Dwight's office called me first thing and asked that I get over to meet with him asap.

When I got there, I was shown straight through to his inner sanctum. He was on the phone, he held up one finger. I stood to attention at Dwight's desk. He was Acting District Attorney after all. He might have been Acting D.A. but he was not a happy camper, not by a long way.

"I know he's one of the best attorneys on the West Coast…I went to law school with him. What I want to know is this: How can Mister Brady afford to retain his services if, as you claim, we have frozen all his assets and bank accounts?" The voice on the other end of the line said something snippy, I think. Not a wise move.

"Yes, I agree it does seem likely that he has accounts you weren't aware of you idiot! I'd like to suggest in the strongest possible terms that you find those accounts and quickly. That is if you wish to remain in the employ of the San Francisco District Attorney's Office." Elton Dwight slammed down the receiver. It bounced off the cradle. He slammed it down for a second time. He turned to me.

"Sit down Rick; you look like you're up on a charge." I sat. Luckily there was a chair behind me.

"Job for you Rick…I want you to tail our mutual friend Douglas Patrick Brady twenty-four-seven. I'll pay your usual rate, nothing more, and I'll need receipts for any out of pocket expenses. If he attempts to abscond you call me. Any time of day…you call me. Here's my home number. If he stands trial, I will pay you a bonus and a permanent job within the District Attorney's Office is yours from that date…deal?"

"Deal," says me. We shook on it. I asked:

"Do we know where he is right now?"

"We have an operative watching his house on Vallejo…"

"Tara."

"Sorry?"

"The house on Vallejo is called Tara."

"You cannot be serious…you are being serious! That is extremely amusing I must say…Tara…Ha! You've made my morning Rick, thank you. Keep up the good work." I left Elton Dwight's office and drove to Vallejo to keep up the good work as instructed. I spotted the guy watching Brady's house on my first drive-by. It wasn't hard. It was unusually warm for early October, but this clown was wearing an overcoat and a hat. He was also wearing sunglasses. He stood on the street corner watching the comings and goings over the top of a newspaper. If he'd made a sign saying:

'Undercover Cop, please move along, nothing to see here.'

He could not have been more obvious. I parked a block away on Green Street and walked back to speak to the cop. He wasn't the brightest of recruits but eventually, I persuaded him that I was really there to take over from him. He asked if I needed a 'sit-rep' but as I had no idea what a 'sit-rep' was I gave it a miss.

The house behind me, diagonally across Vallejo from Brady's place looked to be empty. I went around back just to make sure. Then I came back to the front and made myself comfortable and inconspicuous on a handy bench by the front door. I could see the front of Brady's house and more importantly any vehicles entering or leaving the yard to the rear. I had recently invested in some army-surplus binoculars and I used them to scan the upper floor. I'm sure I saw a flash of very blonde hair in one of the rooms, so I guess Inga was close by. I settled down for a long day.

On the way over to Vallejo, I'd called on Sammy Kirk. He'd agreed to take the night shift starting at seven that evening. Hopefully the owners of the house I was using as an observation post were away for a few days and also hopefully Sammy had the good sense to bring a blanket and some hooch. It could get cold at night in October.

Five minutes into my shift all hell broke loose across the street. Three identical limousines pulled up nose to tail outside Tara. What looked like heavy trunks and cases were brought out and loaded into all three cars. I had to make a quick decision. If Brady was leaving in one of these limos, I couldn't follow him on foot. I had to get to the M.G. I crouched down out of sight and scurried to the end of the porch. I jumped over the railing, landing in a strategically placed holly bush. I scrambled to my feet and ran as fast as I could to the car pulling prickly leaves from my pants as I went. I started her up and edged around the corner onto Vallejo. I was just in time. The convoy was just pulling slowly away from the sidewalk.

I followed them, not too close, but close enough to keep all three in view. Traffic wasn't heavy but I still had a major problem. Assuming Brady was in one of these cars…which car was he in? I had no guarantee that the three cars were heading to the same place. I couldn't pull alongside and check every back seat. The M.G. was too well known to most of the people on Brady's staff. I decided I would have to get closer, once we got to wider streets. From where I was, I couldn't pick out Paddy Brady in one of the cars. What should I do if they split up?

The three limos turned right down Divisadero. I did the same, being careful not to get too close. After only five blocks they came to Lombard Street, they all turned left. Were they heading for the Golden Gate? Sausalito maybe?

Lombard Street took a turn to the right and became Richardson Avenue. They were heading for the bridge! Houses either side of Richardson thinned out as we entered The Presidio. I could see the Golden Gate Bridge away to my right. As we passed the National Cemetery on the left; the three limousines began to speed up. I took a chance, put my foot down, and pulled alongside the tail end Charlie. I couldn't see anyone in the rear seats. I dropped down into third and accelerated again but as I did so the second limo pulled alongside the first, blocking my way.

We swept around the right-hand bend and onto the approach to the bridge. I could smell the salt air from the bay. For a second a saw a flash of blonde hair in the rear seat of the right-hand limo. I figured Inga would be travelling with Brady, so I decided to stick with that car if they split up. The bizarre convoy slowed right down and inched through the toll booths. I paid my forty cents and followed the right-hand limo. I was followed in turn by the last of the three cars.

We were on the bridge now; I was following the right-hand limo fairly closely; all thoughts of staying un-noticed had been forgotten. All the cars picked up speed and I was soon in the center of a triangle of limousines crossing the Golden Gate Bridge at close to sixty-five miles an hour.

The rear window of the right-hand car was wound down; Inga's trademark blonde hair was clearly visible as was the Beretta in her right hand. Believe it or not our eyes met for an instant. Then I saw a puff of smoke and a bullet clanged off the hood of the M.G. I swerved to the left and tried hard to put the third limo between me and the blonde with the Beretta. Another shot whipped past my head just as I caught up with the left-hand limo. I was able to sit the

M.G. just behind the long trunk of the dark green limo. Every now and then I risked looking over at the car carrying Inga and most likely Brady.

As we roared off the bridge the right-hand car with Inga onboard, and hopefully Brady, took the first exit for Cavallo Point. The left-hand car in front of me sped northward. I decided to let him go. I couldn't follow them all and by now I'd rolled the dice anyway. I was sticking with Inga's limo. I figured they were heading down to the dock by Point Cavallo probably to meet up with the Kilkenny. All the talk about needing the Beaver and a pilot had been hooey! If Brady was taking all these chests with him there was no way he was flying out of here in the Beaver. The limo behind me was still there. I was now the filling in a limousine sandwich. When we got down to the water's edge I was going to be in deep doo-doo. There was no way I was going to stop Brady from getting on the Kilkenny and sailing away. But I had to do something.

My plan was simple…it had to be; I'd just made it up. I would stay un-shot, confirm Brady was on the boat, and then phone in the newsflash to Elton Dwight. He could call out the Coastguard or the Marines or the University Synchronized Swimming Team for all I cared and try to stop Brady. I looked back over my right shoulder as the convoy started down the hill toward the bay. I could see the Army camp and behind it, in the distance the rust-colored towers of the Golden Gate Bridge. I wonder why they didn't paint it gold. I mean, they couldn't call it the Dull Rusty Gate Bridge, could they?

All three cars slowed as we got to the bottom of the hill. I could see the Kilkenny waiting for its passengers, moored at the jetty. My guess was it already had extra fuel and provisions aboard; it was going to be a long trip, wherever they went. But what would be their final destination? And was Ko den Hamer hiding below decks too? I turned away from the water, drove quickly behind a line of wooden workshops, and skidded to a halt. Jumping from the car I ran back toward the waterfront just in time to see Paddy Brady and Inga getting out of the first limousine. Inga looked back as she walked down the gangplank…I'm not sure if she saw me.

I had to find a phone. I ran back along the line of workshops, all of them were locked. I hammered on each door I came to but the empty echoes from inside told their own story. I looked through the grimy windows of the last building in the row. It was a Ship's Chandlers I think and there was a phone on the wall to the right, behind a battered pealing counter. I tested the door, it felt pretty firm. In the dust by my feet, I found a length of piping about eight inches long. I used it to smash the murky glass panel in the door. Trying not to cut my wrist I reached in to find the lock.

That's when a Doberman the size of a small pony came charging round from the rear of the counter. I got my hand out just in time as the massive animal thumped into the door from the other side. The whole building shook as I fell back in the dust.

"You wanna tell me what you're doing there bub?"

I turned around and looked up at a rangy individual, long-limbed, wearing faded; paint-spattered overalls. He was probably in his sixties; he certainly looked the part of the weather-beaten mariner. His white hair was long and straggly.

"Well?" he said. "Don't wanna talk? How about I let Duke out and see if he can persuade you?"

I said: "No need. I'll talk; I was just getting my breath…"

"Duke has that effect. That's why I keep him in the shop."

"I need to call someone, it's an emergency."

"Who you gotta call an' how come it's so urgent you have to break into my shop?"

"I have to call the District Attorney." The tall guy wasn't impressed. He shouted.

"Duke!" and the thudding intensified. Duke began to bark in a booming bass.

"It's the truth; I'm a P.I. working for Elton Dwight."

"Who he? I ain't never heard of him."

"He's going to be the next District Attorney, he's acting…"

"He's an actor?" This was like pulling the teeth out of an alligator's mouth. I explained that Elton Dwight was the Acting District Attorney and he'd be happy to compensate him for the damage to his door if I could use his phone right now. The tall guy thought about that for a while.

"… And I'll give you a dollar for one phone call." That sealed the deal. He opened the door and shouted at Duke to get in his bed. The dog stomped into the rear of the shop, obviously disappointed at missing out on a fresh meal…me. The rangy guy said:

"He won't hurt you now, so long as you're with me." I was very glad to hear that. I phoned Elton Dwight and warned him of Paddy Brady's plans to skip town. Dwight asked:

"Can you get a good look at that boat? Report back when you see which way they're headed?"

"I can do that, for sure. But there's only one way he's going to be going, under the Golden Gate and out to sea. Once he's far enough out we won't have any way of knowing where he's going."

"I'm going to speak to the Coast Guard. They have a cutter stationed at Treasure Island. Maybe we can head him off."

"I'll get down to the dock and give you a call-back."

The Kilkenny was still moored when I got down to the water's edge but the whole scene was one of frantic activity. She was clearly about to set sail. Deck-hands were rolling back the gangplank and her dock-lines were being released. There was a familiar figure waiting for me on the dockside. She was wearing men's jeans, a white T-shirt and a baggy black jacket. She smiled a sad smile as I came toward her. She also pointed her Beretta at my head.

"Hi Rick, how's it hanging?" I should have had a witty one-liner to answer that one, but nothing came to mind.

"Going on a trip?" I asked.

"Not me. I've been canned. Come on Rick, let's take a walk." I asked:

"Where to?"

"Nowhere special; just away from here…Mister Brady's last orders."

"But if he canned you why follow his orders?" Inga pointed the way with her gun, back up the hill away from the water.

"I guess I'm just wired that way, you know…loyal."

"Loyalty doesn't get you shit, you know that? Was it loyalty that made you take those pot-shots at me on the bridge?"

"I didn't hit you, did I? You know Rick you're way too sensitive for this kind of game. I was just following orders. I could have killed you lots of times if I'd wanted to."

"And I'm supposed to be grateful you chose not to?" Inga gave me a little nudge in the kidneys with her gun.

"You do know I still have the gun, don't you?"

"Where are we going?" I asked. We climbed a few hundred yards through a small copse and eventually we approached the top of a grassy slope looking down on Cavallo Harbor. The Kilkenny was already well into the bay, making a wide turn to the west, heading under The Golden Gate. Inga said:

"Here's fine. Sit down, Rick." I sat down in the long grass. The warm early afternoon sun was stronger than I expected for October. The leaves on the trees below us were red and brown and yellow. I could smell the salt air. I heard birdsong from somewhere not too far away. I expected to hear the sound of a Beretta going off from very close by. For some reason, I held my breath. I closed my eyes. After some time, Inga spoke:

"What am I going to do with you Rick?" I opened my eyes. Inga was lying next to me. The Beretta was back in her jacket pocket, I think. I asked her:

"Is Ko den Hamer on the Kilkenny with Brady?" She shook her head.

"He's gone missing; you know…did you ever see him with Paddy Brady?" Again, Inga shook her head.

"I've got to get going…I have to let Elton Dwight know about the Kilkenny."

"Stay with me Rick, just for a while," she said. "You don't owe Elton Dwight anything and I don't owe Brady. If we just stay here for a time nobody has to get hurt."

"By hurt, you mean shot with your Beretta."

"Maybe." The Kilkenny was out of sight now.

"Where's he headed?" I asked.

"You know I wouldn't tell you that; even if I knew."

"Loyal to the end, hey? You know he used you. He's an old school Irish/American gangster. There's no way he'd let a woman run his operation."

"And especially not a Dyke?"

"I didn't say that. You know what I mean."

"Oh, I know what you mean Rick." Inga was looking up at the sky; white clouds meandered slowly above us. "Tell me…I've always wondered…ever since we met, I've always half expected you to make a serious pass at me. You know, the macho guy thinks he can 'fix' a lesbian with one wave of his mighty dick. Most guys I've known eventually get round to it. They start out playing it cool, but you can tell deep down they are thinking: 'what a waste!' You never did. I practically threw myself at you a number of times."

"Are you offended?" I asked. Inga laughed.

"You always could make me smile Rick." I lay back on the grass beside her; pulled my hat down over my eyes. I tried hard to think of the right thing to say. Eventually, this gibberish came out of my mouth:

"Okay…if we're being totally honest here…you know, and I know that you're a looker. Even dressed like a guy you know you have an…an effect on saps like me."

"An effect?"

"You know what I mean…"

"Maybe you're attracted to tall blonde guys?" she said.

"Nnnnooo I don't think so. What I'm saying…what I'm trying to say is this. I have thought about you…in that way, lots of times. And at certain times I have wanted to, you know…"

"What?"

"You know…" Inga sounded like she was trying hard not to laugh out loud. Like an idiot, I pressed on.

"The whole thing with Josephine and Ko has really hit me. It's been tough, for a while I was at my lowest point since the war and…" I pushed back the hat and rubbed my ear. It was a habit I couldn't quit. Any time I talked about the B17 engine fire and my injuries my left ear itched like hell.

"I've had to make some adjustments…"

"…Like living out of your office."

"Like living out of the office."

"And it's been a while since I…Since I've…"

"…Oh, that kind of adjustment," she said. "That must be a very difficult adjustment to make."

"Yes, it's hard all right." And with that choice phrase ringing in the air, we both began to laugh like we'd never stop. Inga looked down at my groin. She said:

"Yes, I can see it's getting very hard for you." The whole situation was bizarre I'll grant you. Infantile dick jokes on a hillside while Inga's ex-employer, a well-known gangster about town was fleeing the country. I didn't care. It was the first time I'd really laughed for ages. Inga slid on top of me and we rolled around in the grass like five-year-olds. Except one five year old still had a massive boner. Inga went on:

"…It's okay Rick. I know I talk tough and maybe I do still prefer girls but maybe, just maybe it might be fun to fool around with a decent guy every now and then. Maybe I can make my own adjustments."

"Wow, you make it sound so casual," I said.

"It is Rick, it's just sex; that's all. Jeez, remember when I put that ticket down my bra at the racetrack? You'd have thought my tits were booby-trapped." Inga really started laughing at her accidental joke. "Booby-trapped! Get it?"

The brain is a very funny thing, I'm sure you know that. But I found it out for sure on that hill overlooking Cavallo Harbor, because it was at that exact point that I realized who had blown up the Lockheed Constellation and why.

Chapter Twenty - Six

And so, the rolling around had to stop. I stood up. Inga lay at my feet looking up at me.

"What's wrong Rick? We were only goofing around. Nothing's going to happen unless you want it to. You know I like you, Rick, I thought we'd just got that clear."

"It's not that, something just came up." Inga ran her hand up my thigh.

"I can see that," she said; then she saw my face. "What's going on Rick?"

"I know who blew up the Connie."

"…And you're going to tell me?"

"I'll tell you on the way. We need to get to the car." I set off down the hill back to Cavallo Point. We drove back up to the highway and I turned right, put my foot down. As we drove, I told Inga all about Second Lieutenant Yuichi Onoda and his ammo box booby trap. I'm not sure if she made the connection but I knew she would when we reached our destination.

I stopped for gas in San Rafael and I took my chance to phone Elton Dwight. He was none too pleased by the head start the Kilkenny had but I explained that I'd been held at gunpoint for an hour while Brady had sailed off into the sunset. Later, as we drove into the town of Napa Inga turned to me saying:

"The Flight Engineer's wife!"

"…widow," I said.

"She booby-trapped his lunchbox!"

"That's what I figure; she worked in a munition's factory during the war, so she knew her way around explosives. He used an old ammo box to carry sandwiches in. My guess is she wired the handle to pull the pin on a grenade inside the ammo box…"

"…Just like the Jap soldier," interjected Inga. "She knew all about his playing around with women at work."

"And she saw a way to get rid of him and get a new home at the same time." Inga was quiet for a moment. I turned left onto Sonoma Road.

"Don't forget she mentioned increasing the premiums on his life insurance. My guess is she hoped he'd not get peckish till the Connie was out over the Pacific at cruising altitude. There'd be no witnesses and the recovery of any wreckage would have been impossible. For some reason, Stu Brown opened the lunchbox just after take-off."

"...and Boom!!!" said Inga. I closed my eyes for an instant and we nearly ran into a ditch. Inga tugged on the wheel and saved our bacon.

"Sorry," she said.

Stu Brown's house was gone, replaced by the wooden framework of a structure five times the size. All the army surplus gear in the yard had now been cleared. An advertising board on the roadside said:

ANOTHER FINE HOME BEING BUILT
BY
FRED BELMONT CONSTRUCTION

I was happy to see that our previous visit hadn't cost Fred Belmont any business. I was less happy to see that Mrs. Brown was not at home to visitors. I asked Inga to slink over and find out where Mrs. Brown was staying while her new dream home was under construction. She took off her boxy black jacket, tucked her tight white T-shirt into her jeans, thus making it even tighter, then she sashayed across the road to a chorus of wolf whistles from the framers working on the house.

She came back over a few minutes later, with more whistles and comments following. Inga didn't seem to mind the attention she was getting; not half as much as I did. We would really have to talk things through about us, and soon. I had to get my head straight. Sure, it was fun getting all flirty and having fun with Inga. She was a great dame. But if she was wired in such a way that I'd never stand a chance with her...

"She's staying with her sister in Santa Rosa."

"Did you get an address?" Inga held up a scrap of paper with an address scrawled in pencil.

"Are we going over there now?" she asked. I'd thought about this as we drove up to Napa. I guess I'd also calmed down a little. So, I said:

"...And do what? We don't have any evidence; we don't have any proof. The only way we can nail her is if we get her to confess."

"Let's go anyway. I'm sure you can work something out on the way."

"Not today," I said. "She's not going anywhere. She thinks she's got away with murder so she's in no hurry to skip town. Don't forget she plans on moving into her dream house just as soon as it's finished." I started the M.G.

"Are you hungry?" Inga nodded. "Let's head back to Main Street and grab a sandwich at your favorite malt shop, maybe your gentleman admirer is working today." Inga elbowed me playfully and said:

"Ass-hole."

When we got back to town, I dropped Inga at the club then headed back to the office. Once there I called Elton Dwight to bring him up to speed on my attempts to stop Paddy Brady's escape.

"Ass-hole." Was the first thing he called me and the conversation sort of went south from there. Of course, the offer of a permanent role in the D.A.s office was rescinded on the spot. Hey, if I'm honest (and my momma brought me up to be a good boy) if I'm honest I wasn't too ticked off about losing that job. There was no way I could work for Elton Dwight month in month out. I'd end up wringing his neck in the first few weeks. So, we both dodged a bullet there.

My next call was to Josephine my (soon to be ex) wife. I wanted to check if Ko den Hamer had resurfaced, he hadn't. Jo asked what I was doing for a meal that night. I said:

"Nothing I can't heartlessly cancel."

"Do you want to come over? I made lasagne." I should have heard the alarm bells right there and then. Lasagne isn't something you just throw together. It takes a little time and planning to get it right. So, I should have known that Josephine had got plans.

"I can grab some beers," I suggested.

"Could you get a bottle of wine instead?" she asked. This was the second time she'd asked me to get wine for a meal. The last time she'd met me at the door only half-dressed. I should have smelled a rat. I said I'd try to find a decent bottle of red. I went to the liquor store on the corner. I'd never bought wine at this store before. I asked the guy behind the counter for a good bottle of red wine and he looked at me real funny. Just like the guy in the last liquor store I'd tried to buy wine at. He said:

"We don't sell wine here, just beer and hard liquor for guys that wanna get drunk fast."

"I know that, I'm not new to this, I'm just new to wine. I got a dame asking for a bottle of wine and I figure it's a good idea to get her one."

"Wish I could help," said Mr. Surly behind the counter. Luckily Mr. Surly's boss comes in through the back door at just that second.

"You're looking for red wine, sir?" I nod. The boss digs around under the counter and comes up with a bottle of red with the name Beringer Brothers on it. "It's from a local winery in St. Helena, that's way north of here, about ten miles north of a town called Napa."

"I was there this morning," I said. That sealed the deal. This guy was a bit of an enthusiast for the grape I guess you could say. He goes on and on about how wine-making is going to take off in the farmlands north of San Pablo Bay. Tells me I should put some money into property up there. What a load of hooey! I'd seen what most of the farms up there were like. I wouldn't put a penny into any of them.

It took me twenty minutes to get out of there! By the time he'd finished, I felt sure that I was stepping back into the street with a gift from the Gods and Mother Nature all wrapped up in one lousy bottle of wine. I put the bottle in the passenger seat and drove out to Oakland. I pulled up behind Mr. Loomis's Chevy and walked across the street carrying my prized bottle of Cabernet Sauvignon which was, I was told, just the thing to serve with home-made lasagna.

Josephine met me at the door. She was wearing her best 'going out dancing' dress and she had her long hair swept over one shoulder. Normally she would be wearing her favorite pearl necklace with an outfit like this. She wasn't wearing it today. I had a good idea why she wasn't.

She took off the tiny apron she was wearing as we walked into the kitchen. She wiped her hands on a towel nervously as I searched in the drawers for something I knew we didn't have...a cork-screw. Finally, I offered to go next door and see if the neighbors had one. Josephine insisted I put my feet up in the front room and she hurried around to the neighbors.

I didn't stay in the front room for long. I ran upstairs and chased around the bedroom and bathroom trying to find Josephine's pearls. Just as I'd feared they were nowhere to be found. I raced back downstairs with an empty feeling in my stomach. Sure, I was hungry, but this was something else. Josephine came back minutes later with a fancy contraption that looked like something you would stick on the top of a Norden Bomb Site. She was slightly breathless as she said:

"The Kleins say this is the best one on the market. They just bought it. Ellie said lots of people are 'getting into' wine now. It's the next big thing."

"No shit," said I.

"It's the truth," said Jo. Eventually, I work out how to use the bottle opener and I get the bottle opened without spilling any. A good sign, I thought. Josephine pulled the lasagne out of the oven.

"You hungry?" she asked.

"Starving, I've been driving around for most of the day."

"In that funny little red car?"

"It's the only one I got at the moment," I said. "Might buy a pick-up if the sight-seeing business goes the way I plan it."

"What sight-seeing business?" asked Jo. I told her all about my plans for a sight-seeing empire and my little spot of trouble, i.e. no plane. Jo served the lasagne, I poured the wine into two tumblers and we ate and drank in silence for a while. It was kinda awkward. It felt like we were two generals at a table and one of us was about to sign a surrender document. I couldn't say which one of us was the victor, getting the spoils of war and which one was going to pay reparations and be occupied. Still, the lasagne was really good. I told her so. She seemed genuinely pleased. In the end, I had to break the spell and there was really only one way to do it:

"So, you've not heard anything from the Flying Dutchman?" Jo shook her head; her eyes remained on her plate. She hadn't eaten much at all.

"And the police haven't been in touch?" Another shake of the head, the conversation ground to a halt again, the occasional scraping of my knife and fork seemed to echo around the kitchen.

"How come the F.B.I. let you go? I thought they were going to lock you up and throw away the key."

"And you'd like that I guess," she snapped.

"I didn't say that." After that little joust the conversation kind of dwindled away to nothing. Jo continued to stare at her plate, every now and then she moved a mouthful of pasta around. I finished up, put my knife, and fork down with a clatter that made Josephine jump.

"Sorry…do you want some more wine?" Jo poured me another tumbler but only put a drop in her glass.

"What are you gonna do?" I asked.

"Get a lawyer?"

"It's a start. Do you want me to talk to Melvin?" I knew by then that Josephine was going to need all the legal help she could find. I knew that if her pearl necklace was found when the F.B.I. searched this house (as they would any day now) Melvin Hammerstein was really going to earn his corn. I knew what Josephine had done but I could only guess why. Sure, things hadn't gone the way she'd planned on that night and maybe, just maybe Melvin could get some mileage out of that.

I promised to keep my good ear to the ground, see if I heard anything about Ko den Hamer's whereabouts. There was nothing more to say. I finished off the wine and helped wash the dishes. For a short while, as we stood side by side at the sink, me washing Jo drying, it was almost like old times. But I knew those days were long gone and they weren't coming back any time soon. I put on my coat. I was going to get out of there and never come back.

I was walking toward the front door when I heard the sound of a key in the lock. The door opened quickly and there was Ko den Hamer, complete with a pistol. He called out playfully:

"Hi honey, I'm home! Oh, I see we have a guest, how nice."

And then something very hard hit me over the back of the head. My vision went grey and I tumbled forward at den Hamer's feet. I remember thinking what ugly shoes he was wearing then, guess what? I passed out.

When I came to, I was back in the kitchen. I was tied to a chair and the soapy kitchen towel was stuffed in my mouth. I tried but I couldn't shake it loose. My head hurt like hell and I thought I could feel dried blood down the back of my neck. Josephine said:

"He's awake."

"No matter," said Ko. "We're nearly finished here. Do you have your tickets?"

"Yes, all set."

Ko came round to face me, standing close he looked down into my eyes.

"So, Mister Detective; you got it all worked out?" I shook my head, tried to say something witty. All that came out was:

"Mmmmffmmf!!!" Ko laughed and yanked the towel out of my mouth.

"Sorry Richard; didn't quite catch that. What were you saying?"

"I said I know you've skimmed a shit-load of cash from the mob and they are going to chop you into little pieces when they catch you. I know my wife killed those two girls in the apartment. I think she went there looking for Rhonda Pearlman but somehow everything went tits up. I know you're planning to travel to Europe on the S.S. Liberte. Have I missed anything?"

"Not bad, not bad." He said. Could this fucker get any smugger?

"What you couldn't know is we killed those lovely young ladies together. Sure, we went to the apartment looking for Rhonda Pearlman. She'd learned a little too much of my plans that night at the bar. She was threatening to go to the cops unless we paid her a considerable sum. Now we couldn't have that, could we? Truthfully, we didn't know about the two girls who shared the apartment. The plan was to kill Rhonda as soon as she opened the door; make it look like a break-in gone wrong. But as you know Rhonda wasn't there."

"You didn't have to kill them both!"

"That's possibly true, but we had so much fun; didn't we darling?" Josephine looked a little embarrassed, which I thought was an odd reaction. She said:

"Do we have to talk about it now? Can't we just kill him and leave?" Ko looked genuinely surprised.

"Well, Josephine, I am shocked…and a little disappointed if truth be told. Did you not enjoy yourself the last time?"

"That was different."

"You mean…he's your husband?"

"I know you enjoyed watching me stab the girl at the door…the one with the big tits. Shit! Remember? There was blood everywhere. You even got some on you and you were standing behind me! She went down without a sound…didn't say a word, if you don't count all that gurgling."

"Come on Ko, shoot him now and let's go." Ko levelled the Luger at my head. Then he snatched it away suddenly. He went on:

"I know you had a great time stripping them and laying them out on the bed. You said the younger girl had really expensive underwear. You were going to take it, but you said it would be too tight. I could tell you were getting horny; you couldn't keep your hands off the girls and you blew me in the alley after, remember."

"I remember…Are you going to shoot him, or do I have to do it?"

"No! It's just too easy. After all the things you told me about this sad, damaged soul you want me to just put him out of his misery like a crippled dog?"

"Something like that," said Josephine. Ko leaned close to my ear and whispered.

"She can be a vindictive little bitch, can't she? Still, she fucks like a nymphomaniac on death row and that means I can forgive her most things. Still, I suppose we should get this over with." I looked at Jo, but she just stared back at me. She could have been in a trance for all the emotion she was showing.

Then Ko also turned to face Josephine. Before she could utter a word, he shot her in the neck. Jo flew backward, a red rose of blood spray bloomed behind her. Her head banged against the wall. She slid slowly down to the linoleum floor leaving a smear of crimson. She sat on the floor as the blood continued to spurt from the through and through wound. Her hand reached up to her throat and was instantly bathed in blood. My ears rang from the noise of the gunshot.

"There's that funny gurgling sound again," said Ko as he coolly took the towel he'd used to gag me and wiped the Luger. Jo's eyes were staring at me for a moment and her mouth opened. She coughed blood then her body slid sideways. Her head hit the floor with a clunk.

"Pity about Josephine; she really was good in the sack, willing to try anything…well you'd know that wouldn't you? Maybe not. But she was dumb as a stump…and I guess you'd know that too…Right," said Ko. "She could never grasp the big picture…anyway; time to go." He pressed the butt of the gun against my hand.

"Now here's what's going to happen next. I'm going to press this gun into Josephine's hand then I'm going to put it out of your reach on the floor…over there, I think. Then I'm going to burn the house down. That should really confuse the shit out of the police, don't you think?" I said:

"I'm going to hunt you down you mad fuck, I'm going to hunt you down and kill you like the rabid dog you are." Ko didn't look to be too concerned by my threat.

"Fine defiant words Rick, I'm sure Josephine would be very proud of you if she weren't as dead as a door-nail, but I don't think you will hunt me down my friend; and here's why." Ko went to the stove and turned on all the burners. I could hear the hiss of the gas even over the pounding in my ears. Ko left the kitchen and I could hear him splashing something around by the front door. He came back into the kitchen holding a cigarette lighter. He said:

"Shouldn't take too long, see you around Rick."

Then he left. Over the hissing from the gas, I heard another sound. A loud whoomph came from the hallway; then the front door slammed. This was not good. I had seconds to save myself. I rocked the kitchen chair back and forth until it toppled backward onto the floor. The impact knocked the breath out of me, but it also broke the back of the chair. In an instant, I could move my hands. They were still tied behind my back, but they were no longer tied to the chair. I rolled around on the floor like a stranded whale and managed to pull my hands over my feet. I stood up, went to the stove, and turned off the gas using my teeth.

I wasn't out of the woods yet. Not by a long stretch. I still had to get out of a burning house and my hands were still tied. I opened a kitchen drawer and pulled out a carving knife. I held it facing toward me and began sawing away at the rope. It took me longer than I'd hoped but eventually I cut through. I could feel the intense heat from the fire in the hallway. I turned; the doorway was already ablaze. There was no way I could get out that way. I picked up the kitchen table and swung it at the window over the sink. It took me three attempts, but I finally succeeded in smashing the window.

I placed another chair by the sink and started to make my way out of the shattered window. Then I looked back at Josephine. There was no way I could leave her there to burn. And yes, I knew she was dead. The large pool of shiny dark blood around her corpse confirmed that. I stepped back down, went over, and picked up her bloodied body. She was still warm. I picked her up as gently as I could. I took a step and slipped in her blood. In that second, I nearly dropped her to the kitchen floor.

"Sorry," I said. I lifted my wife's body as high as I possibly manage and held her up to the broken kitchen window. The heat in the kitchen was becoming unbearable and smoke spread across the ceiling like acrid choking clouds. I apologized to Josephine's mortal remains one more time then I bundled her out of the window. I heard a sickening thud as she hit the ground outside. I climbed on the chair, stepped into the sink with one foot then threw myself into space. As I tumbled through the air there was an instant when I realized I would be landing on my dead wife.

I crashed down on the bloody body. Breathless I jumped to my feet as quickly as possible. My arms and upper body were covered in her blood. My mouth filled with salty red goop. I turned away from her and coughed and coughed until I threw up.

I guess I must have passed out then. I can remember the sound of windows breaking from the heat and the smell of burning timber. I heard the hungry roar of the yellow flames just above my head. I think I remember hearing sirens, but I can't be sure. A few neighbors climbed over the fence into our yard and dragged me and Josephine clear of the inferno. Someone must have called the cops.

I woke up in hospital sometime later. The big cop Grunwald was standing at the foot of my bed.

"You should maybe think about asking for a discounted rate on the room Shamus. You spend more time in here than some doctors. By the way, you are under arrest for the murder of Josephine Marshall."

Chapter Twenty - Seven

"But that's no big surprise, is it? I mean, you were seen throwing her lifeless body out of your home, your prints are on the German gun that shot her dead and you had all the motive in the world because she was fucking her boss and she'd thrown you out of the house. I've never seen such an open and shut case. If I were you, I'd start thinking about what I want for my last meal because you are going to fry for this one Shamus."

Grunwald was having so much fun I could hardly bring myself to piss on his cornflakes. But in the end, I did, just to see his face as he tried to guess if I was bluffing. I told him everything that had happened, and I gave him an excellent description of Ko den Hamer. I passed on his travel plans too.

"Nice try, but I'm not buying any of it," he said, but I could see a tiny grain of doubt had settled down in his booze-addled brain. I put on my best 'cooperating with the authorities' voice' and told Grunwald all about Ko den Hamer's money laundering scheme, I told him all Ko had said about the murders of Lily and Anna in Rhonda Pearlman's apartment. Then I told him to call the Acting District Attorney if he didn't believe me.

"Not that faggot. You got Dwight in your pocket Shamus?"

"Do you think you might stop calling me that? You sound like a bit-part actor in a Bogart film."

"Wise-ass!"

"That's better. So, Detective Grunwald, when do I get my phone call?"

"Look around jackass! You're in a hospital bed, you're not under arrest."

"You see that's what confused me. You are going on about last meals and electric chairs. I got the feeling that I was already arrested, charged, and convicted."

"Don't push your fuckin' luck…Shamus."

At that second a pretty young nurse looked in on us. She spoke to the detective.

"Are you Detective Grunwald?" He nodded.

"There's a phone call for you at the desk."

"Who is it?" he asked.

"Do I look like a receptionist?" was her snappy reply. I loved her for that. Grunwald came back in after five minutes. All the fun and games seemed to have left him.

"You'll have to come in and give us a statement. I'd bring that Jew Boy lawyer of yours when you do."

"So, I'm not under arrest?" Grunwald couldn't bring himself to say the words. He shook his head.

"Can I make my statement in a few days?"

"Just don't make me come looking for you."

"I wouldn't dream of it, Detective." Grunwald went to the door. I called out:

"Thanks for coming in to visit, Detective. Maybe you could bring a bottle next time. I'd love to chat about old cases and the like. You know, chew that fat."

Grunwald slammed the door shut, I heard a passing nurse go:

"Ssshhhh!" I hoped it was the one with the smart mouth. I liked her.

I was kept in hospital for most of the day, under observation. I was released just after four. I got a cab back to Oakland to pick up the M.G. When I got there the air was still heavy with the smell of smoke. The house had burned to the ground. Nothing was left of the place but a few blackened metal appliances and charred beams. The roof had collapsed into a pile of rubble. I stood on the sidewalk looking over the scene for quite a while. Mister Loomis hobbled over from across the street. He handed me a cup of tea.

"Terrible thing…terrible thing," he said. "Sorry to hear about Mrs. Marshall…terrible thing. I just can't believe it." I wasn't sure if Loomis was talking about Josephine fucking her boss, helping kill two girls, being involved in a massive fraud, or the fact that she'd been shot to death in our kitchen in front of my eyes. I didn't ask him to clarify. I took a sip of the luke-warm milky tea. Mister Loomis pulled a hip flask from his jacket pocket.

"Would you like a little something in that?" he asked. I nodded. He topped me up before taking a quick swig himself. I drank the tea. Loomis was obviously struggling for things to say because the next thing he asked was:

"When's the errrm, funeral?" he asked.

"I'll drop by with a note. I've not had a chance to make any arrangements yet. I've been in hospital overnight."

"Well, if there's anything I can do." I handed the cup back to Mister Loomis and he shook my hand. He was still saying: 'Terrible thing, terrible thing' as he walked back across the street. I drove back downtown and checked in at the Sir Francis Drake.

I still smelled like smoked ham and my clothes were smeared and splattered with my dead wife's blood. I turned a few heads as I walked into the lobby. I got some very strange looks from the lantern-jawed matron behind the counter. I can't say I blamed her. I caught sight of myself in the large mirror behind the front desk. I looked like shit, frankly. I smelled like the blitz and I was coughing smoke and phlegm at thirty-second intervals. I paid for two days up-front then I went to the house phone and checked for messages. There was only one…from Inga. She left a number where I could call her back. Obviously, she didn't know what I'd been up to during the last twenty-four hours.

I honestly didn't know if I would tell her when I called the number she'd left. But surprise, surprise as soon as she answered it all came blurting out along with a few tears and an almost incoherent guilt-ridden rant about my failing Josephine. I told her about my plans for the evening.

"I'm coming over," she said. "What's your room number?" I protested feebly but I was happy she was coming. I went upstairs and ran a hot bath. I think I must have fallen asleep in the tub. I was awoken from a seriously weird dream by Inga pounding on the door and yelling my name.

I climbed out of the bath and wrapped the biggest towel I could find around my waist. I answered the door just before Inga kicked it down. Inga stood in the hallway holding a bottle of Jamieson's Irish Whiskey. She was the most beautiful sight I'd seen in a long time. She wore her cream double-breasted suit and a silky dark blue shirt with the top two buttons opened. No-one would ever mistake her for a man from any angle in that outfit. She didn't say anything, but her eyes drifted to the damp towel.

"Sorry, I was in the tub," I said.

"I can see that Rick. You got any glasses?" She waved the bottle at me. I nodded and Inga stepped past me into the room. I closed the door. I hung onto the towel like my life depended on it, made it back to the bathroom, and put my pants back on. They still reeked of smoke, but I had nothing else to wear. Inga was sitting on the bed. She looked at me and said:

"Phew! Now I feel a whole lot safer! A girl has to be careful these days." She filled two glasses with golden syrup and handed one to me. My hands were shaking, and I spilled some of it on the carpet. My hands must have been shaking all day but up until then, I hadn't noticed.

"You okay?" she asked, which under the circumstances wasn't very constructive. I was obviously very, very far from okay. I nodded but I couldn't say anything. So, I took another glug of whiskey. The liquor warmed my throat and chest, eased my coughing a little. Inga said:

"It's okay; you don't have to talk if you don't want to."

"I'm just so tired," I said.

"I know, I know." Inga put her drink on the floor, stood up tall right in front of me. She stepped forward and held me close. Her neck smelled of flowers and vanilla. I could have stayed there all night. Eventually, we sat back down on the bed and got back to the drinking. I told Inga I didn't want to talk about what had happened, didn't want to talk about Josephine at all.

"That's fine. When you want to talk, I'll be here," she said. "I just wanted to say sorry for all the bullshit with the plane and the boat," I said:

"It doesn't matter now, nothing matters…it's no big deal, honest." Inga looked up at me, looked me straight in the eyes.

"…No, it is Rick. I let you down; I don't know what I was thinking. The plane's there for the taking now. You've got all the necessary paperwork. You should just go over and collect it. There's no-one left at the hotel…well apart from the regular staff. There's none of the muscle left."

"What are you gonna do now?" I asked.

"If there's any hot water left, I'm going to have a quick shower, then I'm getting into this bed."

"I meant what are you going to do for work." She said:

"I know what you meant." Inga went into the bathroom; I heard the shower start up shortly after. I sat there like a bump on a log, not sure what to do next. Then I got into bed. The clean, crisp cotton was cool to the touch. Minutes later Inga came out of the bathroom. She had one of those big fluffy towels wrapped around her. She turned off the lights. Neon light from the street outside shone through the thin curtains and bathed the room in blue. Inga dropped the towel.

I think my heart stopped beating for a stretch at that point. She didn't seem too worried that I was staring at her. She looked like a light blue angel. I'm sure I must have tried to say something witty and smart but to this day I can't remember what it was…She pulled back the covers and got in beside me. She put her hand on my chest and said:

"I know we talked about this earlier, but we aren't going to do anything stupid tonight are we?"

"I think it would kill me outright," I said. "Besides I can't stop thinking about Josephine…you know for the life of me I can't work out where things went wrong. I was happy as Larry. I loved her right up to the end. I was still in love with her when she was telling den Hamer to shoot me in the head. Even then I was still trying to find ways to make things work between us…what a jerk! I'm just like all those saps who hire me, you know the adultery cases. They all say the same thing: I didn't see it coming. Now I know just how that feels." Inga said:

“Don’t beat yourself up for being a good guy Rick, that’s my job.” I think she was smiling as she said this. “Look, I didn’t come here to get you in the sack…well not in that way. I just felt that you should not be left alone tonight…I told you before about my experiences with men, it just hasn’t worked for me. Maybe with you, it might be different, in time. But right now, it would be a pointless endeavor.”

“Yes, but as pointless endeavor’s go it might be a very nice one.”

“For you maybe.”

“Well if you put it like that maybe we should just go to sleep.”

“Are you okay with that?” she asked.

“Right now, parts of me are far from okay with that.” Inga lifted the bedclothes.

“I can tell…” she said.

“So, I can’t guarantee that those parts might wake me up sometime in the next few hours and make me do something stupid. That’s what dicks do…”

“Then I might have to defend myself. And you wouldn’t want that, would you? Someone might get hurt.” Inga kissed me quickly then, like you might kiss a child goodnight. Then she moved away from me. I lay as still as I could and closed my eyes. After a few minutes Inga whispered:

“Can we do this Rick? Or do you want me to go? I’m not trying to mess with you, you know that, don’t you? I just think that if we did do it then things would change forever between us and I’m not sure if I could handle that right now. It’s just too soon after all we’ve both been through.” She paused, let out a heavy sigh. “Maybe one day…”

I lay perfectly still and thought about what Inga had said. After a few minutes of deep thought, I took the coward’s way out and pretended to be asleep. I would probably hate myself in the morning for not telling Inga how I felt about her when she gave me the chance.

The next morning Inga was awake before me. I was just coming round when she came out of the bathroom. She was completely naked as she walked across the room drying her pixie blonde hair with a towel. The erection I experienced at that point was beyond description. I was surprised she couldn’t see it by the mountain-sized bulge in the bedclothes. She paced around the room drying her hair, I couldn’t look away…the way her buttocks tensed as she walked; her skin was pale perfection. She had two dimples in her lower back, either side of her spine. Inga dropped the towel and turned around. She stood tall, naked, and unashamed. She smiled at me and said:

“I see you’re awake.”

“I see you’re naked,” I replied.

“I usually am when I take a bath.”

"You're not in the bath now though."

"Would you like me to get dressed?" she asked.

"Don't bother, I'm fine with you just the way you are," Inga asked:

"Are you going to get up?"

"I should probably stay here for a while," I said. "Unless you want to hand me my pants and turn around."

"Don't tell me you've gone all shy on me, Rick. You lie there watching me parade around in front of you for God knows how long but you're too shy to get dressed in front of me, that hardly seems fair."

"But you said you didn't like men. You said last night, 'It just doesn't work for me.'"

"Were you taking notes?" she asked.

"I didn't have to. That sentence is etched in my brain forever."

"Asshole! I'm getting dressed now. You can either watch me, like the pervert I'm beginning to think you are, or you can also get dressed then we can go get breakfast."

"I think I shall stay right here and watch you, like the pervert I am quickly becoming."

Inga turned around and collected her lacy black underwear from the armchair. I took the opportunity to get out of bed, put the pillow in front of my still extremely erect penis, and shuffle sideways toward the bathroom. Inga turned and saw me as she was fastening her bra.

"Chicken!" was all she said.

We went down to breakfast in the hotel restaurant and I'm sure Inga turned more than a few heads as we sat among the sales representatives, businessmen, and captains of industry discussing share prices and trade gossip. I didn't notice. I was too busy staring a hole in my scrambled eggs. Inga commented on my silence.

"How are we feeling this morning?" she asked.

"Better than I thought I would feel thanks. I just don't feel ready to start talking about the whole sordid affair."

"You don't have to. When you want to talk, I'll be there to listen. You know that…"

"Thanks, Inga, you're a pal…and you look steaming hot in that black underwear."

Several newspapers shook. A passing waitress coughed loudly to cover a fit of giggles. Inga smiled beatifically.

Later that morning we hit the shops just like any other recently widowed thirty-four-year-old and his tall, blonde stunningly attractive twenty-two-year-old lesbian friend. I burned through a whole wodge of cash buying another new suit, some shirts and ties, some pants and shoes, and even underwear.

We brought all the new clothes back to the hotel room at lunchtime then went out in the afternoon and started again. Inga was great fun to be with and I think she had a good time too. By the end of the day, I really felt like I should buy her something as a thank-you. We were outside Macy's in Union Square when I said to Inga:

"I think that's enough clothes to last me a lifetime. Maybe I should buy you something…" Inga blushed.

"You don't have to do that Rick. You had to get new clothes; I mean just look at you! But I don't need anything."

"I don't want to buy you something you need. I want to buy you something you want." She thought for a moment then said quickly:

"I want a hat like yours." So, we went inside to the menswear department. Inga tried every hat in the place until she found the perfect one for her. We laughed so much I thought they might come and throw us out. She was like a little girl on Christmas Day; pulling funny faces and poses as she tried hat after hat. In the end, she settled on one the same shape and color as my old fedora. I thought about one day getting Sammy to take our picture, both wearing suits, and the same style hat.

With the last of our purchases made we decided to head for the nearest bar. But as we breezed out of Macy's a funeral happened to be passing ,stopping us on the sidewalk. Reality has a way of jumping all over your good times and this was a real good example of that. I said to Inga:

"I have a funeral to arrange. I'm not sure if the police have rung Josephine's parents with the news. I should call them right away." Inga looked at me with those big blue-grey eyes suddenly sharing my mood.

"Let's head back to the office, you can call from there. Then I'll help you make the arrangements."

"You don't have to Inga," I said.

"I want to help," she said. You don't know how glad I was to hear those words. I waited till the cortege had left Union Square then I hailed a cab. Back at the office, my first call was to Josephine's parents in Bismark, North Dakota. Mercifully for me, the police had called round first thing this morning with the news of their daughter's death, Hank and Marjorie were expecting my call. They were understandably quiet and subdued during it. I guessed that Hank was fighting back the urge to ask me lots of questions about what had happened. I decided to spare them the truth, simply saying I'd got home to find the house ablaze and had rushed inside to look for Josephine. I'd got her out of the house, but it was too late. The real story would come out later.

We discussed what would be the best dates for them to come out and I said I'd speak to a funeral director in the next twenty-four hours then I'd call them straight away with the details. My next call was to Mike Halloran, the engineer at T.W.A. He wasn't in his office. I left a message for him:

"Tell Mike I know why the Connie blew up and I know who did it."

Mike rang me back in less than three minutes.

"Mister Marshall, I knew you were the one guy who could get to the bottom of this..."

"...Hi Mike, I was just lucky really. Can we come out and talk you through what happened? You're not going to believe it."

"Should I tell the company? Is this solid?"

"Oh, it's solid all right. I just haven't found a way to prove it yet."

"Maybe I won't tell the company just yet. Do you want to come out first thing tomorrow? I'll leave a word on the gate. We're pretty busy but I know this will be worth it. We just took delivery of three new Connies. We're doing pre-service checks before a final shake-down flight for all three; do you want me to get you on the flight deck for one of the shake-downs?"

"That would be great Mike but don't get into any trouble on my behalf."

"It's no trouble...You are bringing that little red car and the big blonde babe?"

"I promise I'll bring both Mike and I promise I will get proof about the explosion real soon. Trust me." I rang off.

"I'm heading out to see Mike at T.W.A. tomorrow first thing. He's very keen to see you again. He calls you the big blonde babe...I think you made a conquest there."

"You are just too funny!" said Inga. "Is he married? He's just my type."

"And I'm not?" I asked. My last call before we called it a day was to the District Attorney's office. I wanted to check with Elton Dwight and see if he'd heard anything about the whereabouts of one Jacobus den Hamer. My guess was that he would be following his original escape plan. He'd think Josephine and I were both dead, so he'd have no reason to think the forces of law and order were on his tail. Dwight was in a meeting at the Mayor's office. I left a message saying I'd call back in the morning.

We closed up the office and drove back downtown to the Sir Francis Drake Hotel. We dropped all our bags in the room then went up to the Starlite Roof Restaurant on the twenty-first floor. It was six-thirty and the sky to the west featured a spectacular sunset. We sat at a table by the window and ordered drinks. The Starlite Roof Restaurant was decorated in red and white stripes and had massive windows giving customers breath-taking views of the city and the bay. It was a famous landmark with San Franciscans and visitors alike. I'd never eaten there but I figured tonight was as good a time as any to give it a try.

We ordered our meals as more city lights came on below us and the stars came out above. We both had steak, Inga had a salad with hers I had a baked potato with chives. We talked for hours, about nothing mainly, we just enjoyed being in each other's company. I showed off and ordered her a cocktail I'd had in London during the war. It was called a Sidecar, someone told me it had been invented in Paris during World War One: Equal parts Cognac, Cointreau and lemon juice. Inga liked it. So, we had a few more.

Round about eleven we wound our very merry way back to our room where we both tumbled around a while trying to get out of our clothes, then I think I passed out. It was a hell of a night.

Chapter Twenty - Eight

Mike Halloran had told the company after all. So, when Inga and I turned up at the T.W.A. hangar, we were met by a very odd sight. Mike's office, the one up the stairs overlooking the 'shop,' had been turned into a makeshift boardroom. Elwood Thorpe was there, the guy who worked for Howard Hughes. He was sitting at one end of the table talking to Wallace from T.W.A. Three younger guys in suits looked like muscle (or as they preferred, security). In the middle of the table was a speaker wired up to a telephone. Mike met us at the door.

"Sorry about this Mister Marshall. I mentioned your phone call to Mister Wallace and all hell broke loose. He started calling head office and then Mister Hughes was informed…"

"That's okay Mike," I said. "Where do you want us to sit?"

"I thought Miss err…I thought…"

"Inga."

"…I thought Inga could sit here next to me at the head of the table." All sweetness and light, Inga smiled for the benefit of everyone around that table, she took big Mike's hand and let him guide her to her seat. She was wearing a slinky blue summer dress under my leather jacket. The light cotton slipped across her thighs making a barely audible swishing sound. I almost burst out laughing at the way the whole table turned and beamed at her. She had us all in her power and she knew it…it was sad really, grown men acting like teenage boys full of…well, you know what teenage boys are full of. Elwood P. Thorpe was the first of us…the first of them to get back to business; he cleared his throat and said:

"So, Mister Marshall, I understand you have a theory concerning the explosion on flight 402."

"It's more than a theory," I said. "It's what happened."

"And yet you have no proof and the perpetrator remains at liberty."

"Not for long."

"If you don't mind Mister Marshall, can you tell us what happened to flight 402?"

I didn't want to sit at the table; I preferred to walk around as I spoke. Here's what I said:

"Flight 402 was brought down by a home-made bomb, placed in an army surplus ammo box which was being used as a lunch box. It was wired like a booby trap so that when its owner opened the box it pulled the pin on a hand-grenade hidden inside."

"The lunch box belonged to Stu Brown the flight engineer. The bomb was put there by his wife…"

Everyone around the table started talking at once, asking questions, looking for more details. After some time, the noise level died down and I realized that every one of the suits was looking at the little doo hickey on the table. A tinny voice came from the speaker. I recognized a Texan drawl, but I had no idea who was speaking. My guess was all the suits knew. The Texan asked:

"Mister Marshall, perhaps you can give us your theory on the motive for this heinous act?"

"Stu Brown had been having a string of affairs and one-night stands with numerous women, most from the T.W.A. offices here in San Francisco. His wife had recently increased his life insurance…"

"And how would Mrs. Brown know how to construct such a device?"

"She worked in a munitions factory during the war. She knows her way around explosives."

"And as yet you don't have any proof worth taking to the police?"

It was a little unsettling being questioned by a disembodied voice. So, I decided to find out who was on the other end. I asked:

"Who am I talking to here?"

There was silence in the room and silence on the line apart from an electronic buzzing sound probably coming from the mic at the other end of the line, wherever that was. Eventually, the voice in the box spoke again.

"I'm sorry, has no one told you who you are speaking with?" There was a hush around the table. Everyone looked more than a little awkward.

"No sir," said I.

"My name is Howard R. Hughes. I own T.W.A. and a number of other companies including The Hughes Tool Company and R.K.O. Perhaps you've heard of them."

"I certainly have sir. It's a pleasure to be speaking with you, Mister Hughes."

"Likewise."

"So Rick, what's our next step?" asked the tinny voice on the table. Everyone around that table looked at everyone else around that table. No one said a word. I said my piece:

"Everything we have so far against Mrs. Brown is circumstantial. There's nothing that would stand up in court. I think we need to get a confession from her, or we'll be nowhere."

"Agreed...what do you need from my team, Mister Marshall?"

"I'm putting a plan together, not sure what we'll need until the time comes."

"Mister Marshall I am putting all the resources of T.W.A. and the Hughes Tool company at your disposal. Feel free to call at any time, mention this conversation and ask for my man Thorpe...Mister Thorpe? You hear me?"

"I certainly do sir, thank you, Mister Hughes."

"And you will give Mister Marshall every assistance he requires when he requests it?"

"Yes, Mister Hughes."

"Then there's nothing further to discuss. We'll speak again Mister Marshall. Good day gentlemen." There was a hum on the line. Howard Hughes had hung up. For some time, everyone in the room just looked at each other, not saying a word. Mike Halloran was the first to speak:

"Well if it's okay with the rest of you I've got an engine test to run on a new Connie."

Me and Inga followed Mike down the stairs and into the shop. Mike turned to me:

"Wow, so Mable Brown is a mass-murderer?"

"That's about the size of it," I said.

"She must be some kind of a cold-hearted bitch to kill innocent people just because her husband's a bit of a pussy merchant." Mike blushed and spoke to Inga.

"Sorry, Inga."

"I've heard worse," she said.

"And don't forget the insurance money," I said. "She's currently building her dream house with that," Mike asked me:

"How are you going to get her to confess?" My left ear itched, I scratched it.

"I thought I might drive up there and put the squeeze on her, try a little common or garden blackmail and get her to confess, maybe get it on tape." Halloran asked:

"You got that kind of recording equipment?"

I said: "Nope; but I know a man who most likely does."

When we got back into the city, I called that man. He said that we should head straight over.

Elton Dwight's outer office was full of people holding posters for his campaign and milling around in various random ways. Everyone was talking at once. We eventually made our presence known and were shown into the inner sanctum where there were more people with posters doing the milling around thing. Elton Dwight was standing on a footstool being measured by a guy who I hoped was a tailor. If he wasn't a tailor, he was paying way too much attention to Dwight's inside leg measurement. This did not appear to trouble Elton Dwight too much. The familiar flowery cologne was joined by at least one more gag-inducing concoction favored by the tailor.

"Rick! Do come in. I won't be but a moment," he called. "And Miss Bjarkardóttir, what a pleasant surprise; I thought you'd fled the country with your employer Mister Brady."

"Ex-employer," said Inga.

"Miss Bjarkardóttir, I am very pleased to hear that. Maybe I won't have to throw you in jail and throw away the key after all."

"You're too kind," said Inga. I spoke up:

"I have something to share with you Mister Dwight and it's best shared in private I think."

"Very well, very well, this place is becoming a little too much like Grand Central Station. What with the forthcoming election…I assume I will have your support at the ballot?"

"Absolutely," I said. The room cleared slowly; several large election posters were left propped up against one wall. Dwight stepped down from the foot-stool and started looking over them.

"These are the best three as selected by my team. Which one do we prefer?" Inga took a careful look at each of the posters. She rejected one and put it to one side:

"You look like you're wearing make-up in this one." She took her time looking at the two remaining. Eventually, she pointed at one featuring a close-up portrait, moodily lit.

"This one," she said. Dwight was delighted.

"That's my favorite too. You've just saved me a lot of time and money Miss Bjarkardóttir…thank you very much." Elton Dwight turned to me and his mood became more somber.

"Rick, I assume you are here to talk about your wife's murder. It must have been a terrible ordeal for you." I nodded.

"I want to make sure Ko den Hamer gets the chair for this."

"And how can we ensure that?"

"Here's the way I see it, den Hamer thinks I'm dead alongside Josephine, right? So as far as he's concerned, he has no reason to change his plans."

"You mean he's still planning to leave the country on the S.S. Liberte tomorrow?"

"I'm certain of it."

"So, we get the N.Y.P.D. to put a few men at customs and we apprehend him as he tries to board," I asked:

"What about if he's got himself a fake passport, changed the way he looks?"

"Do you think he might?" Dwight asked.

"I think there's a chance. If only I could be there, I've seen him close up…real close up in the last few days and I've got the picture of him from the brochure he had made. If I was there, I could make damn sure he didn't slip through the net."

"But the Liberte sails tomorrow at 2.00 p.m. New York time. Unless you can turn back the clock there's no way you can get there in time." An idea was forming in my head, a far-fetched idea for sure but an idea that just might work.

"Can you get in touch with New York; get me a name and number to contact if I get there in time?"

"Absolutely…but it's all academic really, you'll never make it." Inga was looking across at me like I was the mad scientist in a horror movie. I smiled at her.

"I think I know a way. We'll have to call in a few favors, but I think we can be there to put a monkey wrench in Ko den Hamer's escape plans. And if there's just the smallest of chances I want to give it a go…for Josephine."

"I'll get someone on it right away," said Dwight. He picked up a phone and asked for an underling to find a contact at N.Y.P.D. Inga asked me:

"What exactly do you have in mind?"

"That would be telling," I said. Dwight put down the phone.

"We should have a name and number for you shortly. Now is there anything else I can do for you, Rick? I do have an election to win you know."

"How would you like to be the one that solves the mystery of the T.W.A. crash?" Elton Dwight looked at me as if I'd just promised to grant him eternal life. He stammered:

"I…I…I would like that very much. It would practically guarantee me the position…not that there's any doubt."

"Here's what I got. I know who did it. I know why they did it. But I don't have anything concrete to hang on them yet. I have plenty of circumstantial evidence but that's not going to be enough to make it stick…What I need to do is get them to talk. Now I'm pretty damn sure I know a way how to do this, but I need some way to record what they say."

"You aren't going to coerce them or threaten them physically? Because if you did the evidence would be inadmissible in court."

"I know that," I said. "No, I'm not going to beat a confession out of them. I just need some kind of portable recording device…if such a thing exists."

"Well, it's funny you should say that Rick, because I just might be able to help you with that. When would you need this 'recording device'?"

"Well, let's see. If everything goes according to plan in New York and I'm still in one piece…I should be back for the weekend. Is that enough time?"

"Plenty, we've been testing a portable wire recorder from a company called 'Minifon.' It's quite something. It looks like a watch. It's connected to a wire recorder by a lead that runs up your arm. The recorder is small enough to go in a coat pocket. We've got two out in the field right now but I'm sure we can lend you one for the weekend." I stood up; Inga did the same.

"Then we're all set. I'll call you as soon as I get back from New York." There were handshakes all round. Dwight was practically dancing around his office; he was so happy. As we got into the elevator Inga said:

"So how are we going to get to New York for two tomorrow afternoon? You know someone with a time machine going spare?" For once in my life, I had the witty one-line answer already to go. This was it:

"No, but I do know someone with a brand-new Connie."

We drove back to the Sir Francis Drake hotel and I started making calls. As I waited for T.W.A. to call me back I did some rough calculations on a sheet of writing paper with the hotel's name on the top. San Francisco to New York is just over two thousand nine hundred miles; the Lockheed Constellation had the range to fly that non-stop. That's what it was built to do. The one factor that might bring us down to earth with a bump was time. Mike Halloran had mentioned that the Connie could cruise at 340 M.P.H. With the time difference that meant that we had to be in the air by ten o'clock tonight if we wanted to make LaGuardia for about ten in the morning, East Coast time. That would give us enough time, even with bad traffic to get down to the docks and set our trap.

But that was if everything went according to plan. There were lots of things that could go wrong: we could hit bad weather or strong head-winds. We might not even get the plane, there was no guarantee one of the new Connies at San Francisco Airport would be ready to fly. My ear began to itch again…

"I'm coming with you."

"You're what?" I asked.

"You heard me. You didn't expect me to just sit on my ass while you chase down the bad guy…"

"…Bad guy? He might look like a matinee idol, but Ko den Hamer is a dangerous killer. I don't want you getting anywhere near him."

"…I'm sorry? You seem to have got me mixed up with someone you can boss around like a mild-mannered simpering housewife. Do I have to whup your ass again Rick? Because if that's what it takes…"

"That might be fun."

"Now don't go all fruity on me, can I come or not?"

"…Okay, you can come, but just to set the record straight you have yet to whup my ass…ever!"

Inga put up her fists and began to dance around me like Rocky Marciano, jabbing away at my chin.

"Come on Rick, put 'em up!"

"If you're coming, you'd better pack a bag."

The phone rang, it was Elwood Thorpe.

"Mister Thorpe…good of you to call me back so quickly; I bet you didn't expect to hear from me so soon."

"What is it we can do for you, Mister Marshall?" This was it. I had to pitch this one right, or we were going nowhere tonight.

"Mister Thorpe, I need a very big favor, one that only T.W.A. can provide…I'm trying to catch a multiple murderer…in New York."

"This is the person behind the bombing of flight 402?"

"No…this is another person entirely. I'm working on bringing the bomber to justice by the weekend. This is another matter. This person has killed three people to my knowledge, including my wife. He's currently traveling across the country by train and plans to sail to Europe on the S.S. Liberte."

"And what exactly can we do to help?" I explained what I needed to happen in order to catch Ko den Hamer before he set sail for Europe tomorrow afternoon. The phone went quiet for so long that I began to think we've been cut off.

Chapter Twenty - Nine

"That's all?"

"That's all," I said.

"You want us to loan you a brand-new Lockheed Constellation and a crew to fly to New York non-stop to catch a murderer."

"That's right," I said.

"I'll have to call you back. I will have to contact Mister Hughes."

"I thought Mister Hughes gave you total authority in this matter."

"Indeed, he did Mister Marshall, but Mister Hughes does tend to… (how can I say this?) He does tend to forget things." He rang off. The phone rang again almost immediately. It was Elton Dwight:

"Everything's arranged with New York. You'll be met at LaGuardia by Captain Baker, N.Y.P.D. He's in charge of the take-down at the dock. I've told him you are there strictly as an observer. You are not to carry any form of concealed firearm in fact no concealed weapons at all. You are to help identify Ko den Hamer to the authorities then you step aside and take a back seat. Do you understand?" I replied:

"Sure, sure…I understand." Elton Dwight wished us luck, gave us a couple of phone numbers to get hold of Captain Baker then he said:

"Please try not to embarrass me, Rick." He rang off. We both packed a few essentials in a small case then sat around in silence waiting for the call from T.W.A. It came at 7.49. It was Mike Halloran:

"Hi Captain; it's Mike. I've got a brand-new Connie just out of the wrapper for you and we are currently fueling her as we speak. We should be good to go about ten tonight, provided I can rustle up a crew for you. So, get your ass down to the hangar as soon as possible. We've got someone working on getting all the clearances you need for this flight. Looks like we just might get you there in time…fingers crossed." I thanked Mike and said we'd be on our way.

"Time to go," I said. We both got changed quickly. Funnily enough, we ended up wearing practically identical outfits, khaki slacks, and a leather zip-up jacket. We picked up our almost identical hats then hurried out to the M.G. We got to the T.W.A. hangar at San Francisco Airport in just under an hour.

They waved me straight inside and I was able to park the M.G. in a corner under Mike Halloran's office. The tiny sports car was dwarfed by the four-engined airliner undergoing its final pre-flight checks. I noticed that the starboard inner engine was missing a cowling. Men were scurrying up and down some portable scaffolding under the wing. Mike Halloran clambered down from the platform and stomped over:

"We have a problem," he said.

"The starboard inner engine is losing oil."

I knew better than to ask Mike how long it would take to fix. The standard answer is: 'it will take as long as it takes.' There's no way to rush these things.

"Okay, Mike I'll let you get back to it. Okay if we get onboard? I'd like to show Inga inside."

"Go ahead. I'll give you a shout when she's ready."

"Do we have a crew?" I asked.

"Should be with us by the time she's cleared to fly. Though I can't promise you any air stewardesses, they are in short supply."

The inside of this Lockheed Constellation was unlike any aircraft I had seen. We walked forward from the entrance at the rear, past row upon row of seats. Then we walked through the galley. The forward end of the passenger compartment was laid out like a lounge on a luxury train with large leather chairs, a couple of couches and wood veneer everywhere. The ceiling was light blue and had a world map printed on it. My feet sank into thick carpeting. I guess this is what T.W.A. called first class. Inga obviously approved. She ran her hand along the back of a leather chair:

"This I can get used to. Much better than that noisy clunker you now own."

I walked forward to the flight deck. I was drawn to the flight engineer's station on the right. I almost looked under the small table for a lunch box. I looked out at the engineers and mechanics working feverishly on the starboard inner engine. I was amazed by the sheer size of the prop. No wonder this plane stood so high. It needed a massive ground clearance for the four propellers.

"I'm going to have to ask you to move back into the passenger's area please Captain." It was Mike Halloran. "We're going to start the starboard inner once the guys are clear; shouldn't take too long now." I did as Mike asked and gave Inga the thumbs up.

"You might want to cover your ears," I said. Inside that hangar, the noise of an engine start was like the starting up of a hundred race cars all at once. Even inside the plane the crackle and boom from the exhausts messed with your head. Inga gave me a look that said: 'Smart Ass!'

"I told you," I said. Mike Halloran ran the engine rev's up. The hangar filled with exhaust fumes and noise. After fifteen minutes of tests, we were ready to go.

With the troublesome engine now running smoothly, the Connie was towed out onto the apron. After a final sign-off, one by one, the other three engines were coaxed into life. The unbelievable noise growing as revs were increased, oil pressures checked, and re-checked. The flight crew came on board and settled in, swapping places with the ground crew one after another. Mike Halloran was the last of the ground crew to leave. With a clipboard under his left arm, he shook my hand and wished me luck.

"We'll have her back to you in one piece by Saturday," I said. Mike leaned in:

"I've had a word with Captain Lacey. He's one of us. You can give her a try if you like." I didn't know what to say…I blurted out a few inadequate words of thanks. Then Mike climbed down the rear ladder. The second officer closed the door and hurried forward. He asked us to grab a seat and buckle up. We were ready for take-off.

The Constellation was the only aircraft moving on the ground at this time of night. It was just past ten. So, we taxied serenely out to the runway and came to a halt on the numbers as the Captain held the aircraft on its brakes. All four engines were quickly brought up to full power and as the captain released the brakes the Constellation pounced forward like a sprinter starting a race. We were soon shooting along the runway faster than I'd ever experienced in any four-engined aircraft. There was a fleeting impression of massive latent power as we picked up even more speed and after what felt like only a few seconds we practically leaped into the air.

I think the captain was showing off his plane's capabilities because we climbed far more rapidly than a passenger aircraft would normally do. I would have done the same. This was one hell of an aircraft. We levelled out over the bay and I could make out the city lights below. Once out over the Pacific, we made a climbing 180 degree turn to head due east. I unbuckled my seat belt and headed back into the galley. I shouted back to Inga:

"Do you think you could work out how to make some coffee?" She came back to join me.

"Just so long as I don't have to put a uniform on."

"Not even if I asked real nice? I bet you'd look great." I said. I walked forward to the cockpit before Inga could come up with a reply.

"We're making some coffee; anyone want a cup?" Everyone wanted a cup. We had broken through cloud cover and the spectacle before me reminded me of why I started flying. Even with the constant drone of the four supercharged engines, there was a feeling of peace. Even though we were flashing through the night sky at close to 350 miles per hour there was also a sense of stillness. I stood behind the two pilot's seats and we talked about our careers in the air for some time; sharing war stories and old jokes.

Inga had worked out how to make the coffee and she brought cups forward two at a time.

The first officer was a Brit who'd moved out here after the war, his name was Colin McHugh. He'd flown Lancasters in the R.A.F. So, he knew his way around four-engined aircraft. He still sported a handle-bar moustache that had been all the rage back then. I had to promise him a go round the airfield in the M.G. with Inga as his co-pilot.

"She's a corker!"

"She's a pip all right," I said, copying a phrase I used to hear all the time back in England, but thought I'd never hear again. It sounded strange even as I said it.

"I'll have a word; see if I can get you her number."

"She does dress a little strange though, looks like a chap from some angles, what with that short hair. Maybe I should buy her a nice dress."

"That might work," I said. "And trust me; underneath the suit, she doesn't look anything like a chap." I moved back into first-class before Colin could ask me how I knew what Inga looked like underneath her suit.

Somewhere over North Dakota, I got to fly the Lockheed Constellation. I didn't get much of a chance to really get a feel for her. If I'm honest I could have been the auto-pilot, just holding the altitude and compass heading. In fact, I could have set the trim and she would have flown herself without the auto-pilot. But it was great to talk with an experienced group of flyers again though. I was happy to see that no-one was using surplus ammo boxes as sandwich tins.

I went back to the cabin after that. Inga was asleep curled up on one of those big leather chairs, wrapped in a T.W.A. blanket. I settled in a second chair, my feet dangling over one arm. The Connie rumbled eastward toward the fast-approaching dawn. I dreamt of Josephine again, mercifully not the electric-chair nightmare. I dreamt I was backstage at a show watching her performing with a Swing Band. I couldn't work out where we were, but the place was jumping with couples packing the dance floor. I was in uniform; I had my cap tucked under my arm. Bright reflections from a gigantic mirror ball danced around and around the hall.

Jo was getting ready to sing. She stepped up to the mic, looked across at me, and smiled. The band leader was sitting at the end of the horn section. Then he put down his trombone and walked up to the front of the stage next to

Jo. It was Ko den Hamer. He pulled a revolver out of his white jacket and in an instant shot Josephine in the back of the head. She fell forward off the stage onto the dance-floor. The band didn't miss a beat, the music kept on playing and the crowd kept on dancing, stepping over Jo's body as they passed the front of the stage.

Ko pulled out a handkerchief and attempted to wipe the blood from his jacket. He looked across at me and winked. He walked over to the mic, wiped brains and bone and blood off it with his handkerchief. The band started a new song and Ko started to sing: 'I Shot a Gal in Kalamazoo.' I rushed forward onto the stage. I was going to kill Ko den Hamer with my bare hands.

I felt the heat from the spot-lights and suddenly I was flying a night bomber caught in a cone of searchlights. Flak burst all around and the plane jumped and fell with every explosion. Inga was shaking me awake.

"They've hit some heavy turbulence; they want us to put on our seatbelts," she said. I sat up, fastened my belt, and took a look out of the window. We were in thick cloud. By the engine tone, I could tell we'd throttled back and begun to lose height. We were on our approach to LaGuardia. I checked my watch. It said 5.00 am. I moved it on three hours. We were going to make it.

We landed in a rainstorm; there was a strong cross-wind which made things interesting for Captain Lacey. He had to side-slip the Constellation almost onto the ground, bringing everything back in line at the last second. We landed with a heavy thump and lots of tire smoke. Taxiing this big bird was tricky too, it stood higher than any other plane and it had a triple tail that caught the wind very effectively. Once we arrived at the terminal we disembarked and ran inside. There was no-one at the T.W.A. desk to meet us. I called the number for Captain Baker; it rang and rang. Eventually, someone picked up saying:

"N.Y.P.D. Homicide."

"Is Captain Baker there?"

"Nope."

"Do you know where he is?"

"Nope."

"He's supposed to be meeting me at LaGuardia…"

"You don't say."

"Is that where he's headed?"

"Could be."

"Will he be calling in for messages?"

"Could be."

"Then can I leave him a message in case he calls?"

"I guess."

I took a deep breath, tried to steady my heart rate, and tried not to call the guy on the other end of the phone all the names I was thinking of at that precise moment. I told him who I was and where I was, and I gave him the number of the phone I was holding. I hung up. Inga looked at me with a 'What the hell?' kind of expression.

"They don't know where Captain Baker is, I left a message."

"Really?" she said. I nodded. We took a seat and waited. The phone rang continuously. It was never for us. At ten-thirty Captain Baker of the N.Y.P.D. arrived. He was a thick-set man in a large grey overcoat that was dripping water on the linoleum floor. He had a burgundy pork-pie hat in his hands. He was very thin on top and tried to hide it by combing over the few strands of lank brown hair he had left. He looked like he hadn't shaved or slept for a week.

"You Marshall?" he asked. I got to my feet, shook his hand, and said:

"Yes, and this is Inga." Baker flashed the briefest of straight-lipped smiles in Inga's direction:

"Ma'am," he said. "Shall we get going?"

"I thought you'd never ask," I replied. We went outside into the pouring rain. There was a squad car waiting for us. Baker got in the front with the driver, we got in the back. As we sped away from the airport Baker turned to face us.

"We have a bit of a problem. The Liberte sails at 2.00 but they start boarding at 12.00 noon. It's going to take about an hour to get downtown if the traffic is kind to us. It never is. You got a picture of the guy we're after?" I showed Captain Baker the photograph from the brochure.

"He's a good-looking guy, you sure he's killed three people?"

"I'm sure. I saw him kill one with my own eyes…my wife Jo."

"Jeezus Christ!" exclaimed Baker. He turned back to see how the road was in front of us. He spoke to the driver:

"You'd better light everything up Hal." Hal the driver turned on the sirens and lights. He put his foot down, heading for the Queensboro Bridge. We made some progress as most drivers pulled to one side to let us through but once we hit the approach to the bridge things ground to a halt. Hal the driver turned off the lights and siren saying:

"It's pointless from here till we cross the bridge. It would only piss people off some more."

For almost half an hour the only things moving on that bridge were the hands on my watch. Eventually, we traversed the East River into Manhattan. Things eased a little and we started to move from red light to red light at a little over walking pace. We passed close to the southern end of Central Park before edging into Hell's Kitchen. Liner Row was just a few blocks away now on the eastern shoreline of the Hudson. At last, we were getting close. It was almost twelve noon. We zig-zagged left and right and left again and came out heading down to the water on West 45th.

Captain Baker flashed his badge at a couple of security gates and soon we were down on the dock at the side of the S.S. Liberte. From where we stood all we could see was a wall of black metal with rows of portholes. We ran along the pier with the ship's hull on our left and a two-story structure on our right. Gantries led to covered walkways onto the ship. At the foot of the main gantry, we were directed inside to the main embarkation desk. There was a long line of well-dressed passengers waiting to board. Captain Baker led the way, holding his badge above his head and shouting:

"N.Y.P.D. make way!" When we got to the head of the line we were greeted by a very official-looking Frenchman, complete with slicked-down hair, an immaculately pressed uniform, and a very snooty look.

"*Passports s'il vous plait*!" Captain Baker showed his badge.

"This is Mister Marshall from San Francisco. I understand you've been informed he's coming..."

"Pardon Monsieur, but I have been informed rien. Now if you will step to one side we shall *continuer a l'embarquement*."

Captain Baker did not look like he was going anywhere.

"I think, mon amie, that you might want to call you supervisor." The Frenchman behind the counter did not seem to get the message. He took a long snooty breath and said:

"I do not think so..." Then he saw Captain Baker's Colt Revolver.

"I think I will call my supervisor," said the Frenchman.

"Good idea," said Captain Baker. After a burst of hysterical Gallic arguing over the phone we were whisked into the manager's office behind the counter. After another ten-minute wait, we were met by a representative from the French Line who confirmed that Ko den Hamer was booked on this sailing. An underling was sent to check all the ticket counters. He came back, breathless, shortly after, and gave us the good news. Ko den Hamer had not yet boarded the ship.

"How many counters are currently checking people on board?" I asked.

"We have eight counters in operation as we speak."

"Is there any way we can watch all the counters?" There wasn't.

"However, once our passengers have checked in, they all have to go across the main gantry to board the ship. You could possibly identify your suspect as he crosses that gantry." Captain Baker spoke in my ear.

"Is there any chance this guy might be armed?"

"Every chance," I said.

"That's what I thought. We can't take him on the gantry, too many people. He could grab a hostage and then all hell would break loose."

"I've got an idea," I said.

"I'm very glad to hear it," said Captain Baker. I turned to the guy from the cruise liner.

"What's Ko den Hamer's cabin number?"

"He's in state-room 803."

"Can you get us onboard the ship quickly?"

"We can get you onboard using the crew's gangplank."

"Let's do it!" I said. As we were rushed to the crew's gangplank, I explained my plan to Inga and Captain Baker.

"We'll need to arrange a tug to meet us as the Liberte leaves the harbor. We can't let the Liberte get outside the 12-mile limit. Once he's in international waters we can't touch him."

Once onboard, Captain Baker went straight to the bridge, Inga and me were shown to the pursers' office where we explained why we were there and what we needed. What we needed were two steward's outfits. They were rustled up in a matter of minutes. The purser left us in his office to get changed. As we did so Inga asked me:

"Are you sure you know what you're doing?"

"Not really. If this goes according to plan, we might still need some firepower. We'll keep Captain Baker close by." I sneaked a look at Inga as she stepped into her white uniform pants. All this getting dressed and undressed together was becoming something I really enjoyed.

"You should see about ordering one of these uniforms. You look great halfway in it."

"And you look stupid in yours," was her reply…ho hum. Once we were fully dressed complete with caps we were taken to the deck where the passengers were being welcomed onboard. There was a five-piece band playing 'Begin the Beguine.' Stewards were milling around with drinks on trays. I picked up a full tray and positioned myself to one side of the main entrance. From there I was able to watch everyone coming aboard. Inga took a tray and, keeping her cap down low, she walked among the passengers dispensing drinks. She kept her eyes on the new arrivals too.

At one-thirty the ship's captain sounded the horn. Preparations were being made for departure. The flow of passengers had thinned considerably, and I hadn't seen Ko den Hamer board. I moved away from the entrance; I was sure he'd spot me if he came aboard now. Captain Baker was back with us, sitting in a large armchair drinking a cocktail with a lot of fruit in it. He kept looking across at me accusingly. I kept shrugging my shoulders and looking back at him. I looked at my watch for the thousandth time. It was 13.50 I looked up and Inga was coming over to me.

"He's here," she said. "He's with a red-head in a fur coat...don't look!" I turned my back on the entrance and Inga watched our target come on board as she looked over my shoulder. She gave me a quick peck on the cheek, pulled her cap down over her face, and walked over to hand Ko den Hamer and his lady companion a 'welcome aboard cocktail.' She came back to me, all smiles.

"Okay, he's heading down to his cabin. When do we do this?"

"We'll give him ten minutes to unpack..."

"Make it twenty. She looks like she's got a lot of clothes."

"Okay, twenty minutes."

The ship's horn sounded two more times and the S.S. Liberte cast off and started to edge away from the quay. Her engines began to rumble louder, the deck beneath my feet vibrated a little. Everyone on board rushed to the outer decks to wave goodbye. Ticker tape flew and the band played Le Marseillaise over and over. Everyone was having a high old time. I did not see Ko den Hamer waving goodbye to the United States.

We were soon sailing south heading for open water just past Brighton Beach which was about 15 miles away. As the cheering and the waving died down, I went through my plan with Inga and Captain Baker. Neither of them was over-impressed.

"That's it?" said Inga.

"I hope you know what you're doing," said Captain Baker. I said:

"He's got nowhere to go...what's he gonna do? Jump ship? Come on, let's get this over with." I went to the bar and took a bottle of champagne and two glasses; put them on a tray. Then Captain Baker and Inga followed me down to deck eight. I asked Inga to stay well back and block the corridor, so no-one walked by. If Ko did something stupid, she'd be safer there. Captain Baker checked his gun and set himself across the narrow corridor from state-room 803. I knocked on the door. There was no answer. I knocked again. I put on my best snooty French accent and said:

"It's the steward, sir, compliments of the French Line. I have a bottle of champagne for you. To welcome you aboard."

"Just a minute," came the answer. I lifted the tray high in front of me, so the bottle hid my face. I pulled the cap down one more time. The door swung open languidly.

"Just put it on the desk, will you?" said Ko. He had his back to me; the red-head was lying on the bed wearing a come-hither smile and come-hither panties and stockings, nothing else. She had pale skin, pale pink nipples, and tiny light brown freckles on her shoulders and chest. I moved to one side as planned and Captain Baker stepped forward, gun held high.

"Ko den Hamer you're under arrest on three counts of first-degree murder, fraud and money lau…"

Without looking back Ko dived forward onto the bed. He grabbed the red-head and pulled her in front of him. He pulled a large nasty looking blade from somewhere and held it up to the girl's throat. Captain Baker levelled the gun at Ko's head.

"Now we aren't going to do anything stupid are we?" he said. Ko said:

"I'm not, but I think you already did." Baker barked:

"Let the girl go Mister den Hamer." Ko said:

"I think not." Then he looked me in the face for the first time since he'd opened the door. He smiled:

"Rick! You're not dead! I thought you were down to be a burnt offering. Last time I saw you, you were tied to a kitchen chair choking back smoke. You are a very hard man to kill Mon Amie. It's good to see you, really…If I'm honest I was quite happy to let you live. Josephine, however, she wanted you dead…I knew then that I couldn't trust her…too emotional, too highly strung. So that's when I decided to kill her, to cut and run, call it a spur of the moment thing. Believe it or not, I am sorry about Josephine, still, I'm sure she didn't suffer; she certainly looked surprised when the bullet hit her in the neck. She had this look; I'll never forget it…kind of like a cow in a slaughterhouse, just as its throat is cut. A look of utter shock; or udder shock if you like." He started to laugh. I hate people who laugh at their own jokes. I felt the neck of the champagne bottle in my hand. I spat:

"Shut the fuck up."

"Or what? What are you gonna do?" To my side Captain Baker was saying:

"Step back out of the cabin Mister Marshall."

"What do you propose to do now Mister New York Policeman? Because by my calculations in about fifteen minutes we will be in International waters. I'm quite comfortable…I can sit here till then; Ginger isn't going anywhere…Are you Ginger?" Ko pressed the knife against Ginger's freckled breast. A thin line of blood dribbled slowly down to her stomach. She whimpered like a small puppy. Ko looked at me.

"Looks like a bit of a stalemate old chum. You know that if either of you makes another move I shall certainly gut young Ginger here like a fish. Now you wouldn't want to see that would you? It would be such a waste too. I've always had a thing for red-heads."

Pow! A shot went off behind my head. Ko's face splattered like a ripe tomato; his head snapped back against the cabin wall. Blood burst up the wall and onto the ceiling. Instantly the stateroom was full of smoke. My ears were ringing, I couldn't hear a word. Ginger started screaming hysterically and shaking her head from side to side. Her head and naked torso were covered in blood. Captain Baker put his gun away and hurried forward, wrapped her in his coat, and pulled her away from the carnage. I turned to look behind me. Inga stood perfectly still holding her smoking Beretta.

Chapter Thirty

So, we all got to find out what if feels like to take part in a major diplomatic incident. The Liberte sailed around in circles just off Brighton Beach until it was ordered to return to New York the next morning. All the passengers disembarked and were flown to their destinations, courtesy of the State Department. We were held for questioning for twenty-four hours and finally release on our own cognizance and only if we swore not to return to New York in the foreseeable future. Over one million dollars in cash was discovered when Ko den Hamer's luggage was searched. Inga was initially going to face charges of manslaughter, possibly murder from the New York D.A. These charges were dropped on the recommendation of Captain Baker who stated Inga's actions had saved at least one life that afternoon.

Captain Lacey and his crew had a fantastic time in New York before flying Inga and me back to the West Coast that following Saturday. We both slept almost all of the way. We later learned that Ko den Hamer had been wanted on numerous charges including murder in Holland and Belgium.

When we landed, I was handed a large envelope with RKO stamped all over it. It was an offer to option the whole story for a movie. They had screenwriters ready to go and even a working title: 'The Flying Detective.' They had Alan Ladd set to play me. I knew that wouldn't work. He would look pretty stupid standing next to a six-foot blonde dame. However, there was a man-sized check stapled to the offer. I took the check and cashed it real fast. The movie never got made.

I called Elton Dwight from the airport and left a message with his service. I wanted to meet him the next morning, collect the undercover recording device from him then head up to the Napa Valley to find Mabel Brown. We had her sister's address in Santa Rosa; I figured that was the obvious place to start.

Sunday morning dawned cold but dry. The late October sun barely bothered to peep through the high clouds covering north-western California. Elton Dwight said he'd like to be on the scene when the arrest was made so we got to ride in his fancy Packard up to Santa Rosa. We were followed by a black and white and an unmarked police car. God knows what the good people of Santa Rosa would think when our convoy rolled into town. As we drove north, I suggested to Elton Dwight that we drive through town without our escort. I didn't want to scare Mable Brown before we got to talk with her. My plan was fairly simple (no surprise there) I was going to pose as a crooked investigator from the Brown's insurance company. The fact that we'd met before would work in my favor. I could tell her I was already investigating her then. I was going to tell her I knew she'd killed her husband and everybody aboard flight 402 and I knew how she did it. I was going to the cops if she didn't pay up. After that, I'd have to play it by ear.

Inga helped me get the Minifon wire recorder in place. I took off my own watch and handed it to her, it would look strange if I was wearing two watches. The actual recording equipment just fit in my jacket pocket. We had to cut a hole in the lining to run the wires through but that was the only hitch. I figured catching the person who downed flight 402 was worth it. Elton Dwight said:

"Now you can't go waving your arms around when she's talking. Try to rest your hands on a table or something solid and point them at the suspect. And keep your jacket buttoned."

"Don't wave arms around, keep jacket buttoned…got it." I said.

"Look; I know that sounds a little infantile, but this is new equipment we're working with here Rick, it's not proven; so, a little care might go a long way."

We drove into Santa Rosa just after noon and pulled up outside a Lowe's store on Fourth Street. The wind had picked up and the sidewalk was awash in autumn leaves and candy wrappers. Further down the street, I could see a large department store with an art deco sign: 'Rosenbergs.'

We found a diner and went in to grab a bite to eat and to look over a street map. The address Inga had picked up on our last visit to Napa was for Mable's sister Laurelai, 382 College Street, Santa Rosa. We asked behind the counter and a very friendly waitress told us a Laurelai Brown owned Breezy Corner Motel on the northern edge of the town. It was just off the highway, maybe three or four blocks away. Elton Dwight had a suggestion:

"Inga and I will check-in at the motel prior to your arrival… In that way, we can be on hand if anything were to go wrong…not that anything will; I'm sure." I said:

"Fine by me, the more the merrier. You got your little pea-shooter, Inga?" Inga pulled her Beretta from the waist-band of her pants. Elton Dwight reached over and took it from her.

"I'll take that if you don't mind…just for safekeeping. We need Mrs. Brown alive and suspects do seem to keep turning up dead when they are confronted by Miss Bjarkardóttir…no offence meant."

"None taken," said Inga. I could tell she was pissed. I could see her jaw tensing and a little blue vein beside her right eye was throbbing. We finished up lunch and headed out. I had my New World Insurance Company paperwork tucked inside an official-looking New World folder. The paperwork was actually my house insurance claim form which I'd collected on my last visit to Melvin Hammerstein's office. I was sure Mable Brown would not want to look at it in any detail.

I was dropped off about a block from the motel. In the time it took me to walk there Inga and Elton Dwight would have checked in. I straightened my tie and strode out in my best 'insurance agent on the make' style. The Breezy Corner Motel was a green and white edifice, with an office building at the end of a row of single-story chalets facing onto a barren parking lot. There was a green and white neon sign on the top of the office and an orange neon sign in the window which flashed: **'VACANCIES'** continuously.

I walked across the dusty parking lot and into the office. There was no-one at the front desk. I rang the bell. Laurelai came out from the rear office. She looked a lot like her sister, she weighed maybe twenty pounds less, but she wore an almost identical housecoat to the one I'd seen her sister in the last time we'd met. Her body under the housecoat was the shape of a very large potato.

"Checking in?" she asked hopefully. I held up the Insurance Company folder.

"Maybe, I'm in town on business. I'm looking for Mable Brown."

"She's my sister; she's out back in the house. What do you want with her?"

"I'm with the New World Insurance Company of Seattle, Washington. There's been an accounting error made on your sister's recent claim. I have a check here three thousand and forty-two dollars, sixty-two cents. It's the outstanding balance on her settlement."

"I can take it if you like," said the potato-shaped sister in the housecoat.

"I'm afraid that won't be possible, you see Mrs. Brown has to sign for the check personally…which way to the house?"

"I'll come with you, show you the way."

"That won't be necessary, I'm sure you're very busy."

"At this time of year? You must be joking; we've only got one room occupied and they just turned up five minutes ago. I doubt they'll stay the night. They'll be in and out in an hour if you catch my drift…this way." I followed her around the back of the chalets to a house standing alone some distance away from the motel itself. As we walked, I attempted to make small talk:

"Do you own the motel Mrs.?"

"Zapruder."

"Mrs. Zapruder."

"Yup, it's all mine since my husband ran off with a cleaning woman seven years three months and one week ago."

"Not that you're counting," I said.

"What? Oh yeah, real funny mister." Laurelai Zapruder opened the front door and called out:

"Mable? Mable! Man with a check to see you; come all the way from Seattle." I heard shuffling upstairs.

"Come through to the parlor, Mable will be a while putting on her face. She doesn't like to meet strangers without having her face all prettied up. Specially strangers with money."

The parlor looked like it had travelled forward in time from the last century. There were oil lamps on the wall and yellowing antimacassars on the over-stuffed chairs. A stuffed barn owl surveyed the room from its perch by an imposing black fireplace. There was a fire crackling away in the hearth. There was a small card table by the window; someone had left some knitting there.

"Have a seat."

"I'll stand if you don't mind, I've been driving rather a long time and my back is not as strong as it was."

"I didn't see your car in front of the motel..."

"Ah, yes. That's because I left it at the garage in town, there's something not quite right with the carburetor...I think. I thought they might fix it while I dealt with this little matter."

"You left it at Gibby's place?" I nodded.

"Gibby's is closed on Sundays." At that second Mabel Brown came into the room.

"Thank you Laurelai, I'll speak with the gentleman now," she said. Laurelai protested:

"But..."

"Why don't you hurry back to the motel? We don't want anyone stealing the bedsheets, now do we?"

"But..." Mabel Brown ushered her sister out of the parlor, closing the door firmly behind her. I moved to the table by the window and sat in one of the two seats placed there. Mabel Brown did not sit down with me.

"I've seen you before," she said. "You came round my old house in Napa."

"You have a good memory, Mrs. Brown."

"Who the hell are you? You selling something?"

"Not exactly Mrs. Brown, I do have a proposition for you but I'm not exactly..."

"...Laurelai said you had a check for me."

"That's not strictly true, though what I have to say will be of great value to you." Finally, Mabel Brown sat opposite me at the card table.

"Well spit it out, I ain't got all day."

"My name's Doolittle, James Doolittle. I'm an insurance investigator for the New World Insurance Company and I've been looking at your claim. I've been looking at it very closely."

"What the hell's that supposed to mean? You've already paid out on it."

"Yes, we did, we certainly did. But I have continued my investigations and I thought you might like to hear what I've discovered." Mabel Brown leaned back from the table, she looked at me in a whole new way, not a way I enjoyed being looked at; eventually, she said:

"Go on," very slowly. I decided to cut to the chase:

"Mrs. Brown, I know you killed your husband and everyone on flight 402. I know you rigged his lunchbox with a hand grenade set to explode as soon as he opened it. I know you upped his life insurance benefits shortly before he died, and I know why you did it."

"You don't say," she said.

"Oh, I do say, Mrs. Brown. It's all in this report." I tapped the file on the table. "And this report is going to one of two places, it's either going to the local police station with my recommendation that multiple murder charges be brought against you…or it's going into your fireplace. What you say next, Mrs. Brown determines where it goes."

"You've got this all planned out you little shit, haven't you?" said Mrs. Brown. "What if I say nothing? You've got no proof, the police have got nothing, or they'd have locked me up by now."

"Mrs. Brown, I'm not the police. I don't want to see you go to the chair. That's not why I'm here."

"So why are you here?"

"I'm here to offer you a way out. All I'm looking for is a little compensation for all my hard work."

She asked: "How much?" I had her now…

"Twenty thousand dollars."

"Twenty thousand!" she yelped.

"That's right," I said. She was quiet and still for a time.

"If I pay you, how do I know you won't be back for more later?"

"Trust me Mr. Brown; I'm not a greedy man…"

"Trust you? Trust you like I trusted Stu? I gave him the best years of my life and all he gave me was the clap."

"I guess nobody's perfect," I said.

"Yeah, a man would say that! You're all the same. He deserved it. He deserved to die. He was always chasing women, couldn't keep his hands off them, anything with a dress and a pulse he would be after it! Sluts! Sluts and whores! I'd known about it for years and he knew I knew but he didn't give a shit. He thought I'd just stay at home playing house while he flew all around the world screwing anybody he liked!"

"Tell me, how did you know how to make that booby trap? I know you'd worked with explosives at the factory during the war but that was something else. That took skill."

"Our younger brother Terry was in the Pacific. He told me all about Jap booby traps in a letter from an island somewhere…we never learned where he was. He was killed two weeks after he sent that letter."

"It was a hand grenade?"

"Two, in fact, their pins strung together with a wire fastened to the inside of the lid. I put a bologna sandwich in there too just to keep the grenades from rattling about."

"You certainly thought it through…how come you didn't think about all those innocent people on the plane?"

"No one is innocent! Besides, I never meant for all those folks to die. I gave him the lunchbox the day before. They were supposed to be going on a short test flight, but it got cancelled for some reason. When Stu came home that night, I thought he'd found out about my plans. But he just fell asleep on the couch as usual. Flight 402 was the next day."

"You could have divorced him, Mrs. Brown," I said.

"Enough talk, are we going to do this or not?"

"You have the money here?"

"I have enough of it, it's upstairs under the bed."

"You have got to be kidding me." I looked at the door. In the instant my eyes moved from her Mrs. Brown grabbed the knitting needles off the table and jammed them into the side of my neck. I fell sideways onto the floor taking my chair and the table with me. I put my hand to my neck to staunch the flow of blood and I felt the warm fluid flow through my fingers. I pulled the knitting needles out and tried to get to my feet. Mrs. Brown hit me over the back of the head with a log from the fireplace and once again, everything started to go black very quickly.

I was on the floor by the fireplace. I think I remember seeing Mrs. Brown's feet leaving the room. I rolled over onto my back. I was looking up at the stuffed owl when I passed out.

I can't have been out for long because as I came to, I could hear Mrs. Brown clomping down the stairs in her farmer's wife's sensible shoes. I tried to stand. The room span around me and I felt like I was standing on the deck of a ship in a storm. I put my hand on the fireplace and took a few deep breaths. The knitting needles had missed their mark. There was still a lot of blood all over my neck and chest, but it wasn't spurting all over the floor like you see when something vital gets hit.

I took a step and my knees started to buckle. I heard the front door slam. After a minute or so hanging on to the wall, I managed to follow her outside. She was heading for the motel parking lot. I went after her as quickly as I could. I shouted to her:

"Give it up Mabel. You can't get away." She turned and shouted:

"We'll see about that. You don't look to be in any shape to stop me." Right on cue Inga and Elton Dwight stepped out of their chalet. I guess the shouting must have alerted them. The two police cars that had travelled to Santa Rosa with us swung into the parking lot, sirens blaring. Mabel stood in the center of the parking lot with armed police surrounding her. I caught up with her and put my hand on her shoulder saying:

"It's all over Mrs. Brown." She screamed at me then:

"I'll say when it's all over!" She swung at me with the heavy case she was carrying. She missed and I think the handle must have broken because the next thing I see is this big case flying through the air. It hit the ground and burst open spewing waves of bank-notes onto the ground. The wind picks up at just the wrong second and the money goes dancing on the breeze all over the parking lot.

We spent the next hour trying to collect all the cash before it blew away down the 'mean' streets of Santa Rosa. With Mrs. Brown under arrest and almost all the cash recovered we went back to the café on 4th Street and I handed over the Minifon wire recorder to Elton Dwight. Inga got hold of a first aid kit from somewhere and she patched up my neck. I looked like a victim of Count Dracula. Elton Dwight had a pair of headphones in his case. He connected them to the recording unit and fiddled with the Minifon for a minute. It began to playback the recording.

As he listened the smile on his face grew broader and broader. By the end, he was beaming. When the recording finished, he clapped his hands, everyone in the café turned to see what was going on.

"You got it, Rick! You got it! Clear as day." He exclaimed.

On the way back to town I had a quick word with Inga about the Beaver. We decided to get Elton Dwight to drop us by the waterfront at Sausalito Harbor. We planned to stooge around for a while and get a good look at the plane. See if anyone was working on it or guarding it. As the Packard pulled to the sidewalk, I saw the Beaver right where I'd left her. Inga asked me:

"Do you have the keys?" I pulled them from my pants pocket.

"Never go anywhere without them," I said. We all climbed out of the Packard and stood on the sidewalk looking out over the water. Eventually, Elton Dwight said:

"We're going to need full statements of course and you'll be my star witness Rick. Solving such a high-profile case will certainly boost my chances come election day." I said:

"Well, you've got my vote, Mister Dwight. I owe you one." He shook my hand.

"No Rick…we owe you," was his reply. "We'll talk soon, maybe about that job."

So, the job offer was back on the table. Things were finally working out. The Packard glided away. Inga and I walked down to the jetty where the Beaver was moored. There was no-one around. I stepped onto the left float and opened the door to the cockpit.

"Climb aboard Inga; slide across to the right-hand seat and keep your head down. I'll get on with the pre-flight checks." Inga did as I asked. There was a little water in the right-hand fuel tank, which was probably condensation, no surprise there. I drained it off and carried on with the pre-flight.

Before starting the engine, I untied both ropes and let her drift away from the jetty as I climbed back aboard. We drifted soundlessly out into the bay. I could hear small waves slapping against the underside of the floats. The wind was nowhere near as strong as it was in Santa Rosa. When we were about fifty feet out, I started up the engine, letting it warm up as I set the propeller and flaps. We put on the headsets…we were good to go. Inga looked back over toward shore. She said:

"You know I don't think anyone is around. No-one at all."

"Suits me." I said. "You strapped in?" Inga gave me a thumbs-up. I opened the throttle and the Beaver started gathering speed. Inga squealed with delight. I eased back on the controls and we slipped into the air after maybe a twelve-second take-off run. We climbed slowly to one thousand feet, making a gentle turn to the west. The Golden Gate Bridge slid beneath us. I thought I saw Elton Dwight's Packard heading into town. I trimmed her out and said to Inga:

"Do you want to give it a try?"

"Do you think I can?"

"Sure, you can, if you can drive a stick you can learn to fly a plane like this. Rest your feet on the two peddles on the floor; you don't need to do anything with them yet…they are your rudder controls. Take the control column in your hands. Just gently, you don't need to yank it around or make any sudden moves, just hold it like it's a puppy or a kitten."

"Okay," said Inga. I took my hands off the controls.

"Right, you have control." Inga whooped with joy.

"You might want to cut out that squealing while we've got the headsets on," I said.

"Ooops, sorry."

We were heading west; the sun was beginning to set; the sea and sky were bathed in a warm orange glow.

"Inga, I need to ask you something; something important."

"Oh God Rick don't."

"Don't what?"

"Don't ask me that."

"You don't know what I'm going to ask you…"

"I think I do Rick and I don't think it's a good idea."

"What's not a good idea?"

"…You know I like you, Rick, I like you a lot and sure we work well together, we make a pretty good team, but it just wouldn't work out."

"It wouldn't?" I asked.

"Of course, not…you know the way I am…and you know I'm happy being me. I'm happy just the way I am." I said:

"I'm very glad to hear it." Before I could go on Inga interrupted.

"…I mean, okay I can't deny it, there has been a bit of a spark between us, sexually…a few times and I must admit I am a little curious to see how things might go between us…in bed."

"So, it's all about the sex. That's what's worrying you?"

Inga said: "It's not just that." Inga wasn't really thinking about flying a plane, we were beginning to lose height. I said:

"I have control."

I took hold of the controls; put on a touch more power, eased in a little right rudder, tilted the control column, and brought us round onto a heading for San Francisco Harbor. Inga carried on talking:

"Don't get me wrong Rick. I'm flattered, really I am, but I think maybe it's all a little too soon…for you I mean…after Josephine. It's got to be tough, but I don't think marrying me on the rebound would be such a good idea."

"You think I'm going to do something stupid because I'm on the rebound?"

"I guess so, and I'd be happier if you didn't say anything more about it today."

"That's your final word on the subject?" I asked.

"I hope you're not too upset Rick. I would never hurt you."

"Apart from beating me over the head with the butt of your gun."

"That doesn't count. I didn't know you then."

I looked across at Inga. Her blonde pixie haircut under the headset, her bottom lip pouting childishly and those eyes. She looked to be in anguish. I almost felt sorry for her. I said:

"That's got to be one of the deepest conversations we've ever had."

"And the hardest," she said.

We were flying over the bridge again. I throttled back, selected some flaps, and prepared to bring the Beaver down. I said:

"Let me get us down safely then there's one more thing I want to say." Inga zipped her lip.

I made a very soft landing across from the Hyde Street Pier, turned to the right, and started to edge in toward the berth I'd rented. About fifty yards out I throttled way back and we drifted in toward the pier. We took off our headsets. Inga looked as if she'd just had to give up a puppy.

"So, Inga," I said. "You didn't let me finish telling you about my proposal."

"Oh, Rick I thought we'd just gone over that. Like I said it will never work between us…"

I took a deep breath; it was very hard to keep a straight face. Eventually, I managed to ask her:

"Inga Bjarkardóttir…Will you be my partner in a private detective agency?"

The End.